ROSIE PRICE

What Red Was

VINTAGE

1 3 5 7 9 10 8 6 4 2

Vintage
20 Vauxhall Bridge Road,
London SW1V 2SA

Vintage is part of the Penguin Random House group of companies
whose addresses can be found at global.penguinrandomhouse.com

Penguin
Random House
UK

First published in Vintage in 2020
First published in hardback by Harvill Secker in 2019

penguin.co.uk/vintage

A CIP catalogue record for this book is available
from the British Library

ISBN 9781529110784

Printed and bound in Great Britain by Clays Ltd, Elcograf S.p.A.

Typeset in 11.25/16 pt Stempel Garamond LT Std
by Jouve (UK), Milton Keynes

Penguin Random House is committed to a sustainable future for
our business, our readers and our planet. This book is made
from Forest Stewardship Council® certified paper.

MIX
Paper from
responsible sources
FSC® C018179

For my parents

1

Kate was sleeping when he knocked on her door. It was early, not yet six, and the sound of banging continued until she was out of bed. She glanced in the mirror over the basin as she passed: her skin was paler than usual, puffy from the cheap wine she had been drinking in her room the night before. The banging started again and Kate pulled the door open. Standing outside was a boy wearing only a towel, his skin still wet from the shower.

'Shit,' the boy said. 'Shit. I'm so sorry. Were you asleep?'

'I mean, it is the middle of the night,' Kate said. She didn't recognise him, but if he lived in this building then he must also be in his first year. 'What time is it?'

'Let me check my pocket watch?' The boy patted his towel. 'Oh, wait. I'm naked.'

'A comedian,' said Kate drily. But she kept her foot on the door so it wouldn't swing shut.

'Can I come in? It's kind of an emergency.'

The boy's name was Max and he'd locked himself out of his room when he'd gone for a shower. He came inside, letting the door slam behind him and adjusting his towel.

'Do you think you could go and get the master key for

me?' he said. 'It's just I can't walk across college in a towel. I'll frighten the tourists.'

'Why are you up so early?' Kate said, ignoring his request. 'I thought lectures didn't start until tomorrow.'

'I was with a friend,' Max said. 'She's across the river. I just got back.'

Kate was annoyed by the disappointment she felt; she tried for a playful tone to disguise it. 'How about I lend you some clothes?'

Max shrugged. 'I'm comfortable with my masculinity,' he said. 'Let's do it.'

Kate gave him a pair of black jeans and a hoodie, looking at her phone while he changed. 'What are you studying?' she said.

'Languages.' Max had gone to her shelf, and was examining the books she had taken all summer to read. They barely seemed to occupy any space. 'Same as you. Don't bother with this, it's bullshit.'

Kate glanced up at the book he was holding out to her.

'I've read it already,' she said. 'And it's not. Some of it's feminism. You have to wash those jeans before you give them back to me, by the way.'

Max shoved his hands in the pockets and grinned. Her jeans were way too short for him.

'Don't worry,' he said. 'I'm very clean.'

After he left, Kate got back into bed but she couldn't sleep. Now he wouldn't come back straight away to return the jeans. She hadn't asked which room he was in, or what time he was leaving for their first French lecture the next morning. In the whole of her long first week at university he was the first person who'd been in her bedroom. Lying there she was aware – as she had been on the day she'd moved in – of the silence of her building, the empty corridors, the sense of new lives beginning elsewhere. Her room, with its wide windows, felt vast and strange compared with her bedroom at home.

That first day Kate had overheard a mother telling her daughter that these halls had been built in the 1960s when the more elite universities were made to widen their access. Walking behind them, dragging her suitcase, she'd caught a glimpse of the girl's profile and wondered if she was living near her; perhaps she would come to her room later, they'd go together to the bar. But then her mother steered her through an archway into the next court and towards the river, where Kate had since discovered the majority of her year were living, in the older accommodation blocks with their winding stone staircases and creeping ivy.

Kate rolled over: she needed to get up and have a shower. She'd been avoiding the canteen but wondered whether she might find Max there. She heard another knock on the door, a light tap this time. It was him, wearing a soft black jumper and his own jeans, his dark hair almost dry.

'Kate Quaile,' he said. 'I like your name.'

Kate frowned. 'How do you know my name?'

'It's above the door.' Max pointed up at the door frame, and Kate saw that on the little finger of his right hand he wore a gold ring. 'So,' he said, smiling brightly. 'What

3

shall we have for breakfast? I'm paying. To apologise for waking you up.'

The following morning he came past on his way to their first lecture and banged on her door until she let him in. She'd only just got up, but he didn't mind that she made him late, showering and then sitting on the floor in the patch of sunlight under her window to put on her make-up. He sat at her desk playing tinny music through her laptop, and came by the following day, and the next. As they walked together Kate observed that he spoke in tangents, so that whenever she asked him a question he would always take the conversation elsewhere without answering her. Other students were always stopping to talk to him, and she soon came to realise that she would not have him to herself for long: he was never alone, always busy, on his way to meet an old school friend or girlfriend. He seemed to know everyone. But she began to listen out for the sound of him bounding up the stairs two at a time to slump in the armchair at the end of her bed, drunk or high and filled with gleeful loathing for the people he'd spent his evening with. On those nights, they would talk until Kate fell asleep, at which point Max would leave, slipping softly from her room. Sometimes, when the door shut behind him, she briefly woke, and wondered if she had dreamt that he'd been there.

A few weeks into term, after the summer had given way to autumn, Kate felt her sense of loneliness begin to lift. It was not so hard, now, to make other friends; she was starting to feel more confident. But when she went out without Max she had to check herself, in case she referred to him too often in conversation, or became preoccupied by the texts that would arrive from him in intermittent bursts, wanting to know where she was and what she was doing. On one such evening, Max had found her just before midnight sitting outside a kebab shop in the centre of town, delicately dissecting her lamb shish. She had been coerced into a night of structured drinking with the other students on her floor, and had managed to give them the slip during the migration from bar to club. Max crouched down beside her.

'This is almost inedible,' said Kate, her mouth full, offering him a plastic fork.

They took the kebab back to Kate's room where she placed it on her shelf next to her cereal: her head was swimming and she was already anticipating a difficult breakfast. Max sat up on the windowsill, pushing the window half open to the cool night air. At the time he was refusing to listen to anything except a single Frank Ocean song, which he started to play now; Kate took his phone from his hand and connected it to her speaker. Max rolled a cigarette.

'You know, a bouncer told me to "get to fuck" tonight,' he said. 'It's been so long since anybody has told me to actually get to fuck.' He sounded almost wistful.

Kate tried to focus. 'Why did he say that?'

'I don't know. I was trying to help with his queueing system. Streamlining it.'

'Oh, Max,' Kate said. 'I'm sure he really needed that.'

'Obviously. Otherwise I wouldn't have had to let people in the side door.'

Kate lifted herself up onto the sill beside him and took his cigarette between her fingers. She was really drunk, she realised, only hazily aware of the window latch digging into her back as she leaned against the frame.

Max sighed. 'This is always the best part of the night, anyway,' he said. 'I don't know why we ever go out.'

'You should have followed my lead.' Kate blew smoke out of the window and turned towards him as she did so. 'If you'd stayed in quarantine for the first fortnight you wouldn't be stuck with so many friends.'

'I know,' Max said. 'I have no one to blame but my abundant charisma.'

'Nothing.'

'What?'

'Nothing to blame, not no one. Charisma isn't a person.' Kate was slurring assertively. The cigarette had made her light-headed.

'It is when it's this abundant,' Max said, as she started to clamber back down. 'What are you doing?'

'Getting ready to go clubbing,' Kate said, crawling under her covers.

'Oh come on – you can't abandon me. It's not even midnight.'

Kate reached for her phone to verify this.

'OK,' Max said. 'It's a little bit after.'

'You can stay but you have to be quiet,' Kate said.

'Can I borrow some pyjamas?' he said, closing the window.

'You can,' said Kate. 'But not because I'm nice. I just don't want you to be naked. They're in my top drawer.'

Wearing Kate's checkered pyjama trousers and a T-shirt, Max got into bed and kicked at the duvet, wriggling down next to her. She shuffled up against the wall to make room for him and Max put his arm around her and nestled into the pillow. He groaned.

'Oh my God. This is fucking blissful.' They lay there quietly, neither of them quite able to relax.

'Kate,' Max said after a while.

'What?'

'You know when people tell you to "get to fuck"?'

'No, but go on.'

'Well, where is it?'

'What?'

'Where is fuck? How do you actually get to it?'

She couldn't tell if he was dozy now or just drunk.

'In your dreams,' Kate said.

Before she'd got into bed she'd felt exhausted, but now the unfamiliar presence of another body had put her on alert, and while Max's breath slowed to the heavy rhythm of sleep, she lay there not wanting to move in case she disturbed him. For a moment, she wondered what he would do if she turned towards him, so that her cheek was on his shoulder. Her chest tightened, and she didn't know if she was more afraid that he would stay sleeping, or that he would respond.

*

In the morning, Kate woke feeling irritated by Max's invasion. She climbed over him, careful to knee him in the thigh as she did so, and went to shower. He still wasn't up when she returned, so she reheated her lamb shish, confident that the smell would drive him back to his own room. She loaded up a forkful and wafted it in his direction. Max groaned, turned his head away.

'You sleep in a girl's bed and don't even have the decency to accept her kebab scrapings the next morning?'

'I'm going out for breakfast,' Max said, squinting and lifting his head from the pillow. His phone started to vibrate, and he scrabbled for it under the covers. 'Hello – are you here already?'

'Who are you having breakfast with and why haven't you invited me?' Kate said, when Max hung up.

'My mother,' said Max, as he pulled off the T-shirt Kate had lent to him. Kate watched him from her chair. There were so many things she still didn't know: Max hadn't mentioned that his mother was coming to visit; in fact he had spoken about his family even less than she had about hers. When she'd told Max she lived with her mother in a Gloucestershire village called Randwick, he'd stopped her, surprised, to say that his grandmother's house was only one village away. She sensed somehow that there was little else he wanted to share. She knew that the Rippons lived in London, and that Max's mother was French-Moroccan and worked in film. Only recently had she realised that Titus was the name of Max's dog, rather than a younger brother – an easy assumption to make from the way Max talked about him.

After he left, Kate got up and put the kebab, which had finally defeated her, in the bin under her desk. The air in her room was stale and she went to the window to breathe. In the courtyard below she saw Max, walking in step with a dark-haired woman. She was wearing a long camel coat, tied at her waist, and she carried a leather bag in one hand. Kate watched Max turn round, walking backwards now, pointing up at their building, to where his room was. The woman turned too, and Kate stepped back a little. She was wearing sunglasses, so Kate couldn't tell where she was looking, but after only a moment she turned away and linked her arm through Max's.

Even more than Max, his mother seemed to Kate to be from another world. For a moment, she tried to imagine her standing among the other parents at her secondary school leavers' night. Somehow she couldn't see this woman making her son pose for excruciating photographs; neither could she see her making small talk with her own mother, Alison, who had arrived after all the other parents in the overalls she wore to her weekly pottery class. Probably Max's school had thrown some glamorous party in London, rather than the 'summer ball' that had taken place in a local farmer's barn.

Later that day, when Kate asked Max how his breakfast had been, he gave her unnecessary detail, starting with the particularly streaky bacon he'd had with his eggs. This time, she interrupted, and asked him straight up.

'What does your mother actually do, in film?'

'She's a director,' said Max.

'A famous one?'

'She's done some big films.'

Kate persevered. 'Like what?'

Max paused. *'Inheritance,'* he said, dropping the deflection. *'L'Accusé, Miel, Blue Bayou.'*

'Shit,' Kate said. 'I've heard of those. I've actually seen some of them.'

'You should have told her. She'd love that.'

Kate did not point out to Max that because he had not introduced her to his mother, she'd had no opportunity to tell her that she liked her films. She already felt as though her questions had become intrusive. But when she got to the library, instead of working on her essay for the next day, she searched *'Blue Bayou* director'. Zara Lalhou – it was a name Kate recognised. In the subsections of Zara's Wikipedia page appeared Max and his older sister, Nicole; their father, William, a vascular surgeon; their west London home; her extensive filmography.

When Max texted to ask how her work was going, Kate closed the web page and cleared her history. But later, when he was out at a dinner, she closed her curtains, got into bed and watched *Blue Bayou* on her laptop. This was one of Zara's later films, and one of her most commercial – English language and Hollywood-produced. Kate had seen it when she was fifteen, around the time that she had started going alone to the cinema after school, when she couldn't face going home. Now that she was watching the film for the second time, she couldn't believe she had forgotten the palm trees bent beneath a summer storm, the sea glittering black in the early hours, the force of the despair that drove the main character into the water. At the end, Kate shut her laptop without closing down the screen, and went to sleep thinking of the woman standing and looking at her reflection in the panoramic window of her Miami apartment, not knowing, not caring, who could be looking in.

2

Though she would never have suggested anything his mother had directed, Kate started to invite Max to come and watch films in her room. He complained about the size and speed of her laptop, though, fussing and trying to minimise the appearance of the smears on its screen. One morning during their second term, after he'd spent the weekend with his parents in London, Max texted Kate to tell her he had a surprise to give her, if she came up to his room. Kate called him.

'Why do I feel nervous?'

'I promise you'll like it,' Max said.

'Can't you come down and show me?'

'Just come upstairs. It'll be worth it.'

As always Max had left his door ajar, but the curtains were drawn and the lights were off. Kate pushed a pair of high heels to one side as she closed the door behind her: she wanted to know who the shoes belonged to, but she wasn't going to ask.

'So? What do you think?' Max said.

'I think it's extremely dark.'

'Look.' Max pulled her by the hand. The two armchairs

that were normally by the window had been dragged into the middle of the room and, balanced precariously on a pile of books, a projector cast a block of white light on the wall above Max's bed, from which he had removed the prints – one of Lana Del Rey and another of a street in Marrakesh, a gift from his mother – which usually hung there.

'I found it at home,' Max said. 'My mum doesn't need it any more.' Kate sat down, and he went to adjust the projector, shifting the books beneath it. 'Is the picture straight?'

They both looked up at the light moving slowly across the wall, as Max tilted the lens.

'It's pretty good,' Kate said, tilting her head to one side, 'I mean, if you wanted a trapezium.'

'A trapezium? Are you sure?' said Max. 'Fuck. Wait, you hold this.'

'I have so much to do,' Kate objected; she did want to stay, but she had an essay to finish.

'This is work. We're watching films. We can even watch foreign films.'

Kate shook her head. 'It's important. It's for Kerrison.'

Max reached over to switch off the projector. 'What are you writing about? I haven't started mine.'

'The usual bullshit,' Kate said, shrugging. 'I actually managed to use the word "synecdoche" to describe the cinematic portrayal of the Parisian insect population.'

Gleeful, Max whipped the curtains open. 'You're a genius. Kerrison will be all over it.' Kate, whose last effort for Kerrison had received simply the word 'WHY' written in its margin, doubted Max's optimism. But in fact he would be proved right: Kerrison did love the essay, and Kate tried her best to look embarrassed as the last paragraph was read out to their class.

'This is the key,' Kerrison said, holding up the essay. 'Write about what interests you. If you love French cinema, write about French cinema. If you have passion, your readers will be able to tell.' She flipped back a page and looked at Kate over her glasses. 'And I love what you said about Zara Lalhou.'

Kate did not make eye contact with Max.

'Is it weird for you,' she asked later, 'if I write about your mother?'

'Why would it be weird?' Max said. The projector was now working and they were waiting for a takeaway to arrive.

'I mean,' Kate said, 'I can't imagine you writing your dissertation on the late pottery of Alison Quaile.'

Max laughed. 'Honestly, it's not weird,' he said. 'I'm kind of used to my mum being . . . you know. Other people's property.'

For Max, Kate realised, it was normal to know that he might have things other people wanted, and to be so secure in his possession of these privileges that he didn't need to guard them closely. It was from this confidence that his generosity sprung: he wasn't worried about what he might lose because he'd always had more than enough. He was generous with his time, as well as his money. Though he was often in demand, he and Kate saw each other several times a week for most of that first year, watching films, sitting in their armchairs – which Max called their thrones – and passing wine and takeaway food, usually paid for by Max, who always seemed to forget to ask Kate for cash. As exams drew closer, and others in their year stopped going out and drinking so much, Kate and Max spent more evenings together, working only when it became absolutely necessary.

'You know what we should actually do,' Max said, on the evening before their first exam.

'Not fail?' said Kate.

'We should go to France,' Max said. 'Go to France and see France and speak French. Otherwise –' he looked glumly at the pile of books on his floor – 'what's the point of all this?'

They finished the year with passes: Kate's better than Max's but worse than she'd hoped for, and two days after they'd had their results they began to pack up their rooms, ready to return home. At the beginning of July, Max paid his sister £100 to borrow her car for a week, promising to return it unmarked and valeted at the end of his holiday with Kate. They met early at Paddington Station and loaded the boot with the four-person tent she had taken from her mother's loft. Max, who had never camped before, had agreed to do so on the condition that Kate didn't complain if he urinated in nearby shrubbery. He had also agreed to drive on the further condition that Kate stayed awake for the whole journey, from London to Dover, and then Calais to the South of France. She had brought a six-pack of tinned iced coffee and a playlist, as well as a series of complaints about her brief return home.

'She treats me like a kid, you know,' she said as they neared Dover. 'Asking what I want for dinner and stuff. I've lived away from home for a year now. I've basically moved out.'

'Isn't it a nice thing that she asks what you want for dinner?' Max said.

'You never ask me,' Kate said. 'We just sort of, know, you know?'

Here Max had to concede. 'We do always seem to know.'

On the ferry they bought playing cards and played Spit until Kate called time, accusing Max of being too aggressive with his technique. When they arrived in Calais, Max opened the car's tiny sunroof and turned Chaka Khan up to full volume.

'Don't crash,' Kate advised, as they pulled out of the terminal. Somewhere south of Clermont-Ferrand the road narrowed and straightened, and they were flanked on both sides by plane trees: it took them ten hours to get to Béziers, and then another hour to find the campsite, which was hidden behind a private estate just north of the beach. When at last they checked in they went straight to the restaurant on site, leaving the car parked under a tree and Kate's tent in a pile in the middle of their allocated pitch.

They sat at a white plastic table drinking beer until it was dark. Pitching the tent, then, was a challenge: Max tried to floodlight their spot with the car headlights, blasting the rest of the campers with a short burst of Chaka before the engine stalled in protest. Instead, they stumbled around in the dark waving their phone torches and tripping over pieces of canvas until they had constructed something resembling a tent.

'Max,' Kate whispered, once they had zipped themselves into their respective compartments. Max was standing up, completely naked, his part of the tent illuminated by the lamp below him. 'I can see your penis.'

'How?' Max whispered urgently.

'You're up-lit,' Kate replied.

'Oh. Sorry.' Max's silhouette, which was magnified across the canvas that separated them, put its hands over its crotch.

Kate snorted, turned so she was facing the other way. 'See you in the morning,' she said.

'The Shadow of the Dick,' Max said. 'Horror classic.'

Every morning for the next four days Kate and Max drank coffee and ate nectarines at their dusty breakfast table, and in the afternoons they swam in the sea and lay on the sand while the salt water dried onto their skin and into their hair. Kate listened to her music, eyes closed and the sun warm on her face; she began to feel as though the wire connecting her ears to her phone was the only thing keeping her connected to the real world. Max dipped in and out of the sea, returning to sleep, or to prop himself on his elbows and read. The breeze would rise and fall, and sometimes his elbow would touch her fingertips. On the fourth day, they stayed there until the sun began to dip, and when it got dark Max went back to the campsite to get his papers, and they rolled a spliff. Lying on the sand, they watched the smoke floating above them, and Kate felt then that she too could float.

The next afternoon, they made plans to drive to a beach a little further down the coast: there was a diving platform Max wanted to try. Kate was in the laundry room, charging her phone and watching a tanned blond man load a tumble dryer with dry, unwashed clothes, when her screen started to flash with an unknown number.

'Kate?' said the voice on the other end of the line. Kate knew straight away who the voice belonged to, but instinctively pretended not to recognise it.

'Hello,' she said. 'Who's that?'

'It's Zara Rippon, Max's mother.'

It surprised Kate to hear Zara use her husband's name, and for a moment she said nothing.

'He hasn't been answering his phone,' Zara said.

'Oh, it's been dead for days,' said Kate. Immediately, she regretted the metaphor: Zara was surely phoning about something serious. 'Is everything OK?' she said.

'There's been an accident,' Zara said. 'Rupert, Max's uncle. He's fine, but he's in hospital.'

'Oh my God,' Kate said. She paused, waiting for Zara to say more, then remembered that it was Max and not her that Zara wanted to speak to. 'I'm so sorry.'

'Thank you, Kate,' Zara said. She sounded a little weary. 'He crashed off the A4, into the front of the Cromwell Road Waitrose. Four times over the limit, no seat belt. Thank God nobody else was in the car. And he was only going slowly; he was swerving to avoid a sheep.'

'A sheep? In London?'

'It was actually a smear on his windscreen, from what I gather. He's conscious, but they're keeping him in.'

'I'm so sorry,' Kate said again. She was nearly back at the tent, now, but part of her wanted to stay on the phone with Zara. Instead she handed over to Max and sat down in the canvas doorway, sticking her feet out into the sun. Watching Max pace slowly along the gravel pathway, nodding as he spoke to his mother, Kate wondered if he was agreeing to change his ferry booking, arranging to come home early. But then he started laughing, shaking his head at something Zara had said. Kate couldn't imagine laughing so freely with her own mother, and she felt a pang of envy.

'What's happening?' Kate said, as soon as Max joined her again.

'He's OK,' Max said. 'Just an accident. He's lucky it wasn't worse.'

'Are you going to go and see him?'

'Yes. When I'm back.'

'Do you think you should go home sooner?' Kate moved the zip back and forth along the bottom of the tent's entrance as she spoke. 'Please don't worry about the holiday, if you have to.'

Max looked down at her. 'Why? There's nothing I can do,' he said. 'And there's nowhere I'd rather be, right now.'

Kate carried on playing with the zip, not wanting to look at him directly in case he saw too clearly her relief at his words.

'OK,' she said. 'You can always change your mind.'

They drove to the next beach as they had planned and Kate kept her phone ringer on in case Zara called again. When she told Max this he looked at her bag and shrugged, a gesture which told Kate that now was not the right moment to ask about Rupert. She hoped that Zara wouldn't call while they were in the car, because Max would see that Kate had already saved her number in her contacts.

That night, Kate thought she would fall asleep quickly, worn out by the long drive and the heat. But as soon as she zipped herself into her sleeping bag, she was conscious of how heavy her stomach felt after their late dinner, of her thighs sticky against each other, of the hard ground against her hips, and she lay on her back looking up at the domed ceiling of the tent. Max had been distant all afternoon, and even though he was less than two metres away from her, she missed him. It was an hour or more before she rolled onto her side. She had been listening out for the sound of Max's breathing, but could hear nothing to indicate he was asleep.

'Max,' she hissed. 'Max, are you awake?'

'Yep,' Max said. He didn't bother whispering; his voice was flat. Kate sighed, and climbed out of her sleeping bag, unzipping her side of the tent. The noise was so loud she thought she might wake the entire campsite, but she did the same for Max's compartment, and climbed in with him.

'Budge up,' she said.

Max sat up grumpily. 'I could have been masturbating,' he said. But he sounded less flat than he had a moment ago, before Kate had invaded his space.

'I knew you weren't,' Kate said. 'You've been far too sombre.'

'I'm not sombre.'

'You are. And that's fine. That's why I'm here.'

Max said nothing.

'Are you close to your uncle?'

'We used to be,' Max said. 'I am still, kind of. But him and my dad.'

'Not so much?'

'No.'

Max shuffled around and turned to face Kate, who had her arms wrapped around her chest. He unzipped his sleeping bag, and threw it over her, so it was half covering the two of them.

'He taught me to drive, in fact. Rupert. In Bisley, at my granny's house. I was fifteen, and we used to take my grandad's car around the fields. We crashed into a fence once. Well, *I* crashed into a fence. But I remember him getting shit for it from my dad, as the responsible adult. He was probably drunk, now I think of it.'

'How long has he been drinking for?'

'A while. Not consistently.' Max took a deep breath. 'He gets down,' he said, weighing his words carefully. Kate could tell this was not something he often spoke about. 'You know. Depressed. It goes in phases, but it seems to have got worse recently. I've no idea why.'

'There's not always a reason,' Kate said. Max waited for more. 'My mum, too. That's why she learned pottery. I'm not saying it's for everyone, but it seemed to help her.'

'Pottery? Really?'

'It's just her thing. Takes her out of her head, and back into the world. And I guess some people just need a bit more help than others, finding their thing.' Kate paused, and when she spoke again there was a touch of pride in her voice. 'I bought her a class for her birthday one year and, well.'

'I don't know what Rupert's thing is,' Max said. 'Drinking, probably.' He laughed wearily. 'That was a nice thing to do, though, Kate. For your mother.'

'It wasn't,' said Kate, momentarily irritated by the assumption that she'd had any option other than to try to help her mother.

'I just meant you're a nice person,' Max said.

Kate looked at Max, and softened. 'So are you.'

'I'm not so sure,' he said.

When they parted back in London, Max went home only briefly before going to the hospital to see Rupert. He found him propped up in bed, surrounded by plastic boxes of fruit and biscuits, with a bandage around his head.

'You look like somebody who's pretending to have a

head injury,' Max said, when he'd sat down next to his uncle. He reached out his hand to touch the bandage, but then thought better of it. Max had his uncle's green-grey eyes, and it was a strange thing for him to see that same shade looking back at him, dulled, even if Rupert was now smiling.

'You know I expect some sympathy, now you've come all this way.'

'It was no effort,' Max said. 'You're not that special.'

'Well. At least you didn't bring me any more fucking fruit.'

'It's good for you,' said Max. They both looked at the withered stalk of white grapes and the wrinkled apricots that had been pushed to the edge of Rupert's bedside table. There were cards expressing sympathy, and a pile of magazines.

'I can't read those, either. Because of the concussion. Can't even watch the football, the pixels get right behind the eyes. Like needles, honestly.' Rupert coughed, and smacked his chest. 'But of course, it's entirely self-inflicted.'

It seemed unkind to agree, so Max didn't say anything.

'Your father is furious with me. Thinks I need to stop drinking, but . . .' Rupert stopped. 'Where've you been, anyway? You look disgustingly healthy.'

'I was on holiday,' Max said. 'France. Just got back.' From his pocket he took the pack of cards he and Kate had played with on the ferry, and cigarettes he had bought from Calais. 'I did bring you some presents, though.'

Rupert's eyes brightened when he saw the two packets

in Max's hand. He slipped the cigarettes straight into the drawer next to his bed before taking the cards and tapping the pack with his knuckles. 'Now we're talking,' he said, shuffling himself upright. 'I hope you're ready to be beaten, boy.'

It was only when they were halfway through a game of 21 that it occurred to Max that perhaps he shouldn't be playing cards with his gambling uncle, but by this point Rupert was on a roll, and Max was putting up just enough of a fight for his uncle to be taking real pleasure in beating him. They kept on playing until Rupert's eyes got tired, and he said that the headache was beginning to return. He sank back into his bed, and Max passed him a plastic cup filled with water.

'You can keep these,' Max said, putting the cards back in the pack.

'Solitaire,' Rupert said. He closed his eyes and grimaced. 'I can smell the fumes from those fucking apricots from here. I suppose I should eat them.' He opened his eyes and looked at Max directly. 'I'm going to tell you something, Max, because I know nobody else will.'

Max leaned forward.

'If, in your old age, you are unlucky enough to have to have a serious operation, it's vitally important that you know the general anaesthetic gives you the worst fucking constipation you will ever have in your life.'

Rupert sighed, dragging the plastic box of grapes towards him.

3

It was October, and Zara was taking the evening train from Paddington to Stroud for her mother-in-law's birthday. Because this year was Bernadette's eightieth, celebrations were imposed on the Rippon family even more forcefully than usual. Nicole and William had set off from London that afternoon, but Zara had been in development meetings all day, and would be the last to arrive. The concourse was packed with commuters, and she sat outside a cafe, the peak of a cap borrowed from her daughter's wardrobe pulled low. It was rare that she was actually recognised in public, but she liked to have her eyes covered, to see more than be seen.

Whenever Zara took the train to Gloucestershire to see William's family she travelled first class. This little luxury meant she could board at the last minute, and that she could delay stepping off London soil for the countryside for as long as possible. When the train was four minutes from departure, she drained her coffee and made her way up the platform. William had messaged from Bisley to ask her to bring flowers, which he'd forgotten to pick up that afternoon, so Zara had bought a bunch of lilies from the supermarket in the station, stripping off the plastic cover and the label to disguise their source. The long-stemmed flowers, with her heavy bag, had the advantage of taking up the majority of her table and so warned off anybody who might try to share it with her.

Zara liked this first part of the journey, when the train passed familiar London landmarks: the car park in Royal Oak whose outer walls were pale pink concrete set with high white slabs that looked like tombstone teeth, the graffitied fence surrounding the tower block in whose shadow she walked daily on her way to the Tube. Here, she was seeing the city in negative, its underside exposed, stripped of the pedestrian's intimacy but somehow, to her, more vulnerable. Zara had been born in Marrakesh, where she lived with her parents for several years until they moved to an apartment in Paris's seventh arrondissement. Grandeur was the preserve of a city, and Zara did not think she would ever comprehend the desire to inhabit these spaces outside of it. Reaching the edge of London made her feel anxious: the horizon gave her a kind of vertigo. She took a beta blocker from the packet she had borrowed from Nicole's medicine cabinet. She put on her glasses, which at least gave her some means of framing the expanse of land she could see from her seat next to the window. It unnerved her to be stranded in this wide, boundless place.

The pill had only just begun to take effect when the train pulled into the station – her heart was at least beating a little less violently – but in the back seat of the taxi to

Bisley she closed her eyes as the driver took her, at a mercifully unhurried pace, through the narrowing lanes.

The large iron gates to Bisley House were closed, and when the taxi pulled up outside Zara could smell woodsmoke on the fresh autumn air. She paid the driver and got out, pushing open the gate and leaving tracks in the gravel as she dragged her bag to the front door. Bernadette's gardener had chopped and stacked logs in the open garage next to Gregor's old Porsche and strung fairy lights across the driveway to the front of the house. It was dark, and the light behind the curtains of the living room was the soft, flickering light of the hearth. Zara opened the front door without knocking: Bernadette never locked it, even when she was out. However impressive the house's exterior, inside it would always remind Zara of the setting of one of those depressingly English post-war films in which soldiers return from the battlefield to the homes of their wealthy families to drink tea and repress their trauma. The rooms were always dark, and though at this time of year Bernadette filled them with soft lamps and candles, the glow seemed to be absorbed by the burgundy sofa, the mahogany, and the coarse, colonial carpets. Zara caught sight of her reflection in the gilt mirror: she was sure that the lighting in this place aged her.

The birthday dinner was in one of the large dining rooms, in which guests were overlooked by the severed and mounted heads of ancient stags. At Christmas, Bernadette put tinsel around the antlers of her favourite, and one year had attached to the end of its muzzle a red nose: mercifully, Rudolph had not yet been dressed for the festive season. On the table were decanters of red wine, and Zara could smell rich beef from the kitchen.

'I'm so sorry I'm late,' she said. Rupert, who was nearest the door, got up to greet her. 'How's your head?' Zara said, as she kissed him on both cheeks.

'The skull's intact,' he said, 'it's just what's inside that's causing me problems.'

'Sara, you're here at last.' Bernadette, who had always taken great care never to pronounce her daughter-in-law's name correctly, was sitting at the head of the dinner table, wearing her evening pearls over a new cashmere twinset and heavily misted with Chanel No. 5.

'Happy birthday. These are from all of us.' Zara handed over the lilies, which Bernadette held from her at arm's length.

'Thank you,' she said. 'William, will you get a vase?' She waved at him, then sat completely still for a moment before sneezing twice, violently, pressing a napkin to her face. Bernadette tilted the bouquet towards her, so she could inspect the flowers: three were in bloom, the rest still tightly closed buds. Carefully, she put her napkin inside the mouth of each of the open flowers, closed it tightly, and tugged, pulling the stamens from each stem. She handed the napkin to William, opening it up so he could see the bright orange. 'Throw that away, will you?' she said. 'Lily pollen stains dreadfully. Not that I'd be able

28

to stand it anyway, with my hay fever. Put them in the kitchen, William.' Bernadette turned to Zara. 'You're next to Lewis.'

Moving to her seat, Zara bent down and kissed Max – who had only in recent years overridden his impulse to flinch at such gestures – and then Nicole. Nicole caught her hand, twisting in her seat and widening her eyes: Zara's daughter was a reliable confidante when it came to Bernadette's mild madness, and the subtle drama over the lilies would be discussed later that night.

Before the beef, there was fish: salmon with lemon and dry bread, and white wine which Zara drank instead of the heavy red that William's brother Alasdair kept trying to pour for her. Everybody was already a little bit tipsy, and Zara needed to catch up in order to endure the evening.

'How is medical school, Lewis?' said Zara to her nephew, as the meat arrived.

'Pretty good, yeah. I graduate this year, so, finals.' Lewis did not often go to the effort of constructing full sentences.

'My first boyfriend was a doctor too, you know,' said Zara. 'A surgeon, like William. I had just moved back to Morocco, and he was something of a hero. I found it all very sexy for a time, but I'm afraid he turned out to be surprisingly stupid.'

'Really?' said Lewis. 'Can't imagine you going out with somebody stupid.'

'Ah, that was a long time before I met your uncle. You can't imagine how different things were.'

In fact, Lewis could imagine, and indeed had – though not for a few years at least. When he'd been at boarding school he had rashly boasted to his friends that his uncle was having an affair with an actress who had appeared in sexy French films. William had not been having an affair with Zara, of course, they were married, and she was not an actress but a director. Fortunately for Lewis, these inaccuracies made his aunt impossible to track down when, inevitably, he ended up searching for pictures of Zara actress; then Zara French actress; and finally Zara sexy French actress – he didn't know her maiden name – during break time with half a dozen pubescent boys crowded around his computer, whose fan made a loud whirring noise as the ancient monitor began to overheat.

A year later, by which time Lewis had realised that it was perhaps not socially acceptable to search the Internet for nude photographs of one's aunt, even if the nudity was artistic, and even if the aunt wasn't a blood relation, he found himself denying flat out that he had ever claimed to have an uncle who was nailing a French actress.

'Sara, wasn't it?' Lewis's friend, Robbie, had said, turning from his computer screen, both hands resting impatiently on the keyboard.

'Don't know who you're talking about,' said Lewis. His right hand twitched.

They were in Robbie's bedroom, which was musty and

windowless: Lewis lying on the floor playing with a book of matches, and Alex on the bed.

'Who's Sara?' said Alex.

'Robbie's imaginary fuck,' said Lewis.

Robbie, wounded, turned back to his computer. 'She's not imaginary,' he said.

Zara certainly was not imaginary. For one thing, had she been, she would still look the way she did in those pictures online which, of course, Lewis had looked at more than once. Her hair would have been smoother: thin and silky, rather than the black, wiry bun into which it was now twisted at the nape of her neck. And her smell: her smell unnerved him. Lewis had not seen Zara for two years at least and he hadn't remembered that slightly musty smell – was it amber? – which smelt to him not like those floral scents with which the girls on his course doused themselves but something more elemental, more threatening. To Lewis, this was the smell of a middle-aged woman.

Across the table, Max was leaning back in his chair so that Rupert, who was sitting on his left, could listen in on the anecdote he was telling his grandmother. As he spoke, Bernadette was gripping the edges of the table, convulsing with laughter that was surely exaggerated for Max's benefit. Rupert was looking down into his glass, glancing up as Max's voice modulated with the pace of the story. He was a little glazed, but he was smiling. Max paused, and Bernadette reached across and took both her grandson's hands in hers, leaning in close.

'Tell me,' said Bernadette, 'is this Kate a girlfriend of yours?'

Max had talked about Kate to Bernadette before, in their fortnightly phone calls and in the letters he sent to her, and he could tell that she had been waiting for the right moment to ask him this.

'I'm going to tell her you said that,' Max said, getting his phone out of his pocket. 'She'll hate it. No, she's just a friend.'

'Ah, Kate. Darling Kate,' said Zara. She and Lewis were both watching Bernadette. 'He likes her too much to go out with her – so will probably end up marrying her.'

'Have you met her?' Lewis said, who was enjoying being in Zara's confidence.

'Who?'

'Katie, or whatever her name is.'

Zara dabbed the corner of her mouth with her napkin.

'I have, yes,' she said. 'Only briefly. But she's been a good friend to Max, this last year, and I have to say it is a comfort to know one's children have support.' Zara nodded in Rupert's direction, discreetly. 'And, you know, there's something in the way he talks about her – he admires her. He speaks about her as though she is resilient, or clever.' Now she rubbed her forefinger and thumb together, taking her time to find the words. 'Just that . . . shiny something. Not love, really. But she is one of those friends you make when you are young, who makes you see the world differently than you did before. Someone who dazzles you.'

Lewis nodded in agreement, but the truth was that he could not imagine meeting somebody who had a better way of looking at the world than he did. Occasionally he had thought that it might be nice to swap places with Max, who seemed to be liked by everyone, and so seemed to get what he wanted. But then, Lewis so often got what he wanted even without needing to be liked.

'What does she look like?' Lewis asked Zara.

Zara shrugged. 'Oh, you know. Hair. Eyes. Pale.'

'She doesn't sound very special.'

'Well, I'm not the one to say, I can't see her through my son's eyes.'

In case there was anybody present who had not yet developed gout, cheeseboards were making their way down the table. William, who had gone to the cellar for port, was now bounding around the room, filling up glasses.

'I'll be sick if I have any more,' Nicole said, pulling a face and waving her father away as he leaned over her shoulder. She pushed her hardly touched dessert towards the middle of the table. Lewis's father, Alasdair, bellowed with pleasure and slapped his brother on his shoulder. There was no danger that Alasdair would be sick; his belly, already distended, seemed only to take on a more solid form the more he filled it, as if he were filling it with purpose. When he came to their side, William put down his bottle in front of Zara, exchanging it for the cheeseboard. Lewis, who had watched the way people responded to William as he circled the table, poured for Zara, and then stood to pick up Rupert's empty glass.

'I shouldn't,' Rupert said, rolling his eyes in Bernadette's direction.

'Come on,' said Lewis, 'you need something for the toast.'

'You're not drinking, are you, Rupert?' Bernadette, who was watching her son, addressed him loudly across the table. 'You know,' she said to Max, only slightly lowering her voice, 'I told your uncle he could only come today if he didn't drink. It interferes with his antibiotics.'

Max glanced over at his mother, who shook her head, ever so slightly.

'The shits,' said Max sympathetically. 'That's what you get if you mix antibiotics and alcohol. Terrible shits.'

Lewis sat down with Rupert's glass still in his hand. Zara took it gently from him and filled it from the water jug.

'Voilà,' she said, passing the glass back across the table. 'Something for the toast.'

Zara patted Lewis's arm, confirming that his humiliation had not gone unnoticed. As her skin touched his, he had a flickering urge to put his hands around her wrist.

4

Bernadette's late husband Gregor Rippon had inherited Bisley House from his father, who had made his fortune in the mining business. Gregor married Bernadette when she was twenty-one, around the time that he started getting seriously involved in his father's company, reinvesting the profits into housing projects on the edges of failing factory towns. A few years after the births of their sons, Alasdair, William and Rupert, Gregor's father died. By the time he was thirty-five the company he had set up alongside his father's had begun work on half a dozen council house estates and municipal buildings whose post-war grey and red exteriors existed in defiance of the glowing limestone houses for which Rippon Stone Ltd had become known.

Kate's mother, Alison Quaile, had long ago ceased to envisage a life in which she inhabited one of those golden-walled, rose-covered cottages, and had rented the same terraced house, built when Gregor's company was still young, for almost two decades. The older houses were more attractive, of course, but even those with working fireplaces had thin windows and draughty doors, and around this time of year the mice would shelter from the cold in the wooden rafters. Alison was not inclined to take on the recurring threat of a rodent infestation, and when in the evenings she settled down on her sofa with a woollen blanket wrapped around her knees and a cushion on her lap she was grateful for the double glazing she'd paid to have installed when she'd first moved in, and for the rubber coating that had been put around the edge of the back door, neither of which would have been authorised by the council as alterations to the listed buildings she'd once coveted.

The house was small, though, and every time Kate came back from university, she brought with her an excess of belongings. Before she left for her first term, Kate's friend Claire had driven her to Ikea to buy new bedding, new towels, and a full set of cutlery and crockery – all of it white – which she put straight into the box at the foot of the stairs. Now, the kitchen cabinets, which Alison had cleared out and organised so that she could easily rotate her own set of hand-painted dinner plates and bowls, to ensure they faded evenly with use, were filled with cheap white plates and scuffed non-stick frying pans. But despite the mess her daughter made of her small home, Alison treasured her presence. Clear-minded, sober, she was now guiltily aware of those blurred years, when Kate had been younger and Alison had been drinking too much, and she was determined to make the most of the time they had now. The first winter without Kate had been particularly hard, especially in December, when there was little light, and little incentive to leave the house. Alison spent two months anticipating her daughter's return, ready to accommodate into her schedule the needs of somebody else. After a full term, Kate was tired enough to acquiesce to the love Alison had to give, and the bowls of pasta and cheese sauce and evenings spent watching quiz shows on television were accepted with neither gratitude nor complaint.

When it wasn't too cold and she wasn't working, Alison spent her time in the tiny shed on the patch of grass at the back of their house. She had been taking pottery and sculpting classes for the last six or so years, initially at Kate's suggestion, and believed the sculpting had been part of what had helped her to stop drinking. She had now been almost entirely sober for three years: it was far easier not to drink, she'd once told Kate, now that she had found a way of expressing herself. Kate, who'd still been at school at the time, had looked at the stricken plaster face Alison had been working on, its mouth gaping open in a silent scream, and had wondered with alarm what exactly it was she was trying to say.

Seeing her daughter at the end of every term reminded Alison of how she used to feel when Kate came back from staying with her father. After the marriage broke down and he moved to Devon, Kate had gone to stay for weekends, for whole weeks over half-term, and she had always returned with a different inflection in her voice, with a smarter pair of jeans or new trainers, and interests to which Alison had no means of catering. David's house was near the sea, and for a while Kate had got into surfing, wearing tight cropped T-shirts and baggy cut-off trousers that showed the braided anklet her father had bought for her one weekend in the summer. But even before Kate began to visit him less frequently Alison could see that this was a phase, just as the guitar had been, and the desire to play the drums – which, despite Kate's double-pronged attack, both parents had refused to provide – and when, on weeknights, Kate got into her pyjamas and sat on the sofa with her mother to watch *MasterChef*, Alison knew that none of these passions would be definitive, that each was just an experiment in identity.

But the changes in Kate after she had met Max felt more substantial. This was not just to do with clothing, or how she spent her time – though she had started dressing differently, in baggy T-shirts and gold hoops and branded sweatshirts – but with her demeanour. When she got back from their holiday to France at the end of their first year, she kept her phone either in her pocket or a few inches away, and she seemed to be constantly in correspondence with him. She had hinted at but not explained what was going on with Max's family, and though sometimes she shared with Alison their less personal exchanges – articles from American periodicals, short films and essays, music by which Alison was baffled – whenever Alison asked about the artist or the writer, Kate snatched back her phone and answered only in short sentences. Though Kate had agreed to come to pottery classes with her mother, she ignored the directions of their teacher and instead started to paint one of the bowls Alison had thrown a few sessions ago while warming up the wheel. Kate sat with her shoulders hunched, the sleeves of her white T-shirt rolled up to the tops of her arms. Her hair was tied away from her face, and she was frowning as she concentrated on the delicate blue pattern she was painting around the bowl's rim.

'It looks lovely,' Alison told her.

'It looks shit,' said Kate, holding up the bowl. 'It's supposed to be this pattern we saw in the South of France.'

Kate came home for Easter of her second year with a subscription to *Sight & Sound* and a new pair of Nikes. Alison decided to ask her if Max was coming to stay in Bisley. She had ascertained that his grandmother owned the large house just over the other side of the valley.

'No,' Kate said. 'He's away.'

'Have you been to the house?'

'No,' Kate said bluntly, which Alison took to mean that she had not been invited.

'He's welcome here any time, you know. We can make up the sofa bed.'

'Thanks,' Kate said, before softening a little. 'I don't know when he'll next be in Gloucestershire. Maybe I should ask Claire to come over. I'm sorry,' she said suddenly. 'Have I been annoying?'

'No comment,' said Alison.

Claire arrived after dinner with a four-pack of fruit cider and a spare pair of pants. 'In case I get too pissed to drive,' she said, waving them, when Alison opened the door. Alison always appreciated Claire's refreshing lack of subtlety when it came to the subject of her former alcoholism.

'They'll help you sober up, will they, love?'

'No, Mum,' Kate said, from the kitchen doorway, 'obviously they're so she can stay over.'

'That was a joke,' Alison said, with only moderate exasperation.

Kate shut the door to the kitchen and they sat at the table, talking and drinking.

'I'm supposed to be revising again,' Kate said to Claire.

'Aren't you just bored with having to do work?' Claire said. 'I would be by now. Jesus, you've got a whole other year.'

'Two,' Kate said. 'And a bit. I've got a year abroad next year.'

'This is exactly why I didn't go to university.'

Claire had instead taken a promotion from waitress to bar manager at a local pub. She was doing a course in hospitality management, and had never expressed disappointment about her decision. But whenever Kate talked about university, she was always careful to focus on the negatives – on the abundance of privilege, the overload of work, the stress – more than the things she valued.

'You were wise,' Kate said wryly.

'How's your mate?' Claire said.

'Max?'

'The one with the drunk uncle.'

'The Drunkle.' Kate, laughing at her own joke, got out

her phone. 'I can't believe I haven't come up with that already. I need to tell Max.'

'Is that maybe a bit insensitive?'

'He won't mind. He's got a dark sense of humour.'

'Humour is a defence mechanism.'

Kate put down her phone. 'His family are all kind of repressed,' she said. 'So I suppose that makes sense. Apart from the mum. She's a film-maker, did I tell you?'

'You did,' Claire said. 'Several times.'

'Oh. Well. She's the exception. As far as I can tell she's the one trying to get everyone to open up. Not sure how well that's going.'

'Max talks to you though, right? Because of –' Claire nodded her head in the direction of the closed door.

'Yeah, he does,' said Kate, her tone casual. 'I'm not really sure if he talks to anybody else, though.'

Since Rupert's car crash, Max had become less elusive about his uncle's addictions, and his family generally. Kate remembered what he had said the year before, about being used to people feeling as though they had ownership of his mother, and she had been careful, since then, to give Max far more than she took. And there was a lot she could give: despite what Claire had just said, Kate knew humour was the way through Max's defences. Whenever he was in danger of withdrawing, or keeping private whatever mishap Rupert had most recently brought on himself, she knew how to put him back at ease, to make him feel as though whatever disaster might have taken place was instead a minor, passing calamity. When Rupert had slipped and fallen down the concrete steps outside his building, when he'd been found wandering down Albert Bridge Road in the early hours of a cold December morning, when he'd sliced open an artery in his hand breaking through the window of his own flat, Kate was always on the other end of the phone. Even though Claire might not have realised it, she herself had always done the same for Kate, when Kate's own mother was in the grip of her addiction.

'Do you remember sitting here,' Kate said now, 'when I got my offer letter? The neighbours came over, you screamed so loudly.'

'Oh, shit, I do remember.'

Kate drank from her cider. Claire never went to the effort of trying to hide her emotions, and once she'd stopped screaming she'd burst into tears. Alison, who did not cry but whose eyes had glittered, had hidden a bottle of champagne at the back of the fridge just in case the news was good. She'd opened the bottle with an expertly soft pop: it had been the only time either girl had seen Alison drink in the last three years, and she had sipped a careful quarter-glass in the time Claire and Kate took to finish the rest of the bottle.

'That was a good day,' Kate said. She felt guilty, now, about shutting the door, and she leaned across and opened it just an inch.

5

Max had missed Easter in Bisley House that year because he'd gone with his mother and sister to southern Italy. Zara had been consulting on a film there and had managed to get a room for Nicole and Max covered by expenses. He had spent most of the week by the pool, he told Kate over FaceTime when he got back, and hadn't done any of the work he was supposed to.

'So there's that,' he said. He was sitting in his kitchen; behind him Kate could make out a tall silver fridge and a cream wall. 'And Granny's cross I wasn't there with her, but then she's always cross about something. How are you?'

'I'm fine,' Kate said. 'A bit sick of home, and I keep being horrible to my mum, I don't know why.'

'That can happen sometimes,' Max said. 'How long have we got left?'

'A whole week.'

'Is it only a week?' He was turning to look at something on the wall, out of view. 'You should come and stay.'

'In Bisley?'

'No.' Max pulled a face. 'I've been exiled for missing Holy Week. Come to London.'

'To your house?'

'Yes! And bring some work as well. I should do some of that.'

'OK,' said Kate. She couldn't stop herself from grinning into the camera. 'When? I'll look at trains.'

'Great, wait, no, don't get the train. My cousin can drive you, he's over at Bisley. Let me find out when he's going back to London. I'll text you.'

He messaged that afternoon to tell Kate that Lewis could give her a lift the following day. Kate gave Max the postcode and waited for Lewis outside her mother's terraced house, with a bottle of water, her backpack and a suitcase full of books. She couldn't tell whether she had equipped herself for a school trip or a romantic mini-break; perhaps, perversely, it was both.

Lewis drove a red Golf with a low, growling engine. He was better-looking than she had expected: a square jaw, straight nose. He had short, sandy hair and his face was clean-shaven. The windows were down – it was one of the first warm evenings of the year – and Lewis stayed in his seat, one of his hands on the steering wheel, the other on his phone, as he waited for her to get in the car. Kate struggled with her suitcase, heaving it into the boot, and got into the passenger seat.

'Hello,' he said.

'Hi,' said Kate.

Lewis took Kate's backpack from her lap and put it on the back seat. As she buckled her seat belt, he pulled away from the kerb and turned down the hill back through the centre of Randwick, whose red-brick buildings and rust-faded cars made Kate feel embarrassed.

'Thanks for coming to collect me,' said Kate.

Lewis said nothing, but leaned across her, and reached into the glovebox, searching with one hand while he kept the other on the wheel. Kate leaned back to make room for him. He was wearing a black T-shirt, the sleeve of which rode up a little to show the muscle of his upper left arm as he reached over her. He found what he was looking for: a cable, which he plugged into the stereo at one end and his phone at the other, while they waited at the traffic lights at the bottom of town.

'My price,' he said, passing Kate his phone and reciting his passcode. 'You have to keep me entertained.'

Kate didn't mind choosing the music, particularly since it meant they didn't have to speak. Lewis seemed like the kind of person who would put the conversational burden on whoever he was with; the kind of man who said things like 'tell me something interesting about yourself'. As they turned onto the motorway Lewis closed the windows and turned up the music. He was driving quickly, but that seemed appropriate to the mood and the music, to the fresh spring evening. Kate chose not to feel anxious whenever he had to slam on the brakes, but forty miles from London Lewis reached behind his seat with one hand and, after a moment or two of rooting around in what sounded like a box of ice, retrieved a bottle of beer from the cooler he had stashed behind his seat.

'Open this?' he said.

'What, for you?' said Kate.

'Oh, yeah,' said Lewis, not looking at Kate but glancing in the rear-view mirror. 'There's probably enough for you to have a couple too.'

'You can't drink while you're driving.'

Lewis shrugged. 'I'll open it, then,' he said, positioning the neck of the bottle in the corner of his mouth between his straight, white teeth.

Kate, who had once had to go to hospital with Max after he'd attempted to open a beer with his teeth and had bitten off the neck of the bottle, slicing open his gum and one side of his lip, grabbed Lewis's before he had a chance to bite down.

'Fucking hell,' she said. 'I'll do it.'

So Lewis drank, and he drove, and Kate, defeated, drank more, as if sobriety were a question of context. By the time they reached the M25 she had relinquished her anxieties, content in the perfect powerlessness of the passenger seat. In fact, Kate liked Lewis. He didn't have Max's warmth, but his reticence made her feel that it was important he should like her. He did use the word cunt more than was comfortable. Somewhere outside Swindon, Kate thought about calling him out on it with a joke she'd once heard.

'Utter cunt,' Lewis said, overtaking a lorry that was sitting in the middle lane. Kate heard the voice of her old Spanish teacher, who she'd stayed in touch with after leaving school: 'He's neither warm nor deep enough to be called a cunt,' she had said serenely, her soft accent draining the word of any threat. But Lewis had already cut back in front of the lorry, which receded in the wing mirror, and she thought the joke would be lost on him.

She did not tell Lewis that this was the first time she had been to Max's house, but she knew they must be getting close when he turned off the main road they had taken into London, and then again onto an even smaller road that curved round into Latimer Crescent. The houses here were large and white-fronted, the road lined with magnolia trees whose large pink petals had not yet fallen to the pavement where they would later turn to mulch in the rain. The cars here were all Mercedes or BMWs or Porsches, parked in gated driveways. Kate leaned forward a little in her seat, trying to guess which was Max's house. Lewis parked, and sat in the driver's seat looking at his phone.

'I'll be there in a second,' he said to Kate.

Kate, who had been waiting for him to get out so she could follow him to the right house, unbuckled her seat belt. 'I can't remember which number it is.'

Lewis looked up at her now, then nodded in the direction of the house closest to them.

'The buzzer's on the gate,' he said.

'Right.'

Kate had not met Nicole before, but she knew as soon as she opened the door that she was Max's sister: she had his thin wrists, green-grey eyes, the same warm skin tone. Nicole looked past Kate to see where Lewis's car was, ignoring the large dog that skittered past her and hurled himself at her guest. Kate crouched down, holding his scruff as his tongue flailed towards her mouth.

'Is this Titus?' Kate said.

'Yes, he's a terror really. Did Lewis drive you?' she asked. 'Did he manage not to crash?'

'Just about,' Kate said.

Nicole stepped back into the hallway. 'I can't get in the car with him. Gives me anxiety. You're Kate, right?'

'Yes. You're Nicole.'

Nicole showed Kate into the kitchen, which was bigger than it had looked on Max's camera: a large, high-ceilinged room with a large iron range and a marble island, in the middle of which stood a large bunch of fresh-cut flowers, peonies and white roses.

'Such pretty flowers. Is it somebody's birthday?'

'Someone Mum worked with,' Nicole said, waving her hand. 'Max is somewhere.' She looked back out onto the road. 'Is Lewis coming in?'

'Oh, I don't know,' Kate said, glancing behind her at the front door.

'So rude.' Nicole went outside, and Kate heard Lewis's voice a few minutes later, the sound of footsteps going upstairs, and Nicole shouting Max's name again. There were no other sounds in the house, so she supposed that Zara and William were out. It seemed slightly absurd, she realised, that she still had Zara's number saved from that emergency phone call last summer, and she felt suddenly conscious of the contrast between her battered backpack and her worn trainers against Zara's immaculately tiled floor.

'Kate!' A door at the far end of the kitchen burst open, and Max came in, wearing gym kit and headphones. He grabbed her, pulling her into a sweaty hug. 'You're here,' he said.

Kate pushed him off. 'I'll hug you when you're less disgusting. Have you been running?'

'Gym,' Max said. He stepped back and, unabashed, sniffed his underarm. 'What's the time? Can we have wine yet?'

After dinner, Max put Kate in the spare room opposite his. She slept deeply and drunkenly, but the wine had been good and in the morning she woke with only the slightest of headaches. She took a long shower in the shared bathroom. There was no lock on the door, but the water was hot and the jet was powerful, and Kate felt so unusually at ease with the possibility that she might at any point be interrupted that she stayed standing under the spray until the mirror had completely steamed up.

It was while Max was making elaborate pancakes that Zara – who had got back late the night before – came downstairs, wearing a long cream dressing gown and with her hair loose around her shoulders. Kate found herself sitting up a little straighter when Zara came downstairs and into the kitchen, half expecting to have to reintroduce herself, but she leaned down and kissed Kate on both cheeks, asked her if she'd slept well in the spare room. She smelt of moisturiser and powder.

'I put out new pillows – did Max change them? The others were very old, I'm sure William and I had them when we moved here. Max, did you give Kate the new pillows?'

'Uh,' said Max. He was pouring thick batter carefully from a mixing bowl into a butter-saturated frying pan.

'I'm sorry,' Zara said. 'It must have been so uncomfortable. Make sure he changes them for you.'

'I slept well, honestly. I was exhausted.'

Zara sat down with Kate at the breakfast table. 'How is your mother?' Zara said.

'She's fine,' Kate said, only a little disconcerted by Zara's familiar tone, which made her feel as though she ought to have something more to offer. She added: 'She's working. I think the routine is helping her.'

'I'm sure she's loved having you home,' said Zara, nodding.

'I think I've probably been a bit of a nightmare,' Kate said.

'Nonsense. She'll have loved having you there, and here we are, stealing you away. Now, what work do you have to do? I'd say you can use my office but I'm afraid I have a deadline. Your exams are next week?'

'Not for another month, actually,' Kate said.

'And you're revising already? You'll have forgotten everything in a month.'

'I've promised Kate we'll work,' Max said. 'It was a condition of her coming to stay.'

'I don't mind,' Kate said hurriedly.

'Well,' said Zara, standing up and adjusting the tie of her dressing gown, 'if you can possibly tear yourself away from your books, there's an exhibition you must go and see.'

*

Now that they were both here in London, it seemed unfeasible that they should study. Apart from their holiday in France, it was the first significant stretch of time Kate and Max had spent together outside of term. From her first morning she knew that this time – in which Max's family passed in and out of the house, too absorbed by their own routines to be fazed by Kate's presence – was precious. On their second night, Max gave her a tour of his neighbourhood, taking her to a Greek restaurant at the end of his road where they drank ouzo and he laughed into his menu while the waiter tried to flirt with Kate. On the third night, they headed to a bar in Soho where Max overrode Kate's embarrassment at the cost of the bottle they'd bought – the cheapest on the menu – by insisting that he'd drunk more than twice what she had, and picking up the whole bill himself.

'You can get a bottle for us on the way back,' he said, as if it were in any way comparable. 'There's a corner shop by the Tube.'

In the mornings they ate pastries and drank coffee, sitting at the kitchen island, listening to music and talking until long after their mugs had grown cold. Each of the family members would come downstairs in turn and make themselves breakfast: cereal for Zara, an English muffin for William, and a kale smoothie for Nicole, who didn't seem to want to go back to her flat in Camden.

'Why are you still here?' said Max to his sister, on the third morning, as if he had only just noticed that she was living there.

'I'm avoiding Josh.'

Nicole had decided that she was breaking up with her boyfriend, but their lease didn't end until September, so in the meantime, instead of telling him that she was no longer in love with him, she had decided instead to disappear for days at a time without explanation. Max asked his sister coyly whether her appearance at Latimer Crescent had anything to do with the fact that it was nearly the end of the month, a few days before pay day, but was ignored.

In place of revision Max and Kate held film screenings in the first-floor living room of the house, which contained a six-seater sofa and the projector that had replaced the older one Max had installed in his first-year room. The image on this screen was bolder and sharper than the one Kate and Max were used to, and speakers surrounded the linen sofa. Now that Kate saw what Max was used to, their grainy projector seemed far less extravagant than when he'd first set it up. On their last night, once they'd worked their way through the films they'd been studying, Kate suggested that they watch *L'Accusé*.

'Do you ever think about making films?' she said, as they waited for it to load. 'You and Zara could be the next Coppolas.'

Max shrugged. 'Maybe,' he said. 'I don't know if it's as fun as it looks.'

Momentarily, Kate regretted putting *L'Accusé* on. But it was not long before Max paused the film and rewound it.

'I love this shot,' Max said. 'It's so intense. Look at the way the camera stays on her while she watches him.'

Lucille's face filled the screen: she was eating spaghetti bolognese, little pieces of minced beef and tomato flecking her chin as she sucked tubes of spaghetti between her lips, watching her lover across the dinner table. Max sat forward in his chair, silhouetted against the blue and red light, and Kate said nothing, not wanting to disrupt his concentration. In that moment the door to the living room swung open, and the lights came on.

'No,' Max said, waving his hand at his father, who stood in the doorway. 'We just started watching.'

'Max,' William said. His voice sounded unnaturally steady. 'Will you pause it, just for a moment? It's your grandmother.'

6

On the way to Bisley William listened to repeats of a
panel show Max had downloaded onto the car's stereo.
Though he was only distantly aware of the voices of the
panellists and the applause of the studio audience, once
or twice he heard himself laughing at a joke he would
not have been able to recount, if anybody had asked
him what was so funny. Thoughts surfaced and sank: the
conversations he'd had with his mother over Easter
about Rupert; her disappointment that Nicole and Max
had gone to Italy instead of coming to stay; her complaints of heart palpitations. William knew that for years
Bernadette had been fabricating ailments that would justify twice-monthly visits to Dr Woodfine, who had kind
eyes and was rumoured to be a distant relation of the
Windsors, but her long-standing hypochondria did not
assuage his guilt. There was little hope of recovery. William, himself a doctor, knew that the ambulance, the
attempts at resuscitation, were only nominal. In his professional life, he had always thought it a cruelty to draw
out a life when it had reached its natural end, but nonetheless he drove at an anxious speed, praying to Bernadette's

God that he would reach Bisley before she was declared dead.

When Alasdair arrived that evening, William had just got back from the hospital. They ate dinner together – a ravioli dish Bernadette's housekeeper had made and refrigerated in a Tupperware labelled with today's date – and Alasdair chose wine from the cellar. As they drank their way through the first bottle of red, the two brothers began to talk instead of their father, who had always been amused by Bernadette's hypochondria. The irony surrounding her unexpected death would have delighted the man who had once convinced his wife that oregano, a distant relation of marijuana, could cause psychosis if consumed in excessive quantities.

'He would have been glad that she didn't see it coming,' William said to his brother. 'She was always so afraid of death.'

Rupert arrived the next day. He'd lost his licence after his car accident, so William picked him up from the station and the three of them read through the will. Afterwards, Rupert took a long walk around the grounds, leaving his brothers with the family solicitor. When they were finished, William went outside to find Rupert, who was sitting on the wall at the top of the garden, smoking. William sat down next to his brother, but couldn't think of anything to say that would comfort him.

The time between death and burial was filled with administration: William and Alasdair took meetings with their accountant, William booked the parish church for the funeral, and Alasdair negotiated caterers' fees. They took it in turns to field calls from Dr Woodfine, who was trying, without integrity, to establish whether he was about to be sued for professional negligence.

At the funeral reception Max sat with Rupert. They were both drunk, but Rupert more so: he was holding on to a glass of the free bar's Scotch as if it were the only thing keeping him upright. Max sympathised. He and Lewis had been among Bernadette's pallbearers, and when they'd stepped through the doors of the church and the Requiem Mass had started to play, his shoulders had tensed beneath the weight of the coffin and, for the first time, he had understood that Bernadette was really dead. Now, though, at the bar with Rupert, he was fully subsumed by his bereavement, free to wallow without being taken by surprise.

'I missed Easter,' he said to his uncle. 'I knew she would be upset, but I still missed it.'

'She was a very sensitive woman,' Rupert said, shaking his head and swilling his glass. The movement was too vigorous, and he slipped a little on his stool. He paused, and righted himself, before he spoke again, and Max did not notice the look Rupert had of biting something back. 'She tended to take things to heart.'

Rupert was drunk the next morning, too, and came down to breakfast wearing Gregor's silk dressing gown tied loosely around his thin waist. He stood swaying by the Aga, peering into the bowl of eggs collected that morning by William.

'Did you know,' Rupert said, turning to face the kitchen

table, 'that if you squeeze an egg like this –' he held the egg at both ends – 'you can't break it. But if you squeeze it this way –' he laid the egg flat on his palm now, and closed his fingers around it – 'it will . . .' He squeezed as tightly as he could, screwing up his eyes as he did so, and they waited for the crack – but the egg remained whole. The noise of William pushing his chair back jolted Rupert, so that he swung his arm down and smashed the egg against the edge of the worktop. The yolk split, dribbling between his fingers as he lifted his hand, bemused. Zara was instantly at his side with a tea towel in her hand, and she wiped his fingers as she would a child's, while Max and Nicole looked on. Nicole bit her lip and caught her mother's eye; Zara shook her head gently. William stood halfway between the table and the counter, momentarily paralysed.

'Have you showered?' Zara said. 'Why don't you have a shower? Come on, William will bring you some coffee.' She glanced round at her husband as she led Rupert from the kitchen. William walked slowly to the sink and put the kettle on, then he stood, his hands resting on the countertop, his head bowed, waiting for the water to boil.

After the funeral, Max returned to complete the final term of the year. During these weeks, he sat with Kate in the library while she passed him notes and helped him memorise them, lifted his head from his hands and made him tea even though he rarely drank it. Kate did not remember her own grandparents, three of whom had died before she was born, but she knew how close to Bernadette Max had been, and his childlike desire to uncover his memories of her – old photographs, letters, gifts she had given him which he had not wanted at the time but which now he treasured – was something Kate was careful to indulge. He was separated from his family, here, and Kate understood that she needed to be more than a friend to him. If she came home from the library late and saw that his light was still on, she would climb the stairs to his room and knock, and, just as she had done when they'd been together in France, she would clamber into bed with him and talk until he fell asleep.

'I just keep thinking that she died angry with me.'

'Surely she wouldn't have actually been angry, would she?'

'I don't know,' Max said. 'She was quite Old Testament, sometimes. One of my earliest memories is of her putting salt instead of sugar in my grandad's coffee. He threw up on the drawing-room carpet.'

'She did that on purpose?'

'Apparently he didn't vote for her roses in the Bisley Blooms Contest.'

'Wow.'

'So, she died with a wrath.'

'Well.' Kate paused. They were both looking up at the ceiling of Max's room, arms tucked by their sides. 'When people are gone it's easy to romanticise them. But I think there is a value in being true to her memory.'

'If she was a cantankerous bitch, you mean?' Max was laughing now.

'I wouldn't go that far. She's gonna have friends in high places,' Kate said, pointing to the sky.

'Granny, mea culpa.' Max turned to Kate. 'I'm tired. Can we watch something? Will you stay here and sleep?'

Apart from his grandfather, who had died when Max was twelve, Max had never lost anybody he'd been close to. The realisation of loss arrived in small, unexpected waves: when Max found a shopping list in her handwriting at the bottom of a carrier bag, when the email address he had set up for her auto-filled on his phone, when old acquaintances of Bernadette's got in touch through William. On one such occasion, when an automated subscription letter for Bernadette arrived at his parents' house, Max took it to his father.

'For Granny,' he said solemnly, holding it out to him.

William, who was drinking coffee and reading the paper, glanced at his son over the top of his glasses, and took the letter. He turned it over and glanced at the addressee but didn't open it.

'We should cancel that,' he said.

During the summer, Kate came up again to stay with Max in London. They would both be abroad for their third year, and because they had no work to do, the July and August days seemed simply to hollow out, each becoming indistinguishable from the next. They needed each other: she him, to escape the monotony of her life at home, as much as he her, and they filled those long days with afternoons on the sofa, curtains drawn against the sunlight, Max circling around Bernadette's memory while Kate nudged him gently ever closer to accepting her loss.

For Kate, staying in Latimer Crescent had lost none of its charm. She loved the evenings when William would cook for them, when the five of them would eat together, Max and William quiet, Zara carrying the conversation, telling Kate anecdotes from the set that her husband and children had already heard countless times, while Kate listened intently. At home, Kate often ate on her knees in front of the television, and every day she was at Max's house she could hardly wait until William started pouring out a bottle of wine and handing round snacks before dinner, which, in its formality, was more intimate than any of the meals Kate could remember experiencing with her own mother. Later, Max and Kate experimented with William's drinks cabinet, inventing cocktails which were only occasionally superior to the cheap red wine they were used to drinking during term time. Max always peaked after the first couple of drinks; his skin flushing and his quick speech quicker still, his reminiscences becoming freer. Kate loved the story of the time he'd fallen from an apple tree in Bernadette's garden and his grandmother had driven him in her Sunday best to the hospital.

'It was the only time I ever heard her swear,' Max said, smiling as he sat back on the sofa. 'She wound down her window and told this woman that I was gravely wounded, and she needed to get out of the way so we could go to the hospital. Then she called her a whore as we were about to drive off, but the window needed winding back up with both hands so it took us ages to actually go anywhere.'

'I would've liked to have met her,' Kate said. 'She sounds brilliant. And mad.'

'She would have loved you,' Max said.

Towards the end of the summer Max went back to Bisley House to help his father and Alasdair sort through Bernadette's possessions. They pulled up into the drive, and Max found that he was expecting his grandmother to open the kitchen door. The house was still and quiet, and Max saw that the ivy had been stripped from the front wall, leaving fossil-like markings on the limestone. On the first afternoon, he walked to the apple tree and found the spot where Rupert had once helped him add his initials to those – Rupert's, William's, Alasdair's and Gregor's – already on the trunk. Later, he moved among the upstairs rooms of the house with a set of cardboard boxes into which he intended to organise both his grandmother's possessions and all the constituent parts of his grief. His grief, though, lacked loyalty, and as he opened up her dressing table, her large oak wardrobe and the embossed shoeboxes stacked against its back panel, it was not Bernadette he thought of but his grandfather, who had died eight years earlier. There was the razor Bernadette had kept in its leather case, whose red handle was engraved with Gregor Rippon's initials, and which felt heavy in Max's hand. He held up the razor, one side of his face reflected in its blade, and it occurred to him that he could not remember what his grandfather had looked like, much less whether he'd been clean-shaven or bearded.

'Just leave it in the cupboard,' said a voice behind him. Alasdair had been standing in the doorway. He had a black bin bag in his hand. 'We'll sort through the bedrooms later.'

7

Kate and Max had both applied to live in Paris for their third-year placements, but when the letters came only Kate had been accepted by the Sorbonne.

'I think it will be good,' Max said to her, when he phoned to tell her that a University in Medellin had taken him at the last minute. 'I think maybe I need some distance. And there won't be many English speakers on the course, so at least I'll get good at Spanish.'

Max was becoming frustrated by the accumulation of family silences around the death of Bernadette. For reasons he did not yet understand, his father had started to avoid mentioning his grandmother by name, and it was somehow impossible not to follow his lead: Bernadette's car became the Polo, her house was now only ever Bisley House, her cherished art collection just a commodity.

He noticed that his uncles had also adopted the new register. When Alasdair came to Latimer Crescent, he spoke with brutal pragmatism of his mother's remaining assets, and more often than not Rupert found a reason to leave the room whenever her name was mentioned. And so before Max had had his visa approved, before he had even booked his flights and had his vaccinations, he was negotiating the euphemistic language of loss.

In Colombia, Max quickly found ways to distract himself. Getting high, or taking party drugs, it was easy to break down the barriers that might have left him isolated. There was always music, reggaeton and salsa, coming from the windows of restaurants and bars into the steep cobbled streets, and he would ride out his highs in a club with a cheap bottle of rum or lying in the hammock of some third-floor apartment, while somebody played a guitar and somebody else rolled a spliff. It was easy, here, not to think too much about home.

Kate could see that a change was taking place, whenever they spoke on Skype. She rarely mentioned Bernadette directly, but whenever she asked him how his family was, or whether he had heard what was happening with his grandmother's house, he would shrug, and Kate could tell that he was looking at something else on his screen. But a moment would pass and his face would brighten again, and he would be smiling straight into the camera, calling her Katherine or Katie, anything but the name everybody else called her, telling her he missed her and that the only thing that would make his life there better would be for her to come too.

'Drop out,' he'd say. 'Drop out and sign onto my course instead – my friend has a spare room in her flat. Come, please come, we'll have the time of our lives.'

Though Kate never admitted it to Max, she would in fact have loved nothing more than to leave the Sorbonne to go and live in Colombia. But something stopped her: she had set herself a challenge, sticking with Paris, and she refused to feel that she could not cope without him. There was no denying, however, that loneliness had so far been the defining feature of her stay: it was as though she was back in her first term again, in the time before she'd met Max. When she'd been with the Rippons in the summer, Kate had asked Zara how she should spend her time in France. Zara had opened her laptop and put on her glasses, and had looked up the addresses of her favourite cinemas, a bar in Le Marais where, she said, all the actors and theatre directors went after their shows, and a market where she could buy macarons better than those sold in Ladurée but cheaper than any patisserie.

There would be grime, Zara had warned, and isolation: Parisians lived alone, not in shared flats like Londoners, but all of this had added to the romance Kate had been expecting. She had never lived in a big city, and she had fantasised about drinking coffee in bars, meeting mysterious strangers, taking solitary, mid-afternoon trips to French cinemas, just like Zara once had. But she was not prepared for the crushing loneliness she would experience in those first months. She drank so many solo coffees that she would frequently feel sick before lunchtime, and her attempts to start conversations in her student French, itself far less fluent than she had let herself believe, were met with bafflement. She tried the cinema and learned not about the nuances of New French Extremism but how best to identify and avoid the audience members – always male, always alone – most likely to start masturbating during the film. When she'd told Max about these guerrilla masturbators, he had responded with incredulity.

'I just don't believe people actually do that,' he said.

'Trust me,' said Kate.

Early in the year, more out of loneliness than desire, she had fallen briefly in love with a Norwegian called Erik who had broad shoulders and was the kind of man who looked forward to reading online reviews of electrical appliances prior to purchasing them. Kate's infatuation had sustained the first two months of their relationship, strengthened by a Christmas of heartache, but then suffered an inexorable decline slowed only by her fear of being alone for the rest of her time in Paris. It was the three-month anniversary present, Kate told Max, that had laid her feelings for Erik to rest. Erik had given her a necklace, and a poem he had written on handmade paper and had folded into a heavy envelope. Kate had read the poem, and, to avoid having to discuss it with him, kissed him before sitting up and presenting the back of her neck so that he could fasten the clasp. Two weeks later she ended the relationship with the very tenuous excuse that it was preventing her from immersing herself fully in French culture. This was a cause to which Erik could willingly martyr himself, and in an ominous gesture of goodwill he wrote and presented to her another poem.

After, determined to make better use of her time here, Kate started going to see films every day. If she went in the late morning, straight after lectures, she could adjust to the grey daylight afterwards with a lemonade and a cigarette in the park between the cinema and her apartment, watching people disperse from buildings for their lunch breaks. The woman who buzzed and waited in front of the apartment block opposite, craning her neck to see whether the shutters on the third floor were open, had finally gone to confront the lover who had stopped returning her messages; the man sitting across from her had lost his job but was still leaving the house to go to work every day. She found frames for these strangers, completed them with needs and secrets and desires, and this way learned to distract herself from her feelings of loneliness.

'Maybe you and I are going through something similar,' Kate said to Max, one evening over FaceTime. 'Detaching from reality, somehow?'

'Are we?' Max said, sniffing loudly and wiping his nose.

Kate, who had assumed that Max would have the insight to recognise this hedonistic phase in his life, shrugged and backtracked.

'Just, you know, being somewhere different. Away from everyday bullshit.'

'Fuck, I don't know if I want to come back,' Max said. He buried his head in his hands for a second before resurfacing, rubbing his eyes. 'But we're still living together, right, next year? You're not going to leave me for Erik?'

'Absolutely not. Erik is dead to me.'

'Well. That makes it bearable.'

*

In their final year Kate and Max shared high-ceilinged rooms on the top floor of one of the old buildings over-looking the river. Living in such proximity, the distance that had opened between them during their year abroad had rapidly closed as they once more got used to the long hours sitting in each other's rooms, talking late into the night. Max's room was bigger, but Kate's had a window which opened onto a wide ledge edged by a concrete bal-ustrade. In winter it was good for smoking, and when the weather started getting warmer they spent hours sitting there on the ledge.

When Max was drunk, he would shuffle right out so that his legs were dangling down below. There was a time when this would have made Kate nervous, when she might have tried to pull him back in, but now she lay on her bed, closing her eyes and feeling the warm breeze on her face as they talked.

'I put on weight in Paris,' she said, her eyes still closed, her fingers pinching her hips. 'It's only just beginning to shift.'

'I think you look really well,' Max said.

'Your dad has said that to me literally every time I've met him,' Kate said. 'Does he think I'm fat?'

Max snorted in dismissal.

'I definitely did put on weight.'

'Next time you should do more drugs,' Max said. 'It's the perfect appetite suppressant, just like loneliness is a stimulant.'

'So if you do drugs alone you'll probably stay about the same weight?'

Max laughed.

'It's true. My dad does always say that to people. It's because he's a doctor: if he tells everyone they look well they forget to show him their moles and foot fungus and shit like that.'

Kate stopped pinching her hips and lifted up her T-shirt, inspecting the birthmark next to her belly button.

'What kind of mole?'

'Freaky ones. It's one of the main reasons I didn't become a doctor. Ruins your social life.'

'And you failed chemistry.'

'I got a D.'

'Is that a pass? How did you even get into university?'

'Charm.'

Kate pulled her T-shirt back down. 'Do you think your mum will help me get into film school, if I ask her?'

'For sure,' Max turned round properly to look at her. 'You're applying, then? Don't you need to have made a film?'

'That's where you come in.'

'Am I going to star in it?' Max climbed back in through the window now and started playing with his hair in the mirror. He sucked in his cheekbones. 'Have you seen my Natalie Portman?'

'Actually, I was going to ask if I could borrow your camera.'

Seeing that she was serious, Max dropped the act. 'Of course you can.'

'It'll be really short, just one shot, no dialogue.'

'What's the shot?'

Kate paused. 'I haven't worked it out. But I had an idea, when I was away. This woman, on the balcony opposite me. Every afternoon she used to come out and roll a cigarette and smoke it. And the whole time she smoked it,' Kate said, 'she would have this milkshake Frappuccino thing in front of her in a plastic cup, piled high with whipped cream and chocolate shavings and marshmallows. And she would just watch it, while she smoked her cigarette. So I was thinking of just having somebody sit there with this big extravagant thing, the camera focused on it and they're looking at it but they're not eating it they're just smoking.'

'Can I audition?' Max said.

Kate shook her head. 'It has to be a woman.'

'I like it. It sounds cool. Mum will definitely help you. Definitely.'

'Thanks,' Kate said. She was smiling: this was the first time she had articulated any of this, to Max or to anybody.

'You two should have a chat about it next time you come over. Perhaps when we're next in Gloucestershire.'

'I'd love that.'

'The house is in a bit of a state, though. I've no idea what's happening. I have a feeling my uncle wants to sell it, but nobody's talking about it.'

'Rupert?'

'Alasdair.'

Max hadn't heard from Rupert in weeks and he knew that if he voiced his fear that his uncle was getting worse, and that he couldn't bring himself to pick up the phone, then Kate would try to persuade him that he needed to intervene. And Max, who suspected he was not up to the task, had begun to wonder whether it would be worse to try and to fail than not try at all.

'That would be sad,' Kate said now. 'It's been in your family for years, hasn't it?'

'It'll all be packed up,' Max said, ignoring Kate's question. He sat down heavily on the bed where she was lying, deliberately squashing her feet and patting her on the leg. 'But you should definitely come and see it. After we graduate, maybe. In the summer you can climb out onto the roof there too. And the rest of our lives will have begun by then. None of these bullshit exams, real adult life.'

Kate groaned. 'I'm not ready,' she said, putting her pillow over her face.

Max turned and climbed further on top of her, pressing down on the pillow.

'I understand,' he said. 'I'll just have to kill you instead.' Kate hit him with the back of her hand, and he lifted the pillow.

'Do you do this to your girlfriends?'

'No,' Max said. 'But I don't love them as much as I love you.'

8

Rupert stopped drinking in the new year, after he'd woken up in A&E with deep cuts in his left arm and a large bruise on his eye. Ostensibly, there were improvements, but sobriety was lonely, and had opened up within him a new, inescapable flatness. Whereas, when he had been drinking, there was always the promise that giving it up might help him to get better, now that he had actually stopped, and was still unhappy, there was neither hope to brighten the future nor drunkenness to dull the past. Rupert was running out of options; or, at least, he believed himself to be, and because he had isolated himself there was nobody trying to persuade him otherwise.

Just after his finals, Max went to visit his uncle. He went to his flat in Battersea with the excuse of borrowing a pair of sailing shoes; Rupert had had part-ownership in a yacht at one point, before Max was born, and he'd heard about the parties. Max had been hoping that Rupert would give him an anecdote or two along with the shoes: perhaps somebody famous had once been sick on them back in the eighties, or Rupert had won ownership of them in a bet. But Rupert had already put the shoes in a bag by the door when Max arrived, and although he invited him in for a glass of sparkling water he struggled to put sentences together as Max sat with him, telling him about his final term. Max never knew, with Rupert, whether to pretend that things in his life were better than they were or worse: much later it occurred to him that it was best just to be truthful, but at the time he was constantly searching for the exact words or story that would put the light back in his uncle's eyes. On this visit, Max had decided to give the impression of being unaccountably happy, despite his recent exams, and told Rupert about the evenings he'd spent watching films with Kate, their late nights up drinking and talking, their plans for her to move to London with him that September. It was important, he felt, to talk about the future with Rupert, to make sure he was aware of its existence.

'You can come and have dinner with us, once we're in the new flat.'

'Hm,' Rupert said, nodding. He was staring at the table; the rims of his eyes were red. He sat there for a while, but Max did not break the silence and instead waited for him to continue. 'She's a good friend,' Rupert said eventually, without looking up. His intonation was flat: it could have been a question or a statement. Max agreed that indeed she was. There was nothing more he could think of to say, and he was starting to feel as if Rupert didn't want him there. He gathered himself up to leave.

'Don't forget the shoes,' Rupert said.

*

It was not long afterwards that Rupert took an overdose. When William called to tell Max that his uncle was in hospital he asked if there had been another accident, refusing to imagine that whatever harm Rupert had come to had been self-inflicted. He had wanted to believe that it was the people who never said they were suicidal you needed to worry about, and that vocalising the desire for death would somehow help to neutralise it. But Rupert had talked about it, and had thought about it, and still he'd reached the conclusion that he no longer wanted to live: Rupert, in short, was weary. He had taken multiple measures to ensure that he would not fail: the pills had been bought online, shipped to his flat from America; he'd taken more than twice what was necessary in his bath with a bottle of whisky.

It was Zara who had heard exhaustion in her brother-in-law's voice when she asked him on Friday what he would be doing the next morning, and Rupert only laughed. She called back a few hours later, and then went to see him. Nobody answered the door, but Zara knew where he kept his spare key, and she was as unembarrassed about letting herself into his flat as she was about calling the emergency services when her knocking on the locked bathroom door went unanswered. For the third time in three years, the Rippons began their weekend in the in-patients clinic, waiting for news. On the Saturday afternoon Rupert regained consciousness, and when his nephew and his brother came into focus against the bright hospital lights, he groaned. Max leaned over him.

'Ru,' he said, trying to keep his voice level, 'Uncle Ru, it's me, you're here, you're safe.'

Rupert put his arm over his eyes. 'Why didn't you let me?' he said hoarsely.

Max stepped back, and when he spoke, it was with less force than he had intended. 'We couldn't have done that,' he said.

Not everybody in the family responded with excessive sympathy to Rupert's hospitalisation. An overdose, Alasdair could not help but notice, was not a particularly assertive means of taking one's own life. It was bloodless, and there was a clear margin for error.

'Somewhat effeminate,' he had said to William, as they sat waiting for Rupert to be discharged.

'It's suicide, not a fucking fashion statement,' William said.

Alasdair's indignation frequently threatened to escalate into anger, and William tried to remind himself that it was only a few years since Alasdair's wife had left him, and he supposed that even attempted suicide could be interpreted as a form of abandonment. Anger, Zara said, was not an uncommon reaction to such a tragedy, and was in some ways healthier than self-reproach or depression.

'Alasdair has never been even remotely depressed,' William said. 'He's only ever been wronged.'

William was out of his depth, but there were at least practical things he could do to help his brother. He paid for his therapy, ordered shopping to his flat, and – perhaps for his own benefit rather than Rupert's – that summer he began in earnest to transform Bisley House into somewhere habitable. The radiators needed bleeding, the boiler replacing and the guttering too, but it wouldn't take much to turn it back into the house they had lived in as boys. This was an investment in the future, William said to Rupert, and he wanted the whole family to be included. Rupert raised his eyebrows and gave his brother that Rippon stare.

Max joined his father at the end of July, and he and Kate met up in Randwick. It was the first time they'd seen each other properly since Rupert had taken his overdose, and Max had just learned that Bernadette had taken Rupert out of her will before she died.

'Apparently she didn't want him to spend it all on alcohol,' he told Kate. 'I think it was supposed to be an act of kindness, but it just comes across as kind of merciless.'

'Shit,' Kate said. 'No wonder he's been struggling so much. Poor Rupert.'

Max didn't say anything for a while. They were walking along the ridge of the common between Bisley and Randwick; he was scuffing stones with his shoes. 'Maybe,' he said eventually, 'I'm wondering if maybe she was going to change it back and then she didn't. Maybe she was upset, he'd just crashed his car and he was drinking too much. I remember how sensitive she was, on her eightieth birthday, when she thought he was drinking again. So she thought she'd just –' He drew his hand across his neck, made a garrotting noise.

'Not just money? He was cut out of the house as well?'

'Everything,' Max said. 'Money, house, all the art.'

'That's harsh.'

Max shrugged. 'It is. And clearly it didn't have the effect she wanted it to. If anything it's made him worse.'

'Definitely,' Kate said. 'I can definitely see how it would make him worse.'

'Tough love,' Max said. 'Different generation.'

'Is that really an excuse, though?'

'I don't see the point in being angry with her,' Max said, a little more bluntly than he had intended. They stopped next to a bench. Max looked at it, considered sitting down, but then kept on walking. 'My parents aren't really helping, in the way they're reacting. Dad just wants to throw money at the problem. And Mum, well, she kind of indulges Rupert. Going over there with groceries, taping numbers to his fridge and his bathroom mirror. Wants him to call whenever he needs to.'

'Isn't that a good thing?'

'Yes and no. It's good that he knows we care, but I can't help but think if he really wants to get better, he'll just get better.'

They'd reached the car park at the edge of the common. Zara was coming to pick Max up, and had offered Kate a lift home.

'I don't know if that's how it works,' Kate said now, careful not to be too forceful, reminding herself that if Max wasn't quite making sense it was because he was in the middle of it all, confused and angry. 'It's an illness, not a choice.'

'Hm,' Max said. 'That's exactly what my mum says.' He got out his phone, held it up for signal in case Zara had texted, and Kate didn't say anything else.

William was glad that Max had come to see the house: he wanted his son to be involved in his plans, to feel that he had a stake. After Rupert had spiralled, and once William had realised – too late – what the full consequences of his mother's actions would be, there was a small part of him that wanted to take a match to Bisley House, and all it had come to represent about his family. Stronger than this impulse, though, was his desire to regain ownership of the place that had for decades been his safe harbour – from boarding school as a child and university as a teenager, every Christmas thereafter – and in which his most precious memories had been formed. To Alasdair he had revealed none of this, but had said only that he wanted to 'sort through' the house, in response to which Alasdair, who was still thinking seriously about selling, had begun looking enthusiastically into skip hire.

As soon as Max left and Alasdair arrived, however, it became clear to both brothers that their immediate exercise was an emotional one. The house's rooms and corridors were contested zones to be taken into the territory of whichever of them was able to prove a greater claim. The experience of trauma, either psychological or physical, carried the most weight in the unspoken hierarchy, so that the concrete step upon which William had lost three and a half of his baby teeth afforded him reign over the wine cellar and all it contained, the red wine symbolic of his childhood sacrifice when, at the age of six, he had hurled himself screaming up the cellar stairs with blood streaming down his neck and soaking into the starched collar of his school shirt, causing the housekeeper to faint. Alasdair had afterwards questioned the business acumen of a tooth fairy that rewarded his younger brother's clumsiness over his own age and experience: a question that culminated in an unsuccessful attempt to negotiate with said tooth fairy a down-payment on his remaining molars.

The spare room, in which Alasdair had lost his virginity at the age of fifteen and three-quarters during a party thrown by the brothers (when Bernadette and Gregor had naively vacated their home for Hogmanay in Edinburgh one New Year's Eve) and in which Alasdair had suffered the intense trauma of having to comfort his then girlfriend Felicity, who wouldn't stop crying after she'd bled on the peach-trimmed floral bedsheets, became unquestionably Alasdair's domain, leaving him well within his rights to strip it of its peach soft furnishings, to unscrew the writing bureau and carry it down to the hallway where he would have it collected and driven back up to his flat in Fulham.

The only rooms considered off-limits were Bernadette's and Rupert's. Though the latter had not been inhabited for decades now, William was surprised to find that this was the best-preserved of the three boys' bedrooms: still the curtains Bernadette had sewn for Rupert herself out of spaceship-patterned cotton, whose edges had been bleached by years of exposure to weak summer sunlight; still the celestial stickers on the ceiling above the bed; still the rickety shelves on the far walls and the broken spines of yellowed books. Alasdair's and William's rooms retained few of their original features, by contrast, the single beds having been replaced by doubles, the patterned curtains with dark blue velvet drapes. William wondered how it was possible, despite everything, that his brother could have lain down on this bed, looking up at what was left of his stickered solar system, and concluded that their mother loved him the least.

9

The summer Rupert took his overdose, Lewis had never been in better shape. When he first started working as a doctor it had been all too tempting to try to survive the ten-day runs of fourteen-hour shifts and nights in the hospital on a diet of energy drinks and doughnuts. But Lewis knew the damage such a lifestyle would do to his physique, and corpulence was an inferior state of being that he was not willing to accept, particularly not in his prime of life. While others in his year had spiralled into a cycle of caffeine and sugar, Lewis had been going to the gym six times a week where, for an hour at a time, he maintained eye contact with himself in the mirrored walls as he sweated over iron bars, sandbags and kettlebells, transforming his body from good into excellent shape. Lewis was a determined man. Once he decided he wanted something, there was little that could stand in his way, and his regime did not just constitute lifting but also cardio in the mornings, high-intensity workouts, plyometrics, and a diet high in lean white meat, leafy vegetables and egg whites, and low in carbohydrate and flavour. Lewis thought of himself as an exceptional cook, and worked under the misapprehension that if he smothered the pale flesh of a chicken breast in powdered spices, parching the already-dry meat of any moisture, and incinerated it under the grill for a full forty-five minutes, then it would taste good. He had nobody to tell him otherwise: Alasdair usually ate out, so he was free to enjoy his arid chicken breast and limp vegetables without criticism.

Lewis would have liked to have cooked more for his father, whose stomach had grown yet larger in recent years, and who found eating so strenuous that he often ran out of breath when tackling a particularly heavy meal. To some extent, Lewis knew that he had his father's poor habits to thank for his high levels of self-discipline; without the memory of Alasdair in his white vest and chequered boxers bulldozing down the stairs at least once a week, stomach first and swearing, to extract his shirt from the laundry, he might not have taken up rugby at school, perhaps would not have had the incentive to join the gym when he started university, or to sign up for the five-aside squad when he left at the age of twenty-four. Alasdair's forehead shone pink and permanently with sweat, he wheezed when he spoke, he never walked if he could take a cab, and he always ate either takeaways or in restaurants. It was at medical school during his first dissection classes, in which Lewis watched the blade of his scalpel slice through the thick yellow fat of his cadaver's stomach, that it had first occurred to Lewis that his father might not live forever. He had always known that Alasdair's robustness was a weakness rather than a strength, and though Lewis found it easy to dissociate from the many patients that passed through his care, he was occasionally struck by similarities in the anatomy, diet or body-fat distribution of the occupants of the beds on his ward and that of his father.

'He's got nobody to look after him,' Lewis had recently overheard Nicole say to her own father. What Lewis inferred from this was not his own inadequacy as a caring son, but the inadequacy of his mother for leaving, and of his father for failing to persuade her to stay. And of course, Bernadette – peace be upon her – for being too self-absorbed to encourage her son to take better care of himself. But in the absence of any other suitable caregiver, Lewis was willing to step up, and to treat his father to his signature breakfast dish: the kind of thing he would have made for the girl he'd been seeing, if they went on another date, or if she ever responded to his texts.

'What is this?' Alasdair said, sticking a spoon into the yogurt piled on his plate. 'Müller Light?'

'They're sweet potato pancakes with low-fat yogurt and blueberry and cinnamon compote,' said Lewis. He sprinkled a little extra cinnamon onto his own portion, bending down so he was eye level with the plate so he could observe as his masterpiece took its final form.

'Jesus Christ,' said Alasdair.

Lewis's phone buzzed in his back pocket. The message was from Nicole: a photograph of William halfway up a ladder in what looked like the main hallway of Bisley House.

'*Tweedledum goes climbing*,' read the text. Lewis showed his father, who squinted at the photo.

'Tweedledum? Who's that? Where's Tweedledee?'

'William,' said Lewis. His father was missing the point. 'They're still at Bisley.'

'I don't know how he has the time,' Alasdair said vaguely. 'Doctors don't work hard enough, clearly.'

'Are you going to start going more often?'

In reply, Alasdair grunted, expending a third of a bottle of maple syrup onto his pancakes.

'William's always there,' Lewis persisted.

'William's sentimental.'

'But it belongs to both of you.'

'Well,' Alasdair said, 'I just can't see how it will ever be worth the upkeep.' He wiped his chin with his hand, catching a watery dollop of yogurt that had slid from his pancake. 'It's been a lot of effort, and it'll only get more expensive. It's a fucking albatross. Look what it did to Rupert.'

Lewis ate the rest of his pancakes in silence. It didn't seem fair that his father should be entitled to shut down a conversation in this way, and he rather envied the ease with which Alasdair had taken to weaponising his own brother's suicide attempt. He felt, not for the first time, as though he had been excluded from this particular tragedy. Sitting in the waiting room after Rupert was admitted, Lewis had found himself thinking about how it would have been if he was waiting for news on his own father. He would have known his role, he thought, if it was his father in the hospital bed: he would be at the centre of the drama, other relatives gravitating around him, adjusting their own concern in appropriate proportion to his. But because it was Rupert, and not Alasdair, Lewis found he was frequently left out of the hushed conversations taking place around him. Even when it came to medical matters, Lewis's expertise did not grant him access. At the vending machine he had found Max deep in conversation with one of the doctors who was looking after Rupert, but when Lewis had approached, the doctor had cleared his throat and stopped talking. Lewis had got a glass of water and gone back to the waiting room, where he'd sat by Nicole, who put her head on his shoulder.

In fact Nicole had been his only reliable confidante throughout the recent crisis. All news seemed to filter through William, and where Lewis was not kept updated, Nicole would text or phone and tell him the latest. Lewis heard about Bernadette's will via Nicole, before Alasdair had got round to explaining what had happened, and about the details of Rupert's overdose, and even about the growing antagonism between Bernadette and her youngest son in the months before her heart attack.

Nicole's birthday was at the end of the summer, the last Saturday of August, and she'd invited Lewis to the barbecue she was having at her parents' house to celebrate. As he walked from the Tube through the park, the air was thick with barbecue and cigarette smoke from the picnickers littering themselves across the grass. At this point in the summer the flesh on show was less pale than it was in late spring, but it was softer and paunchier after holiday indulgence. Some people never tanned, but just layered burn on burn: especially unappealing on the women wearing tight cut-off shorts and sleeveless tops that exposed their dimpled upper arms. Lewis had his sunglasses on, and so was free to look at the bodies of the women sprawled on the grass, sedated by an afternoon of lager and sun. He liked to look.

Nicole had asked him to bring something for the barbecue, and in the chilled aisle of the supermarket, Lewis considered his options. Strictly, he should only be eating lean meat: chicken breast, or, ideally but unseasonably, turkey. Perhaps a fillet steak, though even Lewis understood that it was a cuntish move to turn up at a barbecue with a fillet steak. But he deserved an indulgence. Chicken thighs, perhaps. Or ribs. Ribs would be a popular choice, and he liked to eat meat off the bone.

Lewis had forgotten how brightly lit Latimer Crescent was in summer. The door was open, and downstairs the walls of the living room were lined from floor to ceiling with deep, white bookcases. On the glass table were heavy art books, fashion magazines, a few of which had Zara on the cover, or mentioned in the lead line. Ribs had been a good choice: hazardous to the white walls, the cream sofas, the clean double-page spreads of those magazines. He only wished he'd brought more sauce. He went out through the conservatory to the back garden, which had been filled with thick white candles on silver dishes, and at the far end of which was a large barbecue.

Nicole had told him six, so he'd arrived at six, but as soon as he went outside he saw that he was early – there was hardly anybody there. It was an irritating quirk of Nicole's friendship group that they never seemed to arrive anywhere on time; but he felt his prompt arrival marked him as an insider, as family. Nicole was standing next to the barbecue with Max and a girl Lewis recognised as the friend he had given a lift to, the one he had assumed was Max's girlfriend. Max was bending over and blowing on the coals, while the girl looked on.

'You came,' Nicole said, and he hugged her with one arm, holding the bag of ribs away from her. She was wearing a black dress that was cut off at the tops of her thin arms. Lewis had always been impressed by how well Nicole looked after herself; she had a tan and clearly had not spent her entire summer climbing the attics of Bisley House. She looked a little tired, though, not quite as determinedly energetic as she had been on the phone a few days earlier.

'Do you know Kate?' she said now.

Lewis nodded, but didn't say anything. Max was sending up plumes of ash and Kate was laughing. There was an empty bottle of wine on the table; they had started drinking a while ago. Without saying anything, Lewis leaned past Max and slid the vent on the front of the barbecue open.

'Shit, Lewis,' said Max, 'and you brought us food. You're my favourite guest so far.'

'Oh, thanks,' Kate said, shoving Max playfully. She smiled at Lewis.

'You need to be careful,' Max said to her, blowing on the coals again. Fuelled by the oxygen Lewis had let in, they were beginning to glow red. 'If you don't step up your game I'm renting your room out to Lewis instead.'

'You're a snake,' Kate said.

'You're living together?' Lewis said abruptly.

'We will be, in September. If Kate works out how to stop being so fucking insufferable,' said Max. They were drunk, and showing off, insulting one another to show him how close they were. Kate shoved Max again and this time he stumbled, crashing into the edge of the table where Lewis had just put his ribs.

Nicole was looking at Max with a mixture of amusement and disdain. 'It's *you* who needs to be vetoed, Max,' she said. 'I vote we give Lewis your room.'

Lewis had not known that Max and Nicole were moving in together, and though he laughed along with Nicole, he didn't look at Kate. He would have moved in with them, if they'd asked him. Probably he had been right: Kate and Max were fucking, or at least Max wanted to fuck her – for this, Lewis couldn't blame him.

It wasn't long before people started arriving: Nicole's friends in large, impenetrable groups, and a few outsiders who gravitated to where Max had started grilling. Lewis stood near him with a beer, watching as he started cooking the ribs he had brought: the grill hadn't been quite hot enough when he'd put them on. When the sauce started dripping down into the coals, hissing and turning black, Lewis took the tongs from his cousin and started shuffling the ribs, lifting them from where they'd begun to droop down between the bars so he could rectify the damage Max had done. But as soon as Lewis took over Max disappeared, leaving him there to manage the meat.

From here, Lewis could see Kate over the other side of the garden, talking with her arms folded to a man he didn't recognise; looking far less comfortable than she had been with Max. She was wearing light blue jeans, tight, with a rip above the knee, and a top that showed her arms, which were freckled in the sun. Her nose, too, was freckled, but the freckles were obscured a little by her make-up. He liked her clothes, the jeans made her look younger than she was, like a nineteen-year-old on holiday with her family. He liked her eyes, too. They were intelligent. Probably, she *was* intelligent, in a naive kind of way; 'bright' was the word his father used when describing the women he worked with, or female friends of Lewis's who were not especially attractive.

Lewis stayed at the barbecue until all the meat was cooked. It was getting dark now, and people were starting to get drunk. He noticed Kate was standing on her own. The strap of her brown leather bag cut across her body like a seat belt, and she looked as though she was ready to leave at any moment. He walked up to her, looked deliberately at the strap.

'Are you out of here already?' said Lewis.

'We're out of ice,' said Kate.

The large plastic bucket in which the beers had been cooling was now filled with water, loose corks and labels of wine bottles. Lewis threw his empty beer bottle into the swamp.

'I'll come with you,' he said.

They walked out of the house into the street, where the trees were lit yellow by street lamps. The air was a fraction cooler than in the garden, and it was quiet. The sound of music and of conversation from the back of the house was contained within the garden's four walls; Kate looked at Lewis and smiled and he knew that he was no longer at the margins of a group. The shop was on the corner, two minutes from the house.

'I'll get this,' said Lewis, as they got to the counter, passing a five-pound note to the shopkeeper. 'Actually, and some of that rum.'

Kate fumbled in her brown bag for her purse, but Lewis had already got out his credit card.

'This is on me,' said Lewis.

10

When they returned to the house, Lewis took the bag of ice from Kate and put it in the kitchen sink.

'First rum, ice later,' he said. He took two glasses from the kitchen cupboard.

'Max told me what's going on with Rupert,' said Kate. 'I can't imagine how difficult it must be for all of you.'

It was strange to hear his uncle's name from the mouth of this girl he hardly knew.

'Have you met him?' Lewis said.

'No, but I know he's close to Max. We were just talking about him, earlier.'

Lewis unscrewed the lid of the bottle of rum.

'Was I rude to you, when we first met?' he said.

'I don't think so,' Kate said. She seemed to Lewis to be eager to placate him, and he quite liked it.

'I can be quite shy sometimes,' he said. 'Maybe it comes across as arrogance, but really I'm just self-conscious.' Lewis poured a large measure of rum into Kate's glass.

'Yeah, maybe,' Kate said. She glanced at one of Zara's magazine covers. 'Most people would find it hard not to feel overshadowed, being in your family.'

'Is that so?' said Lewis flatly. It should have been no surprise that Kate was impressed by his aunt.

'Actually, I'm applying to film school,' Kate said, flushing slightly. She had been about to say that she was planning on trying out Max's camera tomorrow, but something in Lewis's expression stopped her.

Lewis sipped his drink, slowly. Between the fruit bowl and water jug on the table in front of him was what looked like an invitation to an award ceremony, embossed and gold-edged. He flipped it over.

'I want to show you something,' he said, picking up the bottle of rum and their two glasses and going through the doorway towards the stairwell. Kate was at the kitchen table, and she looked reluctantly back out to the garden. She was trying to work out how best to say no. 'Come on,' said Lewis. 'They won't even notice we're gone.'

She followed him up the back stairs, kicking off her trainers on the bottom step, out of habit. Alison didn't like shoes on the beige carpet of their little terraced house. Later, she would look back at this moment, when Lewis was so far ahead of her up the stairs; he would not have stopped her had she turned back now.

The thing he wanted to show her, she had already seen. He took her through Zara and William's bedroom to their en suite bathroom. The room was filled with candles, with powders and creams in clean white cartons and blue glass bottles. Behind her, a large copper bathtub with bronze taps stood in the middle of the room, and to her right, the shower, which was marble-walled with a wide, sunken plug set in the middle of the floor. There was a cartoon of Zara hanging above the toilet, a caricature from a New York magazine, which William had hung there and which Max had shown to Kate on her first visit to the house. Because she didn't want to deflate Lewis, who looked so pleased with himself, Kate pretended that it was new to her.

'Wow, yeah,' said Kate. 'That's pretty funny.'

Lewis was looking at the cartoon, at Zara's plump lips, her breasts, which were pushed together and spilling comically out of her low, tight top, with an expression of grim satisfaction.

'I always think of it, when she's fucking with me. This is out there, and there's nothing she can do about it. She might be famous and successful and beautiful but she doesn't have control over how people see her any more. People can fuck with her, and she can't do anything about it.'

'Did you need to piss?' said Kate. 'I need to piss.'

Lewis left her, and waited outside the bathroom. Now she'd got him out of there, she would catch her breath and then go back downstairs. She was feeling drunker than ideally she would have liked, and she knew they were missing the party. From here she could hear voices and music but didn't know how much time had passed already.

He was waiting for her in the bedroom, the door closed and the bottle of rum cradled in his lap. He took a swig, and passed it to Kate as she emerged.

'Tell me something about yourself,' he said.

'What? Why?'

'Tell me something personal. Something about yourself that you've never told anybody.'

'Um,' Kate said, 'how about no? I'm going back downstairs.'

Lewis got up from the bed and stepped towards her. He was tall, her eyes were level with his chest, and his shoulders were broad. The way he was looking at her made her feel as though he knew something she didn't.

'But I want to get to know you better,' he said. 'OK, I'll go first. I've got a tattoo. Right next to my dick.'

'I don't think I'd ever get a tattoo,' Kate said. 'It's too permanent. Or, if I did, it would have to be really spontaneous, so I didn't have time to change my mind about it.'

She didn't want to hear any more about his tattoo: she was trying to steer him away.

'So, tell me something you've done that's spontaneous. It doesn't have to be a secret, but I want to know something personal.'

'Can't I just be boring?' Kate said. She wanted to get closer to the door, to keep him talking as she did so.

'But I know you're not,' he said, 'that's what I like about you. You don't let people tell you what to do. You do whatever the fuck you want.'

She didn't know what to say; everything she said he seemed to twist, and now he was slipping his hands around the base of her neck, so he was covering her ears. He kissed her; instinctively she pushed him. He stepped back, and for a moment she thought he was going to open the bedroom door, but instead he backed up against it, blocking the exit.

'You don't even want to see it?' he said.

'You know what, Lewis, no. I don't want to see your dick. Let's go and find Max.'

He had both hands on the door handle now, behind him. There was a key in the lock; he turned it. Kate knew she wasn't going to be able to leave.

'Come on,' he said. 'You have to see what it says at least. You'll like it.'

He walked her back into the room, took her arms and held them behind her. Kate wanted to tell him not to, but she couldn't find the words – her mind was blank and her limbs numb, so that when he pushed her onto the bed she fell easily, and when he pulled her hair back from her face so he could kiss her again, his tongue in her mouth this time, she couldn't move her arms to push back against him.

There was a point at which she ceased hoping that he would let her leave, only that nobody would come in and see them there. But nobody could come in, because the door was locked. He straddled her, a six-foot man, unbuckling his belt like he was being paid, as if any of this was supposed to be sexy. She could hear the music playing downstairs, but she couldn't remember the song, or the name of the singer.

'Read it,' he said, pulling down the waistband of his boxers. In turquoise ink just below the waistband were the words: *To live is to suffer*. He was hard, and he was close enough for her to smell him, hot and salty.

'Nietzsche,' he said, with a hint of pride, when she said nothing. She wanted to laugh, but her voice choked in her throat, betraying her.

She was betrayed, too, by the hole in her jeans, which tore, a slow, large tear, as he put his fingers through the gap and tugged, sharply. She was betrayed by her waist, her small breasts, which allowed her thin cotton top to slip up to her neck. As he released her momentarily to pull down her jeans she tried to sit up, but he pushed her back down.

'Close your eyes.' He'd pulled his boxers down too, now, and was holding his dick in his hand. 'I'm not going to do anything.'

'I don't want to fuck you,' Kate said.

'I respect that,' he said. 'Let me just see you.'

He tugged at her knickers, pulled them down around the tops of her thighs.

'You're wet,' he said. He put his hand over her face, his fingers in her mouth. They smelt of sweat. 'Taste yourself.'

She could have bit down, then, on his fingers. Bite down. Move away. Scream. But instead she closed her lips and not her teeth.

'You've got a tight cunt,' he breathed.

That was when she closed her eyes. That was the moment at which she shut off her mind, leaving her body to him. Locked out, shut down.

What would later become the icy sensation that spread through her body in moments of retrospective terror she first experienced as pain. Briefly, yes, it was brief, not torturous pain, but a sudden sharpness, like a reprimand, that stunned her to stillness, starting in her cunt, and spreading up through her stomach, settling in and across her chest.

But the pain and the brutality of his dick jammed inside her, transformed after a few moments into a warmth that was almost relief, much like a cold foot stepping into a hot bath that burns then settles.

Lewis moved his hand to her collarbone, his fingers pressing towards her windpipe. His eyes were closed, frowning, as if he were trying to wipe some terrible image that had been imprinted on his mind, and he pressed down harder on her, pressing her into the ancient mattress as he fucked her, his jeans pulled down around his knees.

All the while, she looked not at his face but at his collar, which was at her eye level, and traced the thin red ribbon stitched along the inside of it to where it disappeared with the curve of his thick neck, whose tendons and veins were bulging with the strain of fucking her. She was wet, accommodating, the ridges that ran inside her softening, acquiescing to the rhythm he dictated. But then he stopped, pulled out, opened his eyes, and came on her stomach, the white flesh of which had been exposed, and was now covered in a clear white slime that was warm but turned quickly cold.

'Fuck,' said Lewis. 'Fuck.'

He stood up and zipped up his jeans, buckled his belt. He did not look at her.

'Clean yourself up,' he said, sitting back on Max's parents' bed. As she closed the bathroom door, he put one hand down his jeans and lay back on the cushions, and with the other hand he started scrolling through his phone.

Kate stood in front of the marble basin, looking at herself in the mirror. It seemed impossible to her that the image reflected there was her face, that what she could see still belonged to her.

She took a sponge from the shower, soaked it in water, rubbed it across her stomach, ran hot water through the sponge until it was clean again, soaped it again, and scrubbed her stomach until it was pink. She washed the sponge through until it smelt clean, and of the lavender soap that sat on Zara's glass shelf. Zara would use it later, when she showered. She wouldn't know that it had been used to clean Lewis's cum from Kate's stomach. She pissed, quietly, hoping that Lewis wouldn't hear her, and when she stood up, before she pulled up her knickers, using the same sponge, she wiped between her legs.

She couldn't put the ripped jeans back on, but she couldn't go downstairs again without jeans. She didn't want to go downstairs at all, but she could hear the music still, the laughter, and she longed to be with everybody else, to shatter the sudden isolation. So she pulled the jeans over her thighs, still damp from the sponge, buttoned them up, and straightened her top, then went back out to Lewis.

'You look so fucking hot,' he said, looking up at her. 'Come here.' She didn't come to him, so he stood up and went to her, held her to his chest. 'You smell like sex.'

He led her out of the bedroom, looking both ways before they slipped out into the hall and turned off the light. He left the door open this time. 'Don't tell Zara you were in her bathroom,' he said. 'She'll go mental. But then –' he took a swig of the rum – 'you don't care, do you? You don't give a fuck. You're bad.'

She shook her head. He leaned back, that lazy look on his face, but his hand was still reaching out to touch her, not wanting to let go of her just yet.

'You say no, because you like saying no. But I see through you. I can see through it all.'

He waited for her to react. She did not. He passed the rum. She took a swig, to get rid of the taste in her mouth. When she did not speak, he lost interest.

'I'm going back downstairs. Are you coming?'

Kate stayed there in the hall as he went, taking the stairs two at a time, and when he had disappeared from sight she sat on the top step. Above her, fixed to the walls of the middle landing, were photographs of the Rippon family, iterations of Nicole and Max grinning in varying stages of toothlessness; photographs of Zara and William printed in eighties matt, Zara wearing shoulder pads that must just have been going out of fashion and William in thick-framed spectacles and with an inordinate amount of hair. There was a photograph of Rupert, too, with long hair, standing with his arm around Zara and grinning. He looked well – tanned, lean – probably, he had been happy.

And there was Lewis, she recognised him in among one of the family photographs, flanked by Max and Nicole, their arms linked protectively through his. The three children were wearing green wellington boots and oversized waterproofs, standing at the top of the hill that rose above the house in Bisley. Lewis was grinning, his eyes screwed shut and his little chin and chest thrust forward. Nicole was looking at Lewis and laughing, Max was frowning at the camera, his eyes framed by long, thick eyelashes.

She sat there for a long time, staring up at the photographs.

'I was tempted to do the same.'

A girl wearing a thick beige cardigan had appeared a few steps below Kate. She was looking up at her, amused.

'Hello,' Kate said.

'I think perhaps the best of the party is over, don't you?' said the girl. 'Though, if I were you, I think I would have gone to bed, rather than stopping here.'

'Don't let me keep you,' said Kate, shifting closer to the banister so she could get past. Kate could see up her nostrils, the edges of which were dusted with coke.

'And how are you?' asked the girl.

'I'm fine. I'm just having a break.' Kate forced a smile. 'Are you going to bed?'

'No, no,' she said airily. 'I will continue partying for the time being. I've rather found a second wind. I just came upstairs to shit in peace.'

'Good idea. I can recommend Zara's bathroom.'

She pointed. The girl stepped around her and bowed.

'Thank you,' she said, and disappeared.

Kate stayed there on the step until she heard the flush, and then pulled herself to her feet. She went upstairs and let herself into Max's room. There she undressed, stuffed her knickers in a shopping bag in Max's bin, and then took them out again, and put them in her bag with the jeans and with her top. She zipped up the bag.

She ran her hands over her body. Her extremities – her fingers, the widest part of her hips, her ass – were cold, as though they no longer belonged to her. She put on clean underwear and leggings, stiff cotton on dry skin, then slipped under the weighty sheets. She had left the light on, but she did not get out of bed to turn them off. Instead she lay there, duvet tucked under her chin, her back to the wall, waiting for Max to come up, or to fall asleep: whichever came first.

11

Kate woke early. Max was in bed beside her, curled up, breathing heavily. His skin smelt of alcohol, sweat, antiperspirant. She lay still, her head pounding. Max had turned off the light when he'd come to bed, and the heavy curtains were drawn against the morning sun. Daylight was difficult to contemplate. More difficult was the thought of Max waking and having to face him. She slipped out of bed and pulled on a sweatshirt that had been left on the floor. She took her bag and went down the stairs, barefooted and silent.

Sunlight was streaming into the kitchen through the conservatory roof and front window. She caught sight of her reflection in the oven door and saw that her face was streaked with black make-up and that her eyes were puffy.

The kitchen was a mess. On the marble kitchen island were plates of half-eaten food: overdressed salads, squashed burger patties and hummus that had developed a skin overnight. And drinks, drained mojitos with lime and brown sugar in the bottom of the glasses. Lime gone rancid in the heat of the morning. She hadn't known lime could smell like that, sweet and rotten.

There was a clean pint glass in the cupboard and she filled it with water from the tap. The bags of ice they had bought last night were sitting in the sink, melted, so that the water had leaked out and the plastic was flattened among rind and bottle tops and cigarette papers. She sipped her water. Perhaps she should tidy. Or perhaps she should leave.

There were footsteps upstairs, the sound of a door slamming. Now was the time, if she was going to get out of there. She wondered if it would be Lewis, coming to find her. But it was William who came down the back stairs, neatly dressed and shaved, and found her there in the kitchen.

'You're up,' he said. 'Are you the only one?'

'I think so,' said Kate.

'Well,' he said. 'Breakfast.'

He cleared a space for Kate at the kitchen table, and she helped him to load the dishwasher. He wiped down the table and she sat there, half in a patch of sunlight. William had showered already, he smelt fresh, and soapy. Kate tried to think of something she could say about Rupert: she had not seen William since he'd gone into hospital. She wanted to apologise for the mess that had been made of his house, given what he was going through, but she couldn't remember how to form sentences. He opened a window to let out the stale air and asked Kate if she wanted some coffee. She said that she did and, sensing that William wanted something to do, did not offer to help, but sat quietly as he took a fresh packet of coffee beans from the freezer and cut it open with scissors. He ground the beans, apologising for the noise, and then packed them into the percolator.

'Shall we have some music?' he said. He gave her his iPod, an ancient, chunky thing in white plastic casing, and Kate was reminded of when she had been given that same responsibility, in the passenger seat of Lewis's car as they'd driven to London two years earlier: that had been the first time she'd met him. She turned the wheel of the iPod; the percolator began to steam.

'Milk?' said William.

'Yes, please.'

William heated the milk in a saucepan, beating it with a little whisk which, he told Kate, he considered to be the most ingenious invention he had ever encountered. People spent thousands on these machines, he said, for steaming milk and for making espresso, and they had no idea that all they needed was this little whisk. William seemed to exist in a state of constant amazement, the world a source of unending fascination. It must be exhausting to live like that. By the time the coffee was made, Kate had still found nothing to listen to.

'There's nothing here you like, I'm sure. It's an old man's music collection.' William poured Kate a cup of coffee, and took the iPod from her, and she thought this was just about the kindest thing anybody had ever done. He put on an album by James Taylor, which Kate knew she would not have chosen, but which filled the kitchen with a mellow, calming sound. She drank her coffee, and sat listening to the music as William fried bacon and eggs, singing flatly, and carried on tidying around her, rebuffing her attempts to help him. Breakfast was not a good idea, but it was too late now to refuse it, so when he put in front of her a plate of thin white toast, with the bacon and eggs, she armoured herself with the knife and fork and began cautiously to move the food around her plate, careful not to breach the soft yolk. After the first mouthful, she realised how ravenously hungry she was, and the nausea she had woken with abated long enough for her to eat half of the egg and a piece of toast and two rashers of bacon.

'What time's your train?' said William. In fact she had originally planned to stay another day, but William had just given her a way out.

'I'll have to check the ticket. I think it's open, so, any time.'

William looked at his watch. 'Only eight o'clock. You'll have to wait a while for the others to emerge. I gather it went on late last night?'

'I think so . . . but I might just go. I'll see them all soon.'

Her shoes were where she had left them, at the bottom of the cream-carpeted stairs, and her jacket had been stuffed down the side of the sofa; but she couldn't find her phone. It wasn't in her bag, or her jacket pocket. She was close to leaving without it, suddenly desperate to get out of the house, terrified that somebody other than William, who was so kind with his whisk and his toast, would come downstairs and find her there, as if she wasn't supposed to be awake, standing, breathing. But William found it, next to the white orchid on the shelf above the sink.

'This yours?' he said, passing her the phone.

'Yes, thank you. I must have left it there,' said Kate. 'I went out for ice and must have forgotten it.'

'Oh, right, well, there you are.'

'I went out for ice with Lewis.'

Kate watched William for a reaction, waiting for him to read into this coded statement that which was unspeakable.

'Good,' said William vaguely. 'It's dead.'

She would charge the phone on the train, she said, though she knew her charger was upstairs in Max's room, and that she was not going back up there to collect it.

'Thank you for breakfast.'

'My pleasure. And I shall see you very soon, at the flat.'

'You'll have to come for dinner,' said Kate.

He let her out the front door, and turned and went back inside before Kate was halfway up the driveway. Out on the street, she looked up at the windows. She didn't know if Lewis had gone home last night, or if he'd slept in one of the spare rooms. It was enough for her, for now, to imagine that he was enclosed within those four walls, while she was out here, in the open air, on the road with her keys and with money in her purse, so that she could leave, she could disappear, while he stayed and slept.

12

Even if William had been looking for signs of disturbance, it was unlikely that he would have found anything strange about Kate's mood that morning. He did not know her well enough to read the nuances of her behaviour. Her sudden departure, her unease, the gravity of her silences as she laboured over breakfast: none of this had struck him as particularly unusual. In fact her presence had hardly struck him at all, not least because he was that morning caught up in his own tumult.

Once Kate had left, he abandoned his attempt to clean up the kitchen, and took his coffee to the window seat. Zara would be back soon, at least – she had been away for two nights, at a screening in Maastricht – but still he felt unsettled. The excess of empty beer cans, the sticky smell of alcohol, the light dusting of white powder and loose rolling papers felt like an especially unwelcome invasion. There was a time when a little youthful recklessness would not have bothered William, but in the last year, and in the last two months especially, the excesses of intoxication appeared to him less innocent than they once had.

Last night William had gone for dinner with Alasdair.

Rupert was supposed to be coming, too, but he'd cancelled at the last minute. He was feeling tired, he'd said. William did not know how to get past the euphemism so he'd accepted it without prying further. He had thought, though, that his evening with Alasdair would at least begin with a conversation about how they both thought Rupert was holding up, or whatever other crudely architectural metaphor was most appropriate to Rupert's current mental state. Alasdair greeted his brother with a sturdy embrace, but when they sat down, he started talking not about Rupert but about his own business, the value of his flat, the state of his stocks and the board of his company. William felt like he was having a business meeting.

'Did you go in his room?' said William, when Alasdair stopped talking to tuck his napkin into the top of his shirt.

'Whose?' said Alasdair.

'Rupert's,' William said impatiently. 'She kept all his books.'

Alasdair's lack of response was enough to tell William that he knew what he was trying to say but that he wasn't going to take the bait.

'How can he think she doesn't care?' said William. Hopelessness was beginning to rise inside him; he was nearing the edge of what he could articulate.

'Didn't,' Alasdair said.

'Didn't,' William repeated.

Alasdair paused for a moment before speaking. 'He's a grown man, Willie. Not a kid. Whatever he decides he wants, or whatever he's already decided, he'll do it by himself.'

The starters arrived, and Alasdair used this momentary distraction to change the topic of conversation. As he spoke, wiping lemon juice and fish oil from his mouth with the napkin in his left hand and gesturing with the chopsticks in his right, William struggled to process the image he was painting: a future for Bisley House that had nothing to do with sentiment and everything to do with finance. This was not the conversation William had been expecting and, too wrong-footed to respond coherently, instead he drank deeply from the glass Alasdair continued to fill.

William had come home late, his head heavy with red wine, and there had been no way for him to detect the subtle imprint on his and Zara's duvet where it had been compressed beneath the weight of two bodies: one inert, one active. He had returned to the house not long after the room had been vacated by Lewis and Kate, in fact he had walked in the front door just as Lewis was heading back out into the garden.

No; William intuited nothing, and he had slept dreamlessly while, unconsciously and without guilt, his sleeping body erased the traces of the sins of his nephew. He had been exhausted, and had woken the next morning with the feeling that he was already losing a race in which he had not known he was supposed to be competing, and with a horrid, corporeal awareness that as he had slept, his alcohol-infused sweat had soaked into his bedsheets, his body heating with the effort of metabolising everything he had drunk, his mouth half open against the pillowcase.

*

When Zara got home a little later that morning, there had been only a little movement in the upper floors of the house. William was still sitting by the window where the sun had been.

'How was Big Al?' Zara said, hanging her jacket by the kitchen door. This was a nickname Gregor had still been calling his oldest son when William and Zara had first started dating, and Zara was the only member of the family who insisted on using it now, partly because she knew it upset Alasdair, and partly because she took visceral pleasure in framing the ugliness of those two syllables in her soft French accent.

'Big,' William said, stretching back in his chair. Zara leaned over him, kissed the top of his head.

'Was it bad?'

'Yes,' said William. 'I wish you had been there.'

Zara said nothing, she wanted William to volunteer information without being asked. Alasdair and Zara did not much like one another, but they always made an effort to get along, especially when William was present. It was always very draining, sitting across from Alasdair and watching him ingest food while at the same time regurgitating half-formed, half-offensive thoughts he had picked up with the morning paper; particularly now that she couldn't necessarily rely on Rupert as an ally.

'You never know – he might be the next to go,' Zara said brightly. William looked up at her with an expression of such distress that immediately she was filled with remorse. 'I'm sorry,' she said. 'What did he say?'

William shook his head. 'He just has no sympathy. No understanding whatsoever. That's not to say that I know what it's like to feel that low – that low – but, Jesus, talk about survival of the fittest.'

'It's fine to be angry. Don't forget you're still in shock,' Zara said, 'and that you're a fully functioning human being with more emotional intelligence than a grated piece of Parmigiana.'

'You're too good to me,' William said.

'I said more intelligence. I didn't say how much more. I'm supposed to have Issa over tonight, there's a project she wants to talk to me about. Do you want me to cancel?'

'It's OK,' William said. 'I can just about handle Issa.'

He reached over and squeezed her hand. In the first years of their marriage, he often told her that if she ever left him then she would leave a better person than she'd found. When he said this she always laughed, but never did she disagree. It was true that she had forced William to talk, and to listen when she needed to talk. At first it baffled her, how zipped up he was, and she tried to push him to feel things he didn't want to feel, convinced that there must be more than what was on the surface. About a year into their relationship, confused by the fact that she had not once seen him cry, she took him to see a film called *Left Bank* which began with a cold-blooded murder lost in the violence of the sixties race riots. After that opening scene she had tried to reach for his hand, but he had shifted away from her and sat so motionless that Zara assumed he had fallen asleep. It was only when the lights came up and he refused to look at her that she realised he had been sobbing silently for the duration of the film.

These last couple of months, and indeed the last two years, had tested William's emotional capacity to and then beyond its limits. She guided him as best she could through the sadness that enclosed him, and, distressed though she was by the measures Rupert had taken, neither did she want to ignore those glimmers of pride she felt when William railed against Alasdair's very stunted emotional range. It might have been tempting to use these moments to turn William against his eldest brother, but she resisted, and instead tried to comfort him with the realities of the situation. He needn't worry about the house, for a start: Alasdair wouldn't be able to do anything without their agreement. He should stop worrying about trying to please everybody, and think instead about what he actually wanted.

'Otherwise you'll lose sight of yourself,' she said, 'and you won't be any good to anybody at all. Least of all Rupert.'

Upstairs, she unpacked, and put the clothes from her bag into the laundry basket, on top of the sauce-splattered shirt William had worn the night before. In the bathroom, she noticed that her moisturiser had been moved, and that her facecloth was hanging in a different place from where it was usually kept. Sometimes when William was hungover he pampered himself with the same toiletries he had mocked her for buying, and she assumed that today had been one of those days; though usually he opted for bubble bath and clay masks rather than her age-defying moisturiser. It was possible too that one of Nicole's friends had used the bathroom that morning; either way, and contrary to what Lewis had said to Kate the night before, Zara did not particularly mind. She liked the feeling that the house was lived-in, that her children, though grown, still felt at home enough here to share it with their friends, just as they had done when they were teenagers. She showered, and felt the tension in her body give way beneath the powerful stream of just-below-scalding water, and did not bother to ask William when she went back downstairs, clean-clothed and moisturised, whether any of Max's friends had been using their bathroom.

13

When Kate arrived back at her mother's house, every window had been flung wide. The white plastic front door was unlocked, and it opened with the sound of the rubber seal unsticking. Alison was cleaning; Alison never cleaned. But she had chosen today to put on her old thin denim skirt, vacuum the beige carpet and abrase the skin of her hands with bleach. In the hallway, Kate stood and listened to the sound of the Hoover, waiting to announce herself. There was a bang, the noise stopped, and Alison swore.

'I could have robbed you,' said Kate, as her mother came down the stairs holding a split vacuum bag trailing grey dust.

'You could of,' said Alison, 'I wouldn't mind in the slightest.' She kissed her daughter on the top of her head. 'Hung-over? I thought you were coming back tomorrow.'

'No, I was always coming home today.'

Kate was not sure why she felt it necessary to lie. Years of minor disobediences and deception had perhaps conditioned her this way, but more urgently she felt that her torn jeans were burning a hole in her bag, that she needed to take a shower. Kate went to her room where she closed the curtains, leaving the window open, and lay on her bed. She didn't move for a long time, only when Alison called her downstairs to ask if she wanted pizza for dinner. Kate didn't answer, but went down half an hour later and sat with her mother, who squirted mayonnaise from a bottle onto her plate, and who ate with her body turned towards the television while Kate looked at her food and wondered whether the cardboard packaging hadn't been removed from the pizza or if it just tasted that way.

After showering, she got back into bed and lay there in her towel, her hair still wet. In the dark, she listened to the radio and was reminded by the hourly blips that time continued to move. Kate slept a little, and with her half-sleeping mind conjured shapes into her bedroom that in the light from the radio took the form of intruders who did nothing but stand over her and watch so she was not sure if they meant her harm or if they were there to protect her. Either way she woke with her heart thumping and her palms sweating and knocked her lamp off her bedside table trying to turn it on and spilt a cold cup of tea – a cup that had been there before she'd gone to London, before she had seen Lewis, before – over the carpet, and the shadows disappeared back into the slowly shifting outline of her childhood curtains.

At four, she was woken again by the conviction that she was both pregnant with Lewis's child and had contracted some disease from him, and so she and the baby, to whom she was already completely attached, were sure to die soon. She knew that there was nothing she could do right now, except perhaps go into the bathroom and scour herself out, so instead she lay still – as still as she had lain the night before – and waited to fall back to sleep.

She woke at eleven to an empty house. The windows had been opened again, and there was a note on the kitchen table from Alison, who was working at the council that day. Kate remembered her late-night anxiety and, though in the light of day it seemed far less likely that she could be pregnant, she left the house without breakfast, locked the door behind her, and walked down the hill into the town. It was the last week of the school holidays, and on the pavements were skateboards and bicycles. A house had balloons tied to the door, and chalk on the pavement outside spelt out in white and pink letters, in adult's handwriting, 'Sophie's Seventh Birthday'.

Last night, in her child's bed, she had been struck by the feeling that she was too much a woman to be lying there. Just as when she had lost her virginity as a seventeen-year-old, and had felt a proud perverseness in using a large, yellow duck-shaped sponge to wash in between her legs in her mother's bath, she felt now that she had lost not just her virginity but some essential goodness she'd never managed to appreciate.

The pharmacy was on the high street, and the medicine counter was on the first floor. Kate queued for five minutes behind a woman who insisted on taking three different behind-the-counter eczema creams from their boxes and inspecting their labels before returning all three to the shop assistant and then paying for a packet of lozenges with silver and bronze coins. As the woman emptied out her purse, the assistant asked her if she had a loyalty card.

'I used to have a loyalty card,' the woman said cryptically, before adding, for clarity, 'but I don't any more.'

'That's fine,' the assistant said firmly.

'No I did, I used to have one, I came back from holiday,' said the woman, looking up at the polystyrene-tiled ceiling, 'musta been, 2007, 2008?' She had, at this point, ceased to count her coins so as to give her full attention to the accuracies of her narrative. 'No, 2007. I came back from holiday, and there was a letter, saying that it had been expired due to inactivity. Expired due to inactivity,' the woman repeated, unaware of the queue lengthening behind her.

'Next please!' Another frantic assistant had opened a second till, beckoning towards Kate, who shuffled past the coin-woman towards him.

'Hi,' said Kate, in a quiet voice. 'I need the morning-after pill.'

'You need to wait here for the pharmacist,' said the man, gesturing to a semi-enclosed area filled with plastic chairs. Clearly he was relieved that he could not help her. Before Kate had even moved away, he turned to the next customer. 'Next please!'

It was another fifteen minutes before the pharmacist saw Kate. When at last she nodded that Kate could come into her office, she had seen three other people already, who had all been waiting for less time.

'I'm sorry,' said the pharmacist, 'but they all made appointments.'

'Oh,' said Kate. 'I didn't know you could.'

'Well, only a week in advance. So, no, for the morning-after pill you can't make appointments.'

'Not unless you schedule your sex?'

The pharmacist did not laugh; it was not really a joke. She pushed her clipboard to the centre of the table.

'How many hours ago did you have sex?'

Kate counted. Twenty-four hours since she'd arrived home. Another two since she'd left. Another ten before that since she'd been untouched, unfucked.

'Thirty-six,' she said.

'And did you use a condom?' said the pharmacist.

'No,' said Kate. 'He didn't.'

Pause, tick.

'Is he a regular partner?'

'No,' said Kate. 'He isn't.'

Pause, tick.

'And are you taking any form of oral contraception or do you have any kind of contraceptive implant, coil or mechanism installed?'

'I do not.'

The pharmacist paused again. From a small cupboard above her desk she took a paper cup and a cardboard box, which contained a single pill packet.

'Drink this, and take this. If you vomit or have diarrhoea in the next twelve hours, come back and see me.'

Kate popped the pill from its packet and swallowed it with the water the pharmacist gave her. The pharmacist got up again and took a leaflet from her desk.

'There's no replacement for a condom when it comes to protecting yourself against sexually transmitted diseases, but you might at some stage want to consider the coil.' The leaflet was dark pink, and on the cover was a diagram of a uterus. 'The Giselle is the newest model. I'd recommend it.' She turned the leaflet to face Kate and opened it, pointing to the lists of side effects and benefits. 'A lot of women object to putting chemicals in their body but the dose is really very low; they've developed a spermicide-releasing technology that destroys semen before it reaches the womb, so the protection works on a defensive as well as an offensive level. The installation is painful, but brief, and it only needs replacing once every five years.'

Kate looked closely at the drawing of the piece of metal, trying to fathom where exactly a five-year supply of spermicide might be stored.

'Right,' she said. 'Thanks.'

'Take it,' said the pharmacist. Kate took the leaflet. At the door, she paused.

'Can you give me something to stop it hurting?' she said. Kate watched the pharmacist carefully, for any sign of recognition, and, for a split second, the pharmacist looked back at her. But before she had time to reply, Kate spoke again. 'It was a bit, you know, rough.'

'Paracetamol,' the pharmacist said. She looked back down at her notes. 'You can buy it over the counter. And there are creams, if necessary.'

Kate waited, in case there was anything else.

'Perhaps you should see a doctor,' said the pharmacist, as Kate opened the door.

14

It was hot, and the nights were still. Kate slept with the windows open to let in the cooler air, but even the still air stirred the fabric of the curtains and woke her to the conviction that there was somebody standing over her. A weight on her chest pinned her to the bed and obscured her vision. Though she blinked and opened her mouth, no sound came out, and the figure above her pressed down harder and harder until, unexpectedly and without warning, it released her and she rolled over and turned on the light.

'It's like that painting,' Kate said to her friend Claire, one night when they were alone together in the pub. Other than her mother, this was the first time Kate had seen anybody – or even properly spoken to anybody – since it had happened. Max had texted her a few times, but she'd sent him only short replies back. She did not phone, and neither did Max challenge her distancing. When Kate had arranged to meet up with Claire, she'd half entertained the thought that this might be the moment to tell her what had happened. Claire did not know Lewis, after all. But now that they were in the pub, Kate kept thinking about how long it was since they'd last spoken, and she found it impossible to articulate anything other than dreams. 'It's like that painting, *The Nightmare*, with the little devil thing on the chest of the sleeping woman.'

'My little brother used to sleepwalk,' said Claire. 'Once he pissed in King James's Castle.'

Claire had three near indistinguishable younger brothers, all of whom played rugby for Claire and Kate's old school. Somehow, this anecdote did not surprise Kate.

'Pissed in what?'

'It was this Lego castle he built. Battlements and a moat and everything, with a drawbridge he used to close at night. He was really upset when he realised what he'd done.'

'Yeah, it's not really the same,' said Kate, level.

'No. Yours sound fucked, man.'

Kate had to agree. But the dreams went on, and at night she existed in a state of immobilised terror, while in the day she was restless, exhausted. The deadline for her to put in her film school application came and went, and she did nothing: she had left the camera she'd meant to borrow from Max in its box in his bedroom. Instead, she drank, and disposed of the empty bottles in the skip at the end of their road so that she wouldn't be tempted to count how many there were. Printed on the skip's side was RIPPON, a word which stopped Kate's heart every time she saw it. She threw each bottle into the skip with increasing force so that it shattered on whatever debris was contained there, and walked on, guilty and anxious.

Kate learned very quickly that there was no subtle way of explaining that she had been raped. There was no oblique way of putting it, and because there was no half-way point between having been raped and having not, there were no means of testing the water, of hinting at her condition to measure the response of any potential confidante. There were only the raped and the un-raped.

And so instead she said nothing, hoping that if she chose not to voice whatever it was that lodged itself in her chest, somewhere between her lungs and her heart, it would diminish; that its toxicity might find its own means of excreting itself from her body, in her sweat, her blood, her spit and her shit; that by simply breathing and being, she might gradually cleanse herself without the horror of ever having to give it a recognisable shape and, unarticulated, perhaps it might recede.

In the middle of September Kate moved to London. She had started sending longer replies to Max's messages, and they had arranged to have a takeaway on the night she arrived. There would be a whole week of them living alone together before Nicole moved in, and the flurry of communication in anticipation of their next meeting made Kate feel, at some moments, as if nothing had changed: she would arrive in London in a few days, they would eat Chinese food at the kitchen table of their new flat, they would drink cheap wine. But when she thought about the last time she had seen Max, the excitement congealed. On the designated day, Kate packed clothes and kitchen utensils into a rucksack, to the outside of which she strapped her bulkiest belongings – leather trainers, two pans and a colander – and Claire, who had given her and her enormous suitcase a lift to the station, helped her onto the train.

'You look so fucking intrepid,' Claire told her.

'Come and visit me,' said Kate as the doors closed.

When the train lurched away from the platform, she felt bare, but as soon as she arrived in the high-ceiling two-floored flat she knew that nothing she already owned belonged there, and she was glad that she had only brought two bags with her; Claire would have said that the place resembled an asylum, with its white walls and cream carpets – and they were cream, rather than the ugly beige of Alison's ex-council house – and its windows that opened only halfway so as to prevent its inhabitants from taking the quickest (the easy) way out.

Max had left a key for her under the rug, and he'd forgotten to shut the balcony doors, presenting a challenge to opportunistic thieves. But rapists didn't break in via rooftops, Kate thought, as she searched the house for intruders with one of her kitchen knives held tightly in her right hand; rapists had front-door keys and security codes, so she needn't have worried. Once she'd scouted the flat twice, she took a shit, nervously, watching the handle of the door in case her intruder chose this moment to humiliate her. She still had the knife, balanced on the side of the bathtub, and as she pulled up her knickers, she felt the urge to turn it blade up, and to push it inside herself, if only to remember – really remember, without the sudden panic but with full cogency – what it had been like.

Instead, she unpacked her kitchen things, went out to the shops and bought bread for breakfast, and drank two-thirds of a bottle of wine while she waited for Max to come home, trying to make the television work before giving up and sitting in silence on the floor of the living room, watching the sky darken through the balcony windows and wondering whether anybody was looking in. By the time it was fully dark he still had not arrived, and neither had he replied to her messages. She ate toast to quell her hunger. Several times she half thought she heard a key turn in the lock, and although it was always nothing, she held her breath, waiting for him to enter, to apologise for his lateness, to sense some fundamental change in her: to come to her side, to let her rest her head in his lap and to talk to her about his day until she was at ease, until she could trust him enough to tell him what had been done to her. But she waited, and he did not return. By midnight, he was still not back, and because she had not yet made her bed, she fell asleep on the sofa.

15

Max had not seen Kate since the party at Latimer Crescent. He'd hardly seen her on the night of the party either, and he couldn't remember how much of a state he'd been in. He had a suspicion that he'd abandoned her, as he had a habit of doing when he was a bit too pissed. He knew she'd slept in his bed because the pillow was indented and the cover pulled back when he woke in the morning. She'd left already, William said when at last Max made it downstairs. Max wasn't quite sure how, but he knew that at some point he had ended up at the bottom of the garden, climbing up onto the trampoline – the pride of his teenage years but now long neglected – where Nicole and her friend Elias were doing lines. Max rolled onto the canvas, which bounced, and Nicole and Elias both turned and shouted at him to be still.

'You know this thing is basically a sieve,' Max said, sliding on his belly towards them so as not to disturb the pile of powder Elias was gathering. 'Watcha doing there, sis?'

'My birthday present,' Nicole said, watching Elias beadily.

'You want one?' Elias said.

'Elias,' Nicole said, 'that's my baby brother.'

Elias waved his hand without looking up. 'I won't make him pay,' he said.

'Maxie doesn't do drugs,' Nicole said, pinching him hard on the cheek, 'do you?'

'Yes please,' said Max, batting Nicole's hand away.

Max had done purer coke than this, and the bump Elias gave him was more like a shot of espresso than the buzz he'd been after. Elias, who had been watching him for a reaction, appeared to be impressed by his lack of one, and lined up another. Max stayed on the trampoline with Elias for a while after Nicole had gone back to the party. Elias had been at university with Nicole, but he'd been living abroad, on and off, for the last few years and had only just returned.

'You should have come to see me,' Elias said, when Max told him he'd been studying in Colombia a year and a half ago. 'I was living in Rio then.'

'I've been wanting to go back to Latin America for ages. I tried to persuade Kate –'

'Kate?' Elias flicked the dead ash at the end of his cigarette onto the trampoline.

'My friend. She's here, somewhere.'

'Why doesn't she want to go?'

Max shrugged. 'Money.'

'Go on your own, then.'

That night Elias had stayed in one of the spare rooms, and had hung around for most of the next day, after everybody else had gone. They ate brunch out in the sunshine, and after Nicole had gone to nap, Elias went to find some beers for him and Max. Later in the day, William came out to sit with them, but he didn't take his glasses off and hardly spoke, soon returning inside and shutting himself in his office.

'Did Nicole tell you what's going on with our uncle?' Max said to Elias. He wasn't sure if he needed to excuse his father's mood or to elicit sympathy for it. Elias was wearing sunglasses; it was hard to make out his expression.

'No,' he said. 'What *is* going on?'

Max shook his head. 'Family shit.' They sat in silence for a while before Elias spoke again.

'You know what we should do. Tonight. We should go to the Royal China Club. The duck is fucking incredible – better than you get in Shanghai. I know a guy so we won't have to queue.'

Max started spending more time with Elias, and they would meet in Moorgate when Elias finished work, standing on the pavement outside crowded bars drinking cold beer and smoking. The day he was supposed to move in with Kate, Max had been on his way from the new flat to Latimer Crescent when Elias had phoned, asking what time he was free.

'I can't,' Max said. 'I haven't even starting packing.'

'Just one,' Elias said.

It had got to 10 p.m. before they agreed it was time to schedule a hiatus from drinking and to eat something.

Elias negotiated them the best table by the window of a vegetarian curry house and, without looking at the menu, asked for a lamb biryani.

'Or chicken,' he said, batting away the menu the waiter tried to hand to him, 'chicken is fine if you can't do lamb.'

'This is a vegetarian restaurant, sir,' the waiter explained patiently.

'Oh, yes,' said Elias, with the grace of a self-proclaimed prodigy explaining to his teacher that two plus two equals five, 'but I said I would have chicken.'

Max, sensing that Elias was not quite in control of the situation, took the menu from him and leaned blearily towards it.

'Paneer,' he said, moments before his nose collided with the card, 'we'll have it with paneer.'

'This is gonna be you and me,' Elias said, as the waiter took the menu away. 'When we're rich. Dining out every night on Embers.'

Max frowned. 'Dining on Embers?'

'You've got to start owning this, Max; your idea,' Elias said. He filled up Max's water glass, sending ice cubes tumbling from the jug and skittering across the wooden tabletop. Neither man was aware how loudly he was speaking, nor of how quiet the rest of the restaurant was.

'Oh, yeah,' Max said, and then: 'What idea?'

Elias leaned across the table towards Max, and said, again, in a dramatic whisper: 'Embers. Tinder, but for the over-sixties. The pensioners' dating app of choice. Geriatric romance. It's fucking inspired.' Elias brought his fist down emphatically, crashing through the pile of poppa-doms that had been placed between them, and paused to belch softly. 'But if you don't own it, I can tell you right now, someone else will.'

'Yeah, right.' Max was too drunk to recall whether this had been his terrible business idea or an ingenious joke, but seemingly Elias thought it could be both. 'I can't code, though,' he said.

'I can code, Max. I'd love to code this. I'm gonna learn to code. Let's fucking do this – you're the idea, and the money, and I'll be the executor.' Elias closed his eyes and inhaled slowly, savouring his ingenuity. 'Fuck,' he said.

Max's mouth and hands took the initiative at that point and disregarded the pleas of his brain and stomach, ordering a bottle of the most expensive wine to mark the beginning of their new venture.

After the second bottle, things began to get a little con-fused, and his memory of what happened once they left the curry house was blurry. It was not at all unlikely that he had knocked a drink from the hands of the Goliath fig-ure standing next to him in the Soho bar that he and Elias had stumbled into. Such was his excitement that, instead of apologising, it was also entirely possible that he had attempted to proposition Goliath as a potential investor in his new business.

'Embers,' Max slurred, slapping his hand on the man's upper arm with an unexpectedly dull thud. 'Whaddya say?'

'I'd say you've ruined my fucking shirt, mate,' Goliath said. 'This is dry-clean only.'

'Mate, mate,' said Max, smiling benevolently and spreading his arms wide, 'it's embers under the bridge.'

Elias later told Max that in fact it had been not Goliath but the doorman who had delivered the hefty shove that had sent him crashing out the back door of the bar, his head slamming limply into the brick wall on the opposite side of the alleyway. Elias, who had called an ambulance, and had then cancelled it when the operator refused to guarantee that the driver would be willing to drop Elias at a private address before taking his friend to the hospital, booked a taxi for them both instead.

It was past one when Max got back to the flat. When at last he had remembered the number of the building, he put a deep scratch with his key in the freshly painted door as he was trying to unlock it, before stumbling inside. Because he went straight to his room and passed out on his mattress, he didn't see that Kate was asleep on the sofa.

16

Kate found a job in a cafe bar two streets away from the flat. She didn't want to be a waitress, but she needed to pay rent, and it was the first thing she applied for. She was interviewed on the spot by Mark Cummins, who had her sit and wait while he made himself a cappuccino, before sitting down opposite her, reading her CV, and then tearing it up while looking her in the eye.

'I don't care about your MA or your MBA,' he said, which was fortunate, because Kate had neither, 'the only thing I want to know is this: is your bedroom tidy?'

Suppressing her visceral dislike of this man, Kate said coldly that yes, her bedroom was impeccably clean. He told her to start that afternoon. The satisfaction she felt was only temporary: she reminded herself that if she had managed to make that deadline at the end of the summer, she might have been about to start at film school, rather than a waitressing job. But the work would fill the void that was threatening to open up in front of her: this city was hostile to purposelessness and, unlike Max, she did not have much of a social life to fill her time. Most of the people she knew here were Max's friends and she had no particular desire to make herself vulnerable to new strangers.

'Why don't you move here?' Kate said to Claire, when she phoned to tell her how her first shift had gone. Kate knew her friend was about to move into a flat in Bristol with her boyfriend, but she wanted Claire to know that she missed her. 'You'd love it.'

'And live with your very handsome friend?'

'If you want. You'd have to sleep on the floor, though.'

'Tempting, but I think Alex would be upset.'

Kate was managing to function, but there were bad days. Her new boss was not often in the restaurant, but he did have a disconcerting habit of appearing unexpectedly in the middle of a busy shift. On these days, he would lean on the bar watching how his waiting staff interacted with his clientele, and would sometimes slip behind it to help himself to a Scotch. She could tell that Mark was in a particularly good mood when he met the confused looks of the customers and reassured them that he was the owner and so was entitled to be there. Once or twice, he began pouring out drinks for those customers, which he later made Kate add to their bills – settled, conveniently for him, long after he had gone for the evening.

At times, the unpredictability threatened to destabilise Kate. One day, Mark came in during the post-lunch lull, and was watching Kate, his fingers steepled, as she poured freshly ground beans from the coffee grinder, pressing firmly on the powder with the tamper and wiping the edges so as not to clog the machine, just as he had taught her to do. She surprised herself by how easy it was to keep going, particularly if she'd had a bit to drink, and particularly if she was applying herself to repetitive, mentally unchallenging tasks.

'Do you know who Alexander Fleming is?' said Mark, as Kate started to steam the milk. She did not take her eyes off the quickly thickening milk, determined not to be distracted and to let it boil.

'The scientist?'

'Alexander Fleming was a great Scottish scientist, whose discovery of penicillin transformed the face of modern medicine.'

'Right,' said Kate. She put down the metal jug, which was now too hot to hold in both hands, and turned off the steamer, blasting it once or twice before she did so to get rid of the skin of milk that had formed over its nozzle.

'Fleming discovered penicillin entirely by accident, having left a Petri dish out in his laboratory for three days unattended, upon whose surface a thin mould began to form, and which, during those three days, began to produce the antibacterial substance we now know as the first antibiotic, or penicillin.'

Kate poured the milk slowly into the warm espresso, moving the lip of the jug carefully backwards and forwards to create a creamy marbled effect on the surface of the coffee. Mark was trying to distract her, but she felt quietly triumphant that she succeeded in creating a small masterpiece under his interrogation.

Mark was unperturbed. 'And do you know how they

used to mass-produce penicillin in the early days of its discovery?'

'No,' Kate said.

'Milk,' Mark said. 'Warm milk, in which bacteria thrives.'

Kate looked at him blankly.

'How long did you leave that out for?' Mark said, putting the back of his hand against the milk bottle that stood on the bar.

'I don't know,' Kate said, 'it was here earlier.'

Mark pulled Kate's coffee across the countertop towards him, walked around the bar, and tipped it deliberately down the sink.

'I can't have my staff serving Petri dishes to my guests,' Mark said. 'Start with cold milk. Straight from the fridge.'

When Mark disappeared into his office, she drained his whisky and marked one more and a vodka on the ledger as customer spillages, before topping up her glass. There was something pleasantly annihilative about the bleach-like purity of distilled alcohol. The way it seemed to flood her lungs, counteracting the dull, icy weight there with fiery warmth, spreading to her stomach, satisfyingly empty these days, and sending an obfuscating mist up her spinal cord to shroud her busy brain. She would have to start bringing her own bottle to work, if Mark was going to insist on being so unbearably present.

'Cunt,' Max said, when Kate saw him later that evening, and told him what Mark had done. 'He sounds like a total cunt.'

'And the worst thing is that coffee was for our creepiest customer, so he wasn't even put off by the fact that it was fifteen minutes late. He actually gave me a tip.'

Max shook his head. 'Cunt.'

'It made me feel anxious,' Kate's hand was hovering absently in the space just about her chest, trying to detect the noxious energy lingering there. 'It made me feel like a naughty child being told off by her father.'

Max raised his eyebrows. 'There might be something in that.'

'No,' Kate said, 'I don't mean it has anything to do with my dad. It has more to do with the feeling of being diminished.'

Max grunted indifferently. 'Well,' he said, pouring more vodka into her glass, 'you know what kills bacteria.'

They drank and fell silent. This was not what either of them had envisaged, when they'd decided six months earlier to move in together. They were losing sight of one another, but still they carried on, started using different drugs. For Max, taking coke was liberation: high, he only ever thought as far ahead as the next bump, the next song. Kate was drinking still, but had also gone to a doctor and told him that she had been feeling anxious about travelling on public transport so that he would give her beta blockers. When that did nothing except make her feel more tired, she went into Nicole's cabinet in the bathroom when the others were out and emptied half a bottle of Valium and a packet of Xanax she had brought back from a work trip to America. Prescription drugs, Nicole had confided to Kate, were easy to get hold of in the States. Kate's logic was clear. To survive, she needed to not inhabit herself. Every time she began to think about what had happened, she took another of those pills, another swig of whatever she had hidden in a nearby cupboard, and these, hard in her oesophagus, dammed the memories that rose like a tide whenever sobriety threatened.

17

If Nicole noticed that Kate had been using her medication, she didn't say anything – at least, not explicitly. But when she saw Kate watching her pop three beta blockers out of their packet onto the kitchen table, she began, very casually, to explain to Kate what panic attacks felt like to her.

'Like the pavement is gonna open up and fucking swallow me whole,' Nicole said. She had just woken up and was wearing underwear and a T-shirt and eating peanut butter straight from the jar. Max had stayed at Elias's, so it was just the two of them in the flat. 'I used to just leave work and go home. I don't even get embarrassed about it any more. No point in making things any harder than they already are, you know?'

Nicole looked into the bottom of the jar as she spoke: her openness seemed to be an invitation, but Kate did not know how to take it. This was the closest she'd come to any kind of acknowledgement that there was something wrong.

'I do know what you mean,' Kate said carefully. 'But don't you sometimes think it's easier just to carry on?'

'That's how it gets you,' Nicole said, sucking her spoon,

now looking at Kate across the table. The look felt like a challenge. Nicole stood and lifted her arms to tie her dark, wiry hair into a bun on the top of her head. 'You know who knows a lot about this sort of thing?' she said. 'My mother. She seems so together, but she's been through it.'

'What does she know about?' Kate said. She was aware that she was failing to engage with the hints Nicole was offering, but she didn't know how to be more direct. Nicole was unfazed, though.

'Anxiety,' she said, 'panic attacks. If you want to stop having them. Or maybe just go to the GP. They'll probably try to put you on a million pills, but at least you'll get a bit of rest.' She screwed the lid back on the peanut butter jar and threw the spoon in the sink. 'I slept like a light when I first went on anti-anxieties.'

Kate was confused. 'Like a light?'

'Yeah,' Nicole said. 'Completely out.'

Before Kate had had the chance to ask Nicole if she meant 'log' rather than 'light', she had left the kitchen, and as Kate watched her go she wondered whether the skin on the backs of her thighs was as butter-soft as it looked. At moments like this, Kate feared that she had somehow become a misogynist, that when Lewis had fucked her, he had left something of himself in her. Perhaps that was why she found it so difficult to look away when Nicole walked around the flat in her black cotton underwear, the bones in her thighs looking like they might very easily snap.

Nicole's apparent fragility was, for Kate, another source of anxiety. She had a new boyfriend, and sometimes, when he came over, she could hear them fucking; the sound of the headboard banging against the wall of the room directly above her, heavy breathing, escaped groans: these noises found their way into Kate's bed, and even if she put headphones on and turned up the radio and pulled her duvet over her head, she still felt the thudding in her bones, the screws beneath her ribcage tightening.

Once, when she couldn't sleep, disturbed by the sound of Nicole being drilled to the bed, Kate decided to commit fully to her wakefulness, and went up to the kitchen to make tea. But the noise there was worse – the walls were thinner than the floors – and as the kettle began to boil over the sound of rhythmic thumping, she heard what she was sure was the sound of an open palm colliding with bare flesh, a smacking sound that grew louder and louder, accompanied by a low, animalistic moaning. In that moment she was overcome by an impulse to burst into the bedroom, to tear this attacker from Nicole, to kick him and to stamp his chest into the floor so that he would know how it felt to have his ribs crushed.

The kettle clicked, and Kate, instead of pouring the boiling water into the mug, poured it quickly and deliberately over her bare hand. Her instincts overrode her intention, however, and she immediately drew her hand away and thrust it under the cold tap. When the desire to burn and to be burned had abated, she sank down onto the floor of the kitchen. Only the sudden silence from Nicole's room, and the fear of being discovered there on the floor could move her, and she lifted herself slowly to her feet, pouring what was left of the water into her mug and taking it and her blistered hand back to her bedroom.

Despite the vulnerability Kate had projected onto Nicole, she had insight that Kate did not. Denial, just as she had warned, would only delay the inevitable. In early November, Kate's least favourite customer, the creep she had told Max about, overstepped. He had his little rituals, calling Kate over because he was ready to pay and then spending five minutes rooting around in his pocket for change so she would have to stand there, waiting for him.

'Only you can make the milk so silky,' he would say when Kate put his coffee down in front of him. 'Just how I like it.'

He must have been about sixty, and he walked into the restaurant cock first with his little chest puffed out and his narrow hips jutting forward. His name was Vernon, and he came there once a week every week and sat in his favourite spot by the window reading the paper for a full hour, buying only one coffee before leaving Kate with an inelegant tip and fast-growing nausea. He had a habit of looking at her legs, and she detested this. Today, Vernon had been upset, because his spot by the window had been taken by a mother who was breast-feeding her baby, and Vernon had taken out his venom on Kate, who had refused to ask the mother to move.

'It's Broken Britain, I tell you,' said Vernon, shaking his head, as he threw a ten-pound note on the table, 'it's disgraceful, vulgar.'

Kate said nothing, but took Vernon's money. As she leaned forward she saw that along the inside of his collar was stitched a thin ribbon of red fabric.

'They can't even get staff without ladders in their tights,' he said loudly, as she walked away.

Kate didn't go back to his table. Instead, she took off her apron and, with that particular clarity that only primal terror affords, put on her jacket, detached the key to the front door of the restaurant from her chain and left it on the countertop before ducking out the back door of the kitchen. She was numb, her mind as if suspended in a viscous fluid, disjointed from her body which itself moved without weight, and she crossed the road, following her feet along the pavement and through the alley that led to the front door of her flat.

Time flatlined; she knew then what red was. She was on Zara's bed, she saw the ribbon in Lewis's collar. But this red was not a colour, a warning sign or provocation, the bull's rag; no, red was the filter through which she apprehended everything; it collapsed the time between her present and that moment that refused to remain in her past, so that her whole being, from the dilation of her pupils to the rhythm of her breath and the ice in her chest, recalibrated to respond to the sight of the world through it. And she saw then that if she had been so wrong about what a colour could be, then there was little about the world that she had understood correctly.

Only later, in the safety of the bathtub with blistering water on her skin, did she begin to come back into herself, and still she could not fully comprehend the sudden lunacy that had overwhelmed her. Max. It was time, she knew, to talk to him and to tell him that something was happening to her; it was not possible to go on this way. By the time he came back, maybe an hour later, she was a little calmer. She had managed to get out of the bath and had dried herself gently, cautious because her body was still tender, and still felt like it belonged to a stranger, but anxious to go to Max and tell him before she changed her mind. She put on a tracksuit whose thick flannel material hung loosely around her hips and thighs. But still her body was consumed by that strange iciness, her chest tight and frozen, and the wire embedded within her tautening whenever she thought about what she was going to say; what could she possibly say to Max other than that she needed him, that she needed help?

He and Nicole were sitting together at the kitchen table, arguing about the music Max was playing through his phone. Kate sat down without saying anything, and when he began to draw her into the conversation she found she could neither hear nor speak. She searched for words, and as she did Nicole rose up silently, squeezing Max's shoulder before leaving the kitchen.

'What's happening?' Max said. He shifted his seat closer to Kate, held her shoulder, touched her face. 'You don't look well.'

'I don't feel well,' Kate said.

'Do you want some water? Paracetamol? Have you taken something?'

'No, nothing. Water, please.'

Glad to have something to do, Max got up and filled a pint glass. He sat back down, and he waited for her to speak.

'I think I might have quit my job.'

'Excellent,' said Max, 'why?'

'There's this man,' Kate said.

'What man?'

'I don't know, just a man.' She started before faltering. 'Listen Max, I think I'm going mad.'

'What did he do? What happened?' Max was looking at her intently now. Despite everything, Kate was glad to have his full attention, even if just for this moment.

'It just reminded me of something.'

'Reminded you of what?'

'Of before.'

For some minutes they spoke like this, Max inferring from ellipses and pauses what he could, Kate filling those pauses with as much meaning as she could without speaking, hoping that he would understand, that perhaps by seeing the uncontrollable shaking of her leg, her pale face and the drawn look, he would not only see the whole of her history but would also decide for them both that it did not and could not matter, what had happened to her, what she had done and had been done to her. But he wouldn't engage, it was too terrible a thing to infer, it could not be gestured towards, it demanded to be spoken, and the one thing she could not do was speak it.

'The look he gave me,' she said, 'the man in the restaurant, I've been looked at like that before.'

Max's confused expression told her that she had lost him.

'Looked at you like what?' said Max. 'What did he do?'

Kate picked up the glass of water Max had poured for her, waiting for words to form.

Max took his phone from his pocket – it was vibrating. He put it on the table. Before he silenced it, Elias's name flashed up on the screen.

'Do you need to take that?' said Kate.

The phone stopped vibrating, and then started again.

'Do you mind?' said Max. 'I think he's outside.'

Kate shook her head. She put the glass of water, still full, back on the table.

18

That Christmas, William's family went to stay at the house in Bisley. Alasdair and Lewis were away, but Rupert was joining them for the entire time they were there, and William was determined that this year's Christmas would be on a level with those they'd spent together before Bernadette died, when the house would be lit up with white lights, neighbours ringing round every few hours for mulled wine, the smell of cloves filling the kitchen. Max, who was trying to deflect the pressure William had been putting onto this week, had invited Kate and Elias to come and stay, but only Elias had accepted the invitation. Kate felt the obligation to spend Christmas with her mother, and couldn't bring herself to go elsewhere. Like Max, Zara would have preferred to have Christmas in London but, as she explained to Elias as she drove him and Max from the station, William had insisted on maintaining the traditional family trip to the countryside. Elias was sitting in the back seat of the car wearing two jumpers and a coat, his hands folded under his armpits. As they turned out of the station car park, Zara turned up the temperature.

'Max's father is very fond of his traditions,' Zara said to

Elias, speaking loudly so she could be heard over the sound of the heater, 'even the more absurd ones I really hoped we'd cremated along with his mother –'

'Mum,' said Max.

'– may peace be upon her,' Zara finished.

'I'm just happy not to be spending Christmas alone,' Elias said, with uncharacteristic diplomacy.

'Wait until you see Rudolph,' Zara said. 'And I'm afraid we're having a party tomorrow. All the locals are coming to make sure the roof hasn't fallen in since last time they saw it. I just hope that none of them has a heart attack.'

Straight after Bernadette's death, Zara had expected her distaste for Bisley House and all it represented to diminish, but, in the last couple of years, it had in fact intensified, most likely because William had made the decision to adorn himself with the absurdly English idiosyncrasies she'd always associated with Bernadette and her Estate. This year he had dug out from the attic the same fairy lights Bernadette had had put up for her birthday, and he'd bought what he thought were the same brand of expensive, scented candles and put them in the hallways where they flickered rather than shone and wreathed the house with the smell of cinnamon. He had even tried arranging flowers in the living room. The house now felt even more excessively large and dim and the countryside that surrounded it even more expansive. It gave her the creeps.

It was painful to watch William, so small and insubstantial, attempt to take ownership of the place: balancing precariously on a ladder as he fastened the red nose to the stag head; carefully writing out invitations to their Christmas Eve party on his mother's headed paper, which he then hand-delivered to everybody in the village; even unpacking his suitcase, folding his thin cashmere jumpers and cotton underpants into the bottom of the cavernous oak wardrobe in their temporary bedroom. She had seen this before, in the men in her own family, and in the powerful men they had associated with when she was a child. Their identities were so heavily invested in a past that hardly existed except in their own fantasies that, when it was threatened, they responded with a proprietorial urge to colonise what was left of it.

'I thought you were going to sell it anyway,' said Elias.

Zara sighed. 'If it were up to me . . .' she said, and swung through the open gate and along the driveway. It was dark early now, the winter solstice, and William had wound Bernadette's fairy lights around the leafless trees that lined the driveway, whose branches glistened with raindrops illuminated by the tiny white bulbs. As the house came into view, Elias whistled.

'Fuck, that's nice,' he said.

The west wing was in shadow and the windows in the rest of the house were chequered light and dark: two lamps lit the porch, there was the odd light on the upper floors, and on the ground floor in the kitchen and the living room, where Zara had left Nicole critiquing from the sofa William's wood-fire construction. Rupert was sitting in the armchair nearest the fire, and had been watching Nicole's direction with something that might have been amusement.

He got up when Max came in, lifting himself out of his armchair: he was a little less thin than he'd been last time Max had seen him, and he was clean-shaven.

'Max,' Rupert said, squeezing his nephew's shoulder. 'Merry Christmas.'

'This is Elias,' Max said. 'Rupert, my uncle.'

Elias shook Rupert's hand, smiling briefly, before leaning down to kiss Nicole on both cheeks. 'Who's going to give me a tour?' he said.

Elias made Max show him round the house twice, and they walked its perimeter with the bottle of champagne he'd brought with him, stopping frequently to refill their glasses as Elias burst through the door of each room before circumventing it in awe. Max had learned by now that whenever he went somewhere new with Elias it was necessary to factor in extra time to accommodate the length and volume of his superlatives, and in the doorway to the master bathroom on the second floor he waited with the bottle for Elias to finish.

'This is really beyond fucking incredible,' Elias said. 'That is really the biggest toilet seat I have ever seen.'

Max had to admit that it was an extraordinarily large toilet seat: a winged mahogany throne, complete with a bronze chain flusher, of which he had always been suspicious as a child for fear that he would slide from the polished ledge into the bowl, and disappear into the maze of copper pipes that lined the walls of the house. Elias, who had meanwhile climbed fully clothed into the Victorian bathtub, reached up and opened the window above it, which led out onto a flattened section of the roof. He pulled with a flourish a small clear bag of hash from the top pocket of his denim shirt.

'What time's dinner?' he said.

This time, Elias had not been exaggerating when he said that this was the strongest hash he'd ever got his hands on. When at last he and Max made it down for dinner, they were glassy-eyed and giggly. Zara knew immediately and was quietly envious of their state, but William was busy carving the chicken he had roasted for dinner and didn't seem to have noticed.

Elias was the first to be served. 'Do you mind if I have brown meat?' he said.

'Have as much as you like,' William said. 'I don't eat it myself, reminds me too much of work.'

'Aren't you a GP?' said Elias.

'A surgeon,' William said, nicking the cartilage expertly with the tip of his knife. 'Thigh or wing?'

'Oh, wow. Thigh, please,' Elias said, holding his plate out for William. 'So a surgeon, a film director, a lawyer –' he was pointing round the table – 'a wastrel.' He waved his hand at Max. 'What do you do, Rupert?'

'Also a wastrel,' Rupert said. He was sitting forward in his seat, his packet of cigarettes inches from his elbow. 'I'm not working at the moment.'

'Sensible man,' Elias said. He had started eating already, and took a chunk out of his chicken thigh. 'You hardly need to work, with this place. Why don't you just retire here?'

'I'd love to,' Rupert said. He smiled. 'But it's not my house, unfortunately.'

Zara cut across Elias, whose mouth was too full of chicken anyway for him to ask Rupert any more questions. 'You do work, darling,' she said. 'At the community centre.'

'Ah yes, the volunteering,' Rupert said. He pushed up his shirtsleeves, whose buttons were undone. 'Not quite worth the pay cheque, you see. I need them more than they need me. But –' he leaned towards Elias, who was watching him with suspicion – 'no harm in spreading around the burden a little bit.'

Elias's eyes flickered towards Rupert's wine glass, which was filled with water.

'I didn't know you were working,' Max said to Rupert. Max, who was less expert than Elias in disguising the level of his intoxication, looked as though he'd just woken up. 'How long for?'

'Well, Maxie, we haven't seen each other for a little while,' Rupert said. 'But it's not a big deal. Just to fill the days out a little.'

'That's great,' Max said, 'that's, um –' He stopped, arrested by the sensation that his tongue was about to flop out of his mouth.

'It is,' Rupert said. Zara smiled at him across the table, and William nodded earnestly.

Elias, who was not concentrating but was moving fast

into the snacking phase of his high, reached for a leg from the carcass, which jerked as he tried to detach it.

'Sorry, Elias, did you want seconds?' Nicole said sarcastically.

'Have as much as you'd like,' William said, as Max started giggling. William had been quietly watching his son for the past five minutes, and now he spoke, his voice stern. 'Max. Are you high?'

'No,' said Max, while, at the same time, Elias nodded.

'Obviously,' said Nicole.

'Boys, is that really necessary?'

'They're adults,' Zara said.

'Exactly,' William said, talking to his wife directly now, 'old enough to recognise that it's just a little irresponsible to be getting stoned and drunk in front of a recovering addict.'

'Sorry,' Max mumbled.

'The recovering addict?' Rupert said. 'Is that what we're calling me, now?'

'There's no need to be embarrassed, Rupert,' William said patiently. 'We don't necessarily need to be intoxicated to enjoy ourselves.'

Rupert exhaled, hissing loudly.

'I just want you to be comfortable here,' William said.

'Comfortable?' Rupert started laughing. But it wasn't his old, warm, laugh: this laugh was just a little too loose. 'Have I come here to die? About fucking time.'

'That's in very poor taste,' William said, looking down at his plate sombrely.

'Forgive me, William, for daring to try to lighten the mood,' Rupert said.

Max put his head in his hands. The weed was making him feel heavy; he wished Rupert would stop talking.

'Well,' William said, 'I'm sorry I insisted that you came. I thought some company might cheer you up a little.'

'We just want you to be supported, Rupert,' Zara said, translating – too late – for her husband. She looked across at him in support, but he did not look back.

'No, no, I quite see what you're saying,' Rupert said. He had his hand on his cigarettes. He pushed back his chair and stood up. 'Cheer up. What an ingenious idea, Willie. That's quite the miracle cure. Tell me, have you thought of entering the medical profession?'

Elias, who had been scraping at the bone of Max's demolished wing, put down his knife and looked up at Rupert, then back at William.

'Is there any more of that delicious chicken?'

19

Max managed to endure the forced jollity of William's Christmas Eve party by staying with Elias and the other smokers in the kitchen garden, just behind the house, where they made their way through a packet of Marlboros. Here it was difficult to be seen and so far easier to avoid having to talk to anybody he didn't want to, and because William had dragged two large outdoor heaters up from the garage it was warm enough to stay outside for most of the night. Max stood with his back to the wall of the house while Elias gesticulated, cigarette in hand, complaining about his girlfriend. Over Elias's shoulder, he could see Rupert standing at the edge of the group. He was wearing a long green coat, which Max recognised as having been his grandfather's; the collar was turned up and he had a scarf wrapped protectively around his neck. In that coat, he could have been his old self: the Rupert who'd bought Max bottles of wine when he'd been underage because, he reasoned, he might as well drink good-quality alcohol if he was going to drink; Rupert who hadn't said anything when Max bent the needle on his record player; Rupert who had once picked Max and his friends up from a New

Year's party in his Aston, and hadn't mentioned to his parents when Max threw up in the footwell. It was worth the valet fee, he told Max, just to have material for his wedding speech.

Rupert: collar turned up against the world, but with a sly dimpled smile just visible, as if he was in on a joke that only he understood. Except of course that now he had a cup of tea in his hand, not a whisky. And he'd made no attempt to disguise his sobriety, to drink tonic water and lemon or mulled wine which was hardly alcoholic anyway, as if he didn't mind that he was diminished, as if he had given up all hope of ever becoming that person again.

By ten o'clock, Max, Elias and Nicole had managed to escape to the village pub, leaving Rupert in the garden and Zara to negotiate alone the treacherous space between the canapé table and the downstairs hallway, which was patrolled (incredibly slowly) by Lady Caroline, a local ancient aristocrat who had always resented Bernadette's ownership of Bisley House and so had masochistically attended every Christmas party she had thrown since 1982.

Lady Caroline and her brutal interrogations about the career paths and marriage schedules of the Rippon children were more fearful than even Zara's wrath at being abandoned, and so Max and Nicole endured their mother's anger on Christmas morning in their hung-over state, comforted by the knowledge that they had made it through the night before unscathed. Zara did not attend church, and their exposure to her rage was limited to breakfast, which Max ate quickly with a large milky coffee in an effort to clear his head.

Elias, who had been especially excited about attending church and had worn a blue velvet jacket for the occasion, spent the entire service flicking to the end of his service sheet, checking his phone, and trying to draw Max's attention to the deacon, who had fallen asleep in his seat behind the altar. But Max ignored him; he was thinking of Bernadette, of the last time he had come to see her. He'd driven her to church that weekend, and she had insisted on having the windows down and playing the Requiem Mass at full volume. This was a special treat for Bernadette, who had lost her licence just after her eightieth birthday when the bumper of her VW Polo had triumphed over the village car park's freshly built Cotswold stone wall.

They stood up to sing, and Max stared down at his hymn sheet. William had been having trouble looking Max in the eye since dinner the other night, but now he passed Max his own hymn sheet, which was folded to the correct place, and took Max's from him, turning it to the right page. The singing had always been Max's favourite part. It took him a moment to find where they were, but when he did, he looked straight ahead and sang as loudly as he could, his enunciation crisp, years of public school and childhood churchgoing having trained his voice to a rich-toned tenor that always surprised people. As he sang, he imagined that the little church might become aglow with the faces and memories of his childhood, that he would be carried by the voices of his family in harmony, each only just distinguishable from the next. But neither Rupert nor Nicole were singing – Elias hadn't even looked at his hymn sheet – so he could hear only his own voice and the low timbre of his father, half a note behind.

An hour or so after the six of them had finished lunch and had moved into the living room to recover, Max's phone began to ring. A photograph of Kate, sun-drenched and smiling, leaning out the window of the car they had rented in France a few years before, lit the screen.

'Katherine! Season's greetings,' Max answered, and then, 'Is that actually your name, Katherine? God, I've missed you.'

Kate didn't say anything for a moment. Max heard the sound of a car driving past, and then of Kate exhaling. Her voice was small, far-off: 'Max,' she said.

'What's up?' Max got up from the sofa and went to the dining room, whose table was still littered with the remnants of the Christmas massacre: cranberries, bread sauce, the occasional sprout smashed on the tablecloth. 'Is everything OK?' he said.

'Not really,' Kate said. She sounded as though she was having difficulty speaking. 'I was wondering, well, probably not, but I was wondering if you were still in Gloucestershire.'

'Yes,' said Max, 'I am. What's happened? Where are you?'

'I'm at home,' Kate said, 'well, I'm not at home. I left my home in a bit of a rush. I'm stuck in the middle of

Randwick and, well, I wondered if I could perhaps come and stay with you.'

There were very few taxi companies working in rural Gloucestershire on Christmas Day, but there were even fewer police cars on patrol, so Max, with the confidence of a man who had already crashed his car twice in his life, finished his drink and set off in the VW they still kept in the garage. It was only twenty minutes or so to Randwick, fifteen on a quiet day like today, and as he pulled out of the driveway and turned up his music, he felt intensely grateful to Kate for giving him such a legitimate reason to leave his house.

She was sitting on the wall outside the town hall, and he could tell even from her silhouette that something was not right. Her shoulders were hunched, and in the second before he turned his headlights off, he saw that her face was pale and her eyes wide. She had her hands in her lap, her backpack and her phone on the wall next to her. Max swung the nose of the car across three parking spaces and put the handbrake on. He walked quickly to her, and as he came closer he saw that her right hand, cradled in her left, was streaked brightly with blood.

When she saw him, she started apologising. 'I was going to ring Claire,' she said. 'But her grandparents are there. I didn't want them to see, I didn't want anybody to see –'

'It's OK,' said Max. He squeezed her tightly, and she buried her face in his chest. 'Everything's OK.'

She explained in the car that it was an accident, that she had opened the fridge for milk, and that the crystal platter her grandmother had given her mother on her wedding day, which had been balanced against the door of the fridge and which carried the remains of the Christmas pudding, had fallen to the floor and shattered. She had tried to clear it up, she told him, and that was when she had cut herself, and that was when the ceiling of the kitchen seemed to start falling in on her, and when she felt that she had become detached from her body, that she was no longer in her body but floating several inches above it, as if the shattering dish had shattered too her hold on reality. All of this she said in a level voice and with unexpected fluency. Max did not interrupt but listened quietly as he drove. When at last she paused, he spoke.

'Is it like what happened to you a few weeks ago, in the restaurant?' he said.

'It's exactly like that,' Kate said.

Max spoke carefully. 'And do you know why?'

'I have an idea.'

For the rest of the journey, they didn't speak again about what had happened. It was almost dark, but the sky was streaked with dark pink and the clouds refracted the light of the dying sun. Max asked Kate if she wanted to stop somewhere along the way, and she said that she didn't mind, so he pulled in at the top of Bisley Road and wound down the windows, which were beginning to steam up.

'I knocked out my tooth here, once,' Max said, pointing to the fields below them. 'I was sledging, and I went right into a badger sett. The nose went straight in and catapulted me about ten feet into the air. It was hidden right in the side of the hill. Bastards.'

Kate did not laugh, but she smiled, at least.

'What are you going to tell everyone, when I turn up at your house?' she said.

'I don't know, you had an argument? Your great-aunt threw a Christmas pudding at your head?'

Now she laughed. 'OK. I can live with that.'

'They'll love that you're coming, anyway.'

'Is Elias there?' Kate said.

'Oh yes,' Max said ominously. 'In a big way. And my uncle.'

'Rupert?' Kate said.

'Yeah. Alasdair and Lewis are in the Caribbean.'

Max had already told her Lewis would be away that Christmas, but hearing just how far he was from Bisley sent fresh relief through her body. The panic that had risen in the kitchen at the sound of the splintering glass, at the appearance of fast-flowing blood swelling from her hand, was at last beginning to dissipate. When she got to the house, she would call her mother and tell her everything was all right, that she would be back in a few days. Kate had done her best to clean up, and had left a note for Alison to find when she got back from her afternoon walk: she would have to wait for the full explanation. Now that the tide of adrenaline was ebbing away, Kate felt her energy ebb with it too. She closed her eyes and rested her head against the passenger seat.

20

It was the first time Kate had been to Bisley House, but she hardly registered the significance of this as Max turned into the drive. Max, aware that Kate was in no state to see anybody at that moment, led her up the back stairway to one of the spare rooms on the top floor without turning on the lights. It was cold; the entire house was cold except for the living room, in which the log fire burned, and the kitchen with its wood-burning stove, but the duvet, which had a pale green cover of scratchy cotton and a frilled edge, was thick and heavy, and Max found in the airing cupboard a mohair blanket and arranged it inexpertly on the bed. He asked her if she needed anything, and Kate opened her rucksack, which she had packed at the peak of her panic.

'I brought a sudoku book and three packets of beta blockers,' she said. 'The essentials. I could use a T-shirt, though.'

Max brought her some pyjamas, thick striped cotton, and a spare toothbrush he had found in one of the upstairs bathrooms. He also brought an enormous bandage that he started to wrap tenderly around the cut on Kate's hand before giving up and getting a sticking plaster for her instead. He stood by the door, his hand on the handle.

'Please don't go,' said Kate. She changed out of her jeans and got into bed. Max sat in the chair by the window wrapped in a blanket. 'Tell me about you. Just talk to me about anything.'

Max settled back. 'We can talk about me. My whole family's gone mad.'

'Weren't they already?'

'Yes, but more,' Max said. 'My dad won't make eye contact with me because he thinks I'm going to lead my uncle back into alcoholism, and my uncle is consistently disappointed that he continues to exist. My mother thinks we're all emotionally repressed and need to turn our pain into art. She probably wants to put us all in her next film, we're all fucked enough. Only Nicole seems to be completely unmoved by it all. God, I envy her.'

'Nicole has anxiety, doesn't she?' Kate said. 'Isn't it surprising that she's so level?'

'She used to,' Max said. 'When she was a teenager. I suppose that's it, isn't it? She went through all the extremes as a teenager so all of this –' he waved his hand – 'all of this bullshit is small fry.'

On another day she might have asked him why it was that Max believed Nicole no longer suffered anxiety, but at that moment she did not have the strength to open herself up to his vulnerabilities, as well as her own.

'It must be confusing, being here,' she said. 'There are so many memories.'

'Exactly. And not all of them mean what I thought they meant.'

'In what way?'

'People aren't always who you thought they were.'

For a moment, Kate thought Max might be about to let something slip about Lewis, but in fact he was referring to Bernadette, and the will, and as his voice softened Kate slowly tuned out to what he was saying. In her single bed, with him sitting there like a faithful guard dog in the chair beneath the window, under the warm light of the standing lamp, Kate felt heavy, tired. This had once been a servant's quarters, Max had told her, so it was a walk-through room, with a door on one side and the stairs they'd come up on the other. It made her feel calm to know that if one exit was blocked, there would be another way out, and she fell asleep quickly, her body warming beneath the thick duvet, and Max still there, keeping her company.

She woke in a sweat. It was dark, and Max was gone. She threw off the duvet and reached for her phone; it was one in the morning, she had slept for only a few hours, during which her body seemed to have marinated in its own heat. Her mouth was filled with thick saliva and when she moved she felt a dull pain in her upper abdomen. Spurred by that peculiar vitality available to a person in the moments immediately prior to being sick, she hurled herself from her bed and down the back stairs, through the door of the nearest bathroom on the floor below. She closed the door and crouched over the porcelain bowl of the toilet, where she began to vomit. There was little she hated more than being sick, brought to her knees by her body's violent rejection of what she had chosen to put into it, choking up bile, and pieces of undigested food that had resisted absorption and somehow retained their form.

Instead of climbing back up the stairs knowing that she would only have to run back down again with the next wave of nausea, for a while Kate stayed there in the bathroom, lying on the cold floor with her head resting on the mat beneath the sink, drifting in and out of consciousness, comforted by the certainty that things really could get no worse than this.

By the time morning came, she had managed to sleep for only a few hours in bed and one in the bathroom. When Max came into her room and threw open the curtains, Kate groaned and told him that she would infect him if he didn't leave straight away.

'You do look terrible,' he said, sliding hurriedly out of the room. He went to get her a consolatory glass of water, then left her alone for the morning. Feverishly, she dozed until eleven, thinking each time she woke that she should get up, but she was always pulled back into a heavy half-sleep in which she dreamt that Max was driving her too quickly through the narrow lanes that surrounded the house, throwing her belongings out the back of the car which, when she turned round to look, she saw was completely open.

At midday she got out of bed and went barefoot across

the corridor and down the soft carpeted stairs to the floor below. This wasn't the same way Max had taken her the night before: at the end of the corridor was a large mirror next to a staircase that would lead her to the ground floor. At the top of the staircase she stopped, catching the reflection of the doorway to the room opposite, whose lights were out and curtains were closed. In the mirror Kate could see the edge of a bookcase, and the lower half of a man's body lying prone on the bed; on top of the covers, shoes still on. For a moment she stood there, trying to work out whether whoever was in the room was awake, but there were no noises. She stepped a little closer, and from the room came a low, quick cough: the legs moved. Kate stepped back from the door and went down the stairs as quietly as she could.

There was the sound of the radio playing from the kitchen.

'What have we done to you?' said Zara, when Kate appeared in the doorway. 'Max said you were sick. God, I hope it's not from William. He always seems to be bringing home diseases.'

'It wasn't you,' Kate said. 'I think it was my mum's Christmas dinner.'

'William and Nicole are out walking the dog,' Zara said. 'And Max and Elias have gone for a drive. But they won't be long.'

'Is Rupert here?' Kate asked. She thought that the room she had seen must have belonged to Max's uncle, but she hadn't been sure.

'Somewhere,' said Zara, glancing towards the door. 'Upstairs.'

Kate sat down at the big wooden table in the kitchen, her hands on her stomach. Zara sat down with her and brought her a glass of water. As Kate reached for it, she saw Zara looking at the plaster on her hand.

'You know, when I was first depressed, I used to have all sorts of stomach aches and pains. I used to get sick all the time.' She looked at Kate but did not wait for a response, and spoke in a matter-of-fact tone that made it easy for Kate to pretend she had not recognised the gravity of what Zara was saying, though of course she knew that Zara was telling her that she knew she was carrying something, and that her body was rebelling against the strain it was being placed under. 'Sadness can manifest itself in all sorts of unexpected ways,' Zara went on. 'And it doesn't take much. It doesn't have to be a momentous thing for sadness to transform into something far heavier than simple sadness. It can take one little moment, one small catastrophe that pushes you and then you just tip out beyond the boundaries of normal human emotion. And once you're out there, out of range, it's very difficult to find your way back. People so often forget that emotion is physical; English people in particular.'

Kate did not know if Zara was trying to allude to something specific, when she talked of this one catastrophic moment, but she did not interrupt.

'Think of Bernadette.' Zara gestured at the ceiling, indicating her mother-in-law's presence in the house. 'You didn't meet her, did you? But she was always sick, always thin, and she never understood that her physical illness was the manifestation of her unhappiness. She never completely loved her husband, I don't think, and she felt guilty because part of her was relieved when he died. So instead of mourning, her body became a mortuary, and she grew greyer and stonier until she was drained of colour and filled instead with sickness. William knows nothing of this, of course. He thinks I disliked his mother whereas really I pitied her because she became a stranger to herself.'

'Like in *Margot*,' Kate said.

'*Margot*?'

'Your film. With the hypochondriac who doesn't understand that she's miserable.'

Zara nodded, registering only slightly her surprise at Kate's familiarity with the film.

'Bernadette hated that film,' she said. 'Now you know why.'

The door to the kitchen opened, and Kate turned: it was Rupert, she recognised him from photographs, though in reality he was smaller than Kate had imagined him to be. His green cashmere jumper was too big for him, and the belt on his jeans looked as though it was on the smallest notch. Kate recognised the shoes from the bedroom she had passed upstairs.

'We were just talking about your mother,' Zara said, 'and her hypochondria.'

'Ah, yes,' Rupert said. He was rooting through his jacket, which was hanging on the back of one of the kitchen chairs. 'The only diagnosis she would ever reject.'

'You've met Kate, haven't you?'

'I feel like I have,' Rupert said, still patting his jacket pockets. He found what he was looking for: his cigarettes, and then bent down to kiss Kate on both cheeks. 'Max has told me such a lot about you. What a pleasure.'

'You too,' said Kate.

'Kate has been a good friend to Max,' Zara said, smiling at her across the table. 'She's kept him grounded these last couple of years. I think we rather owe her.'

Rupert went out for a cigarette, and Zara made Kate a dry piece of brown toast, and poured her half a glass of orange juice diluted with water. The smell of toast made her feel a little sick, still, and she was not quite hungry just yet, but she drank the juice slowly, observing the feel of the cold liquid in her stomach, the sugar in her blood. After eating, Zara told Kate to call her mother. Kate had texted already, but it would be better to phone, Zara said, so that Alison could hear her voice. Afterwards, she went into the living room where she lay down in a corner of the sofa. She was awake when Max returned, but she didn't open her eyes when he came into the living room. Instead she listened to him scrunching up pieces of newspaper and quietly moving logs onto the fire, and felt the weight of him sitting down at the other end of the sofa. Kate heard the door and footsteps, as people came into the room, bringing in the smell of bacon frying in the kitchen, and all the while she lay there still, listening to the sounds of the catching fire and Titus's heavy breathing.

21

The day after Boxing Day, Kate woke early. She lay in bed for an hour, unable to move. Now that her sickness seemed to have receded, that other, more familiar sickness was once again dominant in her body, and she was aware of it even before she was fully conscious. It was the first thing she thought of when she woke up each morning and the last thing at night, though at least now, unlike in the first weeks following the rape, she had managed to attach it to phrases which, alone in the dark, she attempted to assemble into a narrative. She had only lately begun replaying her account silently to herself as if in court, picking holes out of inconsistencies, bringing accusations upon herself until she could no longer bear to think of it but neither could she not think of it, until she resolved never to tell anybody because the horror of being disbelieved was worse than the horror of bearing it alone.

She had tried to verbalise it to Max, but she had been cut short. Alone, she had kept on trying and she had even succeeded once, five days before Christmas, looking herself in the eye as she brushed her teeth at her mother's house.

'I was raped,' she said, trying it out. The word was too

shrill, though; she censored herself: 'I said no. I said no but it happened anyway.' No blame apportioned, no specificities, just the barest details. How ridiculous she appeared, in her baggy pyjamas, toothpaste around her mouth, her face pale and round in the merciless light of the bathroom mirror.

But lying in this spare bedroom of Bernadette's house, replaying those fragile sentences over in her mind, she thought that perhaps she could do it, and perhaps now she had no choice but to do it. She could not live like this for much longer, segregated from the world by a cracked pane of glass, at the mercy of the sudden swooping in her chest and fog in her mind that signalled blind panic. Surely there would come a moment when the pain of staying the same would be greater than that of change. In a way that moment came every morning for Kate, it was what forced her out of bed, the moment at which lying immobilised was a greater struggle than to move onto her side, to push herself upright, to feel the floor on her ten toes. And if she could do it, if she had done it every morning since August, then what else was she capable of doing?

The house downstairs was empty. The lights on the eight-foot Christmas tree in the hallway had been left on all night, and the space below it was scattered with pine needles and scraps of wrapping paper. Daydreaming, whenever she'd had reason to pass the iron gates of this house over the past few years, Kate had imagined what it would be like to be on the inside, enclosed by those once-golden limestone walls. She had expected that she would come to the house one day, invited by Max for a week in summer, or for one of the family's dinner parties. She had envisaged endless days and sunshine: not these dusty hallways, this sickness. Kate turned on lights and, as she waited for the kettle to boil, she flexed her right hand, which was beginning to heal. She thought of how Zara had looked at it yesterday, when they'd sat together and talked, and she wondered whether Zara believed that it had been an accident.

Kate made herself black tea, without milk in case it made her sick again, and sat by the window waiting for it to cool. Titus came and sat by her, nuzzling his wet nose on the tops of her bare feet. She could hear, after a few minutes of sitting there, that there was somebody else awake in the house. The water pipes in the walls began to clunk; there were footsteps and there was the sound of a door shutting. She thought the noise could be coming from the room Elias was staying in, but it seemed unlikely that he would be up this early. She hoped it wouldn't be Elias; she wasn't sure she could face him being here, demanding Max's attention.

Titus knew before she did who it was; he leapt to his feet and scuttled to the kitchen door which he nosed open as Zara walked in. Of course, Kate thought, it was Zara who should find her here. It seemed only right that they had both been woken at this early hour, that they should be given this time alone together. Their conversation yesterday had been interrupted, and now she knew that they had to pick up where they had left off.

'You're up early,' Zara said.

'I couldn't get back to sleep,' Kate said.

Zara was wearing an ankle-length dressing gown made from dark blue satin. Her hair was loose, gathered thick over one shoulder. She looked fresh, though she had just woken. She had the same eyes and nose as Max, the elegant bone structure that both he and Nicole had inherited and which made them look like they had been born into a superior breed, a race of natural aristocrats who were so used to being waited upon that, over the generations, all the bulk had been bred out of them.

The rest of the house was quiet. There might not be another moment like this, Kate knew.

'Can I talk to you about something?' she said at last.

Zara sat down at the table and Kate got up to join her. Zara sat with her hands folded, studying Kate's expression with an appraising look that was, at the same time, devoid of judgement. This was a look that told her she was going to be taken seriously. Kate started, for want of a better place, by explaining to Zara the persistent feeling she had of standing on the edge of a precipice, that it was taking all her energy not to fall into it.

Zara nodded: she too had looked into the precipice. 'Do you know what's causing it?'

Now Kate nodded, mirroring her.

'Do you think you ought to talk to somebody?'

'I know what it is,' Kate said, before pausing. Now there

was no path back. She couldn't unsay this, but neither could she not say it, just as she wouldn't have been able to not throw up two days earlier.

'What's on your mind?' said Zara gently.

'I keep thinking about this thing that happened. I can't stop thinking about it.'

Zara said nothing, waited for Kate to continue.

'This guy, I went into the room with him and, you know, I said no, but, you know, it happened anyway.'

'How old were you?' said Zara without missing a beat.

'It was four months ago.'

'I was raped when I was nineteen,' said Zara bluntly, as if she were telling Kate that she had started her period when she was twelve, or had lost her virginity when she was sixteen. Nobody had ever said anything about this third rite of passage, somewhere between virginity and motherhood; but there it was, as ugly as it was undeniable: the first rape. 'It does terrible things. Waves of anxiety and depression?'

'Yes.'

'Yes. I know.' Zara reached out and held Kate's hand. Kate wanted to say more, but before she could, Zara spoke for her. 'You don't have to tell me any more. I understand. Have you told anybody?'

'Not until now,' Kate said, 'not even Max.'

'It's a difficult thing to talk about,' Zara said, squeezing Kate's hand. Kate looked down at Zara's hand, on top of hers.

'He had this tattoo,' Kate said, before she could stop

herself. She put her free hand on her lap, half a gesture, but here she paused: changed tack. 'I feel like I'm going mad.'

'You're not mad,' Zara said firmly. 'I promise you, you're not mad.'

Kate had already said too much. But now that she had started she wanted to keep on talking, to show Zara that she was afraid, but not enough to be silenced.

'I quit my job just before Christmas,' she said quickly, 'I've been thinking about moving home so that I can get proper help, but I realised that would mean telling my mother everything, and I can't bear to do that.'

'Stop,' Zara said. 'You don't need to worry about any of this. You especially needn't worry about money. There will be a way through. For now, we have to take care of you. I'm going to give you some names and some numbers. People you can phone and people you can talk to.'

Kate put her head in her hands.

'You don't have to do it now,' Zara said. 'There's no rush. But for when you're ready.'

From upstairs came the sound of a door slamming. Zara got up and passed Kate a box of tissues.

'You don't even look like you've been crying,' she said, pinching her cheek. 'Brave girl. Your secret is safe with me; as I trust mine will be with you.'

Above them they could hear Max singing falsetto, his muffled voice growing louder, and then his footsteps thundering down the wooden stairs.

'Max,' Kate said, wiping her eyes.

'Are you going to speak with him?'

'I think so,' Kate said. 'I think I want him to know.'

Zara nodded. 'Let me get out of your way. I'll keep the others out of the kitchen. Take as long as you need.' At the door, though, she paused. 'One thing I would say,' she said. 'Max will understand, Max is fine. But be careful who you speak to about this. You never quite know how people will react, and once you've said it, you can't take it back.'

Kate nodded.

'You know where to find me.'

Kate nodded again. 'Thank you,' she said, as earnestly as she could. But as the door closed, she did not feel quite the relief she had been expecting to feel at this first disclosure. She felt instead that in articulating what had happened, she had begun to lose control of it. Zara had not doubted her – and of course Kate had only told her part of the truth – nor had she pressed her on any of the details. She had taken what Kate had said at face value, embellished it, even, with the word that Kate had not been able to muster. Worse, she had warned Kate against what she had spent the last months building up to: the act of externalisation. Words said could not be unsaid.

When Max came into the room, though, Kate's angst dissipated. Zara had stopped him outside the door, had given him some kind of warning, and when he saw Kate at the kitchen table, head in her hands and a box of tissues next to her, he came to her and put his arms around her shoulders, kissed her on the cheek, and pulled up a chair to sit next to her.

'Kate,' he said, 'will you tell me what's happening?'

It was far easier, the second time. She still didn't say the word rape, but she took her time over the narrative, contextualised it a little more, though she lied and gave the impression that the perpetrator was not somebody she knew, and that it had happened when she had been with her old school friends, and not with Max, so that he wouldn't begin to fear that he had been involved or responsible in any way. She was protecting Lewis, she knew, but in doing so she was protecting her friendship with Max, and to her this was far more important. Max was silent as she spoke. When she had finished she saw that he had tears in his eyes.

'When?' Max said. 'When did it happen?'

'Over the summer,' Kate said. She had thought about this moment; she knew what question was coming next.

'And do you know –'

'No,' she said. He could see that she didn't want to say any more: this, he could understand, and an expression that might have been relief passed across his face.

'It's OK, though.' Kate reached out and touched his arm. 'I'm still here.'

Acknowledging how absurd it was that she should be the one to comfort him, he drew away.

'So what does this mean?' he said. 'What do we need to do? What can I do?'

Kate shook her head, put her head in her hands. 'I don't know.'

Max, understanding that his eagerness to help was premature, fell silent.

'I'm sorry,' he said after a while. 'This is fucking shit for you.'

'There are worse things,' said Kate from behind her hands.

'Have you told your mum?'

'No. I don't know how.'

Now she looked up at him, her face grey, blank. Max looked as though he had something he wanted to say but stopped himself.

'There's no rush,' he said. 'Family don't go anywhere. Even if you want them to.' He laughed, harshly.

Kate let Max make her a cup of tea, even though she didn't want one, and he let Titus out, who was whimpering under the table. She was exhausted, her brain tired. She heard Elias on the stairs above them. He barrelled through the closed kitchen door, waving his phone at Max.

'It's a catastrophe,' he said. 'I've got to go back to London. I'm going to be dumped.'

'Oh God,' Max said, 'why?'

'It's the longest story. Julia accused me ages ago of sleeping with her friend, even though I wasn't, but she's started fixating on it again, and now she wants to finish it. Women are fucking crazy. No offence.' Elias nodded at Kate in a generous acknowledgement of her demonstrable sanity.

'None taken,' Kate said, on behalf of all women.

'And you know the worst fucking thing?' said Elias. 'I hadn't even slept with her until Julia started accusing me of it.'

'So you *did* sleep with her?' Max said.

'Well, yeah,' said Elias, 'eventually, but only because she thought I had already.'

'Right,' Max said.

'So there's a train in a half-hour,' Elias said. 'Are you coming with me or what?'

Max shook his head, and glanced at Kate. 'I'm going to stay here,' he said.

22

It was only once she and William had left Bisley House that Zara could make space to think about what Kate had told her: there was no room for her own history in this house already crowded with histories; it would have to wait until they had come back to the sunlit rooms of Latimer Crescent, to which they were returning in time for New Year's Eve. It was while she was sitting on the edge of her bed, that her understanding of what had happened began to clarify. It was as if, unknown to Zara, she and Kate had begun to share the same bodily memory, which could only be fully recalled when Zara returned to the place of its conception, when her own body occupied the invisible outline that had been left there by Kate.

Zara thought at first she must be mistaking the feeling that had surfaced within her, but she had come to know herself too well not to recognise the particular emotion with which she had been burdened since her conversation with Kate. Nor would she quite have believed it had it not been so unmistakably powerful. Just as she had been when William had avoided looking at her at dinner two nights before Christmas, and when at the party her children had abandoned her to go out together and drink instead of staying and suffering with her, she was consumed by a crushing loneliness.

This feeling, which made little sense to her at first, soon began to gather its logic. It was of course to do with Kate, and the fact that she already seemed to have chosen a different path from Zara in processing her trauma, in speaking up not only so soon after the event, in comparison to Zara, but also to a relative stranger. Privately at least, Zara had managed to disclose, but only after years, and only to a very select few; publicly she had never managed it. What stirred in her as she sat on her bed, waiting for William to finish brushing his teeth, was the fear that not only had she been getting it wrong all these years, but that she was entirely alone in having done so.

The week that the London universities went back, Zara had been invited to give a lecture to celebrate the twenty-fifth anniversary of *L'Accusé*. On the Sunday she got up early, and set herself up in the living room, the film on the projector, her glasses on the end of her nose and a notebook by her side. Her intention was to work, but she knew before the film started rolling that it would be near impossible to keep Kate from her thoughts.

When, about a third of the way through, Lucille appeared in the window of her fourth-floor apartment – framed, contained – with her tights torn and her face smeared with make-up, Zara pressed pause. She remembered that day very clearly. She remembered Nadia, the actress playing

Lucille, squealing as Zara had knelt in front of her, pulling at her tights with her fingers, and then, when they did not tear, pushing the blade of her silver-handled costume scissors through the nylon and slicing roughly upwards, grazing Nadia's thigh as she did so.

How she had detested Nadia and the way she allowed herself to be consumed by her dramatised assault, crying in the canteen between shots, allowing herself to be comforted by the second cameraman or third props man or whoever it had been, all for the mere trauma of having to look as though she had been raped. She had been weak, and Zara, at that point violated and entirely silent with it, had resented her for her frailty.

Zara did not know whether Kate had seen this film, but as she wound back and played the scene again, and as she saw the fear frozen on Nadia's face, the genuine tears that had begun to well in her blue eyes after Zara had shouted at her for the second time that day, she found herself picturing Kate's face in the middle of a cinema audience, and imagined that Kate was able to see Zara's image shadowed in Nadia's, and the unbridled resentment of hers that had triggered in Nadia what turned out to be such a convincing performance.

Zara didn't watch the rest of the film, but instead she called her son, who was still asleep when the phone rang.

'I've been thinking about Kate, darling,' Zara said. 'We must make sure that we help her.'

'I know that,' said Max, groggily defensive. 'I am helping. What do you mean?'

'I'm sure you are. But sometimes it's difficult to ask for things, particularly if you don't know you need them.'

'What things?'

'I mean therapy. Professional help. Time to recover. A place to stay.'

'She's going to the doctor,' said Max.

Zara put the phone on speaker and reached for her note-pad. 'Right. Darling, I'm going to send some emails. She was going to apply for film school. Does she still want to work in film?'

'Mum,' Max said. He sounded a little hesitant now. 'I know you want to help, but I don't think it's for you to push her into anything.'

'Meaning?'

'Meaning, well, don't you think that sometimes talking can do more harm than good?'

Zara sighed. 'You've been spending too much time with your father, Max.'

'I'm serious. Why do you think you know what's best for people? Not everybody's the same. In fact –' he lowered his voice – 'it seems like she's worse now that she's having to talk about it. Way worse than she was before. She pretty much shut me down when I asked her about what happened.'

'Or maybe it's because it's worse that she's started talking about it, Max. She just needs time.'

'I'm just saying,' said Max. 'You don't always know what everybody is feeling. Maybe there are some things better left alone.'

'You know that's not true, Max,' Zara said gently. 'No

matter how much you'd like it to be. Your friend needs you. She needs support.'

'Like Rupert needs support, you mean? Even though he keeps saying he'd rather be dead?'

Max's voice cracked a little as he spoke, and Zara waited for a moment, giving him time to compose himself. He was angry: angry that the world was not as comfortable as he'd always been led to believe, angry that things didn't just work themselves out, angry that he might, once in a while, have to do something to help things to the right conclusion.

'None of this is a consequence of what you've done, or haven't done,' said Zara. 'But that doesn't mean you can't be there, when the time is right.'

Max was silent for a moment.

'He hasn't actually said he wants to be dead for a while,' Max said. A note of hope had entered his voice.

'Exactly,' Zara said, as if this had been the point she was trying to make all along.

'Yeah,' said Max, and when Zara imagined his expression she saw him as a toddler: lips pouting, big eyes wet, reaching again for the sweet treat he'd just been denied.

'If you give me her email address, Max,' she said now, 'I'll write to her. I'll send her some numbers she can call.'

'OK,' Max said. She could hear him steadying his breath. It was possible, Zara realised, that he had been on the brink of tears. 'I suppose she'll appreciate it. Thanks.'

After hanging up the phone, Zara wondered about calling Nicole. What Nicole had been through had been very different: the stress of the high-pressure all-girls school William had insisted on sending her to, which in turn had engendered absurdly high expectations of herself and the people around her. It had been Zara who had insisted on therapy then, too. But although it had been she who had driven Nicole to the sessions, and had waited outside while they took place, whenever she'd tried to ask her daughter on the way home whether there was anything she wanted to talk about, whether there was anything that Zara could be doing differently, to make things easier for her, Nicole had turned up the radio and slumped down in her seat. It had worked, though: the therapy, the school transfer, the exercise and the yoga. And you'd never know, looking at Nicole now: with the law degree, the flat, all those friends, what a difficult adolescent she had been. Nicole so rarely needed help, nowadays, and it might even be gratifying for her to help somebody else. But something, perhaps the memory of those silent post-therapy car journeys, stopped Zara from calling.

Instead, that afternoon, she composed and sent several emails: one to a former therapist of Nicole's for a list of recommendations for trauma treatment; one each to the four or five directors to whom she was closest asking if they had any jobs for a young friend of hers who was looking to get work in the industry; and, when she received replies from the therapist and two of the directors, one to Kate with the contact details. She told Kate that she could call at any time, night or day, and that all she asked was that she call one of the therapists and schedule a meeting, as well as going to the doctor for medication. She knew Kate didn't have the money, but she wasn't to worry because Zara was going to pay, and if Kate wrote to either of the directors whose details she had passed on, she would be able to earn the money to pay her rent. This would not end her. Zara would not allow it to end her.

'*We'll find a way through*,' she wrote at the end of her email. '*With love, Z.*'

23

When they'd left Bisley House, on their way back up to
London, Max had driven Kate to her mother's house. While
Kate went up to her old bedroom to pack, Max waited
downstairs with Alison, who was sitting at the kitchen
table. Coloured tinsel had been wound around the banister
in the hallway and there were rows of Christmas cards
strung low across the ceiling here and above the doorway
to the living room. Max could see why Kate had found it
difficult being at home: it was disconcerting, the way the
fluffy carpets and linoleum floors stifled his footsteps, and
he found the density of the decorations claustrophobic. He
did feel sorry for Alison, but he was relieved that she hadn't
asked him why Kate had chosen to spend the end of the
holidays with his family instead of here.

'You're driving all that way?' Alison said now.

'It's a nice drive,' said Max.

Alison nodded, but she was looking towards the door,
listening out for Kate. 'Better, is she?'

'I think it was a twenty-four-hour thing,' said Max,
'such bad luck.' Only after he had spoken did Max realise
that Alison was referring to Kate's mood, and the panic

that had led her to flee the house on Christmas Day, rather than the sickness that had followed. But he didn't say any more, and neither did Alison: she got up and opened the cupboard next to the fridge, her back to Max. Her woollen cardigan was wrapped around her waist, and she was wearing sheepskin slippers with her tights.

'I haven't offered you anything to drink. Would you like some tea? We've got some Earl Grey somewhere.'

Max glanced at his phone for the time. 'We should hit the road, actually, but thanks.'

They kept the radio on all the way back to London. On the motorway, Max turned down the volume.

'I can see how it's hard to talk about,' he said, 'and I don't think you should rush it.' He was thinking of Alison, her skittish energy, and of how much more vulnerable than Max's own mother she had seemed. 'Family, particularly. They always mean well. But sometimes they're too close to see what's best for you.'

Kate shook her head. 'I can't think about it right now,' she said.

After they'd been back a week or so, Kate came into Max's room, dressed in sweats, bashfully holding a bottle of wine and her phone. She told Max that she needed his help: she still hadn't called any of the numbers Zara had given her and she had responded to Zara's email only to say that she would think about her offer to pay for therapy. She needed to try and do this by herself, but she didn't know where to start.

'I've been staring at my phone all morning,' she said, limply. 'I don't know if I can do it.'

'I got it,' Max said. He opened the wine and poured them both a glass, then he took Kate's phone and called the first helpline on the list.

'This is Kate Quaile's assistant speaking,' he said with authority. 'I'd like to speak to the person in charge of panic attacks, please.'

Despite herself, Kate snorted.

'I'm afraid she's otherwise engaged,' Max said. 'She's asked me to speak to you on her behalf. OK, I see, let me put that to her. Please hold.'

Max rolled his eyes and put his hand over the mouthpiece.

'She wants to talk to you,' he said to Kate. Kate nodded, and took the phone, only a little warily. She leaned back on Max's bed with the wine glass resting on her stomach and the phone on speaker, her earlier anxiety beginning to subside now that she was with Max. The woman on the other end of the phone asked her to describe, loosely and briefly, the main symptoms she was experiencing, in response to which Kate found herself under-exaggerating the anxiety, the low moods, the strength of the panic attacks.

'And do you feel low one hundred per cent of the time on seventy-five per cent of the days?'

'I guess it's more, seventy-five to seventy-five?'

'You feel low one hundred per cent of the time on seventy-five per cent of the days?' the woman said.

'No, well, one hundred per cent of the time, well, I'm

asleep some of the time, you know, so maybe, I don't know. Is this assuming I sleep eight hours per day? Because if it is, then I'd say thirty-five, but if it's the time I'm actually awake well, then, it's probably more like fifty, but then I don't sleep too well so maybe forty-five.'

'Thirty-five or forty-five?' said the woman.

Kate shrugged, pulled a face at Max.

'Go for forty,' Max whispered, 'good round number.'

'Forty,' Kate said. She heard the sound of several keystrokes.

'And do you have thoughts of suicide or self-harm?'

'I don't know,' Kate said. Again, she looked at Max, but he was now looking at something on his phone, deliberately not making eye contact with her. 'No, not really,' she said.

More keystrokes. 'Good,' said the woman. She told Kate she would receive a phone call from a psychologist in the next fifteen days, and checked that she had Kate's number correctly, before hanging up.

'You know when your mum emailed me,' Kate said to Max, 'she offered to pay for therapy.'

'Oh, really?' Because Max did not look surprised, Kate assumed that Zara had spoken to him. 'What did you say?'

'I haven't decided,' Kate said. 'Do you think I should say yes?'

Max shrugged. 'Up to you.'

'You don't sound sure.'

'You know best. If you think it will help you, you should do it.'

'It would be less of a wait, going private,' Kate said tentatively. She had wanted his encouragement, not his permission. 'If that phone call was anything to go by.'

'OK, then. Say yes.'

Later that day Kate called to thank Zara and to tell her that she had called one of the helplines and was going to be in touch with the therapists as well as the directors on the list. The conversation felt to Kate less like a crisis talk than she had been expecting, and she could hear Zara running a bath as she spoke, the radio on in the background.

'You really must get in touch with Georgina,' Zara said. 'She's a dream to work for. And she's got the most fantastic imagination. You'll learn a lot, even if you are only running for her.'

'I will,' Kate said.

'And Frieda, too. Brilliant woman. Do send her my love when you talk to her.'

'I don't think I've seen any of her films.'

'No, darling, Frieda is one of the therapists. You know she saved Issa's life after her mother died.'

'Issa as in Issa Moore?' said Kate, incredulous.

'She was in a terrible state. Wouldn't I make an awful therapist, Kate? I'm so indiscreet.'

As well as Frieda, Kate contacted both directors whose names Zara had given her. Neither of them had any work until spring, but one gave her the details of a production company she knew was looking for runners, and Kate managed to get work on the set of a film they were making in south London. On her first day, the set manager gave Kate an industrial-strength Hoover and a pair of padded gloves, and told her that her priority was not to step on any nails when clearing the remnants of the car crash they were shooting. They were in an empty warehouse, filming the final few shots of a climactic chase scene through an indoor meat market.

'Trash,' Zara said gleefully, when Kate told her what her job entailed. 'Pure trash. Exquisite. I dread to think what the budget is for those vans. What's the film called?'

'*Gristle*,' Kate said.

'Exquisite,' Zara said again. 'It will be tough work, though, Kate. Exhausting, and repetitive.'

But this kind of work was exactly what Kate wanted. It took them hours to set up the crash scene: each market stall aligned at the correct angle for the seven waiting cameras; huge hunks of plastic fake meat hooked in the back rows of each stall, bloodied steaks, boards and knives on the work surfaces; then real lamb shoulders, strong with the smell of blood, hanging at the front.

'These have to be real,' the set manager said to Kate, 'because we want them to really splatter the side of the van.' For emphasis, he smacked the back of one hand against the palm of the other, then began adjusting the angle of the carcass closest to him, ever so slightly. He stepped back to admire his work. 'I'm actually a vegan,' he said ruefully.

The two white vans would take less than fifteen seconds to come hurtling through the market, ploughing into the stalls lined up along the middle of the warehouse. Because she wasn't involved in the shooting of the scene, only the set-up and dismantling, Kate stood with the other runners, leaning on the railing of the temporary platform erected behind the camera crew, watching as the first van skidded in an arc through the front of the warehouse, tearing down the fronts of the stalls as it went. For Kate, the choreographed destruction was a welcome break from the scenes of the non-sequential, detached aggression that had been assailing her consciousness in the last weeks. On set, action led to consequence led to action led to consequence. There was a structural integrity to the crash that her own experience of violence was entirely lacking.

During those two weeks, the harder they worked – dragging heavy stalls and stacks of wood, realigning the hanging carcasses and clear-plastic curtains, clearing debris from that morning's work – the better Kate slept, too tired in her body to entertain her mind. Of the work she was doing, she actually preferred the clean-up. It was a comfort to know that nothing she did here had permanence. The more she built, the more she destroyed, the more she understood that there was nothing that would not pass.

On the last day of her first week, Kate stayed on set through lunch, working on one of her stalls. She was squatting on the toes of her heavy-soled trainers, using a screwdriver and her scant carpentry skills to try to prise out a nail that had been flattened in the back panel. Both hands were on the screwdriver, whose tip she was jamming into a knot in the woodwork. She could feel that the waistband of her jeans was riding a little low, that her lower back and hips were exposed, but was too focused on her task to pull them up until she became aware of somebody standing over her, just a little too close. They were men's shoes: Timberland, too clean to have been put to much use.

Kate took out an earphone and looked up. The man was about the same height as Max, perhaps in his late twenties, though he had a rough black beard that made him look older than he probably was. He was wearing a thick hoodie that showed some bulk around his belly and hips, and he was looking at Kate as though he was waiting for something.

'What?' Kate said bluntly. She stood up, hitching her jeans up around her hips, and deciding that if this man tried to say anything about the fact that her ass had just been on show then she would skewer him.

'Oh,' the man said absently, as if he and not Kate had just been in the middle of something. 'That's my screwdriver. I was gonna get it back, when you were done.'

'I thought they were communal.'

'Nah. That one's actually specifically for the rig.' He indicated behind him, to where the cameras were set up. Kate saw now that one of the cameramen was straining to hold a detached piece of rigging in place. The man didn't seem to be in a hurry, though. In fact, he looked as though he was trying not to laugh at her.

Kate glanced down at the screwdriver. Its tip was

scratched, where she had been scraping it. 'Sorry,' she said. She wiped it on her jeans and held it out to him.

'No worries. Try that instead,' he said, pointing to the hammer that had been left on the floor by another of the stalls.

Discreetly, Kate found out from Ben the Vegan Set Manager that the guy's name was Andrew, that he was with the camera crew, and that he'd been working as an assistant to the same cinematographer for the last couple of years. Andrew had left an impression on Kate. Over the next few days, she caught herself looking at him during the takes, watching him instead of the crash scene. That half-laugh he'd had for her had a warmth that she liked, and his brown skin was soft-looking. From the platform where she stood she saw that his frame was substantial but not muscular.

At first Kate had told herself that her constant awareness of this man was because she considered him to be a threat, or had briefly considered him to be a threat the first time she'd been aware of him standing over her. Her instinct was to categorise him as either not safe or safe. But that was wrong. Absurdly, impossibly, she was attracted to him.

'Why is it absurd?' Max said, when Kate told him about Andrew. She'd been agonising all evening over whether to say anything, feeling that this new desire was some terrible sin. She'd found herself unable to resist bringing him up, though, and Max's response took her by surprise.

'Just feels a bit soon,' Kate said, squirming.

'I don't think there are rules,' said Max kindly. 'I think it's great news. I think you should have sex with him as soon as possible.'

Kate put her head in her hands. 'Oh God,' she said. 'Don't. I can't. With any luck I'll never have to speak to him again.'

Of course she did want to speak to him again; it would be mortifying, naturally, but it would be good for her to try to have a conversation with a man who was neither friend nor, necessarily, threat. Ignoring the thrill that rose in her stomach, she reasoned that it would be an experiment – a means of measuring progress – for which it was obviously important to look her best. The next morning, she got out of bed just a little more eagerly than usual, scrubbed her face so that her skin felt clean and fresh, and took out the eyeliner pen she hadn't used since the summer, drawing careful black flicks at the corners of her lashes.

But when it got to the time that Andrew usually arrived and started setting up with the camera crew – he wasn't there. Nor was he there by the coffee van after lunch, around the time she'd seen him there the days before; there were only a few days left of filming, and every day she became less hopeful that she would see him. She was on such high alert that she even forgot to think about Lewis, right up until they got to the end of Friday, and wrapped the final shoot without Andrew having returned.

24

Zara wanted to hear about Kate's first set job, and she promised that after they had wrapped she would take her for lunch. It was no small thing, she said to Kate on the phone, and they needed to celebrate properly.

'We've been meeting with developers all morning,' Zara said, when they met on Greek Street in Soho. 'They're full of shit, bless them. Promising things they don't know if they'll be able to deliver. I'm afraid it's a slippery ladder you're climbing.'

'What were they promising?'

'Money for projects, big names, that sort of thing. Fortunately –' Zara put on her sunglasses as they stepped across the road – 'I've got just about enough influence that I don't have to put up with too much of that, these days.' She got out her phone. 'Is Max coming?'

Kate hadn't said anything to Max about lunch, and because Zara hadn't mentioned him when they'd arranged to meet she had assumed it would be just the two of them.

'I'm not sure,' she said.

Zara was scrolling through her messages. 'No, I think Max is busy. Nicole's in Holborn today, though, so we can drag her away from her desk. And Rupert's meeting us at the restaurant. You've met Rupert?'

'At Christmas,' Kate said.

As they walked north, Zara tried calling Nicole: the street narrowed, and Kate fell behind her. Zara was wearing a large cashmere scarf and impossibly white trainers. She was walking incredibly quickly, turning her shoulders as she slipped through the busy street. Kate caught up with her when she stopped outside a small Japanese restaurant.

'You like sushi, don't you?'

'Perfect,' Kate said. Inside, they waited for Rupert and Nicole to arrive. Kate sat opposite Zara and looked down at the menu, flipping backwards and forwards between its crowded pages. Zara ordered a jasmine tea, so Kate did the same, even though she was hot from keeping up with Zara as they'd walked here.

'So, a fortnight?' Zara said. 'That's good for a first job. Not too full-on.'

'A fortnight,' Kate said, 'and I learned such a lot. Just from watching, you know? I had no idea how many times they reshoot. I really liked watching the camera crew.'

'Good, good,' Zara nodded. She was looking at the menu as she spoke. 'It's very important to observe. So many people want to throw themselves in head first, take charge straight away and they just make a mess of it.

Though, of course –' she winked at Kate – 'those people are usually male.'

Kate laughed. 'Really?' she said. 'That doesn't seem at all likely.'

The tea had arrived, just cool enough so she could hold it in both hands.

'It's because they don't have great big ovens pumping out heat,' Zara said, when Kate commented that it wasn't too hot in the restaurant. 'The skill is all in the knife work, rather than the cooking, you see.'

Kate was not sure if this was true, but she was grateful to Zara for engaging with her mundane comment. She couldn't think of anything to say that wasn't to do with sexual assault, or trauma, unless she started talking about *Gristle* again, but Zara had already called the waiter over and started ordering for everybody. Nicole and Rupert both arrived just as the food began to come to the table. Walking through the doorway they made an unlikely pair: he in his worn navy jacket, she in her high-waisted suit trousers. Rupert sat down next to Kate.

'Delicious,' he said to her. 'What have we got here?'

'No idea,' she said. 'Fish, of different kinds.'

Nicole pulled a plate of sashimi towards her. She couldn't stay long, she said, dousing the tuna in sauce. Kate watched what she was doing, and copied her. It wasn't that she hadn't had sushi before, but it was always in a little supermarket-bought box with pre-assigned sauce, and she usually ate it with her fingers.

'How is he, the slave-driver?' Zara said to Nicole.

'Who?'

'David? Daniel? The partner you're working for.'

'Oh.' Nicole frowned at her mother across the table. 'Duncan. He's long gone. Left about six months ago. Or I should say he was "asked to leave".'

'He was fired?' Kate said.

'No,' Nicole said. 'Definitely not fired. But his departure was negotiated, shall we say, after he got caught in the stationery cupboard with a trainee.'

Zara made a loud noise, which Kate took a moment to recognise as laughter.

'Do modern offices even have stationery cupboards? I thought it was all iPads nowadays. How very eighties of them.'

'It was quite a big deal,' Nicole said. 'They nearly fired her, too.'

'But she got a promotion instead?' Zara said. She still appeared to be amused.

'No,' Nicole said. 'And she definitely won't any time soon. I'm not sure it's entirely fair, actually. He got a pretty tidy severance package.'

'It's an abuse of power, isn't it?' said Rupert. Of the four of them, Kate least expected this observation to come from Rupert.

'Quite,' Zara said, her tone more serious than it had been a moment ago. Clearly, Rupert's comment had surprised her as well.

Nicole stayed to drink the rest of her tea, and before she left she tried to give Zara a twenty-pound note from her purse. Zara brushed it away.

'My treat,' she said, squeezing Nicole's arm. 'You've worked hard for that.'

When it came to paying, then, Kate reached for her purse in what she knew would be only a nominal gesture: Zara refused to let either her or Rupert contribute, and Kate did not argue because she knew it would be ridiculous to insist on paying for lunch when every week Zara put more than three times the amount in her account to pay for her therapy sessions. Rupert smiled wryly.

'I would have been very impressed if she'd let you,' he said. 'I've been trying for years to pay my own way but it's impossible in the company of this woman.'

'That's not even remotely true,' Zara said.

'It isn't,' Rupert said, winking at Kate across the table, 'but you're so easily wound up, I can never resist.'

'You should have come to lunch,' Kate said to Max when she saw him that evening, 'you would have enjoyed it.'

'I think it's nice you hang out without me,' Max said. He was drunk, but fairly steady considering he'd been out with Elias that evening. 'She's helped you, hasn't she? And Rupert. She's very . . .' He paused, unsure of the word.

'Generous?' Kate offered.

'Yeah, generous. That's it.'

Neither of them said anything for a moment.

'Rupert was there,' Kate said. 'He seemed pretty well.'

'Oh, good.'

Max slid out of his chair and opened the fridge. He stared into the bright light, not knowing what he was looking for, or looking for something that wasn't there. He shut it, and opened the cupboard, stared into that, too.

'He looks a lot like you, actually,' Kate said, smiling. 'Same eyes.'

'Hopefully that's where the comparison ends,' Max said. He had found a box of cereal in the back of the cupboard, the contents of which he poured out into a bowl. He caught Kate's expression. 'I'm joking, obviously. I love him. Uncle Ru. Cheerios?'

'No, thanks.'

'Are you sure? They taste almost exactly like cardboard.'

'I'm going to bed,' Kate said. 'I have to get up early tomorrow, I've got another set job.'

'Look at you,' said Max, through his mouthful of Cheerios. 'I'm proud of you,' he shouted, as she left the kitchen.

He was proud: Kate knew this. He'd told her before, would continue to tell her, how strong he thought she was, the way she kept going. But she wondered, as she brushed her teeth, looking at her reflection in the bathroom mirror, how he would feel if she had given up, after that first panic attack. If, instead of stepping onto the train that would take her home, she had simply stepped off the platform instead. Would he be angry with her, like he was with Rupert? What Max didn't understand was that Rupert was in fact stronger than both of them. He had to be, given the depths he had been to, given the fact that he was still standing. There was so much Max did not know: what it was like to have invisible weights around the ankles, a fog in the mind, a clamp on the chest. She looked at herself square in the mirror, as she imagined how she might have cut Max off, so that he'd put down that box of childish cereal and really listen to her, really hear not just the optimism but the dark notes, too.

In the next room, she heard Max bashing around as he put the light on and kicked off his shoes: she remembered the familiar pattern from last year, when they'd lived together at university, how comforting it had been to know that he was home, sleeping just the other side of the wall. That year felt so long ago, now. She spat toothpaste into the sink. It was not his fault he gravitated towards the joyful things in life. She should be grateful that he wanted her to rise to his level, rather than to come down to hers. But as it was, she felt not gratitude but a deep disconnect. Kate heard the light flick off next door, which meant Max had gone to bed without brushing his teeth, which really was none of her business. She splashed water on her face and dried it, and looked at herself once more in the mirror before turning off the bathroom light.

25

A few weeks after Kate's work on the crash scene was finished, the producers of *Gristle* threw a wrap party. Lately, Kate and Max had been on different schedules – out on different nights, asleep at different times – but tonight she had invited him to come with her. Kate, anxiously aware of the possibility that Andrew might also be at the party, had drunk most of a bottle of wine before they left the flat. Her tolerance was high; this much wine wouldn't get her particularly drunk, but it would relax her enough to navigate a crowd of relative strangers.

'How are you feeling about this?' Max said, when they got to the entrance.

Kate groaned.

'We'll be fine.' Max squeezed her shoulder, then checked his watch. 'Elias has a work thing but he said he'll try and come by after.'

'Elias is coming?'

'He said he'd try,' said Max brightly.

This news did not thrill Kate, who tried to avoid spending time with Elias. This could be difficult, since Max saw him most days, and he often stayed on the sofa after they'd been out together, or in Nicole's bed, if Nicole was staying with her boyfriend. Kate couldn't help but notice that Max was sharper when Elias was around: a little less kind and a little more destructive.

'I didn't put him on the guest list,' she said now.

'You know Elias,' Max said, choosing to ignore the subtle hostility of this comment. 'He always manages to talk his way in.'

The bar was dark, but not too grimy, not the kind of all-night place Max had given up trying to drag Kate to, and the people in it were well dressed. After months of being on set, early mornings and late nights spent in torn jeans and old sweats, the production team and crew owed themselves a night of looking good. The atmosphere was loose, familiar, most of the people here knew each other well by now: they'd worked too many hours against too many deadlines for it to be anything other.

'It's quite busy,' said Max.

'I've taken my body weight in beta blockers.'

'Well done.'

Kate took Max to the bar, where she introduced him to Ben the Vegan, and a couple of the crew members she'd be working with on the next film. She surprised herself with her sociability: she couldn't remember the last time it had been her introducing Max to somebody new, rather than the other way round. She supposed that this was the first time in a long time she'd actually been doing something she liked: there had been little incentive to bring Mark

Cummins and his penicillin-infested milk home to meet Max when she'd still been at the restaurant.

'Are you in film?' said Ben to Max.

Max shook his head. It occurred to Kate that he might mention Zara in response to such a question, but she was unsurprised when he didn't.

'I'm actually developing an app,' he said.

Kate took a deep sip from her drink. It amused her, watching people encounter Max for the first time: his buoyancy always seemed to confuse them.

'What's the app?' said Ben.

'Well,' said Max. 'The idea is fucking ingenious, if I'm honest. I just need to get a handle on some of the more technical aspects. But it's a dating app. For older people.'

'Oh, that sounds really good,' said Ben generously. 'Quite a lot of them have phones, you know. My granny's all over Candy Crush.'

'We do have an ageing population,' said Max sagely. 'The name is my favourite bit, though. It's called Embers.' Max paused, waiting for Ben to catch up.

'Like Tinder,' Kate supplemented. 'But for people much nearer death.'

It was when Elias arrived, and Max went to the front entrance to attempt to negotiate his entry, that Kate saw Andrew leaning against the back wall, looking like he was deep in conversation with the cinematographer. She smiled at him and took a step in his direction: he looked at her without recognition, and she turned quickly back to the bar, where she ordered herself two drinks and willed the room to implode. By the time Max was back, this time with Elias, it was difficult to tell which of the three of them was most drunk, and they stationed themselves at an empty table near the bar.

'I mean, it was a charity thing,' Elias said. He was gesticulating as he spoke, unaware of how much space he was taking up, and he hadn't taken off his coat. 'I really don't understand why they had to throw me out. It wasn't like I didn't know anybody.'

'Was that Nicole's friend's thing?' said Max. 'Ellie?'

'Yeah, some bullshit. All because I didn't have a ticket.'

'Those tickets were like, two hundred pounds. For charity. That's the point.'

'Yeah, something like that. They had a free bar though.'

'Uh, maybe that's why they threw you out, then?' said Max. Kate laughed, while Elias looked indignant.

'I'm a valuable contact. A potential investor.'

'Don't most people just donate to charities?' Kate said.

'Well, that's where they're going wrong. We need to set up a charity, Max.'

'Get the app going first,' Kate said.

'Yeah, the app, fuck.'

For once Kate was relieved to have Elias there. His conversational dominance made it easier for her not to think about anything else: particularly Andrew. She found it easier, too, not to notice that Max was buying more rounds than anybody else, and that he seemed to disappear off to the bar for longer than it took to get a couple of drinks. By comparison with Max, whose eyes had lost focus and whose foot was tapping restlessly beneath the table, Elias appeared surprisingly composed. By the time it was Kate's third round, the party was thinning out a little, and she went to get drinks while Max went in the direction of the bathroom. Kate leaned on the bar, booze warm in her stomach, swaying absently to the music, and feeling – as she had not felt in some time – that tonight she might actually be able to enjoy herself. As she was about to order, Andrew appeared next to her. Kate tried not to look at him.

'I didn't recognise you,' Andrew said. He was smiling, not the half-smile from set that had made her feel like he'd heard a joke she wasn't in on, but full, candid. 'You stole my screwdriver, didn't you?'

'I'm sorry about that,' Kate said. She saw that he was wearing headphones around his neck, and that he was chewing gum. 'In case you run out of conversation?' she said, nodding at them.

He laughed, and glanced down. It was a warm, deep laugh.

'Got no pockets. I don't want to look rude, though.' He looked Kate up and down, before taking off the headphones and pointing at the shoulder bag she was wearing. 'You can look after them for me.'

Kate, giddily aware that she was being flirted with, accepted.

'I'm not giving these back.'

He bought them both a drink, and sat on a bar stool: enough to tell her that he wanted to stay and talk to her. Kate sat next to him. When he asked her name, she pretended not to know his. He told her that he had been working on several projects at once, which was why he hadn't stayed until the end of the shoot. He was from south London, he'd studied film at UAL, and his older sisters were both teachers. When she was halfway through her beer, Kate realised that she'd hardly told him anything about herself. But this wasn't because he was self-involved, in an Elias kind of way: his openness was not a performance, more like an invitation, to which Kate responded, involuntarily, by leaning towards him. His knee touched hers.

Andrew seemed quite a lot less drunk than most of the people at the party, including Kate, who was now doing her best to give the impression of sobriety. A woman Kate recognised from the crew came over to them, and flung her arms around him in a sloppy greeting, but he didn't introduce her to Kate, and nor did he show any signs of wanting to take this new arrival as an out. The woman untangled herself and moved towards the bar, and Kate knew that she had his attention, his headphones in her bag, anchoring him there.

When Elias came to find her, Kate pretended that she'd forgotten she'd gone to buy him and Max drinks.

'I thought you'd be with Max,' Elias said, his tone mildly accusatory. 'Do you know where he's gone?' She told Andrew she'd be back, and went with Elias to look for him. They found him, eventually, outside the bar, swaying as he talked to the bouncer who was holding his arms out, pushing him back whenever he stepped too close. Max waved when he saw them.

'See,' he said, 'my friends are in there.'

'Take him home,' the bouncer said, 'and we won't call the police.'

'Hold on, hold on,' Elias said, 'nobody's calling the police.'

'I am.' The bouncer held up the little white bag of powder he had in his hand. 'If somebody doesn't put him in a taxi in the next thirty seconds.'

'That's not his,' Elias said.

'That's why he was snorting lines in the ladies, then, was it?' The bouncer appeared to be more offended by Max's use of the female toilets than of the drugs.

'The signs are very confusing,' Max said, frowning, before adding, assertively: 'gender fluid.'

'They should sell that,' said Kate, who was still flying high from her conversation with Andrew. 'It'll be the new almond milk.'

'Will you take him back?' Elias said to Kate. 'I've got another party.'

Abruptly, Kate landed. 'I guess,' she said wearily. 'Can you wait with him? I just need to give someone something.'

Andrew was where she'd left him. She told him that she had to leave, so she'd come to give him back his headphones.

'That's a shame,' he said. 'Will I see you again?'

As he got up to hug her, she lifted her face to his, not caring that there were still people here they'd both worked with. It was nearly three in the morning, and nobody was

209

in a state to remember anything much. He paused, as if to pull away, but then kissed her, briefly, on the lips.

'You can see me. If you want,' Kate said.

When they'd got back, and Kate had waited for Max to throw up on the pavement outside their flat, she got straight into bed, her chest pounding: not the panic-driven, fearful pounding, but lustful, alive. She put her hand between her legs and, feeling that she was wet, started rubbing slowly, closing her eyes. She could still feel the pressure of Andrew's lips against hers. She pressed her hips into the mattress, not wanting to come, wanting to make this last for as long as she could. Her phone was on the pillow next to her in case he texted her, though presumably he wouldn't tonight, presumably he would wait; she was making herself wait for him, too. Wanted to wait, wanted to make it last, to remember the full softness of his mouth, the smell of mint and something sweet, berry-flavoured. She was close, now, still with him pictured in her mind, hearing his voice. She slipped her fingers inside herself: that was when he flickered, and disappeared, and another voice, clearer, sharper, came into her mind, telling her her cunt was tight, telling her to taste herself. A searing pain shot through her, iciness spreading up through her stomach and her chest, and she pulled her hand away, turned her face into the pillow to stop herself from crying out, rolled onto her side and curled her arms around her knees, her body smothered by the guilty heat it had created.

26

Lewis was putting on weight. It was a fact that he had been trying to ignore – wearing loose-fitting scrubs all day, working full twelve-hour shifts without catching sight of his reflection – until he had seen himself in a photograph one of the nurses had taken, and had seen that he was fat. There was no denying it: his stomach had softened and a full inch of fat had gelatinised beneath the skin of his back, his shoulders and his hips. He'd grown stubble, too, which went some way to disguising what he suspected were the beginnings of a double chin. The causes were clear: his diet was starchy and sugar-loaded; the hours, the lack of sleep and the constant fatigue left him with a shortened attention span and no motivation to exercise. Though in his first year of being a doctor he'd worked hard to keep his weight from increasing, this second year had worn him down. The disdain with which he was regarded by everybody in the hospital from the porters to the consultants, the presumed position of incompetence from which he was constantly trying to elevate himself, the general ingratitude with which his every benevolent act was met: all of this made it extremely difficult for him to be content and in control. He was unhappy, and he was lonely, and it seemed to Lewis to be entirely unreasonable that he might be expected, as well as this, to put up with being over-weight. He realised, when he could no longer fit into his favourite pair of jeans, that it was time to do something about it.

It was a Saturday morning in June, and Lewis was standing in front of the bathroom mirror of his father's Fulham flat, where he had been living for the last two years now, despite having told himself that this was only a temporary arrangement. He was going to meet Nicole in north London for a music festival. She had invited him after the third text he'd sent to tell her that he had his first weekend off in a month and wanted to get out of the flat: with women, persistence paid out. He'd slept for ten hours the night before but even after a shower and a shave he felt uncooked; the bathroom light was not flattering, exposing the dry skin on his chin and jaw, a few ingrown hairs, and the blemishes that had developed on his pale forehead dur-ing the weeks spent sweating and sun-deprived in the hot, concrete cuboid where he worked.

Lewis put the jeans in the laundry basket, and con-sidered briefly raising the subject with his father, since there was the slim possibility that Alasdair's cleaner, who came to do the laundry twice weekly, had managed to shrink them. But he thought better of it, not least because he suspected that Alasdair – who spent most of his time nowadays staying at his girlfriend's flat in Notting Hill – had forgotten how frequently the cleaner came, and might use the opportunity to cut her hours. It wasn't jeans weather anyway, so Lewis put on a pair of elasticated rugby shorts and a polo neck whose thick cotton went some way to disguising the rippling movement of his flesh beneath it. From some angles one might even be fooled into thinking that the swelling of his chest was actually muscular.

The festival was in Finsbury Park. Lewis had never had reason to travel this far north before, so he had taken a taxi, which cut to the front of the ant-crawl of twenty-somethings spilling out of the Underground and towards the park's iron gates. A lot of the men were wearing backwards caps, patterned shirts, pastel-coloured shorts, and the girls were in festival uniform: shorts that hugged tight to their hips and cut high across their thighs, tops with mesh inserts, hoop earrings and faces decorated with glitter like warpaint. At the gates Lewis had spread his arms wide and looked down at the female security guard as she leaned over to frisk him before strolling up the path, following the sound of the speakers.

The afternoon was turning out to be less fun than he had hoped. He was sprawled on the grass next to Nicole and her friends, each of whom was a permutation of the generically attractive and thin twenty-something, skin exposed to a more or less degree, hair more or less glossy, all pleasingly emaciated. He was usually quiet in groups, and he had been led to believe that women understood his silence to signify strength as opposed to stupidity or shyness, and he sipped thoughtfully from his tinny while zeroing in on the girl – who was looking down at her drink, and who had shorter, thicker legs than the rest – sitting to Nicole's left. He caught the girl's eye; there was time yet to brighten this dull afternoon, and after twenty minutes or so of waiting for his cousin to move so he would have an in, Lewis took matters into his own hands and got up.

'Drink?' he said, looking around the group, but pausing pointedly as he looked at the girl, tipping his hand to his mouth.

'Yes!' Nicole said, grabbing his leg to steady herself. 'Four, no, five gin and tonics. I'll come with you.'

On the way to the bar, he asked Nicole the name of the girl who had been sitting next to her.

'You mean Ellie?'

'I don't know, that's why I'm asking,' Lewis said. Nicole could be fairly idiotic, for a lawyer. Oblivious to his condescension, she began ducking through the crowd to the front of the bar.

It was then, as Nicole disappeared, that Lewis saw Kate. It was the first time he had seen her since they had slept together. She was over the other side of the bar, and she hadn't seen him, but he noticed straight away that she was thinner, and it suited her. She looked good. The top she was wearing showed her shoulders, clinging to her small tits, and her hair was tied back from her face to show the freckles that ran from the tops of her cheekbones to the bridge of her nose. She was looking down so he couldn't properly make out her face, but even seeing her silhouetted from the side like that stirred something in him; he remembered her pale blue eyes looking up at him, wide with awe, as he had fucked her, and he had known then that she'd never been done like that before.

The crowd shifted around her, and Max came into view, and another man Lewis recognised as a friend of Nicole's. Lewis hesitated. He didn't know whether Kate had told Max anything about them, whether it was a good idea to approach her with him there. He saw too that Kate was laughing, hanging off Max's arm, glowing. That was not how he remembered her; he couldn't remember what she looked like when she laughed, or what her laugh sounded like. Not for the first time, he wondered whether Kate and Max had slept together.

It was then that Kate turned, and looked directly at him. She froze. Instinctively, Lewis made to move towards her, but before he could, his path was disrupted by a flailing limb and a cry of rage from Nicole as she was jettisoned from the crowd by a pair of angry women.

'I've been waiting for nearly half an hour,' Nicole lied, pushing Lewis in front of her. 'Bitches,' she hissed at the women, before looking up at Lewis, expectantly. Lewis shrugged. Obviously, he was not going to hit a girl.

'Whatever, we'll have to go to the other bar,' Nicole said. She led him away from the crowd, and when he looked back, he couldn't see Kate.

'I think I saw Max,' said Lewis.

'Oh yeah, he's here somewhere. With Elias.'

'He is. I saw him. Why don't you call him?'

'I can't be bothered.' Nicole sounded a little sulky.

'Why not?'

She shook her head. 'He's with Elias,' she said again. 'They'll both be fucked. I can't deal with either of them right now.'

Lewis let it slide after that. By the time they'd got their drinks and gone back to the group, the women had been surrounded by male friends of Nicole's. Even Ellie, the runt of the litter, had some stringy guy lying on the grass next to her. Lewis wasn't in the mood to compete, and he was preoccupied with thoughts about Kate.

He got up, without saying goodbye to Nicole and her friends, and tried calling Max. The line went dead as soon as it started ringing. Either Max's phone was out of battery, or there were too many people here, disrupting the signal. Lewis circled the park a couple of times, looking for them. When, after half an hour, he still hadn't found them, he went to the park's perimeter and called a taxi.

In the taxi he was still thinking of Kate. There was weakness in her which he'd seen in other women before her: the way she'd clung to Max's arm, pulling her body close to his, the way she animated herself when he turned to talk to her. She craved approval, and that was what had led him to her that night last summer – her need to be validated. He'd seen today that very little had changed: she had been clinging to Max in just the same way, was probably letting him fuck her for the same reason, using him, letting him worship her, all the while feeding off his attention.

When he got back to the flat, he resolved that he would have to better himself. He stripped his father's cupboards and the fridge of the family-sized bars of chocolate and overpriced ready-meals and booked a grocery shop to arrive at the flat the next morning: chia seeds, quinoa, bananas, eggs, avocados, chicken breasts and minced turkey, protein shakes and energy powders, some fillet steaks to treat himself at the weekends. Lewis got into bed bloated, filled with beer and a sense of failure, but satisfied with the knowledge that tomorrow would be a new beginning, a fresh start.

He was woken on Sunday morning by the sound of Alasdair banging on his bedroom door.

'What the fuck is this chicken feed you've bought on my credit card?'

'It's our weekly shop,' Lewis said, once he had made it through the shower and into the kitchen.

'You buy this shit every week?' Alasdair picked up a half-kilo packet of linseeds and peered at the label.

'Not every week, we were running low,' Lewis said.

'Christ, don't they pay you anything at the hospital? I thought you were supposed to be saving people's lives. Fucking NHS.'

'I usually use my own card, yours must have been saved on the system,' Lewis said sulkily; somehow he always seemed to revert to his child's self with his father. 'I'll make us both breakfast,' he said, determined to be the bigger man – metaphorically, at least: it would do Alasdair no harm to go back on the diet.

'No, no,' Alasdair said, dropping the linseed back into one of the overflowing shopping bags at his feet. He hadn't taken off his coat. 'I only came back here to get some papers. House stuff.'

'What's going on?'

'Nothing, that's the problem,' said Alasdair. He made his way to the fridge, opened it to look inside, and then closed it again. 'Willie doesn't want to sell. Absolutely no business mind. All sentimentality. Won't get it into his woollen head that some of us could really do with the cash.'

'I didn't realise you wanted to sell it,' Lewis said tentatively.

'I don't see a sane alternative. We'll get a massive payout if we sell it straight to developers. Willie wants to turn it into a guinea-pig sanctuary or a fucking toenail recycling centre.'

'Really?'

Lamenting not for the first time that Lewis hadn't inherited his own excellent sense of humour, Alasdair left his son in the kitchen to make his gruel. In the study was Alasdair's private stash of Fruit & Nut, which he tore into as he began rifling through his drawers. Alasdair had in fact had Bisley House surveyed some years earlier, just after his father's sudden death. At the time he had assumed that Bernadette wouldn't last much longer without Gregor, and he had very charitably invited her to London while, with the help of Lady Caroline, who had kindly offered to keep a set of keys while Bernadette was away, he had arranged for an architect, a chartered surveyor and two rival estate agents to have a free rein on the place over the course of two afternoons.

He had of course been grieving, his ability to make

good judgements impaired by his father's sudden passing, and when, six months later, Bernadette had developed a new appetite for life inspired by a romantic obsession with her physician, fucking NHS, Alasdair had reluctantly called off the second valuation and had filed the documents somewhere safe and, most importantly, secret. It was only now that he really felt he had the strength to look at them again, after everything he had been through.

Absently, Alasdair picked an almond skin from between his molars with his tongue and flicked through the paperwork buried in his desk. He had always failed to understand why they couldn't skin the fuckers before putting them in their products: he ought to write to their investors; perhaps he should just buy the company. Marriage certificate, birth certificate, divorce paperwork, more divorce paperwork. There wasn't one piece of paper in this drawer that hadn't cost him in the thousands, and what did he have to show for it? A son with no sense of irony and a worryingly effeminate fixation on nutrition, an absconded spouse and a set of dead parents whose most valuable assets were being monopolised by his younger brother's prolonged and very expensive grieving process. Only the company had brought him any lasting pleasure, and it was the company that was in desperate need of a large cash injection. Alasdair finished his Fruit & Nut and threw the empty packet in the wastepaper bin. He stuffed the valuation, which he had found at the bottom of the second drawer of his desk, into his briefcase and left, shouting goodbye to Lewis as he slammed the front door.

27

Kate had fled, after she saw Lewis that day. This was the first time she had seen him since the rape, and she had been waiting for this moment for nearly a year now. During this time she had begun to hope, even to fantasise, that if only for this first time, she would be able to see him without him seeing her. She supposed that if she was always waiting for him, then at least he wouldn't be able to surprise her, and so the inevitable violence of her reaction would perhaps be tempered.

When at last she saw him, though, or rather when at last they saw each other, what overwhelmed her was not fear, but simple astonishment at the fact of his presence: the fact that he existed outside the realm of her imagination. What shocked her was how real he was, now that he was no longer just a memory. And if he was real, then the rape was real. When she'd seen him, she'd had no choice but to allow her instincts to take over. As the crowd closed back around him, she put her hand to the ice in her chest, feigning sickness for Max. She told him she was going back to the flat, that he didn't need to come with her, and she ran: getting to the edge of the park as quickly as she could, running out the panic that was rising with her, dulling her senses. Max did not follow her.

Her heart was still pounding when she got to the Tube. She imagined Frieda's voice telling her to breathe, to fill her lungs, and her heart began to slow. She was still foggy, but thoughts, distant and blurred, began to form. Since the rape, and until this point, she had come to believe that there were two distinct world views available to her: either the world was at fault for what she had suffered, or she herself was to blame. If, as she often suspected, the latter was true – for whatever reason, genetic fault, inherent weakness, or the disease or defect Lewis had left in her – then she was deficient.

This image of herself she had thought she could just about accept, if it meant that the world was a place of safety. If she could just face up to her own flaws, weaknesses, then at least this meant she had some measure of control because only she was culpable. But seeing Lewis in the flesh collapsed not only all the time that had passed and the progression she had made between the rape and now, but also this carefully drawn distinction. The look on his face, which to her was something akin to anger, told Kate that she was not safe.

When she got back to the flat, still she did not feel secure. It was possible that he would arrive here, perhaps having followed her, perhaps with his cousins, opening for him the doors she had locked. She needed to call somebody, but she didn't know who. She couldn't call Max, and she didn't want to call Claire: she still hadn't told her what had happened to her, and she couldn't do it right now. Instead she called Andrew; he didn't pick up. Probably it was a good thing: it would be too much for him, too. She'd been guarded, the few times they'd met up, and at this moment she was sure she had the capacity to make the kind of drunken phone call that would end a relationship before it had even begun.

Water. Water would help her pounding head. She took the glass from her bedside table and washed it out, refilled it. The outside of the glass was wet, her hands shaking, and as she turned from the sink it slipped from her grasp and shattered on the floor. Numbly, she looked down at the mess she had created, just as she had on Christmas Day. She stood there for a while, eyes unfocused, balance unsteady, before getting down on her hands and knees. Carefully, she started to sift through the pieces of glass with her bare hands, until she closed her palm around a large piece with a long, sharp edge.

Kate sat back against the cabinet, and ran the piece of glass along her thigh, increasing the pressure and then releasing it again, tracing it below the hem of her shorts, lifting it and then following the groove of her hip bone above. Calmer, she was breathing again. She could have cut her body from cunt to throat, to try to reach the tightening wire that connected the two, embedded in the trunk of her flesh. But even then she could not have extracted it, because to do so would be to extract a terrible, essential part of herself.

She didn't stop as she had when she'd smashed the platter

at her mother's house. Then, she had fled the temptation. But now there was nothing to prevent her, and she pressed down on the glass, pushing it through the soft skin of her thigh, dragging it in a swift line, maintaining the pressure of her hand as best she could as the searing pain shot through her thigh and up her spine. Only when blood began to bead on the glass's sharp edge did she exhale.

By the time it was dark, and Kate had cleared up the kitchen and the cut on her upper thigh, Max and Nicole still had not returned, and nor had Max texted to see if she was all right. This didn't bother her too much; he'd been wasted, and mostly she just felt relieved he had bought her excuse. She filled the bath, feeling calmer still, able to reflect on what she had done that afternoon. She ran her finger along the open wound. It was true that she'd been tempted before now, but this was the first time she had followed through. She supposed the impulse had something to do with expression, like her mother's horrifying plaster-cast faces, but it was more private than that: it was expression that did not travel, expression without communication. What use were words, the image of wire, even slices in flesh, if the receiver did not know and feel intimately the network of raw nerves, the tenderness of the flesh around which those wires were entwined? Without that carnal knowledge, they might as well just be strands of loose thread.

It was while she was bathing that her phone, left on the side next to the sink, began to vibrate.

'What's up?' said Andrew.

'I was just in the bath,' Kate said. 'I called you earlier.'

'I was on set,' he said.

'What are you doing now?'

'Nothing. You wanna come over?'

'I don't feel like leaving. Why don't you come here?'

Andrew hadn't been to the flat before, and Kate made a half-hearted attempt to tidy her bedroom before he arrived. She put a plaster over the cut on her leg, hid the tissues she had used to stem the bleeding at the bottom of the bin, and opened the window to let in the fresh air. The times they'd seen each other since the night that Max had got thrown out of the *Gristle* party, they'd kissed again, had stayed out late enough and been loose enough for it to be easily implied that they both wanted something more, but whenever he'd got to the point of suggesting they go back to his, gripping her hips and pulling her towards him, looking down at her and putting on a low, supplicatory voice, she'd told him no and pulled away, frightened of what would happen.

When Kate had first got back from the park, she supposed that part of her had decided that now was the moment to tell Andrew. Then, she had still been in the flush of panic and felt that she was ready, finally, to talk to somebody who wasn't paid to listen to it all. But that impulse had passed, erased by the pain of glass: she didn't need anybody, didn't need to spill over, she could contain herself, by herself.

*

Kate, when Andrew arrived, thought she was putting on a very good impression of sobriety, but he seemed to disagree.

'Have you just been here drinking on your own?'

'No,' said Kate indignantly. 'Actually I was at a festival.'

'I bought us food,' he said, putting a plastic bag on the table. 'Well, I bought food for me. You can have some, if you want.'

They shared noodles at the kitchen table. Kate, who'd hardly eaten all day, was suddenly ravenous, and she ate unselfconsciously, flicking soy sauce down her chin and sucking salty beansprouts from her chopsticks. Andrew tilted his chair back, taking in the room: the wooden worktops, the large dining-room table, the terrace.

'What did you say your rent was?'

Kate wiped the corners of her mouth, took a big sip of water. 'Max owns it,' she said.

'Oh yeah, mates' rates.'

'Do you want something to drink?' She got up, but he caught her hand, pulled her towards him.

'No,' he said.

'Well, I do,' she said, slipping out of his grasp. She made vodka tonics and came back to where he was sitting, holding one in each hand. He looked at the drinks, then looked at her, looked at her waist, her hips. He leaned forward, put his hands around her waist. She couldn't control his hands, couldn't push him off without putting the drinks down, and he took advantage of her momentary motionlessness, slipping her top up over her navel, kissing her there: her stomach was full, tender. She squirmed; he let her top fall back into place.

'What?' he said.

'Nothing,' she said. She took a sip of her drink; gave herself time to consider. She felt sick, but she couldn't keep stalling. She stepped away and walked out of the room, still holding both glasses, looking back so he followed her.

When they were still both dressed, even when he pushed her into the mattress, kissed her hard, she could handle it. She pulled him onto her. He was heavy, heavier than – she stopped herself. This was not the same; this, she wanted. When he took her jeans off, though, unhooked her bra, and she felt summer air coming through the window onto her skin, she knew she was nearing the edge of what she could tolerate, and became still. She was losing him: his eyes unfocused, his hands busy, breath heavy, all dictated by desire. He would stop, if she told him to. But if they stopped now, she might never be able to start again. She kissed him back, harder now, but now he was the one pulling away: for a moment it was as though he had sensed something was wrong, but she realised he was reaching for his wallet, for condoms.

Kate pushed her underwear to her knees, so that she could move her legs apart but only just, and then pulled his hands to her wrists so that they were pinned above her head to the bed by his weight. The more he resisted pressing down on her, trying to shift his weight, the more she pulled back, pulled him onto her, into her. As he gave in, started to fuck her, both her legs hooked around the backs of his thighs, pushing him deeper, until the beginnings of that familiar, stabbing pain came, and her mind began to shut down, and her body woke into that familiar, constricted space. He'd closed his eyes. He was frowning, pressing his lips together, as though remembering something, his face tilted slightly away from hers, and as he released the pressure for a moment on her right arm, she shifted his hand and closed his fingers around her neck, so that his weight was now moved to her windpipe, and as she tried to catch her breath a gurgling sound came from her throat which stopped only when she surrendered her breath. He didn't resist, gripped tighter, even; came inside her.

Afterwards, he traced his finger along the plaster on her leg.

'What did you do?' he said. They were half under the covers: outside the sky was pink, the air cool on their skin. Kate shuffled so that the duvet was covering her legs, she turned to face him.

'Scratched it,' she said unblinkingly, her face close to his.

He kissed her, deeply, held her chin, then slid his hand back around her neck, but gentler now, no weight behind his grip. When he spoke, his words were meant as a kindness, not a threat or even a friend's warning. This Kate knew, but still what he said stirred within her a sense of profound dread, in a place that Andrew did not yet know.

'You should be more careful.'

28

Max knew Kate had somebody there when he got home the next morning because her feet were definitely not that big. They weren't Elias's trainers, either, because he'd just been with Elias. There were, besides, voices coming from Kate's bedroom. He went to her door.

'Kate?' he said.

'What?'

'Do you, um, want a cup of tea?'

There was silence. Kate came to the door, pulling on a jumper, and opened it a crack.

'You've literally never made me tea in your life.'

'That's not true,' said Max, craning his neck to try to see past her. Kate grinned at him, and opened the door a bit further, so he could see the end of her bed. Max saw feet, which went some way to explaining the shoes.

'Hello?' said a voice – male – from within. Kate, giving up her attempts at discretion, opened the door all the way.

'Hi!' Max said. 'I'm Max. I know exactly who you are.'

Without invitation, he came into the room and climbed into the bed on Kate's side. Andrew shuffled up to make room, and didn't seem irritated by the intrusion. From where she sat at the foot of the bed, Kate could smell alcohol oozing from Max's skin. He wriggled around to get comfortable.

'Man, you've got too much energy,' Andrew said.

'And you're making my bed stink,' Kate said, hitting Max on the leg. He ignored her.

'So, what did we all think of the after-party?'

'I left, Max. Remember?'

'OK, well, it was great, you should have stayed. They had these massive speakers and neon paint all over the walls. Wait, you were sick, weren't you?' Max looked at Kate, and then at Andrew. 'Oh, I get it. Lovesick.'

Andrew looked at Kate. 'Did you bail to come and see me?' he said, half laughing.

Kate flushed.

'Well, next time you should come, you're both invited. Except for Kate. She hates parties.'

'It's true,' Kate said gravely.

Max sat up and ruffled Kate's hair. He was pissed, showing off.

'But we love her, so we don't mind.'

Kate batted his hand away.

'Guys, I'd love to join you for brunch,' said Max, 'but I've got to go and see my parents. I just came back to shower.'

'We didn't invite you for brunch,' Kate shouted after him, as he disappeared upstairs, leaving the bedroom door wide open.

*

By the time Max arrived at Latimer Crescent, he was beginning to sober up. The sky was cruelly bright, the sun burning off the last of his alcohol haze. He put on his sunglasses as he walked from the Tube, hoping to soften the headache that was forming at the front of his skull. At the house, he announced himself by banging around the kitchen, slamming drawers and opening cupboards.

'What are you looking for?' said Zara, coming downstairs to find him.

'Medicine.'

'Hangover?'

'No,' Max lied instinctively.

'That's why you've got your sunglasses on inside, is it?'

Max took them off. His eyes were red, and the rims of his nostrils, too. He sniffed.

'Hay fever,' he said.

Zara didn't mind Max partying, and in fact she rather liked it when he turned up at the house needing care and sustenance. It made her feel necessary. She opened the cupboard next to the fridge, and handed her son a packet of painkillers.

'Here you are,' she said. 'I'll make us some coffee.'

They had lunch out in the garden, Zara sitting back and soaking up the sun that came dappled through the leaves of the plum tree, Max with his sunglasses back on, piling his plate high with Parma ham and fresh bread. After the coffee, he'd moved back onto beer, and the bubbles were cold on his tongue.

'It's from the new bakery,' William said, as Max cut

himself another doorstop slice of bread. 'Wonderful little place. They have all these sourdough cultures.'

'Oh yeah,' said Max.

'You know, every baker's hands carry different bacteria, so no two bakers' loaves will ever be the same. The bacteria mixes with the culture when they knead it, and with all the different stages – pre-ferment, ferment, proving, baking – every loaf is days in the making.'

Max chewed on the bread in a show of appreciation. He feared, given the state his insides were in, that digesting this slice was going to take almost as much effort as had apparently gone into creating it.

'I've started my own sourdough, actually,' said William.

'He has to find a way to keep himself busy, now he's an old man,' Zara said.

'I'm afraid your mother has become insufferable,' said William to Max, in a matter-of-fact tone. 'She's working on a new film and she seems to be under the illusion that she's gained another twenty years of life as a result.'

Max laughed. It was a sign that they were both fairly content, when his mother and father were comfortable enough to publicly insult one another. 'What's the film?'

'It's a gem, Maxie,' said Zara. 'I've got the script on my laptop, I'll send it to you. Fantastic writer. Very dark, very funny. You'll like it, I think.'

'Are you directing?'

'The original director had to drop out, so they got me on board. All very last minute. We film in the autumn, for release next year.'

'She dropped dead, not out,' said William. 'Aneurysm. It's dog eat dog, Max, the film industry. You ought to tell your friend Kate that.'

Even after nearly five years of what Max was sure he had portrayed as completely platonic friendship, William was still in the habit of putting a euphemistic emphasis on the word 'friend' whenever he was talking about Kate. Max chewed, thoughtfully, wondering whether to call his father out.

'Oh, for God's sake. She's not dead,' Zara said. 'Just hospitalised. Kate will like it too. It will resonate with her, I think.' She raised her eyebrows at Max.

'Oh,' said Max, 'you know, she's doing quite well. I think she might have a boyfriend.'

'How wonderful,' said Zara. Max thought that she might have been more pleased by this, but then, he supposed, it would be odd if she were excited by the news that one of Max's friends was sexually active. For a second, the thought came into his mind that both of his parents were now imagining Kate, with a new yet unseen boyfriend, having disinhibited, non-violent sex. He regretted mentioning it.

'Well,' William said, clapping his hands together, 'how about I show you my pre-ferment?'

Inside, William took from the fridge a jar containing a thick, white substance.

'He's quite a specimen,' William said, putting on his glasses and peering closely. 'Only a couple of days old; another day or so and he'll be ready for the next stage.'

He handed the jar to Max, who looked at it. 'Are you sure it's a he?'

'Don't,' said Zara, following them in from the garden. 'He's already attached enough as it is.'

The phone started ringing; Max and William ignored it. Zara went to answer.

'It's just the prototype,' said William. He took back the jar and turned round to double-check that Zara was gone. 'If it goes well, I might open my own place. When I've retired, obviously.'

'A bakery?' said Max.

'It'd be quite something, wouldn't it?'

'That's a great idea, Dad.' Max was genuinely enthused. 'There are loads of good places you could do it around here. And around where my flat is, actually.'

'Not in London,' William lowered his voice conspiratorially. 'That's why we can't tell your mother just yet. In Bisley.'

'That was Rupert,' Zara said, coming back into the kitchen. 'He's coming over for dinner. Will you stay, Max? You haven't seen him for months.'

'Oh, I said I'd have dinner with Kate. But send him my love.'

'I will.'

Max heard himself ask: 'How is he?'

'He's doing well,' William said. 'Still volunteering, some of it paid.'

'Oh,' Max said. 'That's good.'

Both his parents stood, looking at him, waiting for him to say something else.

'We'll send him your love,' Zara said again, when he didn't.

Before he left, Max went upstairs to his old room. He'd come to collect some cables, so he could get the iMac working again. His room, as always, was far tidier than he'd left it, but this time it was more bare, too. The piles of paper that had been on his desk had been put away into a drawer, the books back onto their shelves. The sheets had been stripped from the bed and the coverless duvet was folded at its foot, with the pillows stacked on top, and the lampshade had been taken from the ceiling light, leaving the bulb bare. The walls might have been repainted, too. For a while, he sat on his bed. They were only small changes, and as such they elicited only a muted response in him: he wondered whether he ought to feel more sad than he did about his near-empty room.

He lay back, closed his eyes. Perhaps he should be feeling guiltier, too, about avoiding Rupert. He wasn't having dinner with Kate: he had no plans later. But he was feeling a little tipsy from the beers, and it was a sunny afternoon. He wanted to keep on drinking, not to have to sober up for dinner so he could sit in the conservatory with his uncle, trying to keep his eyes focused. It was exhausting, seeing Rupert. He couldn't ask what he did all day, because the answer would lead them nowhere Max wanted to go, and now Rupert was sober they couldn't rely on alcohol to bridge any gaps between them. In fact, even before Max had turned eighteen, their adult friendship was formed next to the drinks table at family parties, or during trips to the pub or to expensive restaurants, where Rupert would line up different wines and make Max blind-taste them. Max was a natural, Rupert had told him, chuckling and finishing, one after another, the glasses from which Max had sipped. One on one he could see him. Just not today; he wasn't quite ready. Before he got up, he saw that on the ceiling the glow-in-the-dark stars, which William had stuck there for him when they'd first moved into this house, and which still had their glow the last time he'd slept in this bed, had been left.

29

Zara had always been the first to wake, and she had long ago given up waiting for William to stir before getting out of bed. Once awake, she couldn't bear to lie there: the taste of a night's sleep in her mouth, the feel of cold sweat in her armpits and between her legs; no matter how badly she had slept – and lately she had been sleeping very badly – she rose almost immediately, washed and brushed her teeth, put on loose trousers beneath her cold silk dressing gown and went downstairs.

For the last six months or so, she had been waking just after four. When she was younger, this would usually have meant that she'd been drinking, or was high. In the early years of her relationship with William, when neither of them had been able to sleep for fear of missing even a moment's time spent with the other, they'd frequently stayed awake until sunrise, talking, fucking; but now they were only ever intentionally awake at this hour when one of them had to work.

Since Christmas, Zara had been thinking of that time more often. It had been then, in the Maida Vale flat, that she had first told William what had happened to her during the production of the first film she had worked on, when she was still a student in Paris. He was the only person other than Zara, and the rapist of course, who knew the exact details of what had happened: the room it had happened in, the precise progression of his hands from her neck to her waist to her breasts and then her hips, the moment at which verbal coercion had turned to physical force, the angle at which he had positioned himself as he pushed himself inside her. William knew too the name of the director and the name of every award he had won and the films for which they had been awarded.

But they didn't talk about it any more: William understood the past to be just that, and though he had never once been unsympathetic to her, from the start he thought of the trauma as existing in some other life, since Zara had already lived with it for almost a decade when they met, and he saw her as a stronger and a better woman for having resolved herself to it. Zara had come to find it easier to mould herself to his view of her than to confront him with the reality, which was that those memories had never found a quiet place in her consciousness, and that far from being resolved, they were at once their own organism and unwelcome filter through which she experienced the world.

There had been a time when it had looked as though sex, or the lack of it, might threaten their marriage, when, a few years before Nicole was born, Zara found in William's office the rented pornos he'd been watching the evenings she was working. It destroyed Zara to think of him as a voyeuristic male who saw women only as objects of pleasure, and after that she did not want to sleep in the same bed as him. Briefly, she moved out, and Bernadette, who of course knew nothing of what had happened to Zara, divulged, presumably as an attempt to reassure her, that Gregor had had many affairs during their decades-long marriage, and that Bernadette hadn't once tried to leave him. Zara went back to William, and they found their way back to one another's bodies, though it was never quite the same.

It had come at a cost, to live like this. Zara had been drunk when she had conceived Max, and Nicole, well, she couldn't be sure, but in the year before her daughter was born Zara had found she was only able to feel excited by the act of sex if she had William's hands on her neck and bruises on her body. For a while William had accepted this phase as experimental, and it had excited them both to know that although they had been together for years now, they were still impatient to discover the limitations and weaknesses of one another's bodies. But after a while it was all she wanted, and if she was sober she couldn't bear to have him touch her in anything other than a fraternal embrace. In time they came to the unspoken realisation that what she really wanted was for him to rape her, but because it was surely impossible to want to be raped, they both began to suspect that if her fantasy of directing her own violation was an impossible one, then it followed that physicality between them was an impossibility too.

When Nicole was born, it saddened William too much to know that his daughter's mother could only desire him as her aggressor, and he was torn apart with guilt for having made Zara see him that way in the first place. After *L'Accusé* won the Palme d'Or, Zara, who had been retraumatised by a bloody and difficult birth, began to travel more for work. William meanwhile dedicated himself to nurturing the innocence of his only child, cushioning her in the love he felt that Zara had withdrawn from them both, and in so doing, he hoped, sparing her from ever experiencing the fate that had befallen his wife.

He thought himself to be doing Zara a kindness, protecting her from the destructive power of sex, but the unintended consequence was that she felt almost as undesirable, as flawed, as she had in the early weeks that had followed the rape. She withdrew further, through alcohol, through her work, requiring him to be a friend over a lover, more brother than husband, until, when Nicole and Max at last moved out, it became clear to them both that they lived their lives just as they slept and woke, in disjointed parallels, and that they were almost entirely independent from one another.

The appearance of Kate in Zara's life had begun to change things, and now there was the film. When the script had come from her agent at the beginning of the summer, Zara had read the email that introduced it and then the entire script, sitting without moving in the exact spot she'd opened them, at her desk one Tuesday morning. She'd phoned the producer as soon as she'd finished, told him that she was transfixed. She'd been so giddy that her agent had called her and asked her to rein it in just a little: Zara's eagerness was making it impossible for her to negotiate. Later that week, when they'd got the green light, Zara had gone through the script again: more slowly, this time, with a pen and notepad, and the story had moved her no less.

Strangely, it was not the rape, but the sex, which came in the latter half of the film, that Zara was most drawn to. Zara had known before this that there was still a part of her, so long suppressed, that desired to be desired. She knew that she had become more beautiful as she'd aged, but for years had felt that she must remain untouchable. She found it hard to touch herself even, for fear of defiling her body: the thin, moisturised legs, the nude polished nails, the naturally neat triangle of pubic hair and stomach that was slim enough so as not to reveal where her skin was beginning to sag, the long neck over which her dyed hair fell loose in the mornings. It was now so long since she had been able to bear the smell of desire, even on her own hands, perhaps particularly on her own hands, that if ever she masturbated, which she did very rarely, she was troubled for days afterwards.

Lately, though, since she'd received the script, since she'd met Kate, she had begun to question whether this act of self-denial was less wilful than forced. Everything Kate had said to her about her own trauma had stayed with her, and was leading her to a conclusion that was painfully at odds with the rules by which she had lived since the rape. How much she had lost; how much she had sacrificed;

how profoundly she had betrayed herself. Daily she had been robbed since she was attacked: of her autonomy, of her desires, of her desirability, of the pleasure of intimacy with her own body and the body of the man she had once loved, perhaps loved still.

Of course, she'd told none of this to Kate. It was not fair that she should have to bear the burden of Zara's unhappiness as well as her own, and nor did she want Kate to think of her as being so profoundly unhealed. But, in the months that they were close, as she watched Kate work through her trauma, Zara was making discoveries of her own. When she touched herself for the first time since Kate had confided in her, she was alone in her bathtub, and as she lay there trying to coax her body into a state of relaxation, the water grew lukewarm, and when at last she came it hurt her to experience it: still her body associated the sensation of pleasure with intense pain. But she was triumphant nonetheless, and for the rest of the day she glowed with the secret knowledge of her success. And, after that first time, it became easier to re-experience physical pleasure and very gradually she began to hope that she might be able to overwrite years of deprivation and of abstinence with something new.

The day after they'd had Max over for lunch, after she'd told him about her new script and he, in turn, had told her that Kate was seeing somebody, Zara allowed herself a lie-in. Then, when she slipped out of bed, instead of going from the bathroom down to the empty, sunlit rooms of the ground floor of the house, she brushed her teeth and washed her face and, loosening her gown from her waist, got back into bed with her husband. William smelt sweetly of sleep. In bed he wore a white T-shirt and checkered pyjama trousers which she had always thought endearing, and as he turned in his sleep towards her, putting his arm around her, she moved her face closer to his so that she too might inhabit the glow of his skin in the warm morning light. It had once irritated her, the way he never quite fully closed the curtains, but at this moment she was grateful for the gap that illuminated him.

Zara moved closer still, began to slip her cold hands under the soft cotton of his shirt where his torso radiated the warmth of a night's deep sleep, and lifted her head so that she could bury her face in the groove above his collarbone. His neck smelt of laundry detergent, of soap, faintly of cologne. When he opened his eyes, he was smiling, and he held her face sleepily in both hands.

'I missed you,' he said, looking at her as if to make sure that she was really there, and closing his eyes again. She had always thought it sentimental, when he said this to her on waking, as if he had spent his night's sleep searching for her, but it had always filled her with blissful reassurance too, and now she kissed him with intensity that had for so long been alien to them both. William kissed her back, but she could feel as he did so that his hand was on her shoulder, that even as he pulled her to him with his kiss and his words, he was gently pushing her away.

In that moment Zara was struck by the fact of his absence; by the certainty that the man who was kissing her was not really there, and she pulled back. Almost immediately, William rolled over and reached for his phone, which he kept on the bedside table, and Zara knew then that he was not able to meet her in her desire. In stark possession of this knowledge, she could not bear to lie there beside him and she got out of bed, and went downstairs to where the light was not filtered through half-closed curtains but fell coldly and without interruption on high white walls.

30

After Kate first slept with Andrew, she had phoned Claire. This was a tradition of theirs from school, which Kate had kept through university, but had of course dropped after what had happened with Lewis. Now, she was longing to relive that old giddiness. She spared Claire the details she needn't know: the closed windpipe, the pain. But she would at least give herself the pleasure of recounting in detail the build-up, the intimacy, the brief moments of embarrassment she had done her best to hide from Andrew but could now reveal.

'So are you, like, seeing each other?' Claire said.

'I don't know. Maybe?'

'Well, at least one of us is having sex.'

'Oh,' said Kate. Clearly, things had not been going well between Claire and her boyfriend, since they'd moved in together. Claire didn't volunteer any more information, and Kate did not ask. She had been doing such a poor job of keeping in touch and she didn't feel she had the right to demand any details Claire did not want to give. But she promised to call again soon, and told Claire – and meant it – that she should come and visit if she needed to get away.

She realised now that she needed to tell Claire what had happened to her, and she didn't know when she would next see her face-to-face. After that phone-call, though, Kate resolved to speak to Andrew. The morning after they first slept together, she hadn't wanted to be touched, because the daylight was too bright and her body was too heavy. But the next time she saw him, she went to his flat instead, and when he started to pull her towards the bed she told him to stop, sat down beside him, and told him what had been done to her.

'Shit,' he said. 'When?'

'Last summer. August.'

'Shit. So when we . . .'

'Yeah.'

'You'd . . .'

'Yeah.'

'Man.'

That was enough, for now. They were only just getting to know each other, and neither of them knew the limits of the other. That evening, instead of fucking, they made lasagne. Kate was charged with making the béchamel sauce, Andrew the bolognese. He put on a playlist so they didn't need to talk, and when the sauces were ready they layered them with pasta. While the lasagne was in the oven, Kate heard the front door open.

'Shona,' Andrew said to Kate, before shouting: 'Shona!'

Shona, when she came into the kitchen, refused Andrew's offer of dinner.

'You're making her eat lasagne? It's too hot for lasagne.

I can't believe you have the oven on. You need to widen your repertoire, we're going on a cookery course or something.' She looked at Kate and smiled. 'Hi. I live here.'

'I'm Kate.'

'I know,' Shona said, winking. Kate couldn't remember the last time she had seen somebody wink and actually look good while doing it. 'It smells quite good. But I don't eat Italian food.'

'That's why we're having lasagne,' Andrew said quietly, as Shona went to her room. 'So she won't have any.'

Shona came back in briefly, wearing a white dressing gown and complaining that her bedroom smelt of garlic. Before she disappeared into the bathroom she flashed a bright white smile at Kate, behind Andrew's back.

'Is she cross with you?' Kate said.

'Nah,' he said confidently. 'It's her way of showing affection.'

They did not speak as they ate, Kate trying to decide whether she should pick up the conversation she had started earlier, and Andrew focusing on his food, sometimes pausing to inspect the mouthful he had impaled on his fork. When he was finished, he pushed his plate away from him and folded his arms, watching her work her way through her portion.

'What does it do?' he said.

'What do you mean?'

'What happened to you. What does it do to you? Now, I mean.'

Kate shrugged. 'I get low. I get anxious. Panicky, really. Flashbacks, sometimes.'

Andrew nodded. 'Panic attacks?'

'Sometimes.'

'I feel for you.'

'Thanks.'

'Really. I used to get those, for different reasons. But I feel for you.'

Kate was surprised by this: she hardly knew any men who had had panic attacks, or at least any men who would have admitted to having panic attacks. Stage fright, he told her.

'What, when you were filming?'

'Acting. That was what I wanted to do, for years. Always at school, even went to drama school for a year. But when it got to auditions, stuff that actually mattered, I'd freeze up. Feel like I wasn't in my body. It was humiliating, sweating like that over a few pieces of paper. I know it's different, but . . .'

'But you don't get them any more?'

'No.'

'What's your secret?'

'No secret. It passed.'

'You stopped acting.'

'I found something I was better at. I'm too fat to be an actor, anyway.'

'Not true.'

'Nah, I like food too much for that shit.'

Andrew got up now, and brought the rest of the lasagne to the table, dug his fork in.

'So you remove the cause, and that fixes you,' Kate said, 'but what if you can't?'

'Then you learn to live with it.'

After this first conversation, Kate knew she had licence to bring up the topic whenever she wanted. It was not often that she felt the need to talk about it. But the knowledge was there that she didn't have to censor herself, that if she needed to refer to the rape then she could. With Andrew she could use it as a reference point when talking about the chronology of her life: being able to recount something minor and irrelevant that had happened 'before the rape' was significant for her, because it helped her to smooth out that rupture, to incorporate it into the fabric of her existence. Sometimes, she gave him details. She hinted, more than once, that the man who had raped her was somebody she knew. She didn't say who, or how she knew him, but she said enough for Andrew to know that although she was not in immediate danger, neither had the threat completely passed.

He noticed the plasters that sometimes appeared at the tops of her thighs, and the half-healed cuts which, in time, she was willing to bare. Once or twice when he saw a new injury he asked her how she had done it and she told him she'd scratched her leg on some thorns, outside; on a loose piece of metal, at work; it was an accident. The lies were open, empty, intended not to deceive but to tell him they didn't need to go there, and as she told them he ran his fingers along the red-brown lines, tracing the ridge of scabbed skin, before taking his hand away.

The second time they had sex, they were both sober. She'd gone to his flat again, which she was starting to prefer to her own, since there were fewer memories there. Without alcohol to deaden her, it was harder for Kate to slip back into the safety of submission and self-relinquishment: Andrew pulled her on top of him, lay back, and told her to lower herself onto him slowly, her hands on his wrists this time. This way, she found that she could control the rush of pain she had come to associate with sex, and that just as Lewis had broken down the distinction between pain and pleasure, she began slowly to delineate the two.

As they fucked, she used the strength of her thighs to move slowly onto him until she could relax her weight entirely, and when the fear came, the intensity of having him completely inside her, and the flood of icy panic that started at the pit of her stomach and spread upwards to her chest, she leaned forward and made him look at her, his face bathed in deep blue light that came through the curtain in the dark, and he reached out for her, his hands on her hips, her back, pushing his body further into hers but at the same time touching her with both of his hands, silently reminding her that hers was a whole body of skin and flesh and bone, complete, not just the rawness between, and he brought her back to him, moving her on top of him, slowly so as not to bring too sharp an awareness to his presence inside her, then pushing her hips back so that instinctively she resisted him, bringing herself towards him until warmth rushed in and she began to move on him in the same rhythm, faster, more ragged, until she came, the shudder of him in her indistinguishable from her own pleasure.

31

Two weeks after Max had skipped dinner with Rupert at his parents', his uncle wrote to him. His instinctive response, on seeing Rupert's name and email address on the screen of his phone, was dread. But, Max reasoned, it was the middle of the afternoon, not three in the morning. Rupert had been stable for a while now, and email was not his usual mode of emergency communication. Nonetheless his stomach knotted as he waited for the message to load, and when it appeared on his screen he scanned it through once for signs of a pending crisis before slowing down and reading it properly. The message, unremarkable in its contents, was significant only because Rupert had chosen to send it. He wanted to know how Max was, to tell him how sorry he was to have missed him the other day, and to ask him to explain the rationale behind '*this fucking app*'. He signed off: '*Sounds like you're doing splendidly, boy. Do remember me when you've made your first million.*'

Rupert hadn't written to him with such inane chatter for years now. Max saw, when he searched his inbox, that the last email was before his car crash, and for a moment an image came to Max's mind of his uncle hunched over his phone, scrolling through the numbers in his address book. He didn't want to think how many times Rupert might have thought about calling, before calling a helpline instead. He scanned the email once more, trying to read between the lines some deeper significance: reproach, perhaps, for Max's recent distance, or regret, for the role Rupert's own actions had played in pushing Max away. But this was not a reflective message, this was a message about the future: a future in which Rupert appeared to be telling Max he had a stake.

Max didn't reply straight away, but went to charge his phone and to pour himself a drink. This moment felt like something that needed marking, and he needed a little alcohol to numb out the feeling in the back of his mind of having forgotten to do something important. Max's phone vibrated again; it was Elias, this time, texting to say that he was coming over in half an hour and would Max please go and buy some of the branded tonic he liked, from the shop on the corner. Max left his phone charging and took his wallet and keys. As well as tonic, he bought a bottle of gin to replace the one he'd just finished. By the time Elias arrived, Max was more than a little pissed, and he was putting up more resistance than usual to Elias's suggestions. Elias, though, was as stubborn as Max was drunk, and by the time Kate and Nicole had both arrived home from work, they had made little headway on the first point on the agenda Max had optimistically assembled that afternoon.

'I just don't see how you can means-test a dating app,'

Max was saying. Elias, who was sitting next to him at the kitchen table, was leaning over his shoulder and looking at the notes Max had written on the screen of his iPad.

'These people are already very bad-looking,' Elias said. 'They can't be poor as well.'

'They're not bad-looking, they're distinguished.'

Elias zoomed in on the photograph Max had pulled up to show him a grey-haired man's ruddy and multi-jowled face smiling against a grey seaside setting.

'They are bad-looking. He looks like he's been divorced at least three times. And that photograph was probably taken about ten years ago by his ex-wife.'

'Distinguished. And looks like he's rich as well. Guys? Distinguished?'

Max held the screen up towards the sofa, where Nicole and Kate were slumped, watching a documentary about the deep-sea life forms of the Pacific Ocean.

'Loaded,' Nicole confirmed.

'At least get them to submit a health check when they sign up,' said Elias. 'What if they find love one month and then fucking die the next?'

'Elias,' Max said, his voice reproachful.

'Forgive me,' Elias said. 'What if they fucking pass away, I mean. And you're going to have to be careful about promising lifelong partnership when we decide on the tagline, too. It needs to be clear that "lifelong" is only ever as long as the shortest life. Do you think we can fit that under the logo?'

'That seems unnecessarily pessimistic.'

'Whatever. Stick with "lifelong", if you want. Wait, unless you go back to "Stoke the embers of your dying days"?'

'We decided that was too morbid, didn't we?'

'I thought it captured a potent sense of longing,' said Elias. Inexplicably, he had brought with him an avocado and spinach smoothie, which he sipped now, and which Max waited for him to spit out. To Max's immense surprise, he smacked his lips and sat back in his chair, opening his laptop.

Max took his pen out of his mouth. 'What about,' he said slowly, ' "Embers: Find your fire".' Being creative was exhausting.

'Yes,' Elias said, pointing to Max's screen. 'Make a note of it.'

Max, who did not want to dislodge Elias's impression that he had on his iPad extensive documentation of the development of their business venture, opened a blank document and saved it under the title of 'Thoughts'. 'Embers: Find your fire', he wrote. And then, beneath it, 'Stoke the embers of your dying days'. He hesitated, before typing next to this second quotation '(E.C.)', and then adding, in bold, his own initials after the first tagline. It was important to look like he knew what he was doing: he needed to be sure that he was taken seriously. Surprisingly, he had been doing reasonably well on this front. Elias had helped to bring on board a small handful of investors, and they had a developer working on a prototype.

'Have you seen?' Elias got up and brought Max's tablet over to the sofa. He sat down heavily next to Kate, and showed her the screen, which was freshly cracked. 'I'll show you.'

'Did you drop this again?' said Kate to Max, as Elias started typing Kate's name.

Max waved his hand, dismissively. 'Elias sat on it.'

A photo of Kate taken years ago by Max filled the screen, with a short text-box at its foot and an empty white circle in the top left-hand corner.

'What a honey,' said Kate to the photo.

'This is you,' Elias said, 'if you ever get old enough to sign up. So if you get rated by the other person, and you rate them too, then that's a match, and you start glowing.' Elias pressed the screen and the white circle on the screen began to glow red. 'The more embers you have, the more matches. So people know you're in demand, baby.'

'Wait,' said Max, 'let's match her with Andrew. We can see what you'll look like in sweet old age. Do I have any photos?'

'Why would you have photos of him? Let me see.' Kate took the tablet from Elias and began to flick through the boxes displayed to the left of her image. It looked as though Max had uploaded every portrait photograph from his phone onto the app, to make hypothetical profiles. The patination of shattered glass ran from the top left-hand corner across the screen, overlaying both Kate's face and her hypothetical matches. She flicked absently to a photograph of Max's dog.

'Hah. Perhaps I should go on a date with Titus. Do you think Andrew would mind?'

She swiped once more, and a photo of Lewis appeared, face-on, his head tilted slightly backwards as he looked into the lens of the camera. She swiped back to the previous image and put the tablet on the sofa beside her.

The shock of seeing his face forced her to her feet, and instinctively she backed away from the tablet, all the way to the sink. She turned on the tap and put her hands under it; filled a glass, drank it, filled another, felt too sick to drink it. She needed to be outside, desperately needed space. She opened the lid of the kitchen bin, and emptied it of its bag, took it downstairs without saying anything to the others.

The outside bin was always filled by passers-by with miscellaneous waste: tied-up shopping bags, half-eaten fast-food and drinks cartons, empty cigarette packets. There was hardly enough room for her to add the half-empty bag she had brought down, so Kate untied it and began to fill it with some of the bin's contents: the larger plastic bags first, then the polystyrene carton that contained what looked like weeks-old jerk, and the sturdier coffee cups that had not yet disintegrated. But beneath the top layers of fresh rubbish was a mulch of refuse, half decayed and submerged in a thick black liquid from which rose the overpowering stench of shit.

Kate moved the bin, which was heavy with rainwater, saw floating there what looked like the remnants of a barbecue whose coals explained the tarred liquid, more collapsed drinks containers and cans, what she feared might be a used condom, and several of what could have been the bags used to collect dog shit. Something, small and white, just visible on the bloated surface of one of the blue bags, appeared to move. She stepped quickly back and sat on the low wall outside the flat.

More than anything, more than fear, panic or even sadness, she felt weary. She put her heavy head in her hands. She didn't know how long she'd been there when she heard the latch click. She straightened up, quickly, wiped her eyes, felt an arm fall on her shoulder. He smelt of gin, and he held her tightly, with a clinging, drunken strength. He didn't say anything, but pulled her head against his chest, and stayed there, still, watching the street, she rising and falling with his breath.

32

The director who had been originally lined up for *Late Surfacing*, the film Zara had inherited, hadn't begun her pre-production in earnest, and that summer Zara started work on an unmarked script and an empty shot list. On the first day she shut herself in her office on the top floor of Latimer Crescent, read the script again from beginning to end, her pen in her right hand, and found that she was unable to make a single mark. By lunchtime, she'd read it through again, and a hole had opened up in her chest. She thought about phoning her agent, or maybe her producer, but she didn't know how to voice what it was she was feeling: she was not in the habit of asking for help.

As she turned her phone face down on her desk, it started ringing. Zara looked at the screen and saw that it was Kate. She put the phone back down, on a pile of notes, so that the vibrations were softened. She couldn't speak to Kate now. Even the thought of her was a distraction, when she was trying to claim for herself the experiences laid out in the script in front of her. This vibrantly detailed rape, this fiction, lay just beyond her grasp, and she could not counter Kate's claim to it, if she heard her voice. Her phone buzzed with a notification: Kate had left a voicemail, but instead of listening to the message, Zara went downstairs and made a coffee. That afternoon, she stayed with it a little longer, made her first mark on the script: a small question mark in the margin of the fifth page. Still she did not listen to the voicemail, but she kept on working.

Only once she'd finished this third read-through did she listen to Kate's message. She sounded a little nervous, though she was trying to disguise it, asking Zara how she was, explaining that Max had told her about the film and asking whether she needed any help. Zara drafted a text message in which she explained that they would not be at the production stage until the autumn, but that she would let Kate know if anything came up. She reread her message, and saw clearly that it would only invite interest in a few months' time, so instead of sending it she deleted it, and returned to her notes. But now Kate was in her mind, she couldn't stop thinking of her, of the divulgences Kate had made to her, of the vulnerabilities she had exposed both in herself and in Zara. She wrote late into the night, and the next morning she got up and started again before breakfast. That day and the following one she wrote from seven until seven breaking only for coffee, and by the end of the week she'd completed her notes for the first full read-through.

The exertion consumed her. The skin on her hands became dry, and in the mirror her face looked more tired, skin sagging below her eyes and at the corners of her mouth. Because she didn't want to make her usual fortnightly visit to the hairdresser, silvery roots began to appear at her scalp, and she sent William to the chemist to buy some dye. He helped her shampoo the dye into her hair as she knelt on the floor in the bathroom, he lathering it as she held on to the sides of the bath with both hands, her dressing gown loose around her elbows. When she dried her hair it had a synthetic shine to it.

Kate did not follow up on her message, and the more time that passed, the less able Zara felt to respond. Unless it was Max or Nicole calling, or her agent, she would let her phone go to answerphone. One Sunday, though, Rupert rang three times in a row, and on the third time Zara picked up, preparing – just as she had when she used to call Kate – to modulate according to the level of distress she could hear in the voice on the other end of the line.

'She lives,' Rupert said.

'I'm working,' Zara said, taken aback by the levity of Rupert's tone.

'So I hear,' Rupert said. 'William tells me you've shut yourself in the attic.'

'When did he say that?' Zara said. It surprised her to hear that her schedule had been the topic for family discussion.

'I saw him last week for supper, and I realised it's been such a long time, so I thought I'd call.'

'And I'm so glad you did, darling.'

'I don't want to intrude, but I thought, if you wanted company –'

'Oh, that's so kind of you, Rupert, and you wouldn't be intruding. But I'm fine, really. It's just the schedule, keeping me chained to the desk like this. It's nothing sinister. You know, I do my best work under pressure.'

'I'm sure,' Rupert said. 'Well. Call any time.'

Zara knew she would not call, and neither did she tell William that his brother had phoned. How things had changed since Rupert wouldn't even pick up the phone, let alone go out for a dinner: she had been too taken aback by the call to ask him how he was feeling, though from his voice she could tell that he was better than he had been in a while. When William got home that evening she came downstairs to make a sandwich and to speak to him briefly about his day before going back to her office, and it was the same the following day: she wrote, she worked, quietly she read, and gave nothing of herself away, while William waited patiently to receive whatever it was she would be willing to give him, when the time came.

One Thursday in September, while William was at the hospital, the doorbell rang. Zara had been stuck on a scene all week that she couldn't block. Every shot list she compiled had gone in the bin, and her office was filled with scrunched-up paper and angry biro scribbles. She'd been on the sofa since lunch, and unwilling to get up to find the remote, was watching a documentary about the indomitable rise of flat-pack furniture. At the sound of the door, she shifted herself and shuffled downstairs. It was too late for the postman, and only when she knew that her silhouette had appeared on the other side of the glass and it was too late to turn back did she consider that it might be Kate, whose call she had ignored, who she had invited into her life before hiding herself away; Kate, who was the same as Zara, and who Zara did not want to face.

But when she opened the door, it was not Kate but her nephew who stood there, backpack slung over one shoulder, listening to his music. He pulled out an earphone as she opened the door.

'Lewis,' Zara said. 'William isn't here.'

'That's OK,' Lewis said. 'I didn't call ahead, but, I was passing through . . .'

Zara allowed a moment to pass, in case Lewis managed to take the hint and excuse himself, but he did not, so she stepped to one side to welcome him into her home.

Lewis sat at the kitchen table, as he had always done as a child, little legs swinging off the side of the chair while Zara made him hot milk with honey and cinnamon, except that his two big feet were planted firmly on the tiled floor, across which Titus skidded to greet him, and Zara was heating coffee on the stove instead of milk, standing with her back to him. He looked like he'd put on weight.

'I can't think of you as Dr Rippon, I'm afraid,' Zara said. 'Just makes me think of William. Not to mention how terrifying it is to imagine some poor patient putting their life in your hands. If ever I fall sick, promise me you won't come near me.'

'They wouldn't let me anyway, conflict of interest.'

Zara thought that he was being unusually friendly, as she sat with him at the table. But then, she had begun her voluntary self-banishment nearly six weeks ago now, so perhaps even a conversation with her monosyllabic nephew was enough to stimulate a bounteous sense of warm fellow feeling.

'I'm sure you're very good,' she said to Lewis, patting the back of his hand. She'd forgotten how much fun he was to patronise. 'Is it near here, your current hospital?'

Lewis nodded, moving his hand away from her. 'St Mary's. Paddington.'

'Oh, yes, yes, William trained at St Mary's. And I had Nicole there. She was delivered by a doctor called Moses, can you believe it? The Red Sea indeed.'

'Right,' said Lewis, who was not comfortable with such imagery. They talked a little longer about nothing in particular. Zara sensed that there was something he wanted to say to her, but instead of pushing him she waited for him to meet her with it. 'No, yeah, there was something I wanted to mention to you, actually, now that I'm here.'

'Oh yes?' Zara said.

'It's a bit sensitive,' said Lewis.

'I'm listening.'

'It's about the house,' Lewis said. 'The house in Bisley. I want to ask you about it. I don't know if you know but my dad wants to sell.'

Zara raised an eyebrow. 'Oh, yes?' she said again.

'I think it's a mistake. I've tried to tell him, but he thinks I don't know anything about property or money or business.'

'And you want me to talk to him?' said Zara.

Lewis shrugged. 'If you want,' he said.

'I don't know what to tell you, Lewis. There isn't quite as much in the pot as you might think, and that house is a mess. It's a money pit, rotten roof, crumbling walls. It's between your father and William, and I wouldn't be surprised if they have to sell.' In Lewis's face now Zara saw the sullen boy he had once been: sensitive, easily wounded, burdened by the expectations of a father who had always asked too much but had given too little. She softened. 'As it happens, William doesn't want it going on the market either. Something sentimental, which I'm afraid I can't quite understand. Perhaps I'm too used to being a nomad,' she said.

'It just stands for so much,' Lewis said, 'it's been in the family for nearly a century. I think it's ridiculous that he wants to sell. And, you know, it meant such a lot to Bernadette.'

Zara flashed him a glance. It was possible that Lewis didn't know what his grandmother had done to her will before she died. Either way, it was clear he thought that he could manipulate her by invoking Bernadette's memory.

'Sentimentality won't get you very far, I'm afraid, if the house really is the state they say it's in,' she said. 'I will talk to William, but I won't promise anything; in fact I happen to agree with your father. But I'll talk to him.'

Lewis was relieved, nonetheless, by this half promise. 'Appreciate that,' he said. He stayed a little longer out of courtesy, and Zara asked him again about the hospital. Lewis told her about the deadweight medical students, about the stress of being expected to keep track of an entire ward at once, and about the thrill he'd had, the first time he'd been in the operating theatre. He didn't ask her whether she was working, and she didn't volunteer anything about the film. When Lewis finished his coffee he stood up and she walked him to the hallway. At the front door, he glanced up the staircase, like he was checking to see if anybody else was there.

'They've all gone,' Zara said, 'fled the nest. Just me here now. And Titus, keeping guard.'

Titus growled from the other end of the hallway. Lewis looked back down at his aunt.

'I should come by again,' he said. He was half turned away from her, his hand pressed against the door, 'I'm working shifts at the moment, so I don't always have much on in the day.'

Zara reached past him, and twisted the latch. 'It's a devil, this door,' she said. 'Always sticks.' She put her hands on his shoulders, now, and kissed him on both cheeks. 'You must come again,' she said, and opened the door.

After he left, Zara went back up to the living room and switched off the television, then went upstairs to her office, where she swept her discarded notes into the bin and opened the attic window above her desk. She turned her notes to the scene she'd been stuck on, and began to write.

33

When Kate had phoned Zara, she had been on her way to meet Andrew after work. She'd found a regular job on a panel show, which paid the bills but provided little creative stimulation. The work was repetitive: lifting, arranging, tidying, buying coffee for the crew. Occasionally she was tasked with more unusual, last-minute jobs: once driving a van to New Covent Garden Market to collect three fake palm trees and a pineapple plant, and another time negotiating an insurance quote on a hired tortoise. What she liked more than any of this was the building work. She liked to be left alone with the satisfaction of measuring and fitting panels, smoothing joins, the smell of sanded wood and varnish: all of this while knowing that a few days later she would be taking a hammer to whatever it was she had created.

'I like this,' Kate's new set manager had said, before she left that day. He was notoriously cantankerous, and she'd been staying out of his way; this was the first time he'd said more than two words to her. Now, though, he ran his hands over the top of the cabinet she'd been sanding. 'You don't ask too many questions, do you? You just get the fuck on with it. We need to work together more.'

Kate had hidden her smile, and shrugged, which she felt was in keeping with her assigned identity as a diligent but quiet worker. She'd left Zara her message, only faltering slightly, just before she got on the Tube, hanging up as she descended the stairs to the ticket hall.

She met Andrew in the foyer of Covent Garden Odeon, where he was already queueing for popcorn: he hated being late. They were here to see a film Andrew had worked on last year, and Kate was excited. But, as the adverts began, she made the mistake of leaning over and whispering in his ear that she would be disappointed if he didn't get a screen credit. He glanced at her, shook his head, and reached into his backpack and took out a scrap of paper and pen.

'Questions afterwards,' he said sternly, smoothing out the paper and passing it to her, then turning back to the screen. As soon as it became clear that he wasn't joking, Kate made sure she paid careful attention to the film, particularly the scenes she knew he'd been involved in, in case he asked her about any of it.

'Is there going to be a test, as well?' she said, as they left the cinema.

'No,' said Andrew. But she could tell that he was thinking about it. She liked the fact that he cared so much; it made him vulnerable, because it meant that he had things to fear, things to lose. This was a person she could trust, and she wanted to earn his trust in return, to give him the best of herself.

*

In late September, Max insisted on cooking dinner for Kate, and when they'd finished their meal, he told her that he was planning on moving back to Latimer Crescent.

'Obviously you can stay if you like,' he said. 'I'm sure Nicole won't mind. But she'll definitely understand if you want to leave, too. Definitely.'

His reasoning, he told her, was mostly financial. He was taking his business seriously, and he had to free up money to put behind it.

'Mum's going to be away filming for the next few months, so somebody needs to look after Titus. And, well, if I want to make a go of it – the business – I've got to make some sacrifices, just for a while. I'm throwing money down the drain being here.'

Throughout this conversation, Kate kept glancing to the magnetic strip attached to the wall above the draining board and the new set of Avalon kitchen knives, silver-handled and freshly sharpened. Nicole had bought them recently, announcing that she was going to learn how to cook, before Elias came over and started playing with them, throwing them from a few feet away against the metal strip, to see if he could land them blade-flat. Kate knew that they were sharp because Elias was a bad shot, and one or two of the knives had landed, tip first and handle quivering, in the kitchen's oak floorboards though thrown with only a little force. And she had tested the smallest knife later, pushing her finger against it until it slipped through her skin and a bead of blood appeared on its tip.

'Will you be all right, without me?' Max said. Kate realised he was studying her expression; that she must have appeared vacant.

'I'll be fine, of course I will. I think it's good. I think it's a good idea. Definitely if Titus needs looking after.'

She had intended this last point lightly, but in her ears her voice sounded strained. Max, though, didn't appear to pick up any tension.

'Poor Titus – he needs all the help he can get,' he said, then: 'I'll miss you.'

'You too,' Kate said. 'But you're not going far.' She was placating him, telling him what he wanted to hear, and she did not listen as Max continued speaking – it wouldn't be immediate, he told her, a month or so at least – she paid careful attention to the slow progression of panic throughout her body. He was leaving, she would be left here with Nicole, Nicole and one of her friends; perhaps it would be Lewis who decided to move in, or else it could be another man, another threat to negotiate. She knew that she had to leave as soon as possible.

When Max went to bed, she thought about calling Andrew. She got out her phone, looked for a moment at his name in her contacts. He'd told her she should call, whenever she needed, but she wanted to deal with this on her own. So she locked her phone, and instead walked to the metal strip above the draining board and undid her jeans, slipping them over her hips. She chose her knife and tested it firmly against her finger, and then against the flesh just below her hip, in one of the spaces of white skin that was not already latticed, and she pushed in the tip and drew it quickly across the top of her thigh. In a single straight line the skin went white, a canyon in flesh, before a line of bright red blood rushed to fill the cut she had just created, and as the blood rushed to the surface of her skin she was euphoric, exhaling loudly, triumphant.

The blade was sharper than she had realised, though. A cut like this she would have expected to be stemmed with a single tissue and a carefully applied plaster, but quickly the blood began to gather and to drip into her jeans, and she reached with one hand for the kitchen roll while holding another hand over the gash. The white towel was soon saturated, and then, as the adrenaline ebbed away, came the pain.

After pain, as always, there was again panic: the fear that she had gone too far, that Max would have forgotten something and come back into the kitchen, the fear that the blood would seep uncontrollably from the self-inflicted wound. Usually, this was part of the pleasure; the added adrenaline derived from the power of containment, of concealing something so potentially destructive. She especially liked to cut in places where there was a risk of being discovered; in a quasi-public place, or in a room like this, whose back windows were almost level with the backs of other houses.

Today, though, she had perhaps taken too great a risk: from downstairs came the sound of a key fumbling in the front lock, and of Nicole speaking loudly to somebody on the other end of the phone. Quickly, as the landing lights were switched on, Kate shoved the kitchen towel down the front of her jeans and refastened them over it. The pressure sent a dull pain through the top of her thigh to her bone, and she shifted her leg so that the denim was as loose as it could possibly be over it. She had been cheated of the full pleasure of watching her cut open, but she also knew that had Nicole not interrupted her, she would have gone on to repeat her ritual with more force but less satisfaction. She turned to face the sink and started to fill a glass of water.

Nicole came into the kitchen, still talking on the phone, and smiled at Kate when she saw her standing there. She was holding a parcel, which looked like a shoebox, under one arm and a shopping bag under the other. Kate did not listen to what she was saying, but moved away from the sink and away from the incriminating metal strip, and pretended to read something on her phone. Her leg ached as she walked. The depth of the ache told her that this would take a while to heal, that it was inevitable that Andrew would see what she had done, and the thought of his disappointment filled her with sadness. She wished she was not so weak.

Nicole put her parcel on the table, and went to the sink, where she picked up the knife, the same knife Kate had just held, and without inspecting it, thrust it blade first into the top of the box, sliding it towards her to slice through the packing. She put the knife in the sink and pulled out the chair at the table, getting herself settled in, and Kate went to her room. She lay there, her hand pressing on the top of her leg, waiting for the sound of Nicole leaving the kitchen, so that she could go back up and check the blade of the knife and wash it, put it back where she had taken it from, but she must have fallen asleep because she woke in the morning with the kitchen paper stuck with dried blood to her thigh, and when she went back into the kitchen she saw that the knife had been cleaned and put back in its place.

34

Kate didn't eat anything that morning. The combination of the pain in her upper thigh and the guilt in her stomach was making her feel sick, so she drank a glass of water and sat on the floor of the shower, peeling the remains of the blood-soaked kitchen towel from the cut. She washed it, swearing as she scalded herself, and then put a plaster over it. The plaster was barely enough to cover the incision which, as well as being deeper, was far longer than she had intended, and when she put her jeans on she could feel her flesh sticking to the fabric. She left early for work, before anybody else had woken up. Taking the bus would only make her feel more nauseous, so she walked. Andrew was still in bed when she phoned him, but she called twice to make sure she woke him up.

'Bad news,' she said, 'I'm homeless.'

Andrew, who was not easily fooled by Kate's false levity, sounded immediately sharper.

'What happened?'

'Max is moving home,' Kate said. 'And I don't want to stay at the flat without him.'

'Shit. I'm sorry.'

'Yeah, me too. He told me last night.' Kate exhaled. She was beginning to feel calm.

'Do you want to stay with me?' Andrew said, before adding: 'Until you find somewhere, I mean. Shona won't mind.'

'Oh,' said Kate, 'no. It's fine. I'll find somewhere.'

She didn't want him to think that she had called to invite herself to live with him, even if the thought that he might offer had been somewhere in the back of her mind. But now Andrew had censored himself she was too proud even to accept his invitation to stay temporarily.

'It's there, if you need it,' Andrew said. Kate could hear his covers moving on the other end of the phone. His wide bed, his warm body, had felt so far away last night. 'When are you coming to see me? I miss you.'

'Soon,' Kate said.

When she rang off, she felt foolish for having cut: for having buckled, in that moment of weakness, for having created such a permanent relic of what had only been a temporary state of mind. At lunchtime, she texted Claire. The first message she drafted consisted mostly of platitudes and excuses – they hadn't spoken properly for more than a month – but she deleted this and instead wrote: '*I need a new flatmate. Time to move to London?*' About ten minutes later, Claire phoned. She'd broken up with Alex two weeks earlier, and on the condition that they found a flat without rats, she would love nothing more than to live in any city where he wasn't.

'Why didn't you tell me?' Kate said.

'I would have, but I know you're busy.'

'I'm really sorry,' Kate said: she meant it.

On their last night in the flat together, Max and Kate sat out on the balcony to smoke, with a bottle of wine kept cold by the chill of the air. Max was wearing a Puffa coat and Kate had her hood up, a blanket wrapped around her knees.

'Do you think this is the beginning of the rest of our lives?' Max said now. 'And when we're rich and famous we'll reminisce about our days living in squalor?'

'I mean, this place is hardly squalid,' Kate said.

'OK. But this is a new beginning.'

'Maybe,' Kate said.

'No? I feel . . .' Max paused. 'I feel like something has shifted, for you. Like you're beginning to put all that stuff behind you.'

'Being raped, you mean?'

'Being raped,' Max said, allowing himself to be corrected.

They had been sitting there for over an hour, neither of them inclined to move, and it was one of the few times that Kate felt that he was fully engaged with what she was saying to him. She wanted to take advantage of the rare and brutal clarity of the moment.

'I don't know,' she said. 'I don't know if you can just "put it behind you". It's not like a normal memory. I wear it, I feel it every day. It's under my skin, in my flesh. We talk about it all the time in therapy. It's because the memory of it is fragmented. It was too intense to process at the time so it's kind of in bits, stuck in my short-term memory. And these little fragments just take over, whenever there are reminders.' She had told Max this before, but she felt now, perhaps because she was leaving or perhaps just because they were alone together for the first time in a while, that she really needed to make sure he understood. 'It could be anything that takes me back there. A colour, a smell. A time of day, an object.'

'What kind of an object?'

'Anything; things that were in the room, things I looked at. The light bulb, and the slight burn on its shell where the filament was too hot. A mark on the ceiling which looked like a tyre mark but couldn't have been, because we were inside and it was the ceiling.' She paused and looked at him for any signs of recognition, but he did not meet her gaze, so she continued. 'All illogical. The things I focused on to take myself out of my body, and the things that return me to that same state of disembodiment. And that's why it's so confusing, and so difficult, because the things that served me at the time, and enabled me to survive, there are moments when they make it impossible for me to be in the world.'

Max nodded. 'But you feel all of that in your body, too?'

'Yes,' Kate said. She was a little drunk, and something about the understated romance of the setting – out on the balcony, overlooking the city, and the authority she had found – made her want to speak more freely than she had before. 'Particularly, I remember pain,' she said, and at this Max winced, and she felt a slight thrill at her ability to shock, and she dug deeper, again using the word she had just made Max say. 'I think people sometimes forget that rape is painful as well as everything else. So much of it is to do with dehumanisation, and humiliation, and power. People forget that it's an act of violence.'

'I guess some people like that kind of power,' Max said, retreating from her point, latching on to the part he could more easily understand. 'But why?'

Kate shrugged. 'It's sadistic,' she said. 'But I wonder whether maybe he was a masochist, too.'

It was the first time she had said anything to Max about what she actually thought of her rapist, and she felt liberated by her freedom to depict him however she wanted, it didn't matter that he was family to Max: he didn't know that, to Max he could have been anybody.

'Why?' Max said.

'He had a tattoo,' she said. She put her hand over the inside of her hip, and watched Max to see how much he understood, whether perhaps he understood too much. Perhaps now would be the moment that he would ask her, for the second time, who this man was; Kate did not know what she would say, and she moved her hand up, so it half covered the top of her pubic bone, where the tattoo had been. 'It just made me think, maybe his feelings about his own body are complicated.'

'Oh,' Max said. 'What was it?'

Kate took her hand away. 'Words. A quote. Something very pretentious. Hilarious, when you think about it.'

Max didn't laugh. But nothing about his demeanour

suggested that the information Kate had given him had gone any way to revealing the identity of her rapist. She thought now of that conversation with Zara, her first disclosure, when Kate had told her about the tattoo. Zara had turned away from this piece of information as soon as Kate had offered it; now, too, Kate allowed Max to steer the conversation away, as he always did, from the intensity and violence of what she was saying. When they finished their second bottle of wine they said goodnight, and Kate went to bed her mind thick with drink, playing over their conversation. She was not fearful that she had said too much, but neither did she feel the old exhilaration she had hoped for: that she could shock him into paying attention to her. Before she fell asleep, she tried to imagine what Max would have done if she had unbuttoned her jeans and showed him the scars, old and fresh, thatching her thighs.

That night she dreamt of Lewis for the first time in weeks. In the dream, he was sitting cross-legged on the floor of the kitchen in Latimer Crescent, holding his hand to his eyes and crying. Kate couldn't quite recall why he was sitting on the floor, but she knew that it was her fault, that she had hurt him, and that she was unsure of whether to ask for his forgiveness.

Andrew had borrowed a van from the shoot he was working on, and he came over the following day to help Kate move. They packed up after lunch, and Max, who hadn't yet seen the flat, came with them. He sat in the middle front seat, twiddling the dials on the stereo, he and Andrew listing things Kate might have forgotten.

'What about that weird fur jacket thing?' said Andrew.

'No. Why,' said Kate suspiciously, 'did you want me to forget it?'

'And that vibrator thing on charge in the bathroom?' said Max.

'That's an epilator. For leg hair.'

'Oh. Well, did you remember your epilator?'

'Yes.'

'And your vib—'

'Oh my God,' Kate said. 'Yes, I remembered everything.' In the driving seat, Andrew shifted, swapping the steering wheel from one hand to the other, and hiding his smile as he did so.

'What big arms you have,' said Max to Andrew.

'I even remembered the butter dish.'

'What butter dish?' said Max.

'My butter dish. You know, the blue-and-white china one.'

'That's the communal butter dish,' said Max, affronted. 'Owned by the flat as a collective.'

'No,' said Kate. 'It's my butter dish. Which I bought. Look, it's here.' She reached into the bag at her feet and took out the butter dish, which was one of the last things she had packed. She turned it over, and showed Max its base: it had been purchased in Randwick.

'Let me see that,' said Max.

'Why is it wrapped in cling film?' said Andrew, glancing at the dish.

'To stop the butter falling out.'

Max gasped. 'You took the butter dish AND the butter?'

Kate shrugged. 'Well, I bought the butter, too,' she said.

Andrew shook his head. 'That's tight. At least leave the butter for the flat.'

'I was going to have toast tomorrow,' said Max ruefully.

'Buy your own butter.' Kate put the dish back in the bag smugly. 'I'm going to have mine with dinner.'

The excitement began to dissipate somewhere south of Shepherd's Bush, after twenty minutes spent at a slow crawl, stuck in traffic. By the time they were driving over Battersea Bridge, it was dark, and rainwater was streaming down the windows. To the east, Albert Bridge and Chelsea Bridge rose from the water below, each strung with yellowish bulbs whose light was reflected in the black surface of the Thames. Being driven through this city, a city she was so used to traversing independently, on foot, by bus or train, made Kate feel like a child again, particularly with the sound of the heater blasting, the fans on full to demist the windscreens. Downriver, away from the city and to its west, the riverbank obscured the view of the water, curving southwards and filling Kate's field of vision with high, half-lit office buildings. There were no crossing points further west that she could see: the next bridge was Wandsworth, and it was far round the bend. And so she tried not to look west, keeping in view the decorative lights of the Chelsea bridges, their warmth and extravagance, and blocking out the sight of the river disappearing into obscurity.

The flat she and Claire had found was in Tooting. The rent was cheaper than Kate had been paying Max, but only marginally, while the flat itself was significantly smaller: a kitchen crowded with a table and a two-seater faux-leather sofa beneath a small, barred window that only opened halfway. Kate liked it. In her room there was a tiny alcove just big enough for the flat-packed desk she'd ordered to arrive the next morning, at which she would sit to mark up the set plans she'd been given, and to work on her own designs. Her room in Max's flat had been more beautiful, without the ominous damp patches or the scrubby school carpet, and there she'd had a double rather than a single bed. But this was hers; there were no discounts, no favours, no obligations. This bedroom, with its low-hanging, bald light bulb and its creaking metal bed frame, for now belonged to her and nobody else.

Max and Andrew stayed to help her unpack, and once they'd moved in all the boxes, Max invited them to come for dinner with Elias.

'I want to finish here,' Kate said. 'But I'll see you really soon. I'll come over before you go back to Latimer Crescent.'

Max hugged her. 'The end of an era,' he said, kissing her on the cheek. 'And don't worry, I'll be back before you know it. I'm coming to reclaim the fucking butter dish and anything else you've stolen.'

Andrew left soon after to return the van to the studio, having said he would come back later that night.

Left alone, Kate's instinct was to find something to drink, but of course the fridge was empty. She put on her raincoat and leather boots and went to the corner shop, where she bought a bottle of wine and a carton of milk. There were no wine glasses in the flat; Claire was bringing those tomorrow. Kate had forgotten what it was like to live somewhere only half made, what it felt like to start from the beginning. But she washed out a mug with her hands and hot water and poured wine into it. Half a bottle down, she hadn't started to unpack, nor could she make the television work, and they hadn't yet installed Internet, so she listened to the same old album on her phone on repeat, the speakers vibrating thinly against the plywood tabletop, their sound half drowned by the Saturday-night noises from the street down below: conversation and laughter, high heels on the pavement, which would later turn into the arguing of couples, the drunken shouts of men, walking in groups of two or three, with nowhere to go and with nothing to fear.

35

On the first morning in her new bedroom, Kate woke late. Andrew was asleep beside her, arms folded over his stomach, his chin tucked into his chest. His chest was moving heavily with his breathing, his breath stale, but she turned towards him and, without waking him, pulled his arms around her, so that her waking body was enveloped in the warmth of his, her breath in his. Today, she knew, was the first time in a while that she had woken to the certainty that she wanted to live.

It was Sunday, and neither of them had anywhere else to be, and Claire wasn't arriving until the evening. They hadn't often had Max's flat to themselves, and Andrew was making the most of not having to worry about waking Shona, who worked long hours and slept late at the weekends. He turned up the Isley Brothers, sang in an irritatingly tuneful mock falsetto. The flat filled with the smell of coffee, and Kate did a little more unpacking while Andrew put bacon under the grill. She came in for breakfast wearing his hooded sweatshirt, which came down over the tops of her thighs, grazing her scars.

'Thief,' said Andrew, tugging at the sweatshirt and

pulling her into him. He looked down at her, kissed his teeth disapprovingly, but his eyes were smiling. Kate pulled away, stuck up her middle finger and slid the butter dish towards her.

'You never let me take any of your shit,' she said. 'Your room is so horribly tidy I never get the chance.'

'I have to be careful, with you there.'

Max, even less than Andrew, was only very sparsely memorialised among her possessions. His absence seemed more remarkable, given the years they had known each other. There were some photographs that had been stuck childishly onto the pin-board in her old room: matt, low-lit images of them at some party together, their arms around each other. There were presents he had brought back from holidays – a dusty bottle of wine whose label was printed with the image of Dali's melting clock, a novelty bottle opener – and business cards he had given to Kate because he hadn't quite worked out what else to do with them.

There was also a poster that Kate had never got round to putting up, a freeze-frame from *L'Accusé* that Zara had given her, the old image that had stayed with Kate all these years, of Lucille looking out of her window, make-up smeared, tights run. Zara had signed the poster in black marker pen for her, a message that read: *For Kate, who would have made this a far better film. Z.* Zara had sent the poster to her after they'd talked about the film on the phone, and Kate remembered that she had sounded rueful that day, but Kate had not asked her why.

'This is cool,' Andrew said when Kate took it out to

show him. 'It'll be valuable, when you've won your Academy Award.'

'She was in a weird mood when she gave me this. Told me she regretted making the film.'

'You're lucky,' Andrew said, looking at the poster. 'Takes some people years of running to get the kinds of jobs you're getting. She's shown you a lot of shortcuts.'

'I know that,' Kate said. She took the poster back, started to roll it up. 'It wasn't just a whim, though, you know. I was going to apply for an MA, but . . .'

Andrew shrugged. 'I'm just saying. I've got mates from film school who stuck at it for most of their twenties. Half of them are training to be lawyers now.'

'Oh, poor them.'

'You're defensive,' said Andrew. He sat back on the bed, made that kissing noise with his teeth again, looked sideways at Kate. There was that slight sternness about him, which she'd seen when they'd first gone to the cinema together: Kate regretted her sarcasm. She climbed on top of him and put her forehead against his chest.

'I'm sorry,' she said, her voice muffled. 'I just don't want you to think I'm like Max.'

His chest rose and fell under her. He put his hand on the back of her head.

'You're not,' he said. 'They treat you like one of their own, though. It's not a bad thing. It's nice. They must like you a lot.'

'Is that so hard to believe?' Kate said.

Andrew was pushing her, not quite challenging her

285

loyalty, but asking her to show him how much of it he was entitled to. It was for this reason, then, as well as the fact that they were in new, neutral territory, that Kate started to talk properly. She sat up as she spoke, and he sat up with her, she not quite looking at him, and told him that she'd known the man who had attacked her. Still knew him – in fact, had even come close to having to face him socially, because he was a cousin of Max's.

'It's good that you're away from him,' Andrew said, and she didn't know whether he was talking about Lewis or about Max. 'I thought it might be something like that.'

'Like what?'

'I thought it might be someone you knew. Or Shona did, anyway.'

'Shona knows?' Kate felt suddenly panicked.

'Well, yeah, we've talked about it. She said she thought you probably know him.' He stopped. 'Why, does it bother you, me talking to her?'

In fact, it did not bother her. It was a relief, even, to know that this did not have to be a secret, and for a moment, she couldn't remember why it was.

'No,' she said. 'I suppose I just didn't think about the fact that you might want to. But now you say it, it makes sense that you would. I'm glad.'

Andrew didn't need to ask her whether Max had any idea who had raped her, and nor did he ask what to Kate was the most obvious question: are you ever going to tell him? She supposed he saw that she didn't have an answer. For the moment, though, the most important thing was that she had trusted him enough to tell him what only her therapist knew. And she realised, after he left, that they had spent nearly twenty-four hours together. She'd asked him to stay another night, tugging the cord of the hoodie he'd now reclaimed. But he was watching *First Dates* with Shona: this was their weekly tradition and he wasn't going to break it for her, even if she had just entrusted him with her deepest secret.

'I'll put in a good word, you might get invited next time,' he said, putting his hand over her face and pushing her back through the doorway by way of goodbye. She liked that Andrew had tested her, but she knew that her alliances had changed long before, even if she'd only been able to admit this to herself when Max had told her he was moving out; when he had given her permission. She had always resented the thought of neglecting a friendship for a relationship, but Kate knew that she had been absent from her friendship with Max for some time now: another thing Lewis had taken from her. As she finished unpacking, ready for when Claire would arrive that evening, Kate asked herself whether she missed Andrew more than Max, and she found she could not answer. For Andrew, her body ached, just as it ought. But for Max, it was something different. She could have wept, if she'd let herself. For Max, there was insurmountable sadness that was most akin to grief.

Claire arrived that evening, laden with possessions that quickly dominated their small shared space. Kate was happy in the afterglow of Andrew's presence, and she helped Claire to unpack while they drank wine and waited for pizza to arrive. They finished their first bottle quickly and, when Kate went to get the next from the fridge, Claire squatted in front of the television, playing with the remote until it flickered into life. With the unobtrusive noise of Sunday-night TV in the background they could just as easily have been at school again, drinking the wine freely provided by Alison up in Kate's room, smoking stale roll-ups out the window and flushing the stubs down the toilet. When they were drunk enough, Claire recounted in detail the disintegration of her relationship with Alex.

'There are just things you can't know about a person until you live with them,' she said. 'I mean, I always knew he was careful with money. But splitting the cost of toilet roll by usage was just too much.'

'He didn't.'

'I know. I'd never really thought of myself as a feminist until then, but I really did feel discriminated against.'

'Just because you don't have a penis,' Kate lamented.

'Exactly.'

'It sucks that it didn't work out,' Kate said. 'But I'm glad you're here.' She paused. 'I'm sorry I've been absent, these last few months.'

They both knew that it was years since they'd been as open with one another as this. But Kate meant what she said. She could think of few people she would rather be with at that moment. That evening, Kate told her friend what she had been wanting to tell her for months now.

'I had no idea,' Claire said when Kate had finished.

'How would you? We've hardly seen each other. I've been doing my best to hide it. But you know, I think that might have made it worse.'

'Does Alison know?'

'No.'

'And Max?'

'Yes. But he doesn't know who.' She told Claire, then, what she had told Andrew earlier that day: that it was Max's cousin who was responsible. It felt like a relief, this time, to say it. Claire was almost more shocked by this piece of information than the news that Kate had been assaulted.

'I suppose,' she said, after a moment's pause, 'this means I probably can't have sex with Max, doesn't it?'

Kate laughed. 'Not necessarily. I mean, he is single, so . . .'

Claire patted her on the leg. 'I won't,' she said loyally. 'I've got your back.'

'It's part of the reason I had to move out,' Kate said. 'The fear of bumping into him has been wearing me down.'

'He was too good to be true, probably, wasn't he? Max, I mean.'

'We were never together,' Kate said.

'I know. Doesn't mean it can't break your heart, though, losing someone like that.'

36

In December, Kate and Claire booked the same train as Max to Gloucestershire, two days before Christmas. The journey from Paddington always felt to Kate like a trip to a former life, but the difference between that old life – or those old lives – and this felt all the more pronounced now she was travelling with Max, as if making the journey together were a futile attempt to travel back to the way things had once been. When she first saw him, slouched on a metal bench in the middle of the concourse, sunglasses on and a weekend bag between his knees, Kate supposed she had been wrong to think that the journey would hold equal significance for him. But he brightened as soon as he saw her, hugged her tightly, and pulled her ahead of Claire with his arm through hers to the platform.

'It might be my last Christmas there,' Max said, as they went through the ticket barrier. 'They've got an offer on Bisley House. Some mad local aristocrat wants to buy it.'

'Next year you can come and stay with me and my mum,' Kate said. 'I promise not to break everything.'

'Thanks,' said Max, though he didn't really seem to be listening. Kate thought of her mother's house: her famous non-alcoholic mulled wine, and was glad that Max had not been more enthused by her invitation.

The train was crowded, the seats and even the aisles filling as soon as it opened its doors, leaving Max, Claire and Kate, who had been at the back of the queue, still on the platform. Kate had been about to suggest that they wait for a later one, when Claire set off down the platform. In the doorway to the first carriage of the train the guard asked to see their tickets, and Claire took out her standard-class ticket and handed it to him.

'It's full everywhere else,' she said bluntly.

'OK,' said the guard. 'But you need to move into standard after Reading.'

'Excellent work,' said Max to Claire. The first-class carriage was only half full, and he pushed his weekend bag up onto the luggage rail above a set of cushy leather table seats. Once they'd left the station, Claire went to the buffet car to negotiate for them free coffee and biscuits, though the man serving her drew the line at champagne.

'Is it just you and your parents, then, Max?' Claire said, when she sat back down.

'And Nicole. She's my sister. My uncle's coming too, with my cousin.'

'Who's your cousin?' Claire ignored Kate, who was widening her eyes in alarm.

'Lewis. You know Lewis, right?' Max looked at Kate, who nodded.

'He gave me a lift,' she said. 'Back from Bisley one year.'

'I remember.'

'And he was at one of your parties. Just before we moved in together. Eighteen months ago.'

'Oh yeah, at my parents' house.' Max fell silent for a moment. 'Bit of a weird guy.'

'Weird how?' said Claire. Kate's heart was thumping, but now Claire had started, she didn't want her to stop.

'I don't know, just a bit tricky. Always on the defensive. He's upset about the house, actually.'

'Why?' said Kate. She couldn't imagine Lewis being upset about anything.

'Just doesn't want them to sell it. Thinks it should stay in the family, and that we're being ripped off. I don't really get it, though. I know my dad's sad about it but he did actually grow up there, unlike Lewis. Like I said, weird guy.'

Claire didn't ask any more, though a part of Kate had hoped that she would. Part of her was enjoying this subtle power she and Claire now shared. Claire put her earphones in, and she and Max both started to doze somewhere past Reading: the guard had forgotten to come to ask them to move. Kate looked out the window, wondering how it would be if they could choose never to reach their destination, and instead remain beneath this rushing sky. People would be upset, she supposed. Not least the other passengers. Her thoughts were interrupted by a loud tapping on the table between them, whose cause, Kate saw, was an ivory-tipped stick held by an elderly woman in a tweed jacket.

'Young Max,' said the woman, peering over Max. Kate shoved him in the shoulder, and he jolted awake.

'Oh my God,' he said, when he saw the face looming above him. 'Hello, Lady Caroline.'

'I thought it was you,' said Lady Caroline. 'I could hear somebody talking about Bisley House, and I thought it must be one of the young Rippon boys. You, or the other one.'

'Granny always said you had good hearing,' Max said loyally. Later, he explained to Claire and Kate that Lady Caroline was always claiming to be deaf in order to lull her bridge opponents into a false sense of security. Lady Caroline reached up and twisted her hearing aid which, Max also claimed, was just for show.

'And are you taking these young ladies to see the house? You must be sure to make him show you the walled gardens,' she said, speaking to Claire and Kate now. 'He'll try to avoid it in this cold weather, but now I've told you that you must see winter jasmine you'll keep at him, won't you?'

'We're not going to Bisley,' Kate said. 'We're both from Randwick.'

'This is Claire,' Max said, 'and Kate. Who I went to university with.'

'Oh,' said Lady Caroline, who had only ever been to Randwick to attend community outreach events.

'Lewis and Nicole are both still working,' Max said, taking advantage of Lady Caroline's momentary speechlessness. 'They're coming down together tomorrow, though. And my parents are already there.'

'And your Uncle Rupert? Has he recovered from that awful virus?'

'Oh,' Max said. 'That was like, two years ago.'

Lady Caroline was not going to be put off, though. 'I know how these dreadful things can persist,' she said.

'He's much better, thanks,' Max said.

'He is often in my prayers,' she said gravely. 'Well,' she went on, 'I shall see you soon. Alasdair has told you I'm turfing you all out, no doubt. I'm coming by next week to value the paintings.'

'Well,' said Max wildly, 'I'll see you really soon, then. That's great.'

When at last she retreated, tapping her stick against every other seat as she made her way down the aisle, Max collapsed back in his seat. 'Maybe Lewis is right about the house. Maybe we should take it back off the market, and install a drawbridge.'

'What virus?' Kate said.

'The Rippon euphemism for depression,' Max said, rolling his eyes. 'Nobody wants to admit it runs in the family, apparently.'

'Really? Doesn't that bother Rupert?'

'I don't know,' Max said, shrugging. 'It was only really Granny who used to say it.'

'And Lady Caroline.' Kate caught Claire's eye.

'And Lady Caroline,' said Max, ignoring the cynicism in Kate's voice. 'So she's the one buying the house. It's a terrible investment, but clearly she hasn't been put off. She's only doing it because she hated my grandmother.'

'I think she's excellent,' said Claire, putting her earphones back in. 'I can't wait to be that old.'

*

Kate and Claire got off the train one stop before Max. Claire's mother picked them up at the station, and dropped Kate home. When Kate got to the door, the old knot in her chest started tightening again. She had avoided coming home for nearly the entire year, and had seen her mother only once or twice up in London. Alison hugged her at the door, and Kate pulled away after only a second or two, fearing that by their proximity Alison would be able to sense the damage Kate had done to her own body, Alison's own flesh and blood, since last they'd seen one another.

'I'll put the kettle on,' Alison said, as Kate disappeared upstairs with her bag.

In her bedroom, she was overwhelmed not by the sense of loss or nostalgia that she had felt when she had been there the year before, but by numbness. There was nothing new for her to feel here, there was only the old sadness of which she would never be rid. Alison brought her a cup of tea and lingered in the doorway while Kate began to unpack. Later, Kate ate half a bowl of pasta while Alison asked her a series of earnest and irrelevant questions. When Kate cleared away her plate, she put up the volume on the radio.

She was sluggish, reticent. Her hands shook as she washed up her bowl, and she thought then of smashing it deliberately, just for the sake of breaking something. She didn't understand her own impulses. This was, after all, supposed to be a place of safety, and here she was, wanting to ruin it. Alison stood next to her with her own bowl,

295

waiting to use the sink, but Kate took it from her and washed it up, too. As Alison cleared the rest of the table, Kate washed and pocketed the knife Alison had used to chop the onion.

Upstairs, Kate locked the bathroom door and turned on the bath taps. She undressed, and looked at herself in the mirror. Her body was pale from months of winter, and her belly and the tops of her thighs were soft, a little rounded, though less so than they once were. How raw she looked, how uncooked. The bath was too hot, and its heat sent a flush of red up her calf, and set sweat prickling in her underarms and on her forehead. She fought with herself for a moment, until her desire for masochism was overridden by her body's protective instincts, which would not allow her to put her foot in the water for more than a second or two, and settled instead on the cold edge of the bathtub, her feet balanced on the opposite side, running the cold tap into the water.

She ran the knife she had taken from the kitchen along her thigh, waiting for the clarity that usually came moments before cutting. But she could hear the radio downstairs and the sound of pots and pans being returned to cupboards. In her mind's eye she saw Andrew, his fingers tracing scars, holding back on whatever it was that he wanted to say to her. She put the knife down.

Once she had dried herself, she rubbed moisturiser into her legs, the tops of her thighs and her stomach. It was coconut-scented and sickly, and stuck to her leggings as she pulled them on over her still-hot skin. Downstairs, her face still pink from the bath, she curled up on the sofa, and pulled a blanket over her. When Alison came in, she turned on the television and sat next to Kate. Alison stroked her hair, plaiting it and then brushing out the plaits with her fingers before plaiting it again.

37

William was waiting for Max at the station with the radio on, and when Max got into the car he turned the volume down only a notch. He was listening to the final five minutes of a panel show repeat that Max recognised from Saturday lunchtimes at Latimer Crescent, when the four of them would sit around the kitchen table and William would laugh too loudly. He wasn't laughing now, just humming quietly to himself, but until the show ended it absorbed all of his attention.

Max turned off the radio as the credits began to play. 'Who's already here?' he said.

'Your mother,' said William, glancing in his wing mirror, 'and Rupert. He's on good form, actually.' Inevitably, there was a note of surprise in his voice.

'And how's the house?'

'You'll see. It's all rather sad, Max. I'm a little cut up about it, to tell you the truth.'

'You grew up there.'

'Quite. And, well. I just can't help but feel things are changing for us, Max.'

'What do you mean?'

William shook his head. 'Straight after somebody dies, you want to keep everybody together. Overlook differences. Forgive. One feels very resistant to change. But, inevitably, time passes, nearly four years now, and we have to let go of some of the things we've been holding on to. Objects, beliefs. Even hope. That's what your mother is always telling me, anyway.'

'Is this about the bakery?' Max said. 'Your sourdough starter?'

'Oh, Christ. No. Little fucker went mouldy,' said William. 'The wrong kind of mould, I mean, pink and scaly. Started to develop some kind of counter-culture, evidently. I had to throw it away.'

'Did you see Lady Caroline at the station?' Max said. 'She had her driver waiting right by the platform. She cornered me on the train, trying to work out whether I was going out with Kate or her friend.'

'Oh, how is Kate?' said William.

Max shrugged. 'Yeah, OK. New flat seems nice.'

William fell silent. 'Good,' he said, after a while.

The 'For Sale' sign outside the house came into view at the top of the lane, before even the high limestone walls were visible. When Max had last been to Bisley House its chaos had at least been contained, boxed behind barely closed doors, hidden beneath dust sheets, none of it visible from the outside; but now there stood a skip on the front drive which was beginning to overflow with broken pieces of furniture, with those same boxes which had themselves split open. It was dark already, and so were the upper floors of the house: they were keeping to the lower floors, William explained, which had not yet been cleared.

William had insisted on buying a Christmas tree, but the decorations had been packed away somewhere obscure, so it was decorated only in the oversized outdoor lights he had brought in from the front – the same lights Zara had watched him wind around the driveway's leafless trees the year before. The books had gone from the shelves, and the large spice rack that had hung next to the cooker was bare. To Max, Bisley House looked far more like an extravagant holiday house than a home. Before he unpacked he circuited the upper floors, and saw that the master bedroom and most of the spare rooms, including the one Kate had slept in last year, had been stripped of their mattresses, their furniture covered in white sheets.

Max was restless. Last year's Christmas, when Elias, who was spending this year's holiday in Miami, had managed to either insult or irritate almost everybody, when Rupert had been mostly bed-bound, and Kate had turned up with a bloodied hand before vomiting everywhere, had by no means been perfect. But he quite liked a crisis, and he had enjoyed the feeling of being holed up in Bisley House, shut away with the people he was closest to, keeping the outside world from coming in. This year the house felt too quiet, too empty. So far his mother had spent most of her time trying to work through the last of her notes before they went on to editing, and William, who looked like he had aged about ten years somewhere between London and Gloucestershire, shuffled around the upper floors wearing his mother's pink woollen hat and gloves and moving boxes from one end of the house to the other.

William had refused half-hearted offers of help from both Max and Rupert, and, on the afternoon Max arrived, the two of them had sat at the kitchen table. Max sat opposite his uncle, who was calmly reading a magazine. Max was waiting for Rupert to say something, but he just kept on turning the pages, sipping the tea he had made for himself, and as Max watched him he felt a sudden urge to rip the glossy pages from his hands. Instead, he got up, and found a beer in the fridge.

'Do you mind?' he said, a little more aggressively than he'd meant to. The question was only nominal: he had already taken the top off.

'Christ, no,' Rupert said, looking up. 'It's Christmas. How else is one expected to survive?'

'Cheers,' Max said, pushing his beer towards Rupert's mug, and clinking it. He paused, and took a sip, studying Rupert's face as he did so. With the first sip of beer, he felt his momentary aggravation begin to ebb. Rupert's greying hair was shorter and neater nowadays, his skin less pink: a symptom of sobriety. 'Will you never drink again?' Max said.

'I doubt it,' Rupert said. He popped gum from its packet and chewed on it, thoughtfully. 'Perhaps a sip, every now and again. Half a glass at a wedding. But I could gladly live the rest of my life without being drunk. You know, properly pissed.'

'Really? Even if you feel one hundred per cent better? Like, even if someone told you you'd never be, you know, depressed ever again?'

Rupert laughed.

'What?' Max felt defensive, and a little bemused. 'You've been doing so well recently. You seem so much . . .'

Rupert shook his head. 'I'm not laughing; it's not funny. Don't worry about me, Max. I'm not missing anything. It might look like it, from the outside, but in fact I see everything more clearly.'

Max wanted to ask his uncle what exactly it was that he could see clearly, but he wasn't sure he wanted to hear the answer. Instead he tried his best to meet him halfway. 'I guess the alcohol does –' he waved his bottle – 'blur the edges a little.'

'It does. And sometimes you need that, until there comes a point when you can't see anything at all.'

'Isn't that exactly the point?' Max said, taking a swig.

On Christmas Eve, Alasdair, Nicole and Lewis arrived from London. Alasdair had driven, and Lewis and Nicole turned up in the front hall dead-eyed and yawning, presents spilling from their bags onto the tiled floor. Max wondered whether it was possible that they'd been forced to listen to the cricket coverage for the entire journey, since they both looked very relieved that it was over. Even Lewis seemed happy to see Max, and for a moment Max thought that Lewis was going to hug him, but he was so surprised by the possibility that he kept his arms by his sides, and Lewis instead slapped him on the back. Because Alasdair had been absent for two of the last three Christmases, and Rupert the other, this was the first time the whole Rippon family had been together for the holidays since Bernadette had died, and William was insisting that they do everything as she would have wanted. Tomorrow, there would be no presents until after the Queen's speech, and no champagne until the afternoon. Max smuggled a bottle up from the cellar on Christmas Eve, though, and he snuck into Nicole's room on Christmas morning before church, wrapped in an old quilt that was making his eyes itch and his nose run, and popped the cork right next to her head.

'Morning!' he said, as she flailed at him in protest, her head still buried in the pillow. Max had been hoping, once Nicole arrived, that things would start to get a bit more lively. It was a promising start: they had time for a glass each before church, and during the service Max stood at the end of the aisle and sang as loudly as he always did. He took communion because it was Christmas, then watched as the priest and his two deacons in their white-and-gold robes went to Lady Caroline, who was sitting on a reserved cushioned chair in the front row, and knelt before her while she took communion. When they got back, though, Nicole refused to have any more to drink until lunchtime, so Max had to disappear upstairs alone every thirty minutes while the turkey was cooking, the alcohol filtering straight through the lining of his empty stomach into his blood. By lunchtime, he was giddy, his mind working through the possibilities of how he might best sustain this excitable mood. Too much food would be a mistake, but he'd have to suppress the inevitable headache somehow.

'When are you going to sign it over?' Nicole said, as they were eating lunch. Her question was addressed to both her father and Alasdair, but it was Alasdair who put down his glass, suppressing a belch with authority.

'In the new year, I should think. My solicitor is still talking to Lady Caroline's solicitor. Or solicitors. She has a whole fleet. She wants to renovate it and actually move in, which seems like madness to me. If I were her, I'd probably tear it down.'

'So we have one more Christmas to wreck the house before we sell it, then?' said Max loudly.

'Absolutely not,' said Alasdair. 'She's already done her best to decimate our asking price. The place needs to be spotless.'

'Not even a little party? Granny would approve.'

'Tell you what,' he said. 'You can have a party, but only if you stay on after Christmas to finish clearing the attic.'

'Oh, I'd love to, but I have to go on holiday,' Max said.

'I'm staying,' said Lewis, glancing at his father.

Alasdair grunted. 'Lewis doesn't have anywhere better to be,' he said.

Faintly, Max registered that Lewis was watching him as he ate. Lewis had worked efficiently and methodically through his meal, both elbows on the table so as to guard his plate. Only when he was finished did he sit back in his chair, both hands resting on the table and making little folds in his paper crown, his wristwatch gleaming in the light of the chandelier above them.

'Might as well make the most of it,' Lewis said now, in response to his father. 'While we still can.'

'Well, if you feel that strongly about it, I'd be quite happy to leave you to finish here on your own,' said Alasdair, 'save me the trouble of wasting another week's holiday in the middle of nowhere.'

'No, no, I'll stay too,' William said. Zara looked at him sharply, but William didn't look back.

Max, oblivious to these loaded looks, took the opportunity to slip out of his seat, mumbling that he was going to the toilet, but turning left instead of right at the door to the dining room and up the back staircase to his bedroom. There, he rifled through his things and found the little plastic bag he was looking for. He hadn't brought it here on purpose, and it did seem like a bit of a waste, but it was Christmas, after all, and it was raining. He deserved a treat. Max tapped out a little of the white powder onto the wooden chair at the end of his bed, and sat cross-legged on the floor rolling a ten between his thumbs and forefingers. He wished Elias were here. Or Kate, she'd never really been into this, but she would at least have been in on it. He needed this, just a hit of energy. That was what Rupert didn't understand. It was real life that was blurred around the edges, real life that contained ambiguity. Intoxication: this was real, tangible clarity. He leaned over, snorted the line, sat back as his thoughts came into focus, senses came alight. In this state, there was nothing but the perfect geometry of his surroundings. Crisp corners, clear edges. He put the bag in his back pocket, and went back downstairs.

Max was relieved to leave Bisley House, once Christmas was over. On Boxing Day, he'd hardly left the sofa, but the next day he walked the lower floors one last time, and then went down to the walled garden, which in the summer was heavy with the scent of roses and freshly turned earth. He'd always hidden here when they'd played hide-and-seek, because Nicole had hay fever and would be doubled over with a sneezing fit as soon as she came close to finding him. The far wall was covered by a creeper with white blossom, which Max supposed was Lady Caroline's winter jasmine. Nostalgia threatened, but he shook it away. Lady Caroline would be here, soon, pushing her own grandsons to take unsuspecting local girls to view the jasmine. Quite how this plant was supposed to inspire romance, Max was not quite sure. Things must have been very different in Lady Caroline's day. Somehow, he couldn't imagine her downloading Embers.

He'd texted Kate to ask her if she wanted a lift back to London, but she told him she was staying a few days longer, which was a surprise to Max, as he knew she usually tried to shorten her stays in Randwick as much as possible. Zara was driving him and Nicole, while William stayed at the house to help clear it out. Rupert was already back at his flat, having taken the first train running on Boxing Day. Nicole sat in the front, inflicting her music on

Zara and Max, while Max speculated about Alasdair and Lewis's relationship.

'I think they both have abandonment issues,' Max diagnosed, slumped in the back seat of the car, 'after Aunt Sylvie left.'

'Wouldn't that mean they're both really clingy?' Nicole said. 'I've always thought that Alasdair didn't like Lewis that much. God, that sounds awful.'

'Maybe abandonment issues that manifest as a deep-seated distrust of women?' said Max, astounded by his own insightfulness.

'Sylvie was a bitch, though,' Nicole said. 'Do you remember when she threw my dinner in the bin because I complained about the olives?'

'That was you,' said Max. 'You threw the dinner she'd cooked for you in the bin, after you complained about it.'

'That does sound a bit like me,' said Nicole. 'I hate olives.'

'Seriously, though, I think they're both a bit fucked. Maybe you should introduce them to some of your therapists, Mum.'

Zara raised an eyebrow at Max in the mirror. 'Don't drag me into this,' she said, mockingly defensive. 'I'm not even related to them. This is your family, your flesh and blood. Take it up with your father.'

'You married into it, though,' said Max, who was in the mood for a debate. 'That makes you even more responsible, if they're all fuck-ups. You chose to be part of it. The rest of us didn't.'

'Responsible?' said Nicole. 'How?'

38

In Kate's bedroom there were blackout curtains, and on the morning of Christmas Eve she slept until ten o'clock. She woke to the sound of Joni Mitchell's *Blue* playing from the living room. *Blue songs . . .* she heard *. . . are like tattoos.* Kate had put this album on every morning one summer, had left it playing through the house when she'd packed her bag and gone to school, on those days when Alison couldn't get out of bed. She buried her face in the pillow. Why she had thought this album might help Alison, she had no idea.

Alison soft-boiled eggs for them both, and they sat in their little kitchen with the door open so she could hum along with Joni's voice. Kate got up, and turned the music down without saying anything, and then felt sorry that she had done so. After breakfast, Alison went to the corner shop to buy milk and bread. She came upstairs to find Kate sitting on her bed, looking around her room.

'I feel old,' she said. 'I'm too old for this room.'

It took her all afternoon to clear it out. Alison helped by filling plastic bags with clothes and belongings she would take to the council to be recycled, and boxes with possessions of Kate's she could not bear to throw away. As they sorted their way through everything, Kate thought how strange it was to have another person piece together a history of her own life which was to her unknown; that Alison's memories of Kate's childhood, of her pre-verbal existence, had a life to which she had no direct access. When her wardrobe and chest of drawers were clear, and the pile of possessions on the armchair had been condensed into a few boxes, Alison helped Kate to push the bed from the middle of the room to the alcove in the corner of her room.

When she went to bed that night her room smelt faintly of polish, but the air was thinner, colder: cleared of the dust that had built up over the years. Again that night she slept deeply, falling quickly under, too quickly for her to turn off her bedside light even, and when she woke her skin was clean, her pyjamas and her sheets smelling of her mother's laundry detergent, and the duvet over her feet heavy where Alison had crept in in the night and left a stocking on her bed, just as she'd done when Kate was little. Downstairs Alison was listening to Joni again.

She opened her gifts at the kitchen table: a pack of cards with pictures of her university on the back, a bar of lavender soap and some plastic-coated earrings she knew she would never wear. Once she was washed and dressed and smelling of soap they drank coffee and listened to music loud enough to negate the need for conversation. They had chicken this year; there were only two of them, not enough to justify a turkey, and Kate watched her mother stuff it with the pork meat and herbs she'd bought from the supermarket a few days earlier. The fridge was glut full, and the pre-packaged sauces, puddings and creams made Kate feel slightly nauseous. So too did the chicken, whose freshly plucked skin was stretched so thin that it had begun to tear over its fatted torso. Alison thrust handfuls of pork meat up inside the chicken, pressing into the moistened meat half a lemon and two peeled cloves of garlic, rubbing butter and salt into its skin.

At lunch, Alison slowed her eating pace to match her daughter's.

'You do seem better than last year,' she said, when Kate pushed away her half-finished plate: she had picked over the breast meat but hadn't quite been able to dislodge from her mind the image of raw flesh, bound and pierced. Her mother had spoken as if picking up an earlier conversation.

'What do you mean?' Kate said.

'You were so very sad, this time last year,' Alison said simply. 'I didn't quite see it at the time, but I can see it now, now that you seem a little happier.'

Alison's incisiveness came as both a surprise and a relief to Kate. It was much like the feeling she'd had when she'd first got drunk as a teenager, and when, after being driven home by her mother and put to bed, believing herself to have behaved with the perfect impression of sobriety, she'd woken to find that Alison had gone to work leaving a packet of paracetamol and a packet of bacon out on the kitchen counter. Then, just as now, Kate had realised that her mother had deduced far more than she allowed herself to believe. In the afternoon, when they went out for a walk, Kate told her mother that there was a sadness she could not name, and Alison kissed her on the top of her head, looped her arm through her daughter's. When Kate grew weary, and the sky began to run, they went home and Kate lay on the sofa with her head resting in Alison's lap, her eyes closed, listening to the voices on the television, not yet ready to sleep.

Claire rang Kate two days after Christmas to complain of weight gain and boredom.

'There are no good-looking people in Randwick,' Claire said, sighing. 'I'm wasted here.'

'Haven't you just been with your family?'

'Well, exactly.'

'We can go somewhere but you have to come and collect me. And you know nowhere will be open.'

'It's fine, I'll take Mum's car,' said Claire. 'I've got an idea.'

When Claire first suggested that they go to Bisley House, Kate refused. If there was even the smallest chance that Lewis was still there, she told Claire, she wouldn't go. Once they'd set off, though, Kate agreed to drive through the village, so they could catch a glimpse from afar.

'Aren't you curious to see it?' Claire said.

'I've already seen it.'

'Yes, but to see it now, wouldn't it be different? Now they're moving everything out?'

'What, you think it would be cathartic, seeing it empty?'

'Yeah. I dunno. Some symbolic shit.'

The sky was pink, just as it had been when Kate and Max had driven this way the year before, and the houses on the lanes were lit with Christmas lights. By the time they got to Bisley it was almost dark. As they rounded the corner at the top of the lane above the house, Kate began to feel excited. They wouldn't be seen in this light, particularly if they parked in the lay-by opposite. They could get out of the car, perhaps get close. She knew it was possible that Lewis was still there, but it was more likely that he would have gone back to London at the same time as Max.

'Actually,' she said to Claire, as casually as she could, 'I think Max might have said they were all going back yesterday.'

Claire smiled. 'So you do want to see it.'

'Maybe,' Kate said. 'I don't know. I don't want anybody to see us.'

They parked, as Kate demanded, in the lay-by. There were no street lamps on the lane, and the hedges were thick and high. The gates were open, and Kate crossed the lane, stood at the entrance. It was Claire's turn, now, for hesitation.

'Are you sure?' she said.

Kate put up the hood of her coat and stepped onto the driveway. The house was less glowing than she remembered it, more grey, its bricks dirt-worn. Her feet crunched on the gravel as she moved closer, and she saw that there were lights on in some of the windows, and a car, a four-by-four she didn't recognise parked out front next to a yellow skip. On the cool air she could smell faintly the smoke of a wood fire. There were people still, but it was dark out here, so even if he was there, she would see him before he saw her.

'I've been here before,' Claire whispered to Kate. 'They held the village fair here when the school fields were shut with foot-and-mouth. We were about twelve. Do you remember?'

Kate shook her head, without looking away from the house.

'They had to evacuate the paddling pool after David threw up in it.'

'Why does he always throw up?' Kate whispered back.

'He has a weak constitution,' whispered Claire.

Kate took another step forward, and the motion sensor above the doorway blinked, flicking on the security lamp and flooding the driveway with white light. Instinctively, Kate pulled her scarf up around her face, and they both shielded their eyes. With black dots in her vision, Kate loosened the scarf and looked to the uppermost window, her face bathed in light. For a second she stood there before she turned, and walked back to the car.

'It's like being in a thriller, this rape stuff,' said Claire, as she pulled her seat belt across her chest and slammed on the accelerator. She glanced sideways at Kate. 'Sorry, that was a bit insensitive. I just don't have any real enemies, you know. Not since school, anyway. I miss that, having enemies.'

'I hope it was him in there,' Kate said quietly. 'I hope he saw me.'

39

By now there was little left in Bisley House of either senti-mental or financial value, but both William and Alasdair knew that this would be their last chance to retrieve any-thing they wanted to keep. William started in the attic, shining his torch into all the corners, but the light revealed only loft insulation, in places chewed by what were most likely rodents, and the odd loose nail. He worked his way through the top-floor bedrooms, checking cupboards and drawers, to his parents' old room, in which the only remaining furniture was the bedframe with its bare mat-tress, lumpy and yellowing. Here William stopped; he knew he was only making himself feel more raw. He went down the back stairs to get a signal on his phone so he could call Zara.

Alasdair, meanwhile, was finishing up on the lower floors, whose communal spaces were a little more clut-tered than the empty rooms William had been roaming above. Lewis, who was driving back with his father that evening, found him in the dining room, standing on top of the mahogany cabinet. Alasdair was lifting the stag head from the wall, and as it came away from its fixings he showered himself with loose plasterboard, sending himself into an asthmatic frenzy.

'You can keep this at the flat until Phoebe and I find our new place,' Alasdair told his son. Lewis, who didn't want to give the impression that there was anything in the house to which he was not deeply emotionally attached, didn't ask his father how he expected him to persuade a girl to sleep with him while there was a stuffed stag watching over them, but instead took the head and carried it to the hallway.

It was not a pleasant job. He'd stayed, though, because he wanted Alasdair to know that he was taking something from him in selling the house. Not just the memories, but a future Lewis had imagined for himself. If he'd had the opportunity, he would have brought girlfriends here, friends every other weekend. It would be a good place for a wedding, or a stag weekend. Rudolph caught his eye; Lewis did his best to ignore the irony. All the medics he knew went off to Eastern Europe, to strip clubs, but he could have done something really different: a big group of guys down here for the hunting season, shooting partridge in the morning, having it plucked and cooked by dinner. Lewis turned Rudolph to face the wall.

'Did you have many parties here?' Lewis said to his uncle, as they were boxing up what was left of William's room. 'Like friends, girls, you know.'

William looked at him with an unreadable expression. 'Sometimes,' he said. 'Mostly when my parents were out of the country.'

'Did they mind?'

'Christ, no, well, they didn't know. Apart from the time all the silverware ended up in the upstairs bathtub. Alasdair tried to pretend he was trying to polish it, but . . .'

'I think this is the nicest room,' Lewis said, 'not the master bedroom. I'd sleep in here, if this were my house. Which I guess it won't ever be, now.'

'Rupert's was always my favourite,' said William.

Rupert's room was the smallest, and its ceiling was slanted, making it feel like a little girl's bedroom. To Lewis it had always seemed the least grand.

'I imagine it's hard for him,' Lewis said, in a serious tone, 'seeing the house being sold, after everything that's happened.'

'Oh, he stopped coming down here years before your grandmother died,' William said, flicking the light off as he shuffled the last box out of the door with his foot. He kicked it a little harder than he intended, and something inside made a clanging noise. 'Unless he absolutely had to. Couldn't stand the woman, God rest her soul.'

This place to Lewis was like a favourite wax jacket; not only did it signify the wealth and quality of its owner, but its character was derived from the tears and the scuffs that were yearly repaired by an expertly discreet seamstress so that only she and its owner ever knew of their existence. But now that they were challenging its integrity the house was beginning to fail. Once the sale was finalised the builders would be here, sending dust from its lining, beams creaking in the rooftops, panes of glass splintering under the vibrations of the drills that disturbed the house to its foundations.

It was as Lewis was descending the main staircase that the driveway below lit up and, looking out of the little window on the halfway landing, he saw Kate Quaile standing there, another girl at her side. Kate's white face was illuminated in the bright floodlight as she stared straight up at the house. She did not look away.

If the light hadn't come on, he wouldn't have seen her. But there she was, standing in her fake-fur coat only metres below. Lewis stepped quickly to the side of the window frame. He did not want her to see him. Kate, to Lewis, was dangerous. He did not think much about their night together, which had lost its sepia romance more than a year ago. Lewis knew that he had been wrong about her; he had seen it in her when he'd glimpsed her at the festival in Finsbury Park, fear and suspicion that had hardened into something more like anger. He should have known better than to have played this game with somebody so close to the family. Before and since, it had always been relative strangers.

The problem, Lewis knew, was that these women were ashamed of being what they were, and though he was adept at disinhibiting them, there were women everywhere – women like Zara, women, he feared, like Kate – who wanted to turn other women into victims, and use them as pawns in this war they were waging. Lewis peered back around the window frame. By now, Kate and the other girl had gone. He hoped that she had only come to show off the house to her friend, that her being here had nothing to do with him, and he hoped that she thought of him only ever fleetingly, if at all.

The three men went back to London that evening, and on the way Lewis texted a few of his old university friends, who he hadn't seen for a while. He needed distracting, didn't want to go back to the flat on his own. He wished he were driving, rather than sitting in the back like a child, while Alasdair and William sat in silence, listening to the low tones of the radio. His phone vibrated in his pocket, three times in fairly quick succession. All three of the friends were away, unable to meet. He wondered whether they were together, but dismissed the thought: they would have invited him. They'd talked about going skiing, last year, but the plan hadn't come together.

He needed to do some exercise. It would make him feel better, releasing some of the pent-up, anxious energy coursing through his body. His chest felt tight, as if he'd been doing press-ups. Probably, it was from lifting those boxes. Nicole was always telling him to try yoga – but the thought of Nicole brought into his mind the image of Max, and then of Kate staring up at him, and he felt a little sick.

Lewis didn't normally drink alone, but when Alasdair left him at the flat with the stag head and a box of belongings he had collected from the house, he opened a beer and sat on the sofa with the television on, scrolling through his phone. One of the friends he had texted had uploaded a picture of himself wearing salopettes and skiing goggles. Lewis opened another beer and tortured himself a little by looking at photos of the holiday, before he found himself looking at Nicole's Instagram, then Max's. He'd been sitting here for nearly half an hour, now, and was three bottles down. When, scrolling down Max's page he found pictures of Kate, he slowed down, holding the phone close to his face, trying to erase from his mind the vision of her looking up at him, replace it instead with these stolen images.

While with one hand he kept on flicking through the photos, pausing and zooming, with his other he undid his jeans and slipped it into his boxers, feeling the subtle ridges of his tattoo. He thought about fucking her, putting his hand around his dick, closing his eyes and then opening them to look at those pictures every time his thoughts were interrupted. He was too drunk and too numb to stay hard, though, and eventually he fell asleep with his jeans still on and unbelted and his right hand down the front of his boxers.

40

Zara had finished shooting just before they went to Bisley House for Christmas, and in the new year they'd moved on to edits. It was the end of January when at last she got in touch with Kate, asking if she wanted to meet. She'd given herself the afternoon off because she needed to recuperate, she said. It was a cold, bright day, and they met at the Sun Gate of Battersea Park. 'Equally inconvenient for us both,' Zara had said when she'd suggested it. She was wearing a knee-length fur coat and sunglasses with a baseball cap.

'It's second-hand,' she said, brushing the coat, 'I couldn't buy fur new. Titus would never forgive me.' Kate was not sure what she'd been expecting, but Zara did not offer an apology for having fallen out of contact, but rather an explanation. To Kate, this was a relief. The thought of the message she'd left, and the fact that she had assumed some kind of right to work on the film, just because of the charity Zara had already shown her, made her feel embarrassed.

'We were terribly behind,' she said. 'We've had to work like dogs to catch up, which is why you haven't heard from me in rather a long time. I'm sure I'm overestimating my own importance, but I wonder if you were at a very vulnerable stage, when all of this started. The film.'

'You know how it goes,' Kate said. 'Sometimes it's fine, sometimes it isn't.'

'I do know. I don't mind telling you I went into the worst depression I've had for years, when I first started trying to map it out. I don't know whether Max told you, but there's a rape scene. Right at the beginning. Very graphic, very violent. It brought me right back to the day it happened, I thought I'd never find my way out.'

'He didn't tell me,' Kate said, surprised. Zara, though, was not.

'He probably chooses to believe it doesn't exist,' she said. They were walking towards the river, along the gravel path that crossed the park, and by the fountains Zara stopped to buy coffee for them both.

'It's made me very angry,' Zara went on, 'which I think is good. It's healthy. It's made me think of you rather a lot, which is why I suppose I don't feel that we've been out of touch for very long. You've been in my thoughts.'

They were walking side by side, up the steps towards the river. In the flower beds the crocuses had forced themselves through the cold, winter soil, and were just beginning to bud, white and light purple.

'I wonder if you mind me asking,' Zara said, 'do you feel angry?'

'I don't know,' Kate said carefully, 'which means probably I don't.'

Zara nodded. 'Fear is far easier to live with. And if there

is anger, it's safer turned inwards. It's taken me years to realise that. Too many years.'

'Better late than never,' Kate said, because she couldn't think of anything less trite.

'You see, I'm not sure that's true,' Zara said. She looked sidelong at Kate. 'Did I tell you that mine is dead? The one who raped me. And I never confronted him. So it really is too late; I have no outlet, no living cause. It's all buried, and now that I'm here to excavate it, it's too late to really matter.'

'Not necessarily. Maybe that's why you're making the film.'

'Maybe,' said Zara. 'But I can't help but wonder, what if I'd spoken up at the time, before it was too late? Who might I have helped? Who else suffered because of me?'

Kate did not answer. She had no answer. They walked in silence a little longer, to the edge of the park and along the riverfront. Zara took Kate's empty coffee cup from her and threw it in the bin. Kate pulled her scarf up around her face. They were a long way from the entrance to the park.

'What about your boyfriend, are you still with him?'

'Yes,' Kate said. 'You've never met him, have you? It's been about six months now.'

'You'll have to come for dinner soon.'

Andrew hadn't even met Alison yet. She imagined him now, sitting down for dinner at Latimer Crescent, elbows on the table and playing with his wristwatch, taking in the posters and the awards, wearing a half-smile behind his hands that only Kate could see. She flushed, warmth flooding her stomach at the thought of him.

'I'd like that,' she said, before saying, dumbly: 'He likes food.'

'Sensible boy,' said Zara.

Thinking of Andrew made Kate want to know more about the film. She wanted to be able to tell him about it, when they saw each other later that night. He would be interested, impressed by what Zara had divulged to Kate.

'What's the film called?'

'*Late Surfacing*,' said Zara.

'I like it.'

'I didn't come up with it,' Zara said. The film seemed no longer to be at the forefront of her mind. 'Have you thought about whether you would confront him?'

'Who?'

'Your rapist,' Zara said. 'Hypothetically. If you saw him again.'

'I don't think I would,' Kate said. 'I don't see how I could.'

Zara's silence widened the distance between them: she walking at a serene pace, wrapped in her vintage furs, her arms crossed at her chest and leather gloves holding the edges of the coat around her: Kate, her hands thrust deep into her pockets, drew her shoulders up around her ears.

'I can see why you're thinking about it,' Kate went on, 'now that you've been forced to. But I've been trying all this time to escape what happened. Or at least to find a way to live with it so that it doesn't dominate me. And

I don't see how making myself lose more than I already have is going to help.'

'Why would you be losing more?'

Kate had led them to the other side of the park, now, the side that was closer to her bus stop.

'Just emotionally,' Kate said. 'It's exposing. Makes you so vulnerable.'

'Particularly if you know him.'

Kate tensed, but kept on walking. She only ever remembered giving the impression that her attacker was a stranger, but perhaps she had said something to make Zara think otherwise. Or perhaps Zara was talking about her own rapist. She felt a little queasy, the taste of foamed milk and coffee coating her tongue, caffeine in her system.

'I don't know,' Zara was saying now, 'it's just that I regret never saying anything, that's all. There could have been countless others.'

'That's his responsibility, not yours.' Kate was only repeating what she'd been told, but in fact it was far easier to believe it, when she wasn't talking about herself.

'Did you know that you can report to the police anonymously?' Zara went on. 'I didn't know that. I found it out, while I was doing research for the film. They keep it on file, but they don't even need to take your name, a friend can do it for you, just over the phone, and leave their details. They just need a way of getting hold of you if there are any other reports, and they want to use your evidence.' She paused. 'If you wanted to, you know, I would be happy to do it for you,' she said.

Kate had been watching her shoelace loosen as Zara spoke. She stopped, now, and knelt down to retie it. Zara stopped too, stood by and waited as Kate slowly wound the lace back into its bow. Kate glanced up at Zara's black leather boots, the thick heels, looked down at her own muddied trainers. There were so many worlds between them. She stood up.

'I didn't know that,' Kate said. 'But the principle is the same. It's his responsibility to stop, not mine.' Her voice, now, was louder than she meant it to be. 'It's not my problem.'

Zara bit her lip, then nodded. 'If that's how you feel,' she said.

41

When she saw Andrew later that night, she didn't tell him about her meeting with Zara. She didn't want to think about their conversation, much less encourage any curiosity about what it had been like to see her after all this time. Since she'd got back to London after Christmas, they had both been working long hours, he on a film he would be entering for festivals in the summer. That evening, he didn't call until nearly ten to say he was finished, and she arrived at his flat half an hour later with leftovers and a half-bottle of wine. When he opened the door he looked exhausted, dark circles beneath his eyes, sweat marks on his T-shirt.

She heated up the chilli while he showered, and he came in wearing joggers and a thick blue sweater, smelling of soap and aftershave.

'You didn't have to make yourself smell nice just for me,' she said.

'Trust me. I really did.' He put his hands behind his head, inhaling appreciatively. 'I smell good.'

'That's my chilli con carne,' said Kate.

They were hungry, and they ate quickly, he shovelling

chilli onto his fork while she asked him about the shoot that day. The film was only twelve minutes long, and the crew was small, but it was the first time since he'd been a student that he'd been able to get the funding together to make something of his own.

'We're going to the Ponds, tomorrow,' Andrew said. 'In Hampstead. I really regret that scene. It's gonna be freezing.'

Kate knew the scene he was talking about – he'd shown her an early version of the script, back in the autumn. It was the first in which the two main characters were filmed together. Kate had met both of the actors, at Andrew's flat before Christmas. Megan had a slender neck, long, thin legs, and probably no scars on her thighs. Kate could not imagine her putting her eye to the open top of a bottle she'd emptied alone, or bolting upright in the middle of the night, chest seized, gasping for the light. She thought of Megan breaking the still surface of the pond with her bare feet.

He was looking at her. 'What's up?' he said.

'Nothing, I was just thinking about when it's finished,' she said.

'I can't even contemplate it,' he said. 'Feels like an impossibility.'

After they'd eaten Andrew got into bed. Kate brushed her teeth with the toothbrush she'd started leaving at his house, which neither of them had acknowledged, and got into bed beside him. He turned towards her, kissed her a little, put his hand under her T-shirt in a gesture of sleepy arousal, but left it resting there on her belly without moving until his breathing deepened and he was asleep. Kate lay still, eyes open, looking up at the ceiling, not wanting to disturb the warm hand on her stomach. Now, his hand was covering the breadth of her waist, offering desire and protection. It took her a long time to fall asleep.

Kate liked to let him in, but only so far. She was glad she hadn't told Andrew about seeing Zara. She hadn't even told him that she and Claire had gone over to Bisley House in December, since part of her knew that he would consider such actions to be a form of self-harm. He didn't understand the need she had for recollection, and nor did he understand the sense of control it gave her.

She didn't quite put her meeting with Zara to the back of her mind, but she did at least find a way to rationalise it. She told herself that Zara had resurfaced not to force some kind of a confession out of Kate, but because she genuinely believed that Kate would feel better if she put her status as a victim to good use. Zara did not know about Lewis. It was possible that she suspected, but she had no way of knowing for sure. She knew that if Zara ever asked her outright, she would deny it. In protecting him, she was protecting herself. This had always been her instinct, and she was more certain of it than ever.

In early Spring, Kate invited Max and Nicole for dinner. This, she told Max over the phone, was as close to a flat-warming as she was willing to offer.

'You can even bring Elias,' she said, and then immediately regretted.

Neither Nicole nor Elias had been to the flat before, and they both did their best to find nice things to say about it as Kate showed them round. Elias unfurled the blackout blind in Claire's bedroom.

'These are really good,' he said earnestly. 'They really don't let in any light whatsoever.'

Kate felt unexpectedly moved by his sincerity, and took him to the bathroom to show him the window from which it was possible to see the fruit and vegetable shop on the street below while showering.

'You've lost weight,' Nicole said to Kate, when they were back in the kitchen. 'You're a shadow of your former self.'

'That's not what that means,' said Max.

'No, I mean it. You look really well,' Nicole insisted, ignoring Max.

'Yeah, but a shadow of your former –'

'Where's Andrew?' Nicole cut across Max. 'Did Max tell you I'm heartbroken? George and I broke up.'

'Oh, I'm really sorry,' Kate said. She did not know who George was.

'It's fine, actually he's much more heartbroken than I am. Poor guy. But you're still with Andrew?'

'I am. But I don't know if he'll be able to come,' Kate said. 'He's working on this film. He'll come if they finish on time, though, and he might bring his flatmate, too.'

Kate had invited Shona for dinner when she'd been at Andrew's flat the week before, but she realised now that she was half hoping Andrew wouldn't bring her. She'd made a curry she knew Shona would like, just in case she did turn up, but she wasn't at all sure what she would make of Nicole and Elias, or even Max. Elias was wearing his velvet jacket again, and Kate was relieved that she'd managed to manoeuvre Claire into the seat next to Max. Nicole wanted to know all about Andrew's film, and Kate told her and Elias the gist of the story as she understood it, playfully pulling a face when she got to the part about the semi-naked woman walking into the water.

'Does that bother you?' Nicole said.

'Oh no,' Kate said, shrugging. 'It's just a film.'

'Hm,' Nicole said.

Opposite, Claire was giggling at something Max had told her about his app. Kate reached for the wine and topped up Nicole's glass, and asked her what had happened with George, knowing that this would fill the time between now and dinner being ready. As she set the timer for the rice, she checked her messages, but Andrew hadn't texted, so she turned her phone face down on the table.

When the doorbell rang, they'd nearly finished dessert. By now, Kate was no longer expecting Andrew to arrive, and had stopped checking her phone, but at the sound of the bell she leapt straight up to get the door. He was drunk, and he grinned when he saw her, picked her up in a bear hug.

'I'm here!' he announced. 'Happy birthday!'

'It's not my birthday,' Kate said, 'so you can put me down. Is it just you?'

'Shona says she's very sorry she can't come,' Andrew said diplomatically, 'but she has somewhere better to be.'

He carried her across the threshold and then dumped her, with a dull thud, in the hallway.

'You've had a head start,' Max said, as he got up and found himself gathered in the same bear hug with which Andrew had greeted Kate. Max patted him on the back, a little desperately. 'Put me down and I'll get you some food.'

Andrew sat in Kate's chair and started to eat. Kate, who was a little startled by his drunken apparition, went into her bedroom to get another chair. When she came back, Max was asking Andrew about the shoot that day.

'Big day today,' Andrew said, his mouth full of food, 'big shoot. It was so fucking good, oh my God.'

'So you've been celebrating?'

He nodded enthusiastically. 'Yuh,' he said.

'Kate was just telling me about your film,' Elias said, sitting back in his chair.

'Yeah, it's really good,' Andrew said, nodding again.

'You look a bit demented,' Kate said. Andrew ignored her.

'It *sounds* good,' Elias said. 'Particularly with all the nudity.'

Andrew turned to look at Elias, noticing him properly for the first time.

'All the nudity?' he said.

'The scene in the pond.'

'Oh, yeah, but that's only a bit.'

Elias smiled knowingly. 'Sure. Did you get to pick the actress, too?'

Andrew frowned, put down his fork. Kate looked at the fork. She'd never seen him interrupt a meal before. He turned back to Elias.

'What are you saying?' he said. 'It's not a porno.'

'I know, mate,' Elias said. 'I'm just interested in the casting process.'

'There is some really good feminist pornography, actually,' Nicole said breezily. Andrew and Elias both turned and looked at her. 'What?' she said. 'Women wank too.'

Max took advantage of the momentary stunned silence to swoop in and grab Elias's arm.

'Let's have a cigarette,' he said.

'I've given up,' said Elias.

'OK, so come and watch me have a cigarette,' Max said, jerking Elias to his feet.

'Who's the wanker?' Andrew said, as Max and Elias went downstairs.

'He's a liability,' said Nicole imperiously. 'I don't know why Max still hangs around with him. Probably makes him feel better about himself.'

It wasn't long after their cigarette that Max and Elias left, Max hugging Kate and apologising to her.

'We'll do something just the two of us, next time,' he said. 'Come to Latimer Crescent. You haven't been there for ages.'

'Years,' Kate said, knowing that Max would not understand what she meant by this. She was tired, and she was glad that everybody was leaving. 'Thank you for coming,' she said to Max. Not long after they'd gone, Claire went to bed, and Andrew went to have a shower. They could hear him, singing and colliding with the walls of the cubicle. Nicole, though, stayed with Kate to finish the rest of the wine. She sipped at her glass, unhurried.

'I could see that what Elias said upset you,' she said, when they were alone. Her directness reminded Kate immediately of Zara. 'I'm sorry about him.'

'It's OK,' Kate said. 'There are people like him everywhere. I'm glad Max took him outside, though.'

'He's a good boy,' Nicole said. She sounded a little more like a proud pet owner than sister, but Kate saw that she was being sincere. 'He's really got his shit together, these last few months. I think you helped him, you know.'

'I don't know if that's true.'

'You did. He looks up to you. And you getting back on your feet after, you know, whatever you've been dealing with. I think he wanted to do the same.'

Kate was touched.

'He's always had a sore spot for you,' Nicole said.

'You mean a soft spot.'

'Precisely. I don't think we need to worry about him, though, Kate. He's going to be fine. Well, so long as he doesn't get a freaky tattoo. That's when we know shit's getting bad.'

Kate looked at Nicole. 'What?' she said.

Nicole laughed. 'Oh, hah, didn't Max ever tell you? That's what Lewis did when he had his little breakdown a few years ago. Just after his parents got divorced; he was still a teenager.'

'Max never mentioned it to me,' Kate said cautiously.

'Some pretentious quote,' Nicole said. 'Right next to his dick, so he says. I've never seen it, obviously.' She grimaced; put her wine glass back on the table. 'Lewis only told me about it because he was pissed. But that's real breakdown territory. Can you imagine?'

42

Kate had not been back to Latimer Crescent since the rape, and when Max messaged her the morning after the dinner party to ask again if she would come and see him, she replied that she would meet him in town. She had avoided returning to the house in order to protect herself from the inevitable reminders it contained, but she also knew that while she stayed away, there were parts of her memory she could not properly access. Without returning, there would be no means of recovering that part of herself that she had left there, embedded in Zara's mattress, two summers before.

She knew that she could not avoid it forever. At the beginning of summer, when Max had mentioned that his parents were travelling, she phoned and asked him if she could come and visit. She'd hardly had reason to go to west London this past year, and as she walked from the Tube to Max's road she realised that she had forgotten its contradictions: the bright white mansions dwarfing tower blocks, hash cutting through the smell of expensive perfume, the ubiquity of dog shit.

As she turned onto Latimer Crescent she knew that she was seeking some form of completion, rather than an ending. But to her frustration, she found that she could not remember whether it had been this side of the street or the other that she'd walked on, when she and Lewis had come back from the corner shop that night. The road did not curve quite as she remembered it, and the houses, which she always thought of as standing alone, were in fact semi-detached. She had not realised how little care she had taken over her memories.

When Max opened the door he was wearing a fleece-lined sweatshirt and tracksuit bottoms, and even though it was sunny that morning his skin looked pale, a little grey beneath his eyes, which were bloodshot. He stretched and smiled, and hugged her; his neck smelt of roll-ups and laundry. He apologised for the state of the house: he'd been inside all week, working on a deadline. She followed him through to the kitchen, where the sink was full of dirty dishes and cold cloudy water. Max made Kate a coffee by pouring an undetermined quantity of instant granules from an open jar straight into a mug, the rim of which he rubbed on his jumper before filling from the kettle.

'Mum went mad, doing this film,' he said. 'But it's finished now, so they've gone away. It's been quite fun without them.' He brushed the kitchen table with its light dusting of white powder.

'She told me about the film,' Kate said. 'You didn't say it was about rape.'

'Didn't I? I think I thought it would be triggering,' Max said. 'Cigarette?' He looked at her.

The air inside the house was sticking in her throat, and

Kate did not want to disrupt the delicate balance of their interaction, so she went with him out to the table in the back garden, where Max rolled them each a cigarette. Kate hadn't smoked in a while, didn't really want to now, and the tobacco gave her a light head rush which settled quickly in her stomach as sickness.

'So Embers is going well,' Max said. 'We've been trialling it in Bisley – they've got the right demographic. I'm thinking of pitching it a little bit more like a social network for the older generation, rather than a dating app. Sort of Friends Reunited but with the potential for romance.' He flicked his ash. 'You and me, maybe, meeting on Embers in our seventies.'

Kate was struggling to concentrate. She had been out here, over there, by the wall, when she'd told Lewis she was going for ice, when he'd told her he was coming with her. Or had he asked her if he could come? She stubbed out her half-smoked cigarette. She realised that Max had stopped talking; silence grew between them.

'I need to piss,' she said.

She went back through the kitchen and instead of using the ground-floor toilet she climbed the carpeted stairs. She climbed as she had climbed before, but with the knowledge now that this was an act of self-determination, that she was acting both out of herself and for herself. And she saw her body and her clothing not as it was now, but as it had been that day two summers before: ripped jeans, bare feet, face fuller and rounder, hair longer, the flesh of her thighs unmarked by the knives she had since put in it. That woman had been so much a child, but more vulnerable for her belief that she was already fully grown. Twenty-two, still living at home. How she wanted to warn away that soft shadow, gather it up and carry it back down the stairs, away from this place. But it could not be discouraged, and its home, if it had one now, was the ground beneath her feet, the path they were taking.

On the first-floor landing, she pushed open the door to Zara's bedroom. Still the crisp white sheets, still the softly piled cushions, the glass-topped dressing table with its neatly boxed powders and creams, and the far doorway to the glistening white bathroom closed. The smell was the same, too, of amber, spiced powder, the window opened just a crack to let the fresh air circulate. It had been through that crack that Kate had sent her soul to join the voices in the garden as Lewis had moved on top of her, so that it might carry on without her. In her mind the room was always in the half-light, as it had been that night. But now of course it was late morning and it was bright and she saw that the room was sparser: only the radio by the bed, dimmer lights set into the white ceiling rather than the lampshade she had pictured. What else had she misremembered?

From the window, she could see Max playing with his lighter. Kate stepped back into the middle of the room and lay down on the bed, looking up at the ceiling. She had been lying like this, perpendicular to the edge of the bed. She had thought afterwards that if they both had wanted this to happen, rather than just him, then they might have got into the bed, lying with their heads on the pillows, or bodies under the covers, rather than at this perverse angle, her legs hanging off the side of the bed, pressed together but pulled roughly apart.

The anxiety grew, as she lay there, but she inhaled slowly and deeply, blanketing the metallic tautness with new breath so that it dulled just a little. Memories crowded. The smell of aftershave, the burden of an immovable weight. That red ribbon, that rawness. But they did not undo her. If her perception really was so delicate, if it had been shattered once before, then she could shatter it again. There would be other shades of red, other filters through which she could apprehend the world, and she would be more powerful for her knowledge of them. These images would never leave her, but they could be reshaped, written into new narratives, overlaid with new meanings – meanings that were not the end of her.

Slowly, still breathing deeply, she unbuttoned and unzipped her jeans, pulling the waistband down around her hips, and putting her hand in the front of her knickers. Taste yourself, he had said, and she did so now, rubbing where she had become wet and then putting her fingers in her mouth. Your cunt is tight, he had said. Your cunt is tight, those words a knife, any of the knives she had held since then. His readings of her body, of the involuntary welcome it offered him: tight, wet, warm, this was what she could stand the least, and where the memory of those words seared through her body there was pain, guilt and pain, mingled indistinguishably with the horrors of bodily pleasure.

Afterwards, she went back downstairs, giving Max

no explanation for her prolonged absence. She wondered whether she was somehow using him by apparently coming here to spend time with him when instead she was creeping around the upper floors of his house, exploiting his openness to gain access to her own obscure memories. But she did not care; she was feeling reckless. Max opened beers for them both, and Kate sat back, watched him as she swigged her drink.

'Do you know,' she said, 'I think the last time I came to your parents' house was for that party. Do you remember?'

'Christmas?' said Max.

'No, not Bernadette's house. The last time I was here.'

'Didn't you come here last Christmas too?'

'No,' Kate said again. 'It was summer. Two summers ago.'

'Oh,' Max said, 'is that really the last time?'

Kate nodded. 'And do you remember, I left in the morning before you woke up.'

Max shook his head. 'Maybe,' he said. 'Not sure. I remember a lot of limes. I think that was at the height of my mojito era.'

'A good era.'

'Among the best. That must have been just after Rupert tried to kill himself.' His directness took Kate by surprise; he, unlike her, usually avoided using such blunt markers. 'You looked after me, that year.'

'Did I?'

'Yes, oh my God, yes. You remember all those slasher films we watched?' He pointed up. 'Right here, in the living room.'

'Were they slasher films?'

'I don't know, but everybody died.'

Kate laughed.

'You should come to the premiere,' Max said suddenly. 'Of Mum's film. They're screening it at one of the film festivals next month. Say no, if you think it's a terrible idea. But you know, maybe it will help. Or maybe it will just be fun, which is the same thing, really. What do you think?'

43

Kate left Max's house feeling lighter. She had needed to do this: to make herself revisit the scene of the crime, to confront it without fear. That was progress, surely. Being in the house had not quite overwhelmed her, and already she felt she could go back and face it again. The second time would be easier, and then the third. And if she could be in the place where it happened, perhaps she could once again be wholly at ease in Max's company. No longer would she baulk at the mention of Lewis's name, no longer would she freeze up or flee whenever she was reminded of him.

She didn't quite know why she had mentioned the party. There were moments when she felt like she wanted to expose Lewis. But it wasn't because she wanted justice, rather there was a perverse part of her that wanted Max to feel responsible for what had happened to her. For so long he seemed to have been able to detach himself from her suffering, which for all its strength had only ever belonged to her and not to him, and she wanted him to carry the burden with her, but only temporarily, just so he could feel for himself just how heavy it was, so that he would give her the respect she felt she deserved for having borne it all herself these last two years.

It was the same part of her, she knew, that had spoken up the night before she had moved out, and had told him about the tattoo. She had been playing a dangerous game, just as she was playing precariously with their shared memories when she'd started quizzing him about the night of the party. She had given him shards, only shards of information, she would not give him all of it. Even though she sometimes longed to, she could not bear to surrender this most private piece of her history, which she knew she would have to do if she revealed to him the whole of it.

When Max had asked her if she wanted to see *Late Surfacing*, Kate had said yes straight away. He said that she could bring Andrew, if she wanted, but she told him that she wanted to see it with him: just the two of them. It was Andrew's sister's birthday, and she knew he was annoyed that she was going to the premiere instead of coming to celebrate: this would have been the first time she'd been for dinner with his family. She'd apologised, told him she would make it up to him, but that this was something she needed to do.

She was nervous about the film, particularly after her last meeting with Zara. She did not want to see too much of her own experience reflected there, or any of the details she had divulged to Zara in the months following her disclosure. But she was sure that Zara would have drawn on some of those conversations for her material, however loosely, and if she was right about this, she didn't want

Max to see it without her. She was not sure whether this was because she hated the thought of him imagining her being raped, or because, if that was what was going to happen, she hated the thought of not bearing witness.

She knew there was a strong risk that Lewis would be there. She had to prepare herself as best she could. Before she left the flat, she swallowed three beta blockers, and then took another two on the Tube. Three was the prescribed daily dose, but three was never enough; she stopped at five because six would make her too tired. She put on lipstick which was almost exactly the same shade as her lips, and perfume, both of which provided her with invisible protection.

Kate had borrowed from Shona a pair of dark pink silk trousers and green block-heeled shoes, which were a size too big for her. It was a cool summer evening, and the coarse silk moved roughly against the tops of her thighs as she walked quickly up the steps of Leicester Square Tube station and towards the Odeon. Though she had worked on the sets of half a dozen films by now – and many more television shows – she had never yet been invited to a premiere. Max was waiting for her; she met him at the edge of the railings.

'So handsome,' she said, as she kissed him on the cheek. He did look good in his dark suit: his black hair was thick and clean, and his skin looked a little less grey than it had the last time she'd seen him. Though the entrance to the Odeon was cordoned off there were few spectators: the film did not have a starry cast and the people who had gathered round to watch seemed mostly to be tourists. There was an air of excitement to it, though. Kate caught sight of her and Max's reflection in the glass doorway – both of them sharp, well turned out, fooling everybody, including themselves – and she was glad then that she'd come. She owed it to herself not to punish herself, and as Max put his arm around her shoulders and hugged her to him, she felt that with him beside her there was very little they could not conquer.

The foyer smelt of popcorn, faintly of bleach, and as Max gave their names at the box office Kate watched the holograms spinning across the carpet. Because this was Leicester Square, Kate had expected something grander than the usual carpet tiles and stacked paper cups, but the familiarity was reassuring. She could easily be in the entrance to the cinema near her mother's house, except that now she was wearing silk instead of a school skirt, and her name was on the guest list.

When they went into the auditorium, though, it was even bigger than she had expected, its ceiling arching high above the red velvet-covered seats, the lights already half lowered. It was only once they were in their seats that she saw Lewis. The dull shock she felt at the sight of him was nothing like the panic she had experienced in Finsbury Park the summer before; here, from a distance, sunk in his seat next to his father, his back hunched and chin doubled as he tore at his thumbnail with his teeth, he was drained of power.

Kate and Max sat in the two seats Nicole was saving for them, Kate on the end of the row. A few seats to their right and behind, Zara was sitting with William on one side and a woman Kate didn't recognise on the other. Rupert was there, too, wearing glasses. Max leaned across and tugged at his mother's arm; she reached out and clasped his hand, before she saw Kate.

'Hello, darling,' she said. 'Max said you might be coming.' She was too far from Kate to touch her, but she reached out her hand anyway. 'I'll come and find you afterwards.'

The lights darkened and the screen widened as the words *Late Surfacing* appeared on it followed by Zara's name in bright white against the black background.

It was not the first time Kate had seen her own experience played out in front of her, and it did not frighten her to know that it was coming. No, this she could handle: she had been right to come here. There was a thrill in knowing that an entire theatre would be witnessing the violence of the attacker, the agony of his victim, and she would see now how they coped with it. She knew that there would be those who wanted to look away and that she was stronger than them. She knew that there would be those who would be fascinated, and that they were weaker than her.

As the screen went momentarily black, Kate imagined first her own face stretched across it, metres high, then her body: all of it, bare. Arms, with a small showing of muscle under fat; the rounded belly and small breasts. Doughy white thighs, pale red ladders leading the way to her cunt. In her seat, she suppressed a shudder, but the image detained her for only a second, before the film began. It opened not on a woman's body but on a street; grey, lightless. The camera followed a man, dark hair and broad-shouldered, as he walked. The rapist was called Jack, Max had told her, and she wondered whether this was supposed to be him.

Max had shared with her what sparse details he knew: the rape would be happening in the first twenty minutes, so they were both prepared. The man stopped, and the camera stopped, and he walked into a shop, whose bell clanged loudly. Music was playing from the basement. He seemed to know the man inside, who was tattooed and bearded, with a bull ring in his nose. The camera, which sat just behind the man with the short black hair, panned around and took in the shop: it was a tattoo parlour, posters and designs lining the brick walls, and the bull-ringed man was leaning on the glass display case in the corner.

'Decision?' said Bull Ring.

'Just show me one more time,' said the short-haired man.

Bull Ring reached behind the till and pulled out a large book, filled with letters in different fonts. In the corner of her vision, in the row behind, Kate saw Zara move, just a little, and Kate thought for a moment that she might be watching her. But when Kate turned to look Zara's gaze was fixed on the screen, where Bull Ring was taking the short-haired man into a back room.

'How many of these have you done?' the man said. He sat down on the chair, and began to unbuckle his belt, pulled his jeans down to the tops of his thighs.

'More than you've had hot dinners. It'll hurt, though, where you're getting it. And you'll be out of action for a little bit.'

To her right, Kate saw Nicole lean across and whisper to Max. She was nodding her head at Lewis, and she was laughing. Max's face was lit up by the screen, briefly bright as the shot showed the man filling in a form in blotchy black capitals, JACK EVANS. For the few seconds that Max was illuminated she saw that he understood everything, and that he possessed in that moment the same brutal clarity from which she had ultimately tried to shield him.

This was her doing. The pieces of information she had fed to Zara and to Max, trading on the now worthless currency of her trauma, had come together at last, and the image they created was all too clear. She knew now why she'd felt that Zara was looking at her. She had taken what Kate had confided in her and, without her permission, she had used it. Zara did not yet know it, but she had sent a fault line through the Rippon family: those who knew, and who did not; those who might forgive, those who would not. And at its centre, Max, who wanted only ever to believe that people acted with goodness and grace, who wanted never to look into the truth of what a man was capable of doing.

Now, Max turned back to Nicole, and Kate knew that he was asking her to repeat what she had just said; of course he would not quite be able to believe it. And in the moment that he turned, she stood, and she walked as quickly as she could back up the aisle, through the double doors, out into the foyer, and into the mass of strangers who moved beneath the electric lights of Leicester Square.

44

Max knew what was coming. After Kate fled, he knew there could be no other outcome than this. He'd made to follow her but had slumped back in his seat, transfixed both by the hope that he might yet be proved wrong, and by the inability to face her. He was immobilised, unable to look away, but unable to process what was happening as the film reeled on. Max knew what was going to happen to the woman on the screen, and who was going to do it to her. Doors closed. Keys turned, and as each exit was blocked he felt his voice strangling in his throat, wanting to shout out at the screen, wanting to tell her to get out, to run, while she still could.

The rape itself seemed to be over very quickly, but it was shot with merciless clarity: a single blow to the face, the crack of a skull against the edge of a step, the sound of fabric ripping. And, in that moment, he imagined that it was Kate who was there on the floor. For a second, just a second, it was not this fictional rapist, but he himself who had pinned her there. The image burned across his mind, filled him with a sick self-loathing, but before he could process any further it was over. It was already over, and he had been unable to look away. Disbelief compelled him to keep watching, and the conviction that surely it could get no worse than this; surely it would be better, once it was all over. But there was worse still to come. It was not the attack in isolation, but what it did afterwards: the way it shattered perception, distorted senses, disabled the ability to trust and love and be loved, drained the world of colour and light.

But then the screen went black, applause filled the auditorium. Behind Max, Zara rested her head briefly on William's shoulder, and then stood up. As she bowed her head to the audience, she looked at Max, saw the seat next to him. A shadow of something like disappointment passed across her face. Surely she did not know; she wouldn't have put it in the film, had she known.

'She doesn't know,' Nicole said. She started to laugh. 'She has no idea. Poor Lewis. He's going to think it's about him.'

Nicole did not know that she had voiced what Max had not yet allowed himself to think. He had not yet turned to look at Lewis, for fear of what he would see. But he had to look. He had already wasted too much time, neither look-ing nor seeing.

'It is about him,' Max said, his voice barely audible over the sound of applause. 'It's about him and Kate.'

Nicole looked back at him blankly. Max did not clarify. Soon she would understand.

'What are you talking about? Max?' Nicole was digging into his ribs. Max didn't answer. He remembered that first conversation he and Kate had had about what had happened to her, when he had tried to ask her. He felt a flicker of anger. He'd asked, but he should have asked again. Perhaps she had seen the relief in his expression, when she had cut him off, but she'd let him believe that she didn't want him to ask. None of this mattered now, though. Nicole was saying his name, pinching his arm. He had always thought that he would be able to recognise a man capable of rape. But Lewis. He had never thought that a handsome man would need to rape anybody. The credits had stopped rolling and the lights came up. Max pushed Nicole's hand away and twisted in his seat. There was Lewis, a few seats away, sitting beside his father, his expression inscrutable. Max stared at him. He ignored Nicole, who was snapping her fingers in his face, and continued looking at Lewis until Lewis looked back at him. Max did not break his gaze until he was sure that Lewis knew.

45

When Kate left the cinema, she walked, blindly, not knowing where she should be going. She was numb, barely aware of the blisters that were rubbing against the backs of her borrowed shoes, and of the fact that it had been raining. At the entrance to Leicester Square Underground, she stopped. This station offered a route home for her, but also a black tunnel. Her phone vibrated; she shut it off, tried to shut off the thought of the train hurtling out of the darkness. At this moment she could see no futures available to her, no possible means for her to continue to exist.

Knowing only that she must keep moving, she found herself at the river. On Waterloo Bridge she stopped and leaned over the barrier, not caring that she was covering herself in filth. Her mind was flying, detached from her body. How this body had failed her; how many more times could she allow it to fail her? No longer did she want to punish it. She wanted to relieve its suffering.

The water was clouded and foaming at the river's edges where debris, feathers, cans, pieces of plastic were caught on the stony shore. She closed her eyes and allowed the pressure of the stone barrier against her stomach to deepen the nausea until she thought she would throw up over the edge of the bridge and into the Thames. The river would swallow up her vomit, could swallow her up, too. A lorry hurtled along the bridge behind her.

Not now.

If she stepped back now, she would only be robbing herself yet again of what Lewis had taken from her, of what Zara's film had also taken – her agency. Of course it would be a kind of freedom, too, to take that step back, or that leap – but what was the point in making such a choice if she disappeared in silence? It was this thought that carried her to the south end of the bridge, and she stood there with her back to the river, head in her hands. If only in this moment, in this small way, she could direct her own path, and for now, this would have to be enough: deciding to step away from the bridge, to cross the road, to walk, and to continue walking.

When she got to Andrew's door, she leaned on the bell and let it ring. The sun hadn't yet set, but she didn't know what time it was. She kept ringing, but there was no answer. Only now did she remember that Andrew was out celebrating, that of course he wouldn't be at the flat. But there were footsteps inside and then Shona opened the front door. She looked at Kate, the streaks of make-up, and without waiting for her to speak, took her inside.

'Andrew isn't here,' she said, though she knew Kate knew this already.

'I forgot,' Kate said. She was standing unsteadily in the hallway, unsure whether to stay. Shona was wearing fresh make-up, she realised. 'Are you going to the dinner?'

Shona checked her watch. 'I'm meeting them for drinks. Do you want to come with me?' She looked at Kate again, glanced down at the hems of the pink trousers she had lent her. 'Why don't you come and sit for a minute?'

Kate sat at the kitchen table, trying to focus on her hands, while Shona got her a glass of water.

'I don't know you that well,' said Shona, sitting down next to Kate. 'But if you want to talk, we'll talk. Or if you just want to sit, we'll sit.'

Kate nodded. 'I don't want to come to the party,' she said.

'OK. Do you want to stay here?'

'Yes, please.'

'You want me to stay with you?'

'No, it's OK.'

'You want me to call Andrew?'

'No,' Kate said firmly.

'He'll want to know something's up.'

'Don't call him,' Kate said. 'Please. I don't want to talk. I'm just tired.'

'I can see that,' said Shona. She reached across, put her hand on Kate's chin, lifted it, and looked at her. 'Hold your head up. And I mean this with kindness.'

Shona's gaze was direct; Kate nodded, sat up just a little.

'You sit here,' said Shona, getting up. 'I gotta do my hair, and that's gonna take half an hour at least. I'll come check on you.'

'I think it looks nice,' Kate said.

'Then you really do need some sleep,' Shona said. 'Go to bed. Get some rest.'

Kate went to Andrew's room, and got under his covers, leaving the door open and the light on. Her head was swimming, her body tugged under by the ebbing adrenaline, and she fell quickly asleep. She woke, briefly, to the sound of the door gently closing. Her eyes flickered long enough for her to register that it was dark outside, and that somebody had turned the light out, before slipping under again.

46

Nothing about the way Lewis behaved that evening made sense to Max. After the screening, there was a dinner. Max waited by the door of the cinema, half expecting Lewis to try to slip away, but he strolled out, nodded at Max.

'Where's the restaurant?' Lewis said to nobody in particular, craning his neck and looking back into the cinema, as if the answer to his question might be hidden somewhere inside. If Max had not known what he now knew, he would not have detected anything strange about Lewis's demeanour. If anything, he seemed more relaxed than he usually was, and as they set off for the restaurant he walked ahead with Zara. Max tried to stay close behind but Alasdair was walking slowly. Zara and Lewis crossed Shaftesbury Avenue and Max followed, dashing out between a cab and a bus, now caught on the island between two lanes of fast-flowing traffic as his mother and his cousin turned off towards Dean Street.

'Mum,' Max shouted. Zara stopped and turned round. 'Wait.' The cars did not stop. 'I don't know where the restaurant is.' His voice was whiny, a child's voice. Lewis caught his eye. His look hardened and the edges of his mouth twitched, before Max slipped into the road, ignoring the blaring horns that hailed him as he crossed.

'Well, Alasdair doesn't know either,' Zara said. She took Max by the arm as they waited for Alasdair to cross, which he did, swearing loudly at a cyclist who swerved around him. The restaurant was not far away, and as they walked Max tuned out the sound of conversation around him, and kept hold of his mother's arm, with Lewis, who was walking in step with Alasdair, at the edge of his vision. When they arrived, the film's producer and some of the cast were already there in the private room downstairs. The table was already beginning to fill and Max could not see how he would have the chance to talk to Lewis alone, nor did he know what he could say if he did. He sat down at the far end, away from Lewis but facing him.

'Max,' Nicole hissed, pinching his elbow as she sat down next to him. She had arrived with Rupert, who was watching them both carefully. 'What's going on?'

'Come to the bar with me,' he said.

While they waited for their drinks to arrive, he told Nicole again what he had said to her in the cinema, but more slowly and more deliberately.

'I don't understand,' Nicole said. 'How would she know all of this? Did Kate tell her?'

'I don't think so. She must have just told her about the tattoo.'

'And Kate told you about it, too?'

'Yes.'

Nicole bit her lip. 'Are you sure you haven't mis-understood?'

Max shook his head. Kate would not have left, if it had been a coincidence. Their drinks had arrived, but neither of them made to sit back down. Lewis had turned in his seat, and was watching them at the bar. Max looked down at his drink, avoiding eye contact, but Nicole was looking right back at him.

'One way to be sure,' she said.

Max shook his head. 'We can't,' he said, but he couldn't remember what his reason was, and now Nicole was beck-oning Lewis. Slowly, he rose, came towards them.

'Am I in trouble?' he said, leaning against the bar next to Nicole, putting her between him and Max.

'Don't fuck around,' Nicole said. 'We're family. But I know what I just saw. What does our mother know about you that we don't?'

'Nothing,' said Lewis.

'Nothing, except that she's effectively accused you of raping somebody. And you're not even going to defend yourself?'

'I don't hear any accusations.'

'Kate,' Max said, finding his voice for the first time. 'That was you, in the film. And the woman was Kate.'

'There's your accusation,' Nicole said.

'Wait, wait, wait.' Lewis held up his hands. 'Kate. Your friend Kate was raped. Fuck. The one with the curly hair? Moony sort of face?'

'The one who lived with us,' Max said impatiently.

'You think I raped her?'

'I know it was you.'

'You know it was me?' Lewis repeated incredulously. 'You know it was me.'

'We're asking you,' Nicole said. 'We don't know, but we're asking you to tell us where this has come from.'

Max said nothing. He could see Lewis clearly now, and he wished he couldn't.

'We fucked,' Lewis said plainly, speaking only to Max now, as if it were Max who was owed an explanation. 'I didn't tell you because I thought you were into her. And she didn't want me to tell you in case you got jealous. We fucked and she wanted it.' He shrugged. 'I don't know what else to tell you. If she's decided it was something else, well, then we've got a problem.'

Denial was always going to be the easiest option. Or rather, partial denial, a part confession that confessed to nothing but only blurred the truth with omissions and distortions.

'It's up to her,' Max said, blunt now. 'If she wants to make it official then that's her decision. But I'm telling you now that I know. We're telling you that we know.' He glanced at Nicole. Nicole said nothing, bit her lip again.

'Nicole?' Lewis said, looking directly at her now.

'I don't know what you did,' Nicole said. 'Probably I'll never know for sure. But right now, I think you're full of shit.' Without waiting for Lewis to respond, she walked away from the bar and up the stairs out of the restaurant.

Lewis was laughing, incredulous again. 'What can I say to that? What's happened to this family?'

'Admit what you did,' said Max.

'I've done nothing,' Lewis said. 'I fucked someone who wanted to be fucked. And I've got a tattoo. So cuff me. It sounds to me like you'll believe what you want to believe.'

He took a slow sip of his drink, and when he spoke again his voice was quieter.

'That's not how you do it,' he said. 'Just so you know.'

Max said nothing, waited for him to keep talking.

'You don't pick it out there, in the shop. You have to decide for yourself what font you want, and the size, the colouring. Send it in beforehand, so they've designed it all before you go. I could have told Zara that, if she'd asked me. But I guess she wasn't particularly interested in accuracy.'

He drained his drink and turned back to the bar; caught the attention of the barmaid. Ordered another.

47

Andrew was still asleep when Kate woke the next morning. She didn't know what time it was. For a while, she watched his chest rising and falling next to her, waiting for whatever it was that was causing the crippling tightness in her own chest to manifest. She could feel that she was still wearing Shona's trousers and the wire of her bra was digging into her armpits. When, eventually, she turned onto her front, she saw that there were black mascara marks on the pillow. There had been a great sadness, she knew. But as the recollections began to surface – the darkened cinema, Max's stricken face, Zara's silhouette – what came with them was relief. No longer was she her secret's sole keeper. First Andrew, then Claire. And now Max, Nicole. Soon Zara would know, and William: the knowledge of this crime was now their burden, not hers.

She found Andrew's charger on the bedside table and plugged in her phone. As she waited for it to wake, she unbuttoned the trousers and took them off, took off her bra. Her phone buzzed, the screen loading with phone calls, a dozen or so, that she'd missed from Max, and messages from him and from Claire. She deleted Max's texts, considered deleting his number, but didn't. Instead, she wrote telling him that she was at Andrew's, that he didn't need to be worried about her, but that she couldn't talk to him. She told him she would call when she was ready to. To Claire she wrote only two words: *They know*, and put her phone back on the table.

Next to her, Andrew had stirred, not quite enough to realise that she was there beside him, and she stayed very still, not wanting to wake him. She didn't know what Shona had told him, didn't know what he'd thought of her turning up here, but already, the thought of revisiting last night made her feel heavy. She would tell him, but not straight away. First there would be breakfast. She was hungry, she wanted him to cook eggs for her, wanted to hear about his night, what had they had for dinner, who had come for drinks afterwards. She wanted to spend the morning at least in his world, before having to return to her own. This momentary contentment would pass, she knew, because there was nothing that did not pass. What she had felt last night had lifted, and although that did not mean it was gone, for now this was enough.

Her phone began to ring but she didn't answer it. The sound woke Andrew, who lifted his head blearily from his pillow, saw that she was there, and put his head back down.

'You're here,' he said, closing his eyes.

Kate had been right not to rush that morning; it would take weeks, and then months, before what had happened would begin to make sense to her. But it would be worth the wait. After a while, there were moments when she felt a levity that she had never before experienced, not even before the rape. The value of contentment grew exponentially. Summer ended, fiery autumn leaves carpeted the ground and then rotted. Kate witnessed the progression of Max's life without her in the slimmest of segments: when she and Claire drove past Bisley House at Christmas she saw that the 'For Sale' sign had been replaced by 'Sold', and in the new year, an automated email arrived to tell her that Embers was now live. It was painful to know that he had, ostensibly at least, continued on much the same trajectory, despite what had happened to her. At such times, she had to remind herself that it had been she and not he who had broken off contact, that she had told him she would call, and still she had not.

A few weeks after the premiere, Kate had gone home to Randwick, and Andrew had come with her for the first time. Through the summer she started visiting Alison far more frequently than she ever had, sometimes every other weekend. That first time with Andrew, Kate had sat at the kitchen table watching her mother climb up onto the worktop to fix a screw that had come loose at the top of the cabinet, holding a power drill in both hands with a pencil tucked behind her ear. Kate wondered then how she had ever thought that Alison, who never leaned on anybody, who never used people as if they were things, who had only ever turned to herself in times of need, was weak. Alison possessed a rare, self-sufficient strength; she existed, continued to exist, without ever requiring approval or encouragement, she gave everything and she expected nothing in return. It was that evening that Kate found the words she needed. And though her voice cracked as she spoke, though she began to sob when Alison asked her why she had waited until now to tell her, why she had for so long carried her burden alone, Kate felt at last that she was safe.

48

His dreams began in the weeks that followed that first screening of Zara's film. Though they possessed many of the characteristics of nightmares – their insistent recurrence, their proximity to consciousness, that just-beneath-the-surface feel, the way in which they wrenched him from his sleep – he would not call them nightmares, because it was only on waking, when he was forced to leave the fantastical for the real world, that he felt truly afflicted. They grew worse as the summer pitched: a feverish mind, perhaps, or heat creating the illusion of two bodies when there was only ever one.

That was how it always ended, reaching out for her lying next to him, only to find that she was not there. He knew before he opened his eyes that she was not, though he thought that if he kept them closed for long enough the smell of hairspray and coconut he was sure he had smelt would return to him. Once he dreamt that she had kissed him, her hand sliding across his bare chest, her hair brushing his cheek, and he had woken aroused and guilty before he turned and saw that the bed was empty. Max had said nothing to his parents on the night of the premiere, but the morning after he'd told them. They were sitting across from him at the kitchen table, William halfway through a bowl of cereal and Zara complaining of a hangover. Max was surprised by how easily the words came to him, but then Kate had done all of the hard work already, and Zara, in the narrative they had created between them. All that was left for Max was to point to the perpetrator, which he did calmly and with resignation.

'He's already denied it,' Max said, before either of his parents had spoken. 'They slept together, he said, but she gave consent.' He paused. 'I believe her.'

'She's your friend,' William said, straightening. Until now he had been looking down at his cereal. By this statement, it was unclear whether William was validating or discounting what Max had just said, but neither of them attempted to expand. Zara was silent, and Max waited for her to say something about the film, to acknowledge her role in what had happened, but she did not.

'Have you tried to call her?' Zara said.

'She's not picking up. Neither is Andrew.'

'We must make sure she's all right. Do you have her address?'

'I'm not going to her flat if she doesn't want to see me.'

'I tried to persuade her to go to the police,' Zara said. Max noticed that his mother's cheeks were flushed; that she was trying to keep her voice steady. But he did not soften his tone.

'Maybe now she will,' he said.

'Where's Nicole?' William said, reaching for Zara's hand.

But Zara pulled it away, brushing her hair from her face, sitting up a little taller.

'At her flat. She knows,' Max said. He looked squarely at his father. 'And somebody needs to talk to Alasdair.'

When Max got Kate's message later that morning, he replied immediately to tell her that he would be there, whenever she was ready to speak to him. But she didn't reply that day, nor the next, and the next day he knew that even if she did write, there was very little that could be said. It was then that the dreams started. If he dreamt of her in the early hours, then he struggled to get back to sleep. He'd had little practice at insomnia, given the ease with which alcohol had always brought on sleep, and he was restless. He would get out of bed and go downstairs where he drank squash and read the papers left on the kitchen table. He read them backwards: starting with the crossword, and then those articles that required the least attention, before working his way up to the heaviest stories of the day, sitting on the love seat in the kitchen, the window cold against his back.

A fortnight had passed since the premiere, and again Max was awake at three in the morning. He knew that William had been up too, because the kitchen had been clean when he'd gone to bed, but now there were empty pill packets collected by the kitchen sink, and a half-drunk glass of water. William had always slept well, but lately he'd been waking in the early hours. He told Max that he didn't want to disturb Zara, which was why he'd been sleeping in the spare room, where the blinds were thicker and the mattress was harder, and Max did not challenge his reasoning. That morning, he wondered again how long he could bear to stay at Latimer Crescent. Nicole had offered him his old room in their flat, but he'd told her he needed to be at home.

His refusal of Nicole's offer had been in large part because of William: Max saw that his father was in an impossible position, and this worried him. Max, Zara, even Nicole could choose to believe what they wanted. They could distance themselves from Lewis. But William had his brother to think of, and Alasdair had as good as refused to acknowledge what had happened, had denied that Lewis had a tattoo, even. Physically he was ailing, heavier and slower than ever, and nobody but William had the strength or inclination to rescue him. The burden was great, and Max could see the strain in his father's sleeplessness, the laboured way he climbed the stairs at night, as if carrying his older brother.

During this time, Lewis continued to work at the same hospital, lived in the same flat. William heard from Alasdair that he'd been dating somebody, but that nothing had come of it: bitterly, Alasdair speculated that his son was too traumatised by previous relationships to trust anybody. William, who did not know what he could say, suggested that Lewis might need therapy, to which Alasdair responded with a coughing fit. For the rest of them, it was far easier just to let Lewis fall, and to spare no thoughts for whoever he might take down with him. William, on one of the rare occasions he spoke to Zara about his nephew, said that he was glad Bernadette was not alive to witness this; Zara said it was a shame that Alasdair was.

Rupert, despite what he had seen on the night of the premiere, had still not been told. It was too easy not to include him, to consider him to be outside of time, too fragile to hear the truth. But one night, when Max was sitting at the kitchen table, his phone started ringing, his uncle's picture on the screen. A late-night phone call from Rupert had once signalled desperation, but he knew this was something else.

'Hello,' Max said, picking up.

'Are you going to tell me what's been going on?' Rupert said. Max could hear him inhaling, imagined him standing in the doorway of his house, cigarette in hand: his last remaining vice.

'I will,' Max said.

'Where are you?'

'At home.'

'Did I wake you up?'

'Can't sleep.'

'It's the air,' Rupert said. Inhaled again sharply. 'It's too heavy. Makes me sticky. I have to sleep in the nude, truth be told. Fortunately I live alone.'

Max let out a dry half-laugh.

'The rain will help, though,' Rupert went on. 'Can you smell it?'

'Can I smell the rain?'

'It's called petrichor. Did you know that? The smell of fresh rainwater on the ground, after a long dry spell. You know, that earthy smell. Like relief. It's Greek, apparently.'

'I didn't know.'

'You knew the smell, but you didn't know the word. It smells like redemption.'

Max found that he couldn't speak. There was a lump in his throat, he wanted to cry.

'Take your time, Max. I'm here when you're ready.'

Max nodded, then remembered that Rupert couldn't see him. 'OK,' he said.

'Get some sleep.'

The line went dead. Max put down his phone. He was close to tears, as he sat at the kitchen table. But he stayed sitting there, his fingers numb and his feet growing cold on the tiled floor. He didn't know what time it was. He stared at the crossword, waiting patiently for the letters he had written out to rearrange themselves into a word that made sense. There were three more clues left to complete the grid; he would not get up from the kitchen table until he had them.

49

August, just over a year since the premiere, and Kate hadn't thought about Lewis once that day. She always took note of the time at which he entered her mind, and it was getting later and later. Seven, a month ago. Last week eight thirty; and tonight it was already dark and she had not yet spared a thought for him.

Kate liked to walk alone, particularly at night, particularly on a Thursday or a Friday when women were standing on the streets in high heels and tight dresses, and men were lurking. Sometimes, if it was particularly late and the women were particularly drunk, she put them in taxis, made sure they had enough cash, that the driver had the right address. She no longer walked with her eyes to the ground but would look at any man who looked at her or at other women, and she wouldn't break eye contact until they looked away, confused. Sometimes, she even saw shame. The ones who kept on looking back were the ones who were dangerous. They were the ones who worried her.

Tonight, though, she was not afraid. In fact she rarely felt fear, not now: at least not for her own safety. She knew that this was reckless, that there were far worse things that could have been done to her or that could still happen to her, but she believed that she could endure it, that she could look in the eye any man who hurt her and tell him, even as he raped her, even as he denied her her humanity, that this was his choice, and not hers; that it was him who would have to live with it, and not her. There were times when she thought she would be glad if it happened again, and this she had told to nobody, not even Andrew. If it happened again, she would get it right. This time she would scream, she would fight, and he would have to hit her. He would have to leave bruises that would correspond to the damage done, and she in turn would take his flesh into her finger-nails, his cum inside her, so that she could walk herself to the police station, wearing his violence, and tell them what had been done. It didn't even have to be the police, or the law: justice had little to offer her except a platform. All that mattered was to speak, and to be heard. And this time, she knew, she would be her story's sole teller.

Kate was taking the long way home. The bus made her feel sick, so she was walking to the Tube instead, taking residential roads, where the street lamps disappeared into the cherry trees. When she reached the turning to Venn Street, she stopped. On the billboard outside the Picture-house *Late Surfacing* was listed. Kate had still not seen it all the way through. She went inside, and bought a ticket from the vendor who gave her a flyer listing the events being held for a Zara Lalhou season. Kate smiled at him, and folded the flyer into her back pocket.

It was hot, that night, but in the auditorium somebody

had opened a fire door down by the screen which let in a slight breeze. She was wearing loose cotton shorts and ankle boots, and as the narrative began to unfold, she began to feel calm. She sank deep into her seat, propping her water bottle between her open legs and letting the cold water sit against her bare thighs. It still made her wet, being forced to think about rape, with a searing pain where the memory of her violation still ghosted inside her.

Although she had deliberately positioned herself near the exit, this time she had no desire to leave. Once she had made it through the opening scene, she knew that she owed it to herself to see the film through to the end, and the longer she sat, the more capable she was of distancing her own experience from what she saw on-screen. The rape scene took place not in a bedroom but in the middle of the day in a brightly lit restaurant kitchen. When he pinned his victim to the tiled floor, he slammed her head against a black-and-white-chequered step so that she bled from the back of her skull. She bled too from her thigh, where he held a knife. Black, white and red. Such clarity, such vibrancy. There was no ambiguity here.

How Kate wished that there had been more clarity when she'd been in this woman's position, but Lewis had moved so slyly, pinned her to such soft surfaces, had stopped short of breaking her skin, of leaving any visible lesions, not like the man on the screen. For Kate there had been only that private breach, the breach that nobody could see, a thick-bladed knife sliding into a cluster of nerve endings, and then swiftly retreating, leaving the body to heal itself before anybody could bear witness to what had been done to it.

When, at last, Kate saw the rapist unmasked, when she saw his brazen lack of guilt, she felt nothing. There was no fear, no loathing. There was only dispassion, and the knowledge that he would eventually find that his narrow view of the world had left him nowhere to turn; that sooner or later his existence would lose all breadth and meaning; that he would find he had only the company of those who had an obligation to him, and in the darkness would be paralysed by the knowledge that there was nobody there who cared who was not already obliged to care.

She was relieved, when the film came to its end, that it was the woman he'd raped who killed him. There was a pleasing symmetry to his death, his blood on her white sheets, the back of his head caved in like an egg from where she had raised her metal lamp and brought it down upon his skull, the expression of disbelief that stayed on his face even after the fact, for as with rape, it was easier not to believe in murder. If only theoretically, structurally, Kate understood the desire for symmetry that propelled this penultimate act. Do to others as they have done to you.

But the problem was that now that the final retribution had been committed, now that the balance had been restored, there was no longer a cause: this woman had brought her story to too neat a conclusion, her existence so narrowed by rage that there was no longer any reason for her to continue to live. As Kate watched, she knew that she would kill herself that way, too, if ever she wanted to. A sharpened knife between the ribs, slipping into flesh as easily as into a sheath: another act of symmetry. If she ever decided to do it, that was. She had not made up her mind about it, and neither would she tomorrow. There was always the weekend; there could be weeks, perhaps decades to come. There was no rush. There was only each day, and the next.

Acknowledgements

Jane Finigan and David Forrer, I could wish for no better champions. Kate Harvey, my editor, for her intelligence, empathy and vision. Lucie Cuthbertson-Twiggs and the Vintage family for their support. Parisa Ebrahimi at Hogarth and Deborah Sun de la Cruz at Penguin Canada, whose wisdom has been invaluable. For their early guidance, Zoë Waldie and Peter Straus.

Sara Adams, Abbi Brown, Madeleine Dunnigan, Charlotte Hamblin, Lexie Hamblin and Emma Paterson – my first readers, who gave me courage. For their love and friendship, Johnny Falconer, James Browning, Hannah Barton, Raffaella Taylor-Seymour and Rosie Faulkner. Guy Edmund-Jones, for the word *petrichor*, and for always believing in me. The incredible women – past, present and honorary – of Number 8. Kace Monney, who has shown me there is more.

My family, above all my parents, for everything.

penguin.co.uk/vintage